Praise for Nicky Shearsby

'Pioneering the 'why-dunnit' '
Sarah Goodwin

'Shearsby's writing will give you goosebumps'
Amanda Cassidy

'The master of villainy, the author of bar-raising'
AJ Law

'Nicky is adept at creating an incredibly dark, surreal atmosphere'
@Calmstitchread

THROUGH BROKEN GLASS

NICKY SHEARSBY

SRL PUBLISHING

SRL Publishing Ltd
London

www.srlpublishing.co.uk

First published worldwide by SRL Publishing in 2025
This paperback format first published in 2026

SRL PUBLISHING
THINKING DIFFERENTLY, DELIVERING CHANGE

ISBN: 978-1-915073-50-1

1 3 5 7 9 10 8 6 4 2

A CIP catalogue record for this book is available from the British Library.

SRL Publishing is a climate positive publisher, offsetting more carbon
emissions than it emits.

Nicky Shearsby titles

<u>The Flanigan Files</u>

#1, Beyond the Veil
#2, The Lost Raven
#3, Through Broken Glass

<u>Other titles</u>
To the Bitter End
Green Monsters
Black Widow
Darkridge Hollow

One

Jack

I'll be dead by Christmas. Or so they tell me. Understandably, I'm still not ready to accept it, unprepared for the haze of uncertainty suffocating my reality. Dead? *Me?* The very concept feels alien, ridiculous, the whole thing laughable. I've recently turned twenty years old, for God's sake. I'm too young to die. It's foolish to admit now, of course, but I always believed myself invincible, immortal, youth on my side, my entire future ahead. Unfortunately, being diagnosed with stage four glioblastoma at a young age is akin to being told you'll never taste the sweet nectar of life, the rug snatched beneath your feet before you learn the value of your own worth. Can you imagine knowing a deep-rooted brain tumour is set to destroy your world before you begin to live? *No.* Sadly, neither can I.

That was almost four months ago. Every breath I now

take threatens to become my last, every tick of the clock edging me closer to something I find genuinely frightening. I haven't told anyone how I feel. Even my mother remains mostly oblivious. But my forthcoming death is not something I ever thought I'd express with such flippancy and I'm not even sure I *want* to know what oblivion will be like. I guess it doesn't matter in the scheme of things. None of us are infallible, no one above death.

All I wanted when I awoke this morning was a little space, time away from my daily routine to imagine what my life *might* have been like, and to breathe fresh air while I still can. Until a moment ago, I was walking along this unassuming canal path, minding my own business, lost in thought, to whatever might now be left of my small, fragile world. However, if there were ever a moment to wish for the ability to go back and do things differently, this would be it. I'm about to do something irrefutably and categorically stupid and there's no way of turning off my emotions. It's unfortunate, but what can I do? My path is leading only one way and I'm powerless to divert its course. I guess something profound happens when your life is about to end, the person you *could* have been swallowed painfully by your own unimagined mortality.

I can confirm nothing significant happened to bring about an imposed wrath I'm wholly unsure where to place. My presence caught a stranger's eye, that's all. A single misplaced glance wrongly aimed in my direction. Yet, it has triggered my anger, my irritation, the tiny hairs on the backs of my arms and neck standing now to unwanted attention. Before my diagnosis, such things wouldn't have bothered me, but inevitably, we find ourselves playing a game of cat and mouse, this fellow and I. He looks at me several times when he assumes I'm not watching, his sideways glares made in not-so-private isolation. I glare back, keeping a much-needed distance at first, my body a cancerous timebomb ticking precious seconds from my existence.

I squeeze the rucksack I've recently taken to never leaving home without, its contents almost as unforgiving as my thoughts. No one knows how far my mind has drifted, hovering somewhere between sanity and delirium, this innocent morning offering nothing of value to my struggling breath or irrational thinking. As it is, I'm armed and prepared, understanding enough about the human brain to make this stranger more like me, if I wanted, enough knowledge of the human condition to change his life forever.

I'd love to claim ignorance over the savage ideas screaming violently in my head, delude myself I haven't somehow *planned* this moment. But I can't. I've been lost for a while to the false hope of an impossible dream, imagining in secret how I might "help" others view the world from my perspective. Cancer has changed me, and not for the better. It has ensured this impossible trajectory shift, spiralling me towards eternal doom. It's difficult to explain how I feel about that. But I honestly don't know how else to convey the fragments of my tainted life, nothing to be done other than follow this path to its end.

I follow the stranger until he turns into Conalton Street, almost losing him to a bush that blocks my view. There are street cameras dotted at incremental positions and I'm cautious to avoid them, my trainers catching misplaced stones and debris as I stumble along in pursuit. The crutches I'm forced to walk with make progress difficult and I struggle to pull my hooded top over my face. It doesn't matter. I'm fully aware this garment won't mask my features or hide my shame. I'm wearing gloves. In the lingering summer heat, it must look suspicious.

Although his pace easily outmatches mine, he shuffles slightly, as if his legs ache from the effort. It helps me retain a comfortable distance, and for that, I'm grateful. But I can't help noticing how his grey hair reflects the late morning sun from patches of exposed skull, *his* appearance nothing special. He has no right to judge mine. I clench my fists, my teeth, the contents of my rucksack taunting, these streets quiet enough to afford the privacy I genuinely believe I'm searching for. After all, there are no other faces to dissuade mine, no voices to tell me I'm wrong. I suppose it will make my ultimate actions easier to ignore.

Eventually, he turns onto Parkside Lane, a quiet neighbourhood, *usually*. Yet, I have a feeling I'm about to change all that. My nerves are raw, my uncontrollable anger almost as unforgiving as my mind. When he steps inside a property, I am behind him, upon him, ready to force my way into his home, his life, his nightmares. The poor bastard doesn't see it coming. To be honest, neither do I. I guess it's too late to change my mind. I'm merely seeking something that doesn't exist, pondering thoughts I *know* aren't real.

'What do you want?' he yells as I lunge towards him, my arms outstretched to shock, that's all, despite my repulsive appearance and cruel intentions. It's funny, the way he reacts, the question asked as if he expects me to say.

Unfortunately, there is no coming back from this moment, no honest hope for me now. I am feigned to appreciate how I must look to him, my distorted features offering the illusion of a madman, my silent mouth offering no comfort to anyone. There are few people like me in the world, you see, my appearance *not* something he will have difficulty explaining. No. Our chance meeting ends things for him, for us.

I discard my crutches against the doorframe and grab him around the throat. He is still yelling, choking vile words I don't appreciate aimed so readily my way, clawing my arms with desperate fingers. I pick up a vase of wilted flowers and smash it across his head, wanting nothing more than to shut him up while I ponder my next move. I don't want to *kill* him. How will he understand my predicament if he is dead and therefore unable to appreciate his own? He falls silent, thankfully, yet the laboured expenditure of his breath is almost as unforgiving as mine.

This house is a narrow Victorian terrace. The type with two or three small rooms downstairs, a similar number above, a staircase tucked behind an ageing front door that has seen better days. I need to think. Despite everything, I didn't anticipate this moment and I've no idea if he lives alone or if more people will arrive and ruin the plan I haven't intended to create. I ensure he's unconscious and compliant before I leave him and go in search of his bathroom, blood far easier to wash down a plughole than it is to wipe from carpets and wood. I find it hidden behind the kitchen at the back of the house, this downstairs space tacked hastily onto the building as an afterthought.

As expected, he is heavy, and I'm forced to drag him an inch at a time, shuffling backwards, out of breath. I stumble several times. I can't help it. My body is screaming in protest, adrenaline the only thing keeping me going. But although I walk with crutches now and need them for stability, they do not represent who I am, will *never* define me. I'm far more than my weakened appearance, my strength forged from an underlying anger that endures even when my body cannot. It allows unfailing sustenance when I need it, and complete invisibility when I don't. Eventually, we make it into his bathroom, neither of us aware of our fate or our future, my wrath called firmly into question. I hoist him unceremoniously into a seated position before manhandling him roughly over the edge of his bath, allowing his heavy legs to slide in after him. He isn't a large man but he lands hard all the same, slumping awkwardly against cold cast iron, his arms crushed beneath his weight.

There was a time in my life when I might have concluded his earlier glance as *fleeting*, nothing more, barely a reason for the provocation it has sadly unleashed. But as I reach into my rucksack and pull out a cordless drill, I'm scarcely able to concede what my mind is willing to do. No one knows I carry this item around with me wherever I go. I doubt many would understand *why*. It has merely become an anchor, if you like, protection from those I can no longer tolerate, a weapon against people like *him*. I think about the books I've read, the hypothetical medical training I've given myself in private, grateful my aunt never goes into her basement. I'm not sure she would appreciate what currently resides down there.

I force myself to take a deep breath. Professionals have specialist equipment for such a delicate job, the drills they use stopping the very instant they reach soft tissue. However, I have no such luxury. I don't assume it matters as long as the outcome remains the same. I simply need to remain calm if I'm to carry out my untimely endeavour. I'm not a psychopath. Or at least, I don't *think* I am. However, I'm armed now with a roll of kitchen paper and my nightmares, my aim merely to mop up the blood as I go. I need to be careful. Drill too deeply and he will die, too shallow and nothing will change. I genuinely hope we can one day meet under different circumstances, this man and I. When he can no longer speak, can no longer tell others what I did, when the forthcoming stroke such damage will provoke makes his face look more like mine. I assume only then will he understand what it's like to be me. As I said, I don't want to kill him.

I turn his head as best I can, kneeling next to his bath to gain a vantage point I fear might evade us both. It's not the most comfortable position to find myself. I press cold metal against his skull, hesitate, almost change my mind. My hands are shaking and my lips are dry, but I *have* to do this. After all, I'm doing him a favour, doing them all a favour. I press the trigger, not expecting the noise to reverberate so violently around the tiny room, my screaming drill biting into soft flesh before I'm ready. It judders wildly as blood sprays into the air, my drill pressed too firmly against bone, too heavy for precision drilling, my unstable hands too weak.

I punch forcefully through his skull, unable to prevent the metal rod from sliding deep inside his brain like a hot knife through butter. He begins to fit, his arms and legs jolting violently, foam spitting from his gagging mouth. I stop immediately and pull the offending item from the hole I've created, but it's too late to prevent blood from spurting across the room like a fountain. I'm genuinely shocked when he bites his tongue clean in half. I try to stem the flow with a fistful of paper towel but it only makes things worse, his body jolting savagely, his head slamming from side to side against his bath. I clamber to my feet, unprepared for so much blood. I don't want to admit it, but I know he won't survive. This is *not* how I wanted this moment to go, not what I had in mind. Yet, he falls silent, already dead, the bath filling readily with blood, much of it over the floor. I don't want to acknowledge the repulsive substance now coating my hands, my clothes, my hair.

The unbearable summer heat begins to attract flies to an oil slick of crimson that mocks my every breath, his blood-soaked hair glued in places to his damaged skull. My cordless drill is still in my grasp. It's still warm, sticky blood coating the surface. I recoil in disgust, dropping the offending item to the floor as each blink of my fear-filled eyes provokes slow-returning clarity, my brain replenishing the very holes my memories are keen to retain. I dare not move as I catch my heinous reflection in a nearby mirror, fearful I will see something I dislike, my parched lips unable to confirm anything of value. My shallow breath is beyond painful. I no longer recognise the hollow figure staring back. Even the diffused sunlight from a nearby window offers little comfort. Surely the balance of my mind has not pivoted so violently that I can no longer appreciate my own awareness? Never in my darkest hour did I assume things would come to *this*.

If I could cast aside the madness, I would, but the noises emerging from my throat add nothing to the churlish nature of my existence. It's not important. Not in the scheme of things. It matters little how long I have wished to convey to others what it feels like to be me, to prevent strangers like *this* one from swallowing distasteful behaviour with closed mouths and blind eyes. I have always believed if others could appreciate my affliction the world would be a better place. Only *then* might they understand what it's like to be me, what I'm forced to deal with each day. After all, we are more than our exterior, our existence far deeper than skin.

Unfortunately, I do nothing more than glance awkwardly at his blood-splattered bathroom, absorbing this stranger's blood-soaked features, passing fleeting looks over his hunched body. I don't stare long, would never wish to become like those who seemingly find it easy to do the same to me. I don't know how old he is but he's too old for the game he has unwittingly triggered. I don't know him. Until today, we'd never met. Sadly, I'm unable to absorb the subtle noises that might calm me if I listened—a ticking clock, an ageing boiler, his unfed cat.

Snippets of a frustrated argument are lodged in my head. It's not ideal. But of everything occurring today, a one-sided conversation with my mother is the one thing I remember. She didn't want me venturing out alone, didn't need the worry. I didn't intend it to trigger a chain of events

I was too incensed to see coming, that moment leading to this. I should have listened, I know, but what's done is done. I will muse over my actions long after this day has ended, the tide turning me into something I can never take back. My destiny will become my reality soon enough. I don't need to overthink what that means for me.

The moment has passed, yet my hands grapple with the hot tap in a desperate attempt to revive him, *save* him, reverse what I've done. I swear he is looking right at me, his bloodshot eyes wide, blank, his final moments on this earth imprinted on the glossy surface. I can't look at his face, can't find the plughole. His arms are suddenly too heavy, most of his bulk covering the drain. The bath begins to fill with water, making the scene appear worse than it is, nothing left for me to do now but to run. I leave the tap running, accidentally kicking my drill across the floor in haste, my mind a playground of screaming voices all yelling at once.

I turn around briefly to check I haven't imagined the chaos, unable to find the strength to go back inside the bathroom or locate my drill. I hover, seconds feeling like hours before I grab my crutches and clamber into the street. I dare not look back. All I can hope is that one day when I'm dead and gone, those left behind will understand my motives, my reasons, my pain. After all, I never set out to *kill* anyone. I hope they appreciate this unfortunate, extremely uncomfortable truth.

Two

Jack

I am trying to piece together this day, if I can, attempting to snatch a memory from the air, to recall a stranger's screams, his terror, wondering what might have happened to bring us *here*. Unfortunately, any salvageable recognition I attempt to uncover is being forcefully withheld, my brain blocking information it doesn't want to acknowledge. I haven't prepared myself for what has happened, did not intend this day to turn out the way it has. But I *was* prepared for the carnage and the self-preservation I now must retain. We were locked in an impossible moment, the two of us, locked in that house. I can't quite believe he's dead. I wished *only* to show him how actions have consequences, how his ignorance affected me. If he could have seen the world from my viewpoint, he would have become a better person, I *know* it. I have, after all, remained locked in my head and my private space for months, attempting to dissect humanity, their thoughts, their actions. He was in the wrong place, that's all. It could have been anyone.

I don't know why, but I have a compulsion to hang around the dead man's house instead of heading home, a desire to watch the inevitable unfold from afar. I find myself hiding inside the entrance of an old cemetery, the opposite side of Parkside Lane unwittingly becoming a protection I'm not expecting to find. It is perfectly positioned, oddly appealing, a fitting location considering what I've done. This place is rarely frequented by the living now anyway, no new bodies to entice visitors, its residents long dead.

I feel sick, unsure of my actions, blood on my clothes that might never wash off. I try frantically to remove it in a nearby puddle but it only makes things worse, my pale features elevating events already complete. I glare at my willowy reflection, the lunchtime sunlight adding nothing of value to this moment, despising what I am and what I've become. An hour passes, a string of missed messages from my mother sounding increasingly panicked with every call I leave unreturned, the steady buzz of my mobile phone threatening to expose my position, my weakness, my stupidity. I failed to tell her where I was going, failed to express my pain. She will want to know where I am, understandably worried by now.

I read her messages, my phone threatening to highlight my position from the shadows.

Jack, where are you?
Let me know you're safe, PLEASE.

I'm getting worried now.
Jack?

I turn it off and place it inside my pocket, certain no one noticed me coming here. My mother aside, I'm sure no one cares. For now, I will remain hidden amongst the overgrowth, this densely populated area temporarily keeping my secrets. I crouch uncomfortably in a mossy hole, sandwiched between the ageing wall of Chapel Halls Cemetery and an unwitting Parkside Lane property. My surroundings smell of rotting wood and a man who died not long ago, threatening to expose my secrets, my spinning mind playing tricks, my huddled body aching.

I'm unsure if it is fate or fortune favouring me today, but there is an undignified hole in this wall, unnoticed and untouched by years of neglect, hidden among brambles and weeds. From an uncomfortable position, I sit and watch, wanting to know the outcome, needing to witness the chaos. I hold my breath, cowering like a corpse beneath an aptly rotting tree, surrounded by dense foliage, my pained skin and dark eyes disappearing into the void of the very thing terrifying me the most. *Me.*

Inevitably, footsteps grow closer. I watch as a female enters the house, holding my breath with misguided anticipation as she calls out to a man she doesn't yet know is dead. The man I killed. I think his name is Alex, her voice travelling towards me on the heavy air, mocking my choices, my actions. She disappears, prompting me to count every passing second. One... two... three. I lose count several times, my heart beating too fast to keep up.

When I see her again, she looks panicked, tears streaming down her face, her frightened screams dancing on the breeze like ghosts. She is frantic, banging her fists against a neighbour's front door, needing attention, someone to help. Raised voices fill the air. For a moment I can't even breathe. Then the street falls eerily silent, their drama taken inside a house that honestly now feels like hell. More impossible moments pass before I see them again, the crying woman tugging the arm of her exasperated neighbour, on her phone in a desperate call for help.

This is the moment I *should* move, get up, get out. But I can't move a muscle for fear of what it might provoke, can barely catch my breath. The police are on the scene within minutes, an impressive undertaking considering the current state of UK law enforcement. Overworked officers are commonplace, according to my university professor, yet murder, it seems, prioritises their attention. Perhaps I am offering a service. I don't know what I'm meant to feel beyond the numbness in my legs, oddly cold now sitting here. It is as if I am watching a movie, everything around me unreal, unnatural—the visions in my head nothing but an impossible show on repeat.

I stare unapologetically through the gap in the wall, watching the police spring into action, cordoning off the street, taking charge, their flashing blue lights hurting my eyes. I'm glad I wore gloves, careful not to leave fingerprints, those blood-stained garments stuffed now in my pocket. When I see my professor walking along the street, I'm ready and willing to chastise my wayward brain, assuming the devil himself has raised him from my thoughts, bringing him into my feigned reality. I try to blink Professor Flanigan away as he strides towards the very house I left a man for dead, ready to believe I've lost my mind. Yet, when he speaks, reality bites hard. I sometimes forget he works with the police when they need an expert opinion. It's the reason I'm profoundly drawn to him. He's standing mere feet away now, close enough to touch, if I tried, talking to a smartly dressed plain-clothed police officer, oblivious to my presence. I can hear the worried tone in his voice, his aftershave drifting in the air.

What will Newton think of the scene inside that house? What kind of mind will he assume capable of such an unthinkable act? I almost race into the street, ready to tell him, desperate, as always, for his attention. But logic and reality stop me. I am covered in a dead man's blood, my clothes as black as my mind, my thoughts as dark as the books I've read in secret. He won't understand my reasoning, my logic, my truth.

I close my eyes against my rebuffed surroundings, needing a moment to reflect upon the day and gather my composure. My memories have been slipping in and out of focus lately, my thoughts sporadic, often fleeting. I blame cancer, the thing in my head spiralling me towards oblivion, often no memory of what happens between large chunks of time that swallow my day. It happens more when I'm stressed, today no exception, *this* moment too hideous to recall. It matters little how often I express my frustration, my indignation. I doubt I will *ever* come to terms with it. Yet, because of this, my family home has unwittingly become a place where death waits in corners, where whispers are met with a lingering silence, where no one smiles anymore. It's not ideal, isn't pleasant to see my family in such unforgiving turmoil. I try not to dwell, try not to overthink what cannot be changed. After all, what happens when we lose part of ourselves assuming humanity? Do we become less human, less tolerable to our species?

Three

Newton

I'm not sure when it happened or how I became aware of the trajectory shift, but somewhere along the line, I began seeing other people's problems as my own, taking on their emotions, their turmoil, their baggage. I *could* link it to age, stress, life in general, my problems formed from an inability to see beyond my monthly paycheque. But I have found myself waking each morning with a knot in the pit of my stomach I can't dislodge, a feeling in my gut I can't describe. I should slow down but I don't know how, each new morning depicting the last, not enough hours in the day for such an indulgence.

It was lunchtime and I was hungry, yet Parkside Lane was alive with activity, the house of a supposed murder victim subjected to much attention. The police were in attendance, catching the attention of several people who stood around in clusters, surprised hands covering shocked mouths, talking in hushed whispers so as not to share their thoughts aloud. I didn't know what I was about to walk in on, the hallway floor covered in plastic sheets to protect any evidence beneath.

'I hope you haven't had your lunch yet,' DCI Paul Mannering called my way, reading my thoughts, the sarcasm in his tone confirming nothing I wanted to acknowledge. I turned to see my good friend striding along the street towards me, his mobile phone in one hand, a steaming polystyrene cup in the other.

'Doesn't usually bother you,' I chided, my voice almost a whisper.

Paul grinned, pulling a face when he was sure no one could see.

'Do we know what happened?' I glanced around, unsure which among the onlookers were connected to the victim and which ones were neighbours being nosy. I needed to bring our conversation back to the matter at hand, to the dead man requiring our attention.

'That's what Bernard is currently trying to assess.'

I craned my neck to see inside the property, chaos swamping every inch of available space, a perfect line of sight created by an open front door and silhouetted figures moving in unison. Photographs were being taken, from what I could tell, attending forensic pathologist Bernard Taylor deep in the thick of it.

'The call came in at around one o'clock after the victim's wife came home from work to find her husband dead in the bath. She's a part-time nurse. Works shifts.'

On the surface it didn't sound so bad. *Plenty* of people died in the bath, our homes unfortunately the very places where most deaths occur. I swallowed, my private musing not something I found comforting considering I lived alone.

'Could it have been a heart attack?' My innocent pondering was more wishful thinking than anything, a melted toffee I'd earlier found in my pocket currently wedged in my teeth.

'More *gruesome* than heart attack, Newt.' Paul took a swig of his tea. I ignored his response, his attempted joke not funny. Someone had just lost a loved one.

'And where's the wife now?'

Paul pointed towards a woman some feet away, her head in her hands, face beyond pale. She was mid-sixties, currently being consolidated by a younger woman, a close friend or a neighbour, no doubt.

'Have you spoken to her yet?'

Paul shook his head. 'Care to join me?'

I nodded. I didn't, but wasn't about to confirm it.

Instead, we headed along the pavement to where the two women stood with their backs to us, a crumbling wall offering no comfort, the dead man's wife shaking violently. She was smoking a cigarette, sucking in gulps of air as if believing the thing in her hand could fix everything, rewind time, make this better.

'Mrs Jefferson?' Paul queried.

The blotchy-faced female turned to face us, her eyes bulging with shock, her lips quivering with fear. 'Who are *you?'*

'My name is DCI Mannering. I'll be working on your

husband's case.' He attempted a smile that did nothing other than pull thin lips towards his reddened cheeks. 'Is there somewhere we can talk?'

Mrs Jefferson looked momentarily unsure, knowing she wasn't going to be putting the kettle on for us any time soon, her kitchen currently filled with strangers and unwanted activity instead of tea and biscuits.

'You can use my front room if you like,' the other female offered, smoothing a caring hand across Mrs Jefferson's trembling shoulder. She opened her front door, unable to ignore the chaos next door. 'I'll be right here if you need me, Carol,' she said, offering Paul and myself a frosty glance. Carol Jefferson handed her friend the cigarette.

Compared to the outside, this quiet space seemed almost normal, a clock ticking softly in the background, the smell of fresh flowers in the still air, hazy sunlight from a small window softening the otherwise harsh decor. The only thing separating this room from the activity next door was a brick wall, both houses identical in layout, yet right now couldn't be more different. Carol Jefferson hovered in the middle of her neighbour's lounge before lowering herself into a cushion-filled armchair, holding onto the sides for support neither of us could offer.

'I'm so very sorry for your loss,' Paul stated, trying as always, to maintain professionalism, his understanding courtesy bordering unease. I wondered if his job ever got to him. It certainly got to me.

Carol shook her head. 'I don't understand what happened.' I could tell she was struggling to appreciate the condition she had found her husband, his sudden death unexpected. I hadn't yet witnessed it, was already nervous by the thought of it.

'That's what we are trying to establish,' Paul pitched in calmly. 'Are you okay to talk us through what happened?'

Carol nodded. 'I came home from work to find the front door open. Alex *never* leaves the front door open, not in this neighbourhood.' She looked at me, then at her trembling hands. 'I still can't understand why he would leave the door open.'

'Alex? Your husband?' Paul was writing in his notebook, the victim's first name not yet even established, this case unfolding before my eyes.

'Yes.' She glanced towards Paul, obviously wondering what he was thinking, what he might tell her about this cruel obscenity.

'When was the last time you saw your husband, Mrs Jefferson?'

'Around five o'clock this morning before I left for work.'

'Did anything seem unusual?'

'No. Why would it?' She was looking at Paul as if he knew something she didn't, unsure why he would ask such a question. So was I.

'I'm merely trying to build a picture of events.' Paul offered another thin-lipped smile, still writing, still unable to shed much light on what had happened. 'And your husband seemed *okay*?'

'Of course. He was having a cup of tea and the bacon sandwich I'd made for him, as I do every morning.' She tried to smile but failed, fresh tears springing forward. 'He likes to get up early. To see me off with a wave.' There was a pause, a moment where Carol didn't make a sound. 'Did my husband *kill* himself, detective?' I could see she didn't want such a terrible thought in her head. None of us did.

'As soon as I know more, you'll be the first to know.' Paul could barely look her way, couldn't begin to comprehend the poor woman's pain. 'What happened when you returned home?'

Carol took in a sharp breath, tears cascading down her cheeks. 'Like I said, the front door was open. I called out, thinking the idiot had forgotten to latch it properly. He likes to go out for a walk after his TV programmes have finished. I didn't even notice the blood at first. Not until I removed my shoes.'

'There was blood by your front door?' Paul was writing again.

'Yes. I panicked, thinking he'd hurt himself and *that* was the reason the door was open. I called out but he didn't answer. That's when I noticed the blood inside the bathroom.' She swallowed, not wanting to continue, not wanting the image in her head.

I often find it distressing what grieving people will focus on during difficult times. To Carol Jefferson, concentrating her efforts on an open front door was more important than her dead husband, because thinking of him that way was just too painful. I've been to homes where loved ones have become delirious over an open packet of biscuits or curtains not properly drawn. *Anything* to distract from what matters. The agony of sudden loss.

'I'm so sorry to make you relive all this.' Paul sighed. So did I.

Carol shook her head.

'It's okay,' he added. *It wasn't.* We all waited. For what, I couldn't tell. Even the clock sounded abnormal.

'He was in the bath. Just lying there.' Carol closed her eyes, her cheeks an odd shade of blue. 'There was blood everywhere. I don't even know what happened.' She began to hyperventilate, sucking in air as if she'd never taken a breath before, unsure how to process what she'd witnessed. I handed her a tissue, unable to make any of this better. She didn't take it, merely waved my hand away. 'He was staring at me,' she sobbed. 'His eyes were wide open and he was holding onto the side of his head as if he had a headache.' She released an awkward laugh and sobbed again. 'I thought he'd hurt himself, even asked what the hell he was playing at. It wasn't until I touched him that I realised he was… dead.' She hesitated before confirming her last word, biting her trembling bottom lip. She burst into a torrent of tears, the thought of it too real, too final.

There was a moment of silence, the brief pause allowing us to absorb her words, the idea of finding a loved one in such circumstances, painfully uncomfortable.

'You didn't move him, did you?' Paul asked eventually.

Another head shake.

'I know this is very difficult. Are you okay?'

By the look on her face, Carol didn't need to answer the question.

Paul got to his feet, nothing more to ask at this point, nothing else to add. We hadn't yet witnessed the scene for ourselves, still couldn't confirm whether it was an accident, suicide, or *murder*.

'What happened to my husband, Detective Mannering?' Carol Jefferson called our way as we reached the front door. She stared at my friend as if she couldn't believe she was asking such a question, her day unfolding so very differently to how she'd imagined.

'That is what we intend to find out,' Paul confirmed as we made our uncomfortable apologies, leaving her in the capable hands of her neighbour and a family liaison officer, our job to look for answers nobody wanted to acknowledge.

***

The inside of Carol and Alex Jefferson's property no longer resembled a home. Filled with investigators, evidence bags, and yellow plastic number tags, the kitchen and bathroom were more suited to a movie set than someone's beloved domain. We covered our feet with paper shoes and pulled latex gloves over our hands before going inside the bathroom, mindful of where we stepped and what we touched.

Alex was still lying where his wife had discovered him, his hands seemingly gripping the side of his head, his blank eyes staring ahead. He was covered in blood, his ashen face bloated and lined with purple veins, the bathtub swimming with crimson water that splashed periodically over the floor. At first glance, it was impossible to reason what could have happened. I'd seen less terrifying horror scenes. The poor man looked as if he was trying to hold his brain inside his skull, his eyes wide in shock, as if he somehow believed he might be *saved*. The entire scene was chaos, the body and bathroom left in a terrible state.

'How are you getting on?' Paul was addressing Bernard, the pathologist currently on his knees assessing the body. I stood back and peered over Paul's shoulder, unconvinced I needed a better view.

Bernard sighed, his gloved hands covered with blood, his mind filled with thoughts he hadn't yet shared with us. 'Good afternoon to you, too.'

I smiled, muffling an inappropriate chuckle with my gloved palm as Bernard shook his head. Paul was never one for small talk. I glanced at both men, a swift exchange occurring between the three of us before we got to the crux of the incident.

'At first glance, it looks as if someone has drilled a hole in the side of his skull.' Bernard was looking at the body as if the poor sod was awake and aware of the event when it happened, the dead man staring at us now in no position to confirm what had occurred.

'*What?*' Paul's twisted face said it all.

Bernard nodded grimly. 'Take a look for yourself.' He got to his feet, allowing Paul to move closer, my own feet taking an automatic step back. 'Just above the right temple is a perfectly rounded borehole. It runs deep, too, by the looks of it.' I couldn't tell from my position, but I assumed he was moving what was left of Alex's hair out of the way, offering Paul a better close-up view.

'And you think it was done with a *drill*?' For a brief moment, I thought Paul was going to throw up.

'Yes.'

'Why?'

'We found it over by the toilet covered in blood.'

Shit.

'It wasn't an accident then? Or a heart attack?' I couldn't help pitching in flatly. I would have loved nothing more than to go next door and confirm to Carol Jefferson her poor husband had suffered heart failure, falling into the bathtub and hitting his head in the process. Unless you looked closely there was no way of determining any other cause of death, the borehole behind his matted hair barely visible beyond the blood. No wonder the woman was confused. I couldn't look too long at his swollen features, veins standing to attention like rows of bloated soldiers.

Paul glared at me. He didn't have to say anything.

'I can't conclude having his skull drilled *wouldn't* have brought on a heart attack, but you can clearly see the damage.' Bernard pointed towards the body's inflated head. 'It looks as if the blood tried to clot but gathered in the periosteum space above his skull, swelling his head like a balloon. I'll be able to confirm an actual cause of death once I've done the post-mortem, but I'd state my career on what killed him.' Bernard looked as if he was offering us a smile, his eyes crinkling at the edges beneath his face mask. 'I'm fairly sure he didn't do this to himself. He bit his tongue in half, too. I have it in a bag over by the sink if you want a look.'

I didn't want a look, didn't want the idea in my head.

So, it's definitely murder then?' I asked.

'Well, I can think of better ways to kill myself.' Bernard was no longer smiling.

No one responded.

'How long has he been here?' Paul was looking at the dead man as if he expected the poor sod to answer.

'Oh, only around an hour or two, I'd say, give or take. Not much longer.' Bernard returned his attention to Alex's body, a colleague waiting in the kitchen to take further photographs before they could move him. He lifted a lifeless hand to inspect it. 'His skin has barely absorbed the water.'

Paul checked his watch. 'So that puts the time of death between eleven and twelve.'

Bernard nodded. 'Give or take.'

We thanked Bernard and stepped outside, the air out there no better.

As a psychologist, I couldn't help thinking about temporal lobe damage, a weird idea springing to mind of Alex's attacker either wanting him *dead* or to live with a condition I unfortunately knew far too much about. I recalled a serial killer from a few years ago, dubbed "The Gimlet" who drilled holes into his victim's skulls because he thought it would be fun. The man had no personality to speak of, his nickname created because of the drill he used and the fact he was a perpetual *bore*. I didn't mention this to Paul, or that I'd personally interviewed the guy. Briefly. It didn't matter how hard I'd tried hard to forget all about him. Not until I could check into this further.

Four

Jack

I don't know how long I watch, but I eventually get to my unsteady feet, my only aim to leave this place and go home, attempting to locate something of value beyond what I can't yet accept. I don't know how I manage to sneak away unnoticed, but I slip out of the cemetery like a cat, those currently in this street thankfully busy elsewhere. My legs are like jelly, my body too heavy to walk far, so I find myself waiting for a bus around the corner, trying to slide between the cracks of a life I no longer believe is mine. I don't have to wait long, luckily. However, there are seven people in my presence now who could easily identify me if asked. The driver, an elderly lady, four teenage boys, and a skinny young girl—mouths agape, eyes on stalks, my appearance the reason for their sudden unwanted attention. I try to ignore their sideways sniggers and blatant stares, just kids out to cause trouble, teenagers with nothing better to do. I sit in silence, hoping the journey might pass quickly, listening to the jolting engine, the rattle of ill-fitting windows, disjointed chatter.

The driver is less concerned by what is unfolding than he is of getting through his day unscathed, more stops to make, more travellers to collect. I can't blame him for self-preservation. Yet, despite a brief glance in his rear-view mirror, he does nothing to prevent the chaos erupting behind him, words he could halt if he wanted, violence he could prevent if he chose. These kids toss pieces of chewed paper towards my head, attempting to dislodge the hooded top I have pulled over my face in an attempt to deter attention and any blood still lingering, no real protection from a world I should have avoided today. I don't want confrontation, I swear.

They mock my appearance because they don't know how else to react, my inability to respond to their musings something they find amusing. They see me as a game, a toy to play with while they wait for something better to enlighten their day. In fact, no one other than the thin-lipped old lady does anything to curb the unwanted attention aimed my way. I *am* grateful, her open annoyance displayed behind sharp words and a mop of pure white hair. She notices my discomfort, my silence, receiving an ear full of lip for her efforts, the kids on this bus believing themselves stronger, wiser, *better* than the rest of us. The poor woman is forced to expel their bullying ways with defiance, the shaking of a flustered head, much tutting and underhand muttering.

Embarrassed, I get to my feet, pressing the button three times in quick succession to halt our unwanted journey, easing attention none of us need. I keep my gait purposefully calm as I amble away, my head low because I don't wish to draw attention. I assume those kids will settle down soon enough, their limited focus shifting once I'm gone. I don't expect them to decamp at the next stop, kicking metal panels with outreaching feet, veering off in different directions before one inadvertently heads towards me.

I don't remember much after that. Everything is hazy, too much happening today for my brain to keep up. I find myself standing inside yet another hallway, my aunt's home unwittingly the one place I have considered a sanctuary. I don't recall how I got here but the boy from the bus is lying at my feet. He can't be much older than fifteen, his fresh face unable to produce the stubble that will one day turn him into a man. I shouldn't be surprised to find myself in this unforgiving position, the position of the boy at my feet entirely of his own making. His disjointed attitude shunned me from afar, repelling me from accepted society, seeing a monster instead of a man, something ugly where beauty once lived. It is little wonder I reacted so violently, his blood now on my hands too, if I look. I glare at him, knowing I *should* feel sorry for him, but I don't. Like Alex, he got what he deserved. There is nothing more to say about that, no surprise my mind has chosen to block out the details.

The truth is, I try not to look at my face if I can help it, my appearance little of what I remember, my body nothing more than a target of a selfish drunk driver. He left me for dead, the impact of his vehicle triggering a stroke, highlighting my tumour, ultimately placing me in a coma. No one expected me to wake up. Yet, it caused this shift, changing my looks, my fate, my attitude.

My right eye is now set much lower than my left, blinded by pressure on several nerves, my mouth tilting violently to one side. It looks as if an invisible force is tugging my cheek for fun, laughing at what I can no longer change, laughing at *me*. Because of this, I can't smile. My facial muscles are damaged, the imposition of a reckless drunk creating a chain reaction no one saw coming. I guess I should be grateful. That stranger's selfish disregard for my existence uncovered my cancer. I should probably seek him out, shake his hand, *thank* him. As it is, the collision is now a constant reminder of my pending doom, a continued decline I must face alone. I try not to think too long about that. The doctors shaved my hair at some point too, my once dark curls growing now into a style I no longer recognise — unruly, untidy, difficult to tame. A bit like me. I used to love my hair. It's a shame it will never be as it once was, my face no longer retaining the shape it once did. My left side is bizarrely normal, though, still the *Jack Monroe* I remember, still beautiful. I still feel like me sometimes, if I close my eyes long enough. If I dare hold my breath and dream.

When the boy begins to stir, I take in a lungful of choking air that makes me dizzy, the two of us sucking life-affirming oxygen from our surroundings. I'm thankful he lives, attempting in vain to reclaim the lucidity missing from this day. It's strange. Until this morning everything seemed normal, yet I can no longer go outside without attracting the wrong type of attention. Looking how I do now, it's unsurprising strangers with blank faces and unfeeling eyes watch my every move, expecting the worst, my presence provoking the very reaction that has led us here. Before the accident, those same strangers barely noticed my existence, yet there is nothing left now of the kid who laughed often and loved deeply. The irony is not lost on me.

When the boy stumbles to his feet, there is nothing I can do but watch, unable to understand his incoherent voice, his angry glare set my way through a mop of blood-streaked hair. Like me, he doesn't fully appreciate what has happened, his eyes inflamed, his mouth quivering with an unspoken fear neither of us can ascertain. A few painful seconds pass in stunned silence before he regains his bearings, staggering through my aunt's front door, my misplaced company no longer appropriate. He is clutching the side of his bloodied head, in shock, in pain, his eyes wild with panic. I don't prevent his escape. I can barely look at him.

Instead, I observe from a distance, absorbing how sunlight catches his baby blond hair as he races into the road, his baby-faced cheeks glowing hot, a chilling reality biting into my thoughts when I notice another drill in my trembling grasp. I didn't mean to start this thing, yet I find myself witnessing his demise now, too, my own uncertain, my eyes littered with unthinkable distortions making me feel sick. I would like this day to be nothing but a product of my overactive imagination, a dream, a nightmare, an unfazed entry in my diary. But anger is slowly infecting my memory, the way people seem to find it easy to taunt me, sneering from afar, making me feel like *nothing*.

I take several unsteady steps outside, cautious, careful, all composure and logic gone, that young man's plight distant yet oddly vivid, like the man I have since left dead in his bath. I swallow, wishing only to prove all is well, that I haven't lost my mind to the ravages of this declining world and cancer devouring my soul. Nothing happening from this point on will bring peace to this day, trapped too deeply inside my head, my destiny set in stone. Even the friends I once claimed knew me will never understand what I'm going through, my life almost over, theirs barely begun.

I stagger backwards, closing the door with a slam, locking it in place, sliding the bolts, top and bottom, too upset to appreciate anything else, a flood of emotions encasing my thoughts like treacle. If I hadn't stormed out of my mother's house this morning, things might have been different, today's endeavour not the innocent undertaking I'd hoped. I guess I will never know now. I can't go back and change the past, can never retract emotions spilt in anger.

Five

Newton

We waited for Alex Jefferson's body to be taken away before the police could close the crime scene, unfortunately leaving most of the tidying for Carol, her neighbour, and the family liaison officer. The contents of her bathroom was recorded in photographs, her husband's body heading for the morgue.

Paul was on his mobile, a frustrated look on his face. 'I'll meet you at the station,' he called my way, already walking towards his car.

'Everything okay?' I yelled after him.

'I've been called to another crime scene. I hopefully won't be long.'

This was Paul's job, his life, each day relentless.

I found myself driving across town to the police station

to help with the Alex Jefferson case, if I could, much-needed fresh air eluding me in the lingering heat, my semi-operational fans and uncooperative seatbelt clip doing nothing to ease my troubled thoughts. The stagnant air pumping against my face only added to my discomposure and the thoughts I wouldn't easily get out of my head.

My mobile rang. Paul.

'Sorry, Newt. I *do* need you after all.'

'Oh?' It was rare for my presence to be required twice in a week, let alone twice in a day, my brain not even yet recovered from the last incident. My mobile was on loudspeaker, balanced on the dashboard, sliding across the sun-beaten surface every time I turned a corner.

'Yeah. You might want to take a look for yourself.'

My interest was piqued and I took too long manoeuvring my ageing Volkswagen Beetle around in a quiet street, heading back the way I'd driven.

Tolbert Street was inaccessible, stationery cars bumper to bumper as far as the eye could see. I was forced to park my car along a side street and walk, unable to get any closer, wading through a crowd of stunned faces, my clothing clinging to my skin like a leech. The heady temperature of a lingering summer had given way to frayed tempers and untamed turbulence in the form of frustrated drivers, it seemed, several now aiming their wrath my way. There was a breeze, but it added to the humidity, a haze of swarming insects offering no respite from traffic tailing onto the high street.

Paul was already in the thick of things, the exhausted look on his face nothing new. He glanced my way, his approach slow, his knotted features almost as stressed as mine. I assumed the heat was to blame, the afternoon air stagnant, our sluggish movements brought about by the day's traumas and dust that clung uncomfortably to my lungs. I offered a deflated smile, unconvinced I wasn't about to add to his problems, a headache threatening my patience, my thoughts, my sanity.

'Sorry,' he breathed, his reddened cheeks a by-product of his stress-induced existence. 'I can see this turning into a *very* long day.' He was searching the scene as if to apologise for the carnage surrounding us, disgruntled drivers hovering impatiently next to open car doors, honking horns set against a sea of beet-red faces.

'I don't understand why you need me.' I didn't for one second assume my presence was required. From what I had gathered, this was a road traffic collision. They happened daily, nothing unusual in *that*. I couldn't rationalise what Paul expected me to unpick from this one, nothing out of the ordinary from what I could see. I glanced around, failing to understand the commotion or my friend's blank expression. A witness was speaking with DI Tony Avery. They were trembling, visibly shaken by what had happened, the victim unmoving on the ground. A young lad, from what Paul had already confirmed, the kid no older than my nephew. Paramedics surrounded him. It wasn't a comforting image.

'I need your opinion on something.' Paul sighed, pulling a piece of syrupy chewing gum from his pocket already melting in the heat, a brief struggle with the wrapper ensuing before he grappled it into his mouth. Under normal circumstances it would have made me laugh, offering a moment of contemplation, a cause for amusement. However, I was too hot to laugh, this location too hectic for sarcasm. He offered me the packet. I declined.

'Opinion on what?' I couldn't fully appreciate my friend's stern expression or the thoughts twisting violently behind his eyes. Sweat was trickling into mine, removing the ability to think.

Paul pulled me to one side, stepping into the road so no one would hear him. 'I don't yet have all the details, but the ambulance crew believe this was not the simple traffic incident we were initially led to believe.'

'How so?' I glanced towards the unconscious lad thankfully now on his way to the awaiting ambulance. I was unsure if it was the heat, my failing mindset or the day in general, but the scene triggered a flashback to my troubled past, to a time long ago I doubt would leave me, my dead brother always in my thoughts, his memory forever in my head. It wouldn't be the first time I'd witnessed carnage like this, probably wouldn't be the last. No one yet knew if the boy's condition was life-threatening, swift intervention critical. Eastcliff was becoming a dangerous place, it seemed, a place unfit for the living. I couldn't help wondering if the motionless kid was dead.

'Several witnesses claim to have seen the young man race into the street, but there is speculation he was injured *before* the vehicle hit him. From what we've been told, the front wing of the passing Audi barely clipped his leg.' Paul pointed towards a car some feet away, the driver visibly shaken. 'The vehicle wasn't travelling all that fast from what we can determine. It wouldn't have caused the injuries he sustained.' He paused. 'What everyone initially assumed was a collision doesn't now appear to be the case.'

'Why?' I still wasn't grasping the urgency of the situation, or why Paul needed *me*. I gave him a blank look.

'The paramedics can't say for certain until they get him to the hospital, but he has a suspicious wound on the side of his head.' Paul was chewing loudly now, his gum sticking to his teeth, what was left of his receding hair sticking to his balding head.

'Suspicious how?' A pool of deep red glistened in the sunlight, mocking us from afar, making me feel sick. I tried not to look.

'Well, this is the strange part.' Paul sighed, placing sweaty hands on his hips. 'They say he has some kind of puncture wound.' He glanced towards the ambulance, its frantic crew no doubt busy trying to save the boy's life. 'That's why I need your thoughts.' Paul didn't look happy to confirm it.

I raised my eyebrows. 'What kind of *wound?*' I was sick of asking questions promising only vague answers. I needed coffee. A cold one. With ice. Preferably before I passed out.

Paul glared at me. 'The kind suggesting someone drilled a hole in the side of his head.'

***

I followed Paul's car to the hospital with a steady hum of full-speed fans keeping pace with my unhinged thoughts. None of us anticipated what today's incidents meant for the unassuming residents of Eastcliff, the police forever entrenched in the impossible, just another puzzle to decipher, another case to solve. No one appreciated the seriousness of the situation, this day set to trigger something none of us could have foreseen. As it was, a forensics team was once more left to access the mess, witnesses questioned at length to confirm anything we didn't yet know. CCTV would be searched, the victim's last known whereabouts checked. We didn't know if the kid was stable, if he could confirm what happened, or if he would live.

I joined Paul along a brightly lit hospital corridor, this indoor space offering no respite from the heat outside. When a doctor appeared, his blank expression and perspiring forehead did little for my lowered mood.

'DCI Mannering?' The doctor's face was almost as red as mine.

Paul nodded, glancing my way briefly before turning his attention to the reason we were here, to the medical staff trained to save lives. No one expected the kid to live, enough blood lost to confirm a potential swift end, his injuries already assumed life-threatening. We had Alex Jefferson on our minds. It wasn't helpful.

'How's the boy?'

'Alive,' the doctor confirmed flatly, shaking Paul's sweaty hand.

'Do you know what happened?' Paul gave him a nondescript look. So did I.

'The damage *looked* far worse than it was, thankfully. The skull injury was superficial. You can blame adrenaline for that. And the heat.' The doctor paused, glancing between the two of us, hoping we'd know what he meant. Blood pumps faster when you're stressed, hot, or both, a paper cut capable of looking horrendous given the right conditions.

Paul sighed. He didn't need to elaborate. 'How's he doing?'

'Aside from a minor injury to his skull, he has three broken ribs, a twisted ankle and some bruising to his chest. He'll be sore for a few days but I'm confident he'll make a full recovery.'

Paul glanced my way, relief written all over his face. None of us were yet certain if his injuries were caused by the moving car or the same attacker who'd killed Alex, confirmation he was in no immediate danger exactly what we needed to hear.

'What can you tell us about his head injury?' Paul was writing in his notebook, too many scribbles and doodles to make sense of.

The doctor narrowed his eyes. 'That's an odd one. The wound mark is clean, precise. If I didn't know better, I would say someone tried to drill a hole in his skull.'

'Are you sure it was *drilled?*' I couldn't help asking. It was the second time today I'd heard the theory, witnessed the carnage. It seemed a crazy concept, a ludicrous suggestion. I glanced at Paul. He didn't look back. I couldn't accept the thought of someone out there, deliberately drilling skulls because they could. The Gimlet popped into my thoughts again.

'Yes, but whatever was used didn't penetrate the bone too deeply, luckily, merely caused superficial flesh wounds, fractured his skull. He will have a headache. Plenty of bruising.'

'You think he was *lucky?*' I raised my eyebrows. No one commented. He was far luckier than Alex.

'Could the injury have been caused by something *other* than a drill?' Paul folded his arms, biting his bottom lip unconsciously until it turned white. It seemed an obvious question, one I agreed with. Maybe the passing car had a protruding implement attached to it. Maybe he'd fallen against something sharp. Anything else meant only one thing. There was a potential nutcase on the loose.

The doctor shook his head. 'That's not for me to assess, I'm afraid, but something definitely attempted to penetrate his skull. Unfortunately, that's all we currently know.' He glanced my way. 'I doubt it was accidental, though. The wound is cylindrical, almost like a borehole. Here, take a look for yourselves.' He stepped to one side, guiding us into a small area lit by fluorescent screens, each displaying X-rays of what appeared to be the boy's skull. 'You can tell by the trajectory the bone was most likely drilled. You can even see the drill marks if you look carefully.'

'Can you tell what *type* of drill was used?' Paul had already consigned himself to the reality of the doctor's words, no reason to believe his theory was as ludicrous as I did.

'No. I'm afraid not.' I could tell the doctor was trying to maintain professionalism. 'I guess that's down to you lot to determine.' It wasn't a comforting thought, not an ideal conclusion. It didn't matter that it happened to be true.

'How deep is the wound?' Paul sounded as if he couldn't believe he was asking such a question. He was busy writing, determining the impossible.

'That I *do* know.' The doctor checked a file on a nearby desk. 'The skull was punctured by approximately four millimetres, give or take.'

'So, not enough to cause any lasting damage?' I needed to ask. It didn't sound much, but the brain is a delicate piece of equipment, easily damaged by the slightest impact. I took a step closer to assess the injury for myself, enough medical training to understand what I was looking at, my degree in medical science not something I spoke about often. A human adult male skull is around six millimetres thick, give or take. I didn't mention this to the doctor, or Paul, didn't want to sound like a know-it-all, a failed doctor who turned his attention to psychology. It wasn't true. I just wanted a change of direction.

'No. He should be all right, thankfully. We'll be keeping him in overnight for observation but he doesn't seem to have sustained any lasting issues. See for yourself?' The doctor stepped into the corridor, peeling open a nearby curtain to reveal the young man in question. He was propped against a plethora of pillows, a bandage around his head, two black eyes, a blank expression on his face. He was very much alive, very much awake. A female was by his bedside, holding his hand, a worried look on her face. His mum, no doubt.

'This is one lucky young man,' the doctor stated, a little too brightly for this moment. He stood by the bed, a look on his face he probably didn't mean to portray, a fake smile welded in place. 'Any deeper and we wouldn't be having this conversation.' He nodded towards the boy's unsmiling companion, failing to appreciate the magnitude of his words or the shocked look the kid now gave *him*. 'I'll leave you in the capable hands of these two police officers, Ben,' he concluded somewhat patronisingly, glancing our way before leaving us to it. I didn't correct him, didn't look at Paul, a knowing smile already planted conveniently behind his overheated palm.

Six

Jack

I have no memory of this summer, the coma I was unwittingly absorbed in for a while nothing more than a passage in time I can't recall, a shifting phase I will never understand—a dreamland, a *nothing*. In fact, the only recollection I have is standing on a kerbside some months ago, innocently crossing the road. I didn't assume I was in any danger, didn't believe such a simple undertaking could change my life and the lives of those I know. Yet, today has triggered a shift I didn't see coming, my mind tipped by events I'm not inclined to recall. I can't even breathe now without unrelenting pain, contrived thoughts crashing over my body like crumbling rocks into a sea of black, dragging me underwater, my overworked lungs convinced I'm drowning. My world has silenced, nothing to remind me of this day other than a hot breeze and shallow breath I'm no longer convinced is mine. My drifting memories confirm today's insanity, that's all, impossible visions of my victims vivid whenever I close my eyes. Even walking back along the canal path offers no comfort, nothing here but murky brown water for company, mocking me, preventing my escape.

I stop. Take a moment. The blinding mist engulfing me earlier has cleared, but I'm uncertain I can take the truth just yet, can barely take a breath. We all do things in anger, things we later regret. Unfortunately, the screams of those people are becoming embedded in my head, any desire for calm coming too late to steady my thoughts or constrain my actions. I could blame my condition, if I chose, my frustration, stress, everyone else. But they don't appreciate my *real* problems stem from the lasting damage I've sustained.

Number one. I can no longer eat without help. This is because the nerves controlling muscles used for swallowing are damaged, and so I was attached to an intravenous drip for a few weeks while they decided what to do. In the end, they did nothing. The tumour is too deep, any attempt to operate too dangerous. They have tried chemotherapy, of course, but it makes me sick and I no longer eat anything beyond tasteless concoctions blended into liquid. If it wasn't for my mother I'd have wasted away weeks ago, no appetite left to speak of, no inclination to drag this thing out much further. Besides, I don't want others to see me like *this*. I want them to remember me as I was; attractive, strong-willed, my private education and extravagant upbringing affording me a bright future, my well-formed upper-class accent affording me much attention. Most of that is now gone, of course, my education and obstinance the only things remaining. I even walk with a stoop, my confidence dwindled to nothing.

Number two. I can't speak. They say this is because of the stroke, but it doesn't help and the only thing I've been doing since regaining consciousness is dribbling into my lap. Being unable to communicate is probably the hardest thing to deal with if I'm honest. I can't tell others how I'm feeling, can't express my growing frustration.

Number three. And this is the big one. I will never recover. Until a few weeks ago most believed I would never wake up. As it is, my condition has incapacitated my ability for facial expression, ensuring people now look at me as if I've gone mad. Maybe I have. Maybe this is how it's meant to be.

I knew something was wrong before the accident, before my diagnosis, a nagging doubt lying in wait beneath the bravado of deluded perfection. I've suffered with headaches for a while. Yet, everyone equated them to stress, overwork, too many late nights studying when I should have been asleep. As it currently stands, I don't know if I will be well enough to complete my psychology degree, a fast-growing tumour ensuring I probably won't live long enough to appreciate the life I *should* have grasped when it mattered. The prognosis is terminal, my time limited now to however many months my body can keep functioning. *Months.* That's all I have left. They say I won't make it to Christmas.

I settle my malfunctioning body on a nearby bench, ducks and dogs unconcerned by my presence, the few humans surrounding me no more appreciative of my appearance than *I* am. They pretend they haven't noticed me but can't hide their shock, forced to witness unforgiving glares and uncomfortable whispers, nothing to disguise their unease. I close my eyes against their indignation, my heart in my throat, my legs like jelly beneath my fractured façade. It is easy to find yourself thinking negatively when darkness is all you have for misplaced company, tangling your mind in knots you can never unravel. Until today, I didn't consider myself aggressive, my thoughts happy to reside in private. Yet, this day has singlehandedly changed that.

I'm trying to recall today's journey, if I can, to the reason things happened in the order they did. But the only thing lingering now is a frustrated outburst that left several broken plates on the floor of my mother's kitchen, unspoken words hanging like rope around my neck, a dead man in his bathtub, a boy staggering into the street. My injuries add to my fury. I can't help it. Who I am *now* and who I once hoped to become is lost forever to the ravages of time I do not have.

The boy called me ugly. I remember *all* too clearly now. I recall how it made me feel, my life meaning nothing to those who will never really know who I am. I'm *not* ugly, although I no longer look in mirrors if I can help it. It helps no one to dwell over things I can't alter and it makes me sad to see what I've become. Every day is the same as the last, every moment a painful reflection of an unresolved existence I will never understand, my body set to dissipate without anyone's help. I had no control over what happened to me, less control over what happened today, those events nothing but a by-product of my unfettered imagination. I keep my head down where possible, skirting acceptance, offhand repose oddly affording me the space I require—to think, to ponder, to dream.

I have no idea if I have luck to thank or circumstance, but finding myself outside my aunt's home felt like fate. I've hardly dared venture outside for weeks, happy to hide behind the sanctuary of thin cocooning walls, knowing all I need to know about the human mind from inside my own. I falsely assumed I'd be glad for the fresh air, a brief solace from my daily battles. I was wrong. Instead, a veil has been placed over my life, suffocating my every breath, my small world turned on its head. I can't express my emotions about how *dying* is affecting me, but I guess you can't unless you're going through it. I merely welcome time alone now, when my family, the world and life take a toll I can't expel—space I'm unable to locate, peace I will never find inside the walls of a bedroom still claiming ownership of my long-forgotten childhood.

I glance skyward, wishing my professor was here. He would know what to say to make me feel better. It's a shame Professor Flanigan doesn't know how I feel about him because if he did, things might be different. He once described me as an angry young man, his words something along the lines of, *'Jack, you're in danger of becoming an angry young man in a world that doesn't care about you.'* He believed his throwaway comment too, didn't appreciate the profound effect it would have on me. I have never forgotten the way he looked at me, can't change his assumptions. The description is true enough, I guess. Looking at me now, he might have a point.

My so-called *anger* stems directly from the cast-off actions of a drunk driver and a tumour devouring my brain—a stranger's fast-moving vehicle ensuring for me and my family, nothing will ever be the same again.

Angry? My professor doesn't know the half of it.

Seven

Newton

Paul's inappropriate grin was set in place as he moved a plastic chair to the side of Ben's hospital bed and lowered himself onto it, grateful for a fast-spinning fan that spat warm air around the room. I couldn't tell what the woman on the far side of the bed was thinking but she looked frantic, if not a little broken. I recognised the pained look in her eyes, the way she fleetingly glanced our way, her twitching legs unsure what to make of this impossible situation.

'Good afternoon, young man,' Paul stated, leaning forward as if he was about to shake the boy's hand, the stifling heat suffocating the conversation before it had even commenced. Instead, he placed his hands in his lap and smiled towards the woman who'd so far offered no acknowledgement, attempting to remain calm, professional, polite.

Ben nodded, the woman's glare fixed on ours, her eyes narrowing defensively at every movement we made. There was little to see of the boy's eyes beyond swollen slits that matched purple cheekbones. The poor kid looked as if someone had inflated a balloon inside his head.

'How are you feeling?' I was grateful for Paul's politeness, although his mannerisms confirmed today's visit was *not* for the sake of Ben's health. He was here to assess what had happened, to uncover who was responsible, how he could hold them accountable—*results* all that mattered, in the end.

'I don't remember much, to be honest,' Ben muttered, struggling to speak through the swelling in his face, in obvious pain yet thankfully alert enough for questioning. His injuries did indeed look worse than they were. The doctor was right about that.

'Can you tell us what you *do* remember? I promise we won't keep you long.'

Ben shrugged, glancing briefly towards the woman who gingerly placed a trembling hand over his, offering a smile she barely managed to sustain. She didn't speak, instead took in a breath and held it.

'It all happened so fast.' Ben's voice was tiny. It matched his build, his uncertainty, the way he chewed his bottom lip with unconfirmed anticipation.

'Just start from the beginning.' Paul took his notebook from his pocket, leaving me hovering in the middle of the room with nowhere to go and nothing to do but watch, listen and hope I wouldn't get in the way. I considered getting us a drink but changed my mind. I couldn't assess this kid's state of mind from a vending machine. I offered the woman a smile. She didn't return it.

Ben looked as if he wasn't sure where to begin or how to explain today's events. I felt sorry for him, unsure what to do with my hands other than clasp them behind my back. I didn't dare move in case I triggered an unwanted distraction.

'Some mad bastard attacked me,' he grunted, shaking his head, immediately regretting his decision by the way he winced, glancing at the woman now as if she was about to chastise him for his foul language. I thought of the headache he would have in the morning, my own steadily worsening with every laboured breath I took.

'Care to elaborate?' Paul was busy writing, his scratchy pen annoying me, this hospital too hot.

'He grabbed me from behind. I didn't see it coming.'

'*Who* grabbed you, Ben?' Paul glanced up, his attention caught.

Ben attempted to close his eyes before realising he couldn't, swelling preventing such a simple task. 'I don't remember.'

'Are all these questions necessary?' The woman pitched in, the room seemingly too imposing for her to remain silent. She rose unsteadily to her feet, the heat adding nothing to her stress levels *or* ours.

'I know this is a difficult time for you, Mrs…'

'*Harris.*' She shook her head as if Paul's ignorance was annoying. 'Ben's *mum.*'

Paul's earlier smile slipped. 'Of course. I promise we will be as quick as we can.' He glanced between Ben, his mum, and me, glad I was still in the room before continuing. 'How did you end up in the middle of the street with a hole in the side of your head, Ben?' The question came from nowhere, no time to skirt around the edges of what none of us yet knew had happened.

'Don't you *care* what my boy has been through?' Another outburst from Ben's mum made Paul suck in a lungful of stale air that made me take a breath in response. I'm sure he was on the verge of asking her to leave the room. If Ben wasn't a minor, he probably would have.

Thankfully my friend ignored her question, keen to ask more of his own, merely trying to ascertain the facts. He was desperate to uncover what had happened and get out of here, a serious attacker on the lose. After all, the police were initially led to believe the kid was hit by a car. It would make things easier for everyone if Paul could help jog his memory.

'Why did you run into the middle of the road?'

'I vaguely remember coming from a nearby house.'

'What house?'

A shrug.

Paul made a note in his book, probably to check any nearby CCTV footage, eyewitnesses, doorbell cameras, home surveillance, conveniently placed mobile phones forever in people's grasp.

'It doesn't matter how much you can recall at this stage, Ben. *Anything* will be helpful.' Paul offered the kid's mum a brief smile, his hope merely to reassure her, confirm he wasn't here to cause distress or place her boy in further turmoil. She didn't respond. Paul stopped writing, his lingering smile as fake as I'd ever seen it. It was probably the heat, but my friend couldn't have looked more irritated if he tried. He was used to people's reluctance, their unconfirmed nonchalance, the police often seen as nothing more than unwanted relatives taking up space at Christmas. But it didn't make it easier to deal with.

'I just *told* you. I don't remember *anything*.' The boy was becoming impatient, picking dirt from behind his nails, biting skin from his parched lips. He looked nervous. I couldn't tell why.

'Do you need to do this *now?*' Ben's mum was annoyed by questions getting us nowhere, still hovering on irritated legs, still glaring at Paul.

Paul sighed, glancing my way, probably wondering how quickly he could unload the burden of this moment onto me. He got to his feet, his bones creaking in the heat.

'Why don't I get us all a cold drink?' He was trying to be nice. If these people knew him as I did, they would appreciate he was trying his best.

Ben's mum nodded, her expression telling me she was glad the detective was leaving. He stepped past me, winked, his thinning hairline rippled with sweat, his shirt glued uncomfortably to his armpits. I could tell he needed to escape this room while he could, nothing of Ben's recent injuries yet verified. I returned my friend's acknowledgement with a nod as I stepped towards the bed.

'Hi, Ben. My name's Newton,' I pitched in, sounding uncharacteristically bright and enthusiastic. Ben didn't acknowledge me, didn't look my way. I sat down, the seat still warm where Paul's overheated body had moments earlier been, my own reeling now in response. I swear, if I didn't get some air soon, I'd be joining this kid in the next bed.

Ben glared at me. If he could have narrowed his eyes further, he probably would have.

'Let's start again shall we?' I wanted them both to know the police weren't here to cause distress. I smiled, provoking a quiver from Ben's mum's uncertain lips.

'I know today must be a day you wish you could forget,' I sighed sympathetically, looking into the boy's eyes, not certain which of the two I was addressing. I didn't expect an answer, merely trying to gauge his mood, his persona. 'Why don't you tell me what happened?'

Silence.

I regarded him for a moment, thankful for the bustling hospital keeping my brain company, the last hour passing in a haze. 'How old are you, Ben?' I was only asking because a kid his age needed reassurance, support, someone beyond his family network to help him through this. Whatever *this* was.

Ben glanced my way, a confused look on his face. 'Almost fifteen.'

I smiled inwardly, mildly amused by how he'd made himself sound more grown up than he was, more responsible than he was no doubt given credit for. He reminded me of my nephew, Peter, around the same age, the same non-compliant attitude in tow, wanting to be treated like an adult instead of the kid he was. *Almost* fifteen. Ben's statement spoke louder than he realised.

'That's a great age. It feels like only yesterday since *I* was fifteen.' It wasn't. A lifetime had passed since then. 'At fifteen you have your whole life ahead of you, so much promise and potential.' My fake smile slipped. I couldn't help it. I was hot. Instead, I glanced over my shoulder to ensure Paul hadn't returned, wasn't listening, couldn't scoff. 'So, how are you, *really?*'

'Why do *you* care?' I was given a dismissive glare, a disgruntled sigh emerging from his mum's mouth in response to her son's outburst.

'Because I'm not a copper, and I have no other motive than to support you, to *help* you.' I was getting the distinct impression he'd done something he didn't want to get into trouble over, more to the story he wasn't sharing. I glanced towards his mum. She looked away.

'You're not a policeman?' Ben glanced towards the door, no doubt wondering whether to believe me or accuse me of something, the doctor's earlier incorrect assumption still in his head.

I shook my own, grateful we'd been left alone to discuss things the poor kid didn't seem keen to share with the authorities. Paul knew I'd fill him in later, anyway. I didn't confirm I was a psychologist paid to dissect degenerates like him, every unspoken word logged, every unconscious movement recorded in my head for later assessment. No one needed to know I rarely dealt with kids.

'Whatever you tell me will stay between the two of us, I promise.' I raised three closed fingers towards him. 'Scouts honour.' I don't know why I did that. Beyond an isolated session I'd attended with Isaac when I was ten, I was *never* in the scouts, my brother the one with all the badges, the achievements, our parents proud accreditation and overbearing appraisal not something I'd forget.

'I think the guy had a drill or something.' Ben offered eventually, glancing sheepishly towards his mum who was thankfully sitting down again now. She shifted uncomfortably in her chair. He didn't look pleased to confirm it, seemed almost embarrassed if anything.

'Are you sure it was a *drill?*' I tried not to look shocked by the consideration.

A nod.

'And can you describe your attacker?' I had a horrible vision of some crazed lunatic on the loose, Eastcliff yet again claiming ownership of an untamed madman. I'd blame the sea air if anyone asked, an overburdened population.

'Just some random on the bus.' Ben sighed. I could tell he didn't want the image in his head. Nobody would.

'What bus?'

Ben shrugged. He glanced briefly at his mum before looking away.

'Don't you want us to help you?' I couldn't understand why he wouldn't want his attacker brought to justice, if he could, why he hadn't already confirmed all this to Paul. It seemed an obvious course of action, a logical next step.

Another shrug.

'Do you know who your attacker is, Ben?' It suddenly seemed a very real possibility he was protecting someone. I couldn't imagine who, couldn't comprehend why. Certainly not a friend.

Ben shook his head. I'm not sure I believed him.

'Did anyone witness the attack?'

'I don't know. Like I said, the guy grabbed me from behind and hit me with his crutches.'

My eyebrows sprang skyward. 'Crutches?' This suddenly didn't sound like your average attacker, a mugging gone wrong, a frustrated grudge thrust upon a passing stranger. I tried not to screw my face into a knot, tried not to show my confusion.

'Yeah. He hit me and kicked me a few times. I think he was trying to knock me out or something.' Ben was becoming frustrated, wincing violently at his own strained words, his injuries still fresh, trying not to notice his mum's pained reaction.

'On the bus?' There would be witnesses, CCTV footage. They were probably being obtained as I spoke.

'No. After we got off.' Ben didn't look my way, could barely look at his mum.

'We?'

No answer.

'You were with someone? Friends?'

Silence.

'Can you describe the man on crutches?'

'Crazy looking. A bit of a freak, actually.' Ben could barely bring himself to look up, instead pressed swollen eyelids towards his cheeks. I think he might have been crying.

'We're done here,' Ben's mum pitched in then, raising a frustrated hand, her already frustrated voice elevating, tapping her foot, chewing her lip, glaring at me as if *I* were the problem.

'What makes a person a freak, Ben? What makes them crazy-looking?' I couldn't help my questions, my accusations, sounding more like Paul than was comfortable. Ben no longer appeared as innocent as we initially assumed.

'I dunno. The bloke looked as if he'd had a stroke or something. Could barely walk in a straight line. Was probably drunk.' Ben scoffed. I ignored it.

I paused, taking a moment to think. A disabled man walking with crutches, appearing either drunk or disorientated did not sound the type of person who would willingly attack unprovoked. Unless he had dementia or a mental illness, and that sounded unlikely. No. There was more to the story, more Ben wasn't sharing.

'Why would you assume he'd had a stroke?'

No answer.

'How did you end up inside his house?'

More silence.

'Can you give me the address, at least?' It was my turn now to take out a notebook, my chewed pencil witnessing better days. Tolbert Street, of course, but what number? Paul still hadn't returned. I was glad. I was usually far better at my job.

Ben shook his head. 'I wasn't taking much notice of where I was. Too busy being beat to shit.' He was becoming increasingly irritated. I ignored that too.

'Why would a disabled man beat you up?'

'I didn't say he was disabled.'

'You said he walked with crutches and he looked either drunk or as if he'd suffered a stroke. Does this sound like an able-bodied person to you?'

Ben shrugged. 'Like I keep saying, I don't know. I was just walking along the street minding my own business when something hit me from behind. He dragged me backwards and before I knew what was happening, I was inside some random hallway with a sharp pain in my head.' Ben was suddenly keen to speak, a little too eager to protest his innocence, his memory making a rapid reappearance.

'But you claim the guy was on crutches?' Ben was lying to me about something. I didn't know why.

A nod.

'So how would he have been able to drag you anywhere?'

More silence, the room now threatening to throttle us all.

'Ben?'

'I don't know.'

'But you claim you did nothing to provoke this person?' I'd narrowed my eyes now too, the heat of this conversation too much.

'*Of course, he didn't!*' Ben's mum's unexpected interruption was annoying, no preconceived presumption her boy would ever do something so terrible. She glared at me, her unspoken grievances apparent. I sighed. I was only doing my job.

'You mentioned you were not alone on the bus. Who were you with?'

A loud sigh. I wasn't sure if it was Ben or his mum.

'Okay, tell me about the drill, then.' I wasn't sure I wanted to know but I was convinced the kid was hiding something. I wasn't about to give up just yet.

Ben reached up and touched his bandaged head, his embarrassment disguised behind the redness of bruised cheeks. He took a breath, the memory of what happened too vivid. 'It all happened so fast.'

'Care to elaborate?'

'No.'

'Why?'

Ben glanced at his mum. He didn't say anything else but it prompted her to jump to her feet again, this time rounding the bed as if she were planning to attack me. 'You need to leave my son to rest. *Now.*'

I was ushered out of the room like an unwanted rat, this woman in no mood to see her injured boy questioned further. I glanced his way as I left the room. Something didn't add up. I just didn't know what.

Eight

Jack

The first thing I do when I get home is stand in front of my bedroom mirror because, despite my frustration, I need to acknowledge how others perceive me. The supposed privacy of my room offers no protection from the world outside, compelled instead to endure the silence of my so-called private space *and* this tortured moment. I can barely look at my damaged reflection, yet I'm unwilling to blink in case I accidentally miss something. Standing in my room like this, I finally understand what it means to be *me*.

'Jack?'

My mother's familiar vocals filter along the landing, forcing me to acknowledge my surroundings, my plight. I wish she wouldn't speak to me as if she expects an answer. I'm unable to engage a smile let alone a conversation, locked inside my head, in this for the duration. She pops her permanently flustered head around the doorframe and smiles, nodding in my direction, her grin slipping slightly in response to my incensed features glaring back. I don't know how else to react, my demonic reflection hovering outside my blurred peripheral vision.

I should take this moment as a sign, a mark of things to come. Blinded by what I have done, the *thing* I see looking back is nothing more than a monster I must now live with, my once blue eyes nothing but hollow grey shapes in a sunken skull. I don't mean to recoil, don't wish to display my distress. Yet, my reproach is firm, my hands gripping the bedframe behind me because I don't know what else to do with them, tears springing from eyes that see nothing but pain.

'*Jack!* Is everything okay?'

My mother races towards me and presses her hands over my shoulders, pulling me into an embrace she believes I need. She means well, but the only thing I need is for her to leave me alone, imagining her reaction should she learn what I've done. I push her away, already having pushed all thoughts of hope from my mind.

'Are you okay?' She takes a step back but strokes what is left of my hair all the same, knowing how much it used to soothe me, hoping to relive those precious days we will never recapture.

I shrug, unconcerned by how I'm making her feel. I am not okay. Nothing about this is okay. I raise my swollen eyes towards the ceiling, unable to look at her, unable to respond. I shouldn't be too hard on her, I know. She only has my best interests at heart and despite our earlier one-sided argument, what happened today is hardly her fault. It no longer matters how long I ignored my instincts and her unfettered words, venturing outside against her instructions, blaming her because of bitter words spilt in vain. I wish I'd listened, wish I'd known then what I know now, wish I could have foreseen the outcome. As it is, two people have found themselves at the painful end of my anger, whether the boy lives or dies entirely out of my control.

I close my eyes, keen to disguise any further irritation as I step forward and take a breath, my mouth close enough to the mirror now to fog the glass, my thoughts dark enough to destroy us all. I can't vouch for anyone's opinion on my existence because my views on such matters are hindered by my inability to communicate. In my head, I can speak with the perfect affluence of all the words I have learned in books, and this is good enough for me. In fact, if it wasn't for what happened less than an hour ago, it would still feel like any other day—the sun shining, birds singing, kids playing in a park overlooking the sea.

My mother hovers behind me for a brief moment before retracting onto the landing. She is no longer smiling. Probably can't. She doesn't say anything else. I dare a fleeting glance at my reflection as she retreats into her room, closing a door that offers no protection from tears forever seeping through these thin walls. I once considered myself a good-looking boy. Everyone did. *Now look at me.*

'You haven't been upsetting your mum again have you, Jack?' The sound of my father's imposing voice jolts me from my private thoughts, standing in my bedroom doorway now too, hovering, looking pathetic. I had no idea he was here.

My estranged father visits from time to time, when so-called important issues arise, when my mother fails to cope with the kids he gave her before alcohol became a priority, offering misguided support whenever he tries to stay sober. I assume today is one of those occasions, my earlier disappearance enough to see him rush to this house when summoned, as if my parents solidarity is unmoving. I despise how people *always* make things about them. I'm the one going through this, the one suffering, no idea what will happen beyond treatment unable to prolong my life, barely any future to speak of. They say I could have died. Maybe I should have. I glance down and grunt. It's the only controllable thing I can get my body to do.

My father's unexpected presence makes me reach up and touch my damaged face. I don't know why. I can feel him staring, that's all, saliva already leaking from my mouth. My uneven skin is rough in places, sore. It's embarrassing. I part my lips, willing my brain to communicate something of value, *anything* to make me feel normal. Yet nothing emerges and I can't look at my father, can hear nothing beyond the noise in my head or the children in the street, the adult in this room looking at me as if he's waiting for a miracle.

I should have known something was destined to change things, change *me.* It's not my fault. I couldn't have anticipated what that was until now, could never have determined what was coming. But it was bound to happen, I guess, in the end. Someone was eventually going to push me too far, shifting the balance from what I once considered normal to someone I still don't believe exists.

I pick up a discarded mug, noticing a thick rim of green around the top before I throw it against my mirror in disgust. It cracks, shattering the glass into several pieces, showering cold tea over me and a nearby wall. I have no idea what I'm planning to do, but I need to *fix* my face, my problems, remove all traces of what I've become from my own pained glare. My father dives forward, rushing to help, but I'm too swift, already retrieving a shard of mirror from the carpet. I'm a madman possessed, attempting to cut my wrists, my arms, my face. There is so much blood. I can't tell where it's coming from but I can't stop, unconcerned for the damage I'm causing, unconcerned for myself. My legs struggle to cooperate without my crutches, of course, my arms flailing wildly in response to my surroundings. I've drawn blood, drawing attention. Eventually, my father grapples it from my hand, assessing my wounds.

He yells something I don't initially grasp, grabbing my arms, my wrists, my world blinded by my impending death, the entire room robbing me of rational thought. Someone is crying. It isn't me. I can barely make out a shape in the doorway, my mother trembling, sobbing, alerted to the commotion by my yelling father. He tells her it's okay, yet offers no comfort to me.

I can barely understand his words over the noise in my head, my sister still at summer school club, out of earshot, out of the way. He is crying now too, for some reason, unwilling to accept what his son has become, none of them willing to see me as I am.

I have no idea what they would think of me if they knew what happened today. They will not understand, yet neither do I. I am not even certain how I got home.

Nine

Newton

The following morning came around quickly. I was still half asleep as I headed across town to the police station, the place busy, as always, ringing phones and chattering voices ensuring it was beginning to feel like my second home. Each desk told its own story, officers too busy to keep track, thoughts as muddled here as they were on the street. I'd been asked to offer insight on the second crime scene, the Alex Jefferson case seemingly not the isolated incident we'd hoped. Bernard had assessed the dead man, preliminary findings now in Paul's possession. It was a shame his poor wife was left to pick up the pieces of yesterday's tragic event. I could still see the look on her face if I closed my eyes.

The first thing I did was grab a coffee, the bitter texture

eased only by sugar I loaded into my cup. It was already warm, every window cranked wide to invite illusive air. I was trying to recall what I knew about temporal lobe injuries, damage to this part of the brain often causing problems with speech, paranoia, aggression, memory loss, attention disorder, seizures. I concluded whoever was responsible for drilling skulls must have appreciated the damage it would provoke. If it didn't kill them, they would never be the same again. I stared at the whiteboard, wondering if the attacker *knew* about "The Gimlet". Was he copying him? Was it some kind of sick game he was playing?

I picked up a packet of biscuits, my belly growling, no time for breakfast, still pondering impossible thoughts as Paul turned to address his team, his large voice booming into the heat-induced space.

'Good morning, everyone. Thanks for coming in so early. I'll try and make this brief.'

Everyone stopped what they were doing, the room already too hot for anything else. I was acutely aware of the silence as the biscuit packet rustled in my grasp. I slid a digestive from its wrapper and placed the rest on the table, offering Paul a blank smile he didn't seem impressed with.

'Don't mind me,' I muttered softly, urging Paul to continue. The biscuit was halfway in my mouth now anyway, too late to spit it out, the thing already crumbling, the incoming crunch too loud.

'Alex Jefferson was, from what we can so far tell, attacked in his home after going out for a walk yesterday morning.' Paul was holding a glass of water, too hot for the tea he lived for, every officer soon to be assigned duties to follow up any new information found. He glared at me. I tried not to notice, tried not to chew. 'CCTV puts him walking along Conalton Street at around eleven-thirty but cameras only cover part of the location so we don't know if he met anyone between there and his house, couldn't tell if anyone was following him. We are currently trying to track down anyone seen in the location but, unfortunately, it's not proving an easy task. The blood found inside his front entrance points to an attack happening after he got home.' He pointed to an image of a wooden floor, pink in places with muted blood, several footprints and circular indentations on a nearby rug. 'To be honest, if his wife had come home any earlier, she probably would have walked in on the killer.'

The room was eerily silent. The only sound, in fact, was me, chewing as slowly as I could, dunking my biscuit periodically into my coffee cup to soften the texture until the thing broke in half and sank to the bottom. I tried to fish it out with a spoon but it only made things worse, the continued clack of metal against paper doing nothing for the silence engulfing the room. Paul walked casually up to me and removed the offending items from my grasp, placing my half-eaten biscuit and my contaminated cup on a nearby table.

I muttered an apology, swallowing a lump which had nothing to do with my melted biscuit. I would blame the heat, if anyone asked, the fact that I hadn't had any breakfast.

Paul glared at me as he continued his vivid confirmation

of the way Alex's body was found. It was *not* something any of us wanted to consider. There seemed no logic to the attack, no immediate reason we might acquire. We were all used to seeing discarded bodies, but they were usually found on waste ground, dumped where no one would find them, where their killers wouldn't be disturbed. To hear of such a vicious attack happening inside the supposed safety of your own home wasn't something any of us wanted to acknowledge; no comfort in knowing it could happen to *us*.

'We don't yet know what these are.' Paul pointed to the circular rings I'd spotted a moment earlier. 'Could be anything, and forensics are looking into it now.'

I raised my hand in the air. It wasn't necessary. 'Does CCTV show him entering his house?' I don't know why I asked. I was hungry, looking longingly at my coffee mug, pieces of soggy biscuit now floating on top. I had crumbs on me.

Paul shook his head. 'There were a small number of people walking along Conalton Street we need to track down and eliminate where possible. But unfortunately, there are no cameras along Parkside Lane and, at this stage, we have nothing concrete to go on.' It was indeed unfortunate, the area mostly forgotten now, discarded by the community, crime on the increase. The street was named after a long-closed park once dominating the area, most of it houses now, a forgotten cemetery overlooking it all.

My friend was focusing on the whiteboard, my question already discarded, assessing a second case we all initially assumed unconnected.

'Ben Harris was found yesterday afternoon along

Tolbert Street, having been run over at low speed by a passing car. At the time, we believed this to be an isolated incident, yet in both cases, the two males had holes drilled into the sides of their skulls.' He was writing on the board, two red circles denoting two separate locations.

'Drilled?' Someone at the back of the room asked, this piece of information not yet openly confirmed. He didn't look impressed.

'Yes, drilled,' Paul confirmed flatly, placing his unwanted glass on the table next to my coffee cup.

'As in, drilling a *hole?*'

'You catch on quick, Bates.'

'The drill found inside Alex's bathroom has traces of blood on it. *Old* blood. Blood unlikely to have come from yesterday's attack. We don't, at this stage, know if it is someone else's blood or the killers, but we *will* in a few days.'

Everyone fell silent. The idea the killer had done this before was not a comfort.

'So,' Paul continued with a loud clap of his hands, not missing a single breath, not wanting unrequired banter to deter his thoughts. 'One single question remains. *Why?* Why drill a hole in someone's skull unless you intend to kill them? And why *these* two males?' Paul pinned an image of Alex next to Ben, jabbing a fattened index finger against both faces with uncomfortable force. 'Alex was sixty-four. Ben is fourteen. From what early findings indicate, they didn't know each other, didn't have anything glaringly obvious in common. Alex was found in his bathroom, whereas poor Ben was left on the street. Ben lived. Alex didn't. What's the connection? I need answers, people.'

Everyone was writing notes, myself included.

'Any fingerprints on the drill?' I asked, my question emerging innocently enough, my belly still rumbling.

'What do *you* think?' Paul glared at me.

'Do you need Ben Harris questioning again, Guv?' DS Alice Baker raised her hand in the air now too, following my lead. She perched uncomfortably on the edge of her desk, chewing the end of her pen. She looked hot. *Sexy* hot. Her hair was glued to the sides of her temple in places, her skin dewy with sweat. I tried not to stare at the way her dress clung to her shapely body.

'I'm glad you asked.' Paul turned his attention to Alice. 'Because you have just assigned yourself that very job. He was discharged from the hospital this morning. Newt, can you go with her, please?' He looked at me with a wink I didn't find appropriate.

'Now?'

'Yes, now.' He was serious. 'The rest of you, get to work. We have a murder to solve.'

Chairs scrapped and chatter began as Paul's team headed back to their desks. I glanced up, stood up, my heart leaping uncomfortably into my coffee-deprived throat. I opened my mouth to speak but changed my mind. I liked Alice Baker. It was no secret, everyone *knew* it. Yet, we had never spoken about it, had never brought it up. I cursed Paul silently for plunging us together so readily, this morning already too hot for my bumbling conversation. She turned my way and smiled. I smiled back. What else could I do?

Ten

Newton

Ben Harris's home was a ground-floor maisonette, a nice enough place on the surface despite a distinct lack of kerb appeal and a strong smell of sewage probably due more to the heat than the neighbourhood. I parked outside the property, embarrassed I hadn't cleaned my car in a while, several packets of half-eaten sweets littering the interior. Alice pretended it didn't matter until a wayward toffee welded itself to her leg. She peeled it off and wrapped it in a piece of tissue, offering me a smile I gladly took as amusement. My car had no air conditioning, an open window and noisy fans the only ventilation we were getting this morning. Yet, Alice managed effortlessly to maintain an unchallenged dignity I could only dream of, smoothing her dress over her long legs as she stepped into the sunlight.

I, on the other hand, looked as if I'd been running in a sauna, upside down. She smiled, thanking me for the lift with a nod, unconcerned by my appearance and obvious distraction. I couldn't help but assume we should have taken her car. She didn't comment. Instead, we turned our attention to a young man who'd survived what appeared to be attempted murder. An overgrown path greeted us as the front door creaked open, highlighting a woman in a nightgown, her hair wrapped hastily in a towel as if she'd just stepped out of the shower.

'Mrs Harris?' Alice produced her police badge on cue, offering a smile.

Ben's mum nodded, her face stern, lips tight, the poor woman no happier now than she'd been the last time we met. 'What's wrong now?' She sounded frustrated, the look on her face saying more than words ever could.

'I'm DS Baker and this is my colleague, Dr Flanigan. Are we okay to speak with Ben, please? It won't take long.' Alice was still smiling, still pretending the increasing heat was of no consequence.

Mrs Harris nodded, glaring my way, her reluctant recognition not something I missed. 'Sorry about the mess. It's been a bit hectic, as you can imagine.' She stepped sideways into the property, sounding troubled, as if she believed we might tell the authorities she was doing a bad job, take her kids into care.

'Don't worry,' Alice soothed, stepping inside the front door to the sight of two young children racing around, waving cardboard-shaped swords in the air and stabbing them aimlessly towards our legs. Twins, by the looks of it.

'You two, go and get dressed, please. And be quick about it.' Mrs Harris sent the boys to their room, undisturbed laughter filling the air as they ran. They reminded me of my nephews. Laughing one minute, arguing the next. The place was surprisingly tidy considering it was full of kids.

'Don't mind those two,' she concluded, picking a discarded toy from a nearby chair. 'Can I get you a drink? Tea? Coffee? A glass of water?'

Alice shook her head. 'We don't want to put you to any trouble and we promise we won't take up much of your time.'

'Haven't the police already asked Ben all the questions they need?' Mrs Harris's response was protective. I liked it. It was good to know even in a broken society like ours, there were still good parents in the world.

'Only briefly, I'm afraid.'

'So why *now?*' Mrs Harris's tone tensed, her body following suit.

'Is Ben here? We really do need to ask him a few more questions.' Alice was trying to remain calm, cool, collected. She was still smiling, her cheeks still glowing. I liked the way she was able to put those she spoke to at ease, her job to *help* them, not make things difficult. It might have been the reason I liked her so much.

'He's in his room. I'll go and get him.' Ben's mum left us temporarily standing in her lounge, several muffled voices filtering along a hallway confirming she was both talking to Ben and telling off the twins at the same time, the boys still messing around, still ignoring her requests. I'm sure a baby was crying in the background somewhere, too. A few moments later, Ben ventured into the room. He was dressed in Spiderman pyjamas too young for him, his face more swollen than it was yesterday. I felt bad we needed to question him again. The poor kid looked exhausted, as if we'd just got him out of bed.

'Sup?' Ben asked from the doorway, his nervous persona not going unnoticed. He didn't seem to want to come inside the room, didn't look as if he wanted to offer anything of value.

'Hi, Ben,' Alice stated brightly, offering him an even brighter smile. 'May we have a moment of your time?'

Ben nodded, hovering briefly before he stepped forward, sitting next to a large fan spinning aimlessly in a corner.

'Can you take us through what happened yesterday again, please?'

'Nothing to say.'

There was a pause, a couple of seconds where Alice seemed to contemplate her next words. 'Unfortunately, you are not the only victim, Ben. And we need to clarify a few things.'

'What do you mean?' Ben stiffened, turning off the fan so he could pay us better attention. The room instantly felt hotter, closed in, oppressive, despite an open window and a fly buzzing against a window pane.

'A male was found dead yesterday at his home in Parkside. It seems someone drilled a hole in the side of his head.'

Ben looked shocked, his brow furrowing. 'Was it the

same person who attacked me?' He looked at Alice, then at me.

'That's why we are here. To see if there is any more you can tell us about your attacker.'

Alice glanced towards a family picture on the wall. I couldn't tell what she was thinking.

'Did the guy want to kill *me*?' Ben's mouth had fallen open. He touched his bandaged head, unwanted memories spinning in his mind.

'We can't say for certain at this stage what the motives were. That's what we are currently trying to assess. Are you able to describe him for us?'

Ben shook his head. 'I already told the police. I can't really remember much about it.'

'And I appreciate that.' Alice was still smiling, although I saw a flicker of something pass over her eyes. Was it stress? 'But any information you can give us will be helpful.'

Ben shook his head.

'I can't help you, Ben, unless you cooperate.' Alice glanced my way, her face flashing with frustration.

'My nephew, Peter, is around the same age as you, Ben,' I stated as brightly as I could muster, cutting into the conversation, my nephew at an age where he now assumed he was all grown up, knew everything, had nothing left to learn from the adults around him. I sat down, trying to act casual, accidentally sitting on a lumpy cushion that turned out to be a sleeping cat. It glared at me in disgust before sauntering off into the kitchen, my company about as welcome as a slap to the face.

'So?' Ben didn't seem interested, didn't sound

impressed.

'So, I understand it isn't always cool to talk to outsiders, especially the police.' I was trying to see this from Ben's perspective, appreciate what he'd been through.

Ben stared at me. So did Alice.

I shrugged. 'I get it. You probably did, said, or saw something you shouldn't have, and now you don't want to land yourself in the shit.' I probably shouldn't have swore. He was just a kid. I glanced around, glad his mum hadn't heard the profanity.

'I didn't do *anything*.'

'I don't believe you got beat up for no reason.'

'I don't care.'

'And I'm sure when we find your attacker, he'll be able to collaborate your story. The police are going through CCTV right now.'

Ben shook his head, his confidence disappearing. 'We were just having a laugh.'

'A bit of fun.'

'Yeah.' I swear I saw Ben physically relax, my words hitting the right tone.

'Care to elaborate?' I automatically sat forward, glad the cat had gone.

Ben took a breath, realising too late he'd said too much.

'You bullied him, didn't you, Ben?' It was obvious.

No answer.

'Because he was disabled?' He'd already confirmed as much. It didn't take a genius to work out what had happened.

A shrug. 'We didn't do anything. Not really.' Ben

looked at Alice, then me, a pleading look in his eye. 'It was just meant to be a laugh.'

Alice sighed. I wondered how often she'd seen incidents like these, dealing with kids who hadn't yet learnt how to treat others. 'What was?' she asked softly.

Ben shook his head.

'There's no difference between physical and verbal provocation. Bullying is still bullying, Ben, no matter how you dress it up.' Alice was right, as always.

For the first time since we'd met, Ben looked his young age, unwilling to express the words we already knew, unwilling to confirm his involvement.

'I know,' he muttered, hanging his head shamefully. He looked broken.

'How much do you remember *exactly*?' I stood up, my knees creaking with the effort.

Ben was staring at the floor. 'I'm not landing my mates in the shit.'

'No one is asking you to.'

'And I'm not a bully. If that's what you're thinking.'

No one was.

'But we are dealing with a killer, Ben. I hope you know that.'

I could hear Mrs Harris in the kitchen speaking to the twins, clattering pots and pans, the kids chattering, no doubt making a mess. 'I'll be back in a sec,' I said, leaving Alice to speak with Ben in private, assuming he might open up if I wasn't in the room.

I padded along the hallway into the kitchen, the twins busy eating cereal at a narrow breakfast bar flanking one side of an equally narrow room. They were dressed in shorts now, the baby I'd heard earlier seated in a high chair, spooning thick liquid into its sticky mouth.

'Is everything okay?' Ben's mum wiped her hands on a tea towel as she turned my way.

I nodded. 'I'm sorry for the intrusion. But I was hoping to speak with you in private.' I glanced at the twins. 'About Ben.'

'What do you want to know?'

'Is he okay? After what happened, I mean.' It was a miracle no lasting damage was caused. His superficial head injury would need monitoring over the next few weeks, of course, just in case. I wondered if he'd confided in his mum about the attack, the bullying, the unsupported bus journey.

'I'm not sure. The hospital confirmed there's no real damage, but he has been very quiet since we got home.'

'How so?'

'Well, he's usually the loudest boy in the house.' Mrs Harris went to smile but changed her mind, lowering her voice instead. 'He's a troubled young man. Typical teenager.' She shrugged. I didn't buy it.

'What's his story?' I probably shouldn't have asked. It was none of my business. I knew there would be one. There always was.

She glanced at the twins. 'You two, go and clean your teeth.' The boys groaned as they jumped from stools to the floor, leaving their dirty bowls for their mother to clear away. 'I'll be along in a minute,' she called after them before turning to me. 'Ben's mum was a drug addict. The poor kid was found trying to look after himself and his younger sister after she overdosed.'

'Sorry, I thought Ben was yours.'

'We foster. Troubled kids, mostly.' Mrs Harris glanced towards the mess the twins had left her, then at the baby making its own. 'But nobody wants teenagers, so we've been trying to pick up the slack of a broken system.' She ran a cloth under a warm tap and began wiping baby food from the child's hair.

I don't know why I found it surprising. I'd dealt with plenty of foster parents and their wayward trustees. I assumed the police already knew about this.

'When you say Ben was *found* trying to look after himself—'

'The kids were at the house for two months before social services got involved. The mother was still in the bedroom where she died.'

Shit. I wasn't expecting that, didn't need the thought in my head of a rotting corpse lying discarded and forgotten in the next room. What a hellish situation to find yourself in. Ben must have been terrified of being taken into care and separated from his sister. Leaving his mother's corpse to rot might have felt like his only option. I opened my mouth to speak but no words came out.

Mrs Harris glared at me. 'When the smell got too much it alerted the neighbours.'

Jesus. I glanced behind me, wondering what might have gone through Ben's young mind during those horrific months of his short life, trying to look after his sister alone, knowing their mother was dead. His silence suddenly made sense, his lack of communication part of a personal wall he'd built around himself, the protection he no doubt felt he needed. I didn't know what to say.

'I'm sorry to hear that. And Ben has your surname now?'

'Yes. We wanted him to know he's not alone, that we *are* here for him. It was my husband's idea. He will be too old for us to adopt soon so as a compromise we asked permission to change his name so the poor kid would feel like he's finally part of a real family. We don't intend to kick him out when he turns eighteen.' She was firm about that, had probably seen far too many young adults tossed into the world once the care system was done with them.

'Has he ever been in trouble with the police?'

'Plenty of times.' Mrs Harris didn't look happy to confirm it, but it explained his non-compliant attitude.

'Ben wasn't in a good place when he came to us,' she confirmed, placing her now folded tea towel on the sink, the baby cleaned and fed, seemingly content. She refrained from adding "still isn't".

'Did they not have any other family to step in?'

'No.'

'What happened to his sister?'

'Jennifer is currently with another family pending adoption. The kids don't see much of each other now. She's only six.'

I glanced towards the lounge again.

'Does Jennifer know what happened to their mother?' What kid wouldn't question a missing parent, wouldn't smell rotting flesh in the next room?

'No. Ben kept her in the dark about all that, kept her

away from their mum's bedroom.'

The thought made me feel sick. I sighed. 'Thank you,' I offered, just as Alice stepped through the kitchen door.

'I think we're all done for now,' she confirmed, an entirely different smile on her face from the one she'd displayed when we arrived. Young Ben stood in the hallway behind her appearing just as frustrated. I wanted to ask if she was okay but refrained.

'If you need someone to talk to, Ben, I know someone who might help,' I pitched in, instead. I was thinking about a student of mine, Jack Monroe, wondering if, in my crazed consideration, I could get him to help me help the police. He might be the one person who could get through to Ben, on some level. Although Jack hadn't suffered a direct attack like Ben had, his temporal lobe *was* damaged. If Ben could understand what Jack had been through, he might appreciate just how lucky he'd been. Jack was fascinated by the human mind, always asking questions about the people I helped. Although unethical and probably illogical, I assumed Jack would understand Ben. Ben might see Jack and realise he isn't so alone in this world after all, isn't so damaged.

'Who?' Ben narrowed his eyes. So did Alice. I didn't even look at his mum.

'A friend.' I didn't know if calling a twenty-year-old a "friend" was helpful but I went with it anyway. 'He suffered temporal lobe damage a short while ago. You guys might have something in common.' Jack might get him talking.

'I haven't suffered *shit*.' Ben glared at me as if I was an idiot.

I smiled. Teenagers never fail to make me smile.

'I'm sorry,' I found myself apologising. 'I just want to help.'

I was, in fact, hoping Jack would jump at the chance to help me. After all, he claimed he wanted to follow in my footsteps, the *Happy Place* he often spoke lovingly about nothing but a quiet lecture room we dissected the world in once everyone else had gone home.

Eleven

Newton

I can't recall where I was when I heard the sad news about my student, Jack Monroe. He had been hit by a drunk driver, the impact changing the kid's young life in a way no one could comprehend—left him for dead, his parents left to pick up what was left of his broken existence. The family struggled to deal with a fallout they could barely process, three months before he emerged from his coma, changed, damaged, unrecognisable from the boy I once knew.

I first met him one dull September morning after he'd arrived late to one of my lectures, the first day of a new term not enough to provoke punctuality. He had the brightest smile of anyone I'd ever seen, the biggest character, his laughter not something I thought I'd miss until it was gone. I could never remain angry with him for long, no matter what he did to push my buttons. He had the type of personality that drew you in, made you roll your eyes in a non-committal way, made you smile.

As much as I have tried to convince myself teenagers are annoying and *all* my students are a nightmare, it isn't true. I *like* kids, despite having none of my own, despite what I tell myself before heading to the university each day. My students are good kids, beneath the bravado, most of them hard-working, decent. I was devastated to learn what had happened to Jack. Before an otherwise uneventful day changed everything for him and his family, the boy was a brilliant student, every one of his assignments handed in on time and of impeccable quality. He once told me his main ambition in life was to follow in my footsteps, to work with the police if he could, to become the best psychologist possible. It made me smile, if not a little embarrassed. I did the best I could with what was given to me. I was nothing special.

Jack, on the other hand, had everything he wanted, his entire future ahead, his private education and devoted mother actively propelling him towards greatness. He merely needed to reach out and grab it, always the first to ask questions, his hand forever in the air, his enthusiasm unwavering. It is a shame the last few months have blurred the line, the rest of us destined to move forward now without him.

I'm not sure why Jack was on my mind today. I assumed it was because of young Ben and the trauma he'd suffered, the kid not much younger, the look on his mother's face something I'd grown painfully accustomed. I was also feeling guilty. I hadn't seen him for a while, the coma he had been in seeing me on the end of a telephone far more than was appropriate, consoling his mum more than she wanted. Ben was lucky, in a way, his attack confined to a near miss with a would-be psychopath, his brain matter still intact. I couldn't think too long about Alex Jefferson, or Jack, neither so lucky, the damage to the poor boy's temporal lobe only *half* the story, his tumour highlighting the fragility of life to us all.

I dropped Alice off at the police station and headed to Jack's home, a large property set on the edge of Eastcliff — a sea view and sweeping gravel driveway completing the perfect image of family life. His mum was a director of a company she'd built from nothing, had climbed the corporate ladder to the top. She had done well for herself, well for her kids. I wasn't sure how his father factored into their lives, though. Jack rarely mentioned him other than a passing comment he'd left them a few years earlier. He didn't say why.

I climbed out of my car and headed towards the front door, my dusty shoes crunching loudly underfoot. I didn't belong there, of course, forever dithering, uncertain of my motives. I didn't know if I was doing the right thing by this impromptu visit, didn't now know what to say. I glanced through the family's porch windows to ensure my appearance was adequate before ringing the bell. In my defence, the last twenty-four hours were becoming a blur, everything blending as one, recent events too frustrating to make this about me. This visit was about *Jack*. I took a breath, my lungs ingesting stale coffee and sweat, my otherwise empty belly making me dizzy. I still had biscuit crumbs on my clothes.

I didn't know if it was a lack of caffeine, nerves, or a combination of both, but I was unsure how I felt about standing outside Jack's front door after all this time, my wavering hand outstretched in misplaced anticipation. I hadn't seen him in months, the poor boy too unwell for visitors, according to those brief conversations I'd had with his mum. I'd even missed his birthday. It wasn't common knowledge, but Jack and I shared a birthday. It meant we had something in common, cementing a friendship that wouldn't have otherwise existed. Yet, I saw something in Jack I liked. I saw Isaac. I saw my brother. I didn't tell anyone about that. Not even Jack.

'May I help you?' Jack's mother opened the front door before I was ready, her arms folded across her chest, the look on her face matching mine. I appreciated her pained frustration, the way she took in my unwanted appearance, her eyes glancing twice towards the carrier bag in my hand, my dusty shoes, my fake smile. She hovered in front of me, her look defensive, her presence enough to prevent my innocent quest and the potential friendship I might have offered her son.

'Mrs Monroe. It's Newton,' I confirmed with a nod when I realised she didn't recognise me, a strange crackle forming in my throat I'm sure wasn't there a moment ago. I was confident she would remember me, appreciate my visit, recalling those phone calls I'd made in haste. Her name was Rachel, but I didn't want to appear overly familiar. We barely knew each other.

She shot me a vague look, a strange expression creeping

over her sallow face. She swallowed, looking momentarily crestfallen, as if my sudden intrusion had the potential to upset her son and ruin her day.

'Professor Flanigan. I'm terribly sorry. I didn't recognise you.' The sound of my name sounded as hollow as the look on her face, her failed memory adding to my own perceived invisibility. She tried to smile but I could see she was struggling to cope with such an emotion, her son's illness taking a toll she didn't need me to see. I felt guilty for not visiting earlier, for not insisting on providing the support I should have realised she needed. She was usually well presented, her appearance flawless. Today, however, something was amiss; her glossy dark hair tied back in a hurry, her makeup not quite covering her distress.

'How is he?' My question sounded ridiculous, my feigned utterance unwanted.

'Very poorly, I'm afraid.'

'I can imagine.' I nodded. Rachel didn't have to say anything else. 'May I come in?' I felt like a child about to be sent away with scolded cheeks and slapped legs, my unfounded presence no more wanted than Jack's unforgiving illness. My carrier bag was brimming with items I'd purchased on my way here, things I hoped would cheer the boy up, ideas I now assumed above my station.

'Jack hasn't had a very good couple of days,' Rachel confirmed flatly, glancing over her shoulder towards a flower-scented hallway bigger than my lounge, purposefully keeping her voice low so he wouldn't overhear. I could tell my arrival was ill-timed. 'I'm afraid he tried to hurt himself yesterday and I've instructed him to rest.'

'Oh?' My face had formed a tight knot.

Rachel didn't answer, instead hung her head, still staring at my shoes in disgust. I refrained from rubbing my toes against the backs of my trousers, knowing they needed a clean. I didn't exactly blend in with this neighbourhood or these people, didn't measure up to their impossible standards.

'Can *I* help at all?' I was a psychologist after all. It was my job.

Rachel glanced behind her, her hesitation not something I missed. I wondered if I should have stayed away after all.

'I promise I won't stay long if you don't want me to.'

There was a moment of hesitation. 'Well, he's in the lounge if you want to come in and say hello.' Jack's mum reluctantly stepped aside, allowing me access to a room with a closed door, this uninvited journey something I now wished I'd avoided. Jack and I should be sitting in the sunshine, putting the world to rights, drinking coffee, having a laugh. Instead, I was about to see him at his worst, no idea what I could say to lift the boy's mood. I didn't need to be a mind reader to appreciate what his mother was thinking, her voice emerging as a painful whisper.

'Actually, I'd appreciate it if you could try and get through to him. He hasn't been himself for a few weeks and I honestly don't know what else to do.' Rachel glanced my way briefly, forcing a thin, painful smile. The poor woman looked as if she hadn't slept in weeks.

I nodded. She didn't need to elaborate.

Twelve

Newton

The Monroe lounge was a fairly large space set back from an otherwise quiet hallway. It overlooked a beautiful garden. Yet, the house masked a story of a family torn apart, tragedies yet to unfold behind closed doors, impending death set to swamp every corner, every creaking floorboard doing nothing for my already ravaged senses. The room was dimly lit, the expensive curtains kept closed, medical equipment and prescription drugs laid carefully on a nearby table. I ignored the blatant stare Rachel gave me as she hovered in the doorway, her arms still folded tightly across her struggling chest.

I always avoided sick people, if I could, unwilling to absorb the negative emotions that followed. Besides, I never knew what to say. What if I made them feel worse, or if my attention was met with malice? I'd even avoided my mother, to my peril, my brother and his wife taking on the role of her carer, her dementia seeing his anger aimed my way long after her passing. I couldn't change it.

I stepped forward, my carrier bag suddenly heavy in my grip, although it was probably my imagination, nothing more. It was too warm in here, despite an open window behind swaying curtains. I needed to be strong for Jack, yet my gaze fell everywhere but on the frail body lying motionless on the other side of the room. I stood back, my head down, private emotions in turmoil.

'It's okay,' Rachel whispered, her voice softer now. She sounded almost broken. 'You *can* say hello.' I wasn't sure if she was serious or merely wanted me to hurry up so I would leave.

I didn't dare look at her in case I saw something I didn't want to see, the poor woman unaware of how her vacant lip chewing highlighted her stress. Instead, I hovered by her side for a few painful seconds, unsure what I was meant to do now I was here. I didn't wish to acknowledge her emotions or see Jack in such a terrible place. Rachel had been crying, her eyes swollen and sore from lack of sleep, the usual well-presented image Jack spoke lovingly of slipping rapidly beneath her hastily assembled attire—bare feet, jogging bottoms and t-shirt, tousled hair pulled roughly into a haphazard ponytail. I wished I could provide the comfort devoid of this place, tell these people it *would* all be okay. As it was, I could do no such thing, my concern merely for the kid I liked more than I realised. I was here. For now, that would have to do.

Noting my discomfort, Rachel muttered something

about putting the kettle on and headed into the kitchen, leaving me to focus on Jack. She didn't need to confirm my obvious embarrassment. I'm sure she was used to the reactions people gave her son. I didn't mean it. It was a shock, that's all, seeing him like *that*. It wasn't as if I hadn't dealt with damaged people before. I had. But this was Jack. *My* Jack. The kid who always stayed late after every lecture to share his thoughts on the day, who always handed his assignments in on time, always keen for input. Looking at him now, I barely knew how to react.

He looked comfortable, at least. I was thankful. Pillows had been plumped, a blanket tucked around his fragile body despite the heady temperature contradicting his frozen features. I tried not to look too long at the bandages around his arms or the cut beneath his right eye, tried not to muse over the unfounded reasons for these fresh injuries or the unhinged thoughts going through his head.

His usual vibrant glow was muted. It was the first thing I noticed. His cheeks had taken on an ashen appearance, ageing him somehow, making him look frail, thinner than I remembered, my shredded nerves adding nothing constructive to this moment. When Jack turned my way, his cheeks were flush with apologies he didn't need to give, his eyes swimming with pain I didn't want to see. I raised my hands, shaking off an impulsive desire to hug him, expelling emotions not of his making. I hadn't realised he was watching me, lingering too long over his damaged body to notice. It took everything I had inside to smile, my facial muscles almost as unmoving as his.

'How are you feeling...?' I trailed off. Jack couldn't

reply. He didn't need to try. 'I wanted to come before now but thought I'd wait until you were feeling a little better before I brought the assignments you've missed.' I was trying to act normal, trying not to blame his mother, the accident, or my uncertainty for the reason I'd stayed away.

Jack shifted uncomfortably, already aware of the truth, an awkward silence lingering between us. I didn't miss the sideways glance he gave me. I ignored it, choosing instead to nod energetically.

'I can't have my best student falling behind, can I?' I laughed. I shouldn't have. I sounded a little too enthusiastic, my voice hollow, any attempt to take Jack's mind off his condition, futile, irrelevant. I wanted to keep the conversation light, that's all, race across the room, hold his hand, make everything better.

Jack nodded. He looked depleted, almost as saddened by the concept of seeing me as I was of seeing him, several months passing between our last meeting and this, mere hours, in fact, before an unwitting incident took everything he knew. I could tell he was holding back tears, terrified of exposing emotions he didn't want me to see, the damage he'd endured on full display. He looked genuinely sad, obviously just wanting to remain strong for me, his mum, *himself*. I opened my mouth to express my understanding but thought better of it. I didn't assume he would discern how I really felt, couldn't imagine he'd want to add my problems to his.

I stepped towards a nearby armchair, automatically hovering my hands above his, his injuries more apparent the closer I stood. I reached forward. Should I touch him?

Would it help or hinder? I considered it might do more damage, provoking a commotion neither of us needed, so instead I pretended I was moving a cushion before lowering my creaking legs onto the awaiting chair. I couldn't help passing fleeting eyes over his tenuous skin, the smile I'd firmly planted on my face slipping in response.

'I thought I'd bring you something to cheer you up.' I swallowed, my voice painfully dry. 'Lying around all day can't be doing much for your brain, believe me.' I was feigning a grin, going overboard with my unwavering enthusiasm, trying the best I could. Jack couldn't respond and when Rachel returned with a tray of tea and biscuits, I could barely look at her, could not even look at Jack. His eyes were glistening red with unwanted tears, his mouth quivering with a smile he was unable to present. He used to have such a lovely smile. It wasn't a comfort.

I thrust the bag I'd hastily brought with me across the coffee table, tipping the contents everywhere, ignoring the sideways glare Rachel gave me as several items fell to the floor, almost unbalancing a vase of fresh flowers in the process. I couldn't help my reaction, my nerves firmly on the edge. Aside from a few assignments I'd cobbled together in a hurry, I didn't know what he was interested in beyond an insatiable obsession with the human mind. I'd bought him a couple of magazines on the subject along with two video games my nephews no longer played. I wasn't sure if he owned an Xbox, didn't really know what he was into. A random bunch of grapes completed my offering because *everyone* brings sick people grapes. They were threatening to shrivel and rot in the heat, mocking my stupidity and my inability to deal with this impossible situation.

Jack shuffled forward, struggling to sit upright. I could tell he was pleased, found my gifts amusing, the glint in his eyes something he couldn't deny. Despite not being able to express his thoughts, I knew him well enough to appreciate he was still in there, somewhere. I just wasn't used to his silence, that's all, his chatter usually filling my lecture room, my ears, his mind on a perpetual journey of discovery. He was beautiful once too, with flawless skin and curly dark hair, his smile and infectious lust for life lighting up any room. Now, he could barely blink, could hardly move his mouth beyond a lopsided collection of damaged muscles tugging his face to one side.

I didn't know which had caused the most damage—the stroke or his tumour. I felt sorry for the kid, perplexed I couldn't help him. I swallowed an uncomfortable lump, unsure what else to do, uncertain how much he knew about his inoperable cancer or the looming death sentence hanging over his head. I didn't wish to remind him, didn't want to be held responsible for his reaction.

Thirteen

Jack

Regardless of the problems and difficulties I'm now saddled with, I am immensely grateful for my unexpected visitor today. It has the potential to lift me from the depths of a despair I might not otherwise handle, from a journey I never intended to endure. My professor is unaware of this, hovering on the far side of the lounge, my mother by his side and a pained look in his eyes. Neither look comfortable. I conclude it's the heat, nothing more.

I watch Newton watching me, yet he doesn't initially notice, unconcerned his eyes are not what they used to be. He hardly ever wears his glasses, doesn't appreciate how much he needs them. I notice a fleeting uncertainty, but it dissipates quickly, leaving my anxiety exposed, my thoughts muddled. He flinches, assuming I haven't noticed, the sight of me like *this* provoking haunting images of the very ghost I've become since our last meeting. His nerves are shredded. I can tell by the trickle of sweat running along his brow, the way his adam's apple continually moves, swallowing words he doesn't know how to convey. I understand why. He's concerned for my health, my wellbeing, no doubt exhausted by relentless taunts from those who should know better.

Oddly, of all the people living in this challenging world, Professor Flanigan is the one person who understands me, the *only* one who genuinely knows who I am. In the twenty short years I have existed on this planet, Newton alone has shown the most empathy without regressing to the same disparaging level of incomprehension most around me now do. Yet, he retains an uncomfortable distance between us for a while, his unbearable silence made worse because I can't speak.

Luckily, the stifled atmosphere shifts swiftly, although Newton still struggles to find a conversation to appease us, nothing conveyed that would mean much anyway. I get a strong sense of foreboding, as if he is holding back. I don't know why. If I could smile, I would. If I could ask him to sit down, I would already be by his side. Thankfully, I see no judgment on his face, no hidden thoughts or poisonous emotions to tip my mood further than it already is. Professor Flanigan is a pure soul, a gem, a diamond amid a mountain of broken glass, his light shining far brighter than mine. It's a shame there aren't more people like him in this world.

Newton notices me looking at him and smiles. There has never been a crossed word between us, never more than the laughter I sorely miss. I *want* to laugh, to rid myself of the nightmare that has since become my existence, to feel normal again. If I can.

'How are you feeling...?' His question is honest, genuine. He trails off. I try not to react to his concern, barely refraining from reaching my hand towards his.

Instead, I nod, wishing I could speak, anything to break this impossible moment, my outer appearance as much of a hindrance as my inner. I'm unable to express anything of my feelings, my emotions hidden behind pain he assumes he can already see. I swallow. I can't tell him I *love* him, of course. Will never be so bold. It's a shame it happens to be true. I have never told anyone how I feel about him, *especially* to Newton, can barely acknowledge it myself. I have instead poured my soul onto paper, explaining my feelings within the written word. I keep those words to myself, fearing the repercussions such a declaration might provoke, the rejection my honesty may trigger. It has forced me into perpetual silence, ironically, my limited functions mocking everything I want from the life I should have lived when I could.

Newton leans forward, looking as if he wants to plump my pillows, this sofa made all the more comfortable because of his efforts. I remain still as he leans towards me, holding my breath so he won't notice my elevated pulse, saddened when he merely moves a cushion and sits down. I consider leaning over to kiss this cheek. Only then will he appreciate my story, the full truth finally revealed of who I am. It's a shame I didn't tell him how I felt when I could, the man in front of me now unaware of the desires swimming in my head. I don't care about the age difference, don't care about much anymore, if I'm honest.

He talks for a while about items he's purchased, assignments we both know I'll never complete, tipping a carrier bag of gifts across my mother's coffee table. He is hoping to cheer me up, I know, but I can tell he's nervous by the twitch of his jaw, the way his hands tremble in response to my presence. Despite only having one functioning eye, I can still see more than I should, listening intently to his chatter, knowing deep down what he wants to say. He talks about the weather and nothing in particular. Yet I read between the lines, barely hearing his words, too busy focusing on his smile, his hair, his scent, just glad to be in his company.

'Everyone misses you in class, Jack.' His sentence is innocent although it provokes something that jolts painfully across my heart. I'm reading too much into this, I know, but I can't help it. wanting him to simply say, "*I miss you, Jack*". Because I miss him. Every day. He notices my shifting position, my changing disposition. He doesn't say anything about that. Instead, he turns his attention to a discarded book left open on the last page I turned, nothing I read in print easing what's going on in my head. 'What are you reading?' he asks, picking it up and turning it over, glancing twice at the cover. '*The Mind of a Killer*.' Newton raises an eyebrow. 'I have this very book but haven't read it yet. Is it any good?'

I nod enthusiastically while wanting to tell him I'm struggling with it, struggling to appreciate the author's viewpoint on a killer he blatantly has not understood. By the second chapter I'd reached the dire conclusion the writer never *really* got inside his subject's head, despite studying the killer to some extent. These were the types of discussions we used to share, Newton and I, the types of conversations I miss. I find it devastating those days are gone.

From my limited experience, there are two types of people in this world. Those who understand, and those who don't. Newton fits neatly into the former. He has taught me everything I know about the human mind, helping me appreciate the unexplained when the outside world shuns it. He appreciates my views, knows what makes me tick. The very reason I own a copy of *The Mind of a Killer* in the first place is because my professor owns the very same book.

I stare at the floor. The idea of him seeing my innermost emotions is unbearable. He motions towards me but hesitates. I have no idea what he's thinking. We used to talk happily for hours about life, the universe, everything in it, everything I assumed *mattered*. Now I can barely look his way, can't confirm strongly enough how I'm finding it hard to cope in this world without him, lost without his chatter and unwavering enthusiasm.

I've learned to be afraid of the world around me, fearful of the people in it. Yet, I'm far more alarmed by my own image than I will ever openly admit. People don't understand me, probably never will, and no matter how hard I try, I *cannot* understand them. Only when I'm with Newton does the world makes sense. It's a shame I've been forced into silence, grateful my professor doesn't look at me like everyone else.

I *am* thankful for the time Newton has given me, a

simple pleasure, no distractions to take us from what we used to call our "happy place." He doesn't understand the significance of his gentle soul, how much I *love* him, how much I appreciate what he has no doubt sacrificed by being here today, his life taking a backseat to the needs of a young man who is *not* his responsibility. I close my eyes. My only hope now is to muddle through my remaining days unscathed, *this* moment the best things will ever be.

'I hope you'll forgive me, but I came here with an ulterior motive,' he states calmly, his eyes closing against the weight of unspoken words.

I shuffle forward, my attention forever on him. I find myself listening to events leading to a boy on a bus being attacked. Newton is careful in his statement, leaving out details about the man called Alex, his intention only to help a kid, *not* land himself in trouble. Murder cases can't be discussed until the police are ready to release the details. Alex's body is not yet even cold.

I lean forward, grabbing the first thing I can find to write on.

NO!

I have written the word in capital letters on the back of a tissue box, much to my mother's annoyance. She reaches forward and takes it from me with a tut, placing it back on the table.

'Why?' Newton sounds incensed, his irritation prickling.

I shake my head. No. It's my final word on the subject,

my *only* word, getting up from the sofa and heading upstairs to my room. I slam the door as loudly as I can, unconcerned by how my abrupt exit must look.

I lie on my bed watching sunlight move dappled shadows across my walls, a warm breeze lifting my curtains that threatens to spill the untidy contents of my desk onto the floor. I can't believe Newton thought I would *speak* to the boy, bizarrely assuming I would help him. I can't have him see me. He will recognise me, confirm my involvement, highlighting the very reason he will have a scar on his head for the rest of his life. I scoff, knowing I didn't drill far enough, didn't cause any lasting damage, the memory of Alex's blood spilling across his bathroom now haunting my every waking moment. There's a balance, it seems. A delicate harmony between good and bad, my ill-planned calculations off, my intentions not yet weighed responsibly. I think he said the boy's name was Ben. Despite everything, I'm glad he's alive.

Fourteen

Jack

I hate to admit it, but this house feels oppressive once Newton is gone, my mood a rollercoaster ride of loops and dips leaving me irritated, borderline nauseous. I'm sure he hasn't meant it, but his illuminated presence has highlighted my own, his infectious company bringing my prolonged suffering to the surface. As much as I love my family and the privacy these walls afford, such close proximity to my professor has left my head spinning, the world closing in around me, my wellbeing not open for debate.

I find myself still thinking of him as the day passes into evening, only leaving the sanctuary of my room when I grow weary of my own company. With sleep in my eyes and my devoted dog, Star, by my side, I hover at the top of the stairs, a cavern of impossible thoughts littering my cluttered mind. I used to believe most people were good, when it mattered, honest even, decent. Yet, in my limited opinion, negative energies override the positives, life too complicated to live unencumbered. No one is without fear or incapable of committing random acts of unkindness.

For as long as I can remember, I have been fascinated by the unusual, those who, like me, have found themselves skirting normality. Serial killers, murderers, unfortunate souls locked inside damaged heads, no way to communicate honest emotion beyond actions no one understands. I've felt this way for a long time, unfortunately, thoughts sliding in and out of my head where no one can see them, snippets of conversation I have with myself in the privacy of my room and my aunt's peaceful basement. I'm thankful Newton shares my misguided appreciation, at least, allowing something within me to cling to his every word. It's a shame he doesn't know how I feel about him, destined to be forever misunderstood, it seems, abused and forgotten by society because I'm different. It matters little how much I want to feel part of the world again, to connect with Newton on a deeper level. I probably never will.

I creep into my mother's room and close the door, leaving Star pacing and panting on the landing. I stand in front of her dressing table, staring at my hands, my face. I look out of place now, I know—faded denim jeans, plain grey shirt, a black hooded top unable to cover my hideous features, my trainers seeing far better days. It hardly fits with the lifestyle I remember, designer outfits left unworn in my wardrobe, friends I haven't seen in a while.

I pick up a discarded lipstick and slide off the cover, a simple idea forming in my head. I'd like to become someone else for a while, if I can, to create a genuine smile, to see something other than my pained reflection looking back. I used to have such a lovely smile. If I have to paint on the expression, I will; *anything* to aid my mission to be viewed by the world as more than a damaged freak, a forgotten invalid in a society who will never accept people like me.

I stare wildly at my reflection as I cover my lopsided cheek with crimson, my pale skin and sallow cheekbones reflecting nothing but contradiction. I must look ridiculous but I can't stop, my unsteady hand making the task difficult, my unhinged mind making this moment possible. I see nothing but a skeletal face staring back, ashen cheeks matching sunken eyes, my weight loss a painful side effect of my illness. Fresh cuts from a piece of misplaced glass now pepper my face and my arms, but I ignore the tears I blink away, my tumour on a relentless painful rampage. When I'm done, I still can't smile but my face has symmetry, at least, almost as if I have planned it this way. I wonder what Newton would think if he saw me like this, the man oddly fascinated by me, curious, even, almost as if he *wants* to see the person hiding behind the pained façade.

I notice a box of antidepressants on a nearby chest of drawers, exasperated by my mother's need to exist on such medication. The innocent, unassuming Jack would have dreamt of helping her through this difficult time, contemplating some ridiculous notion of easing her daily struggles with ideas above his station that, to me, now sound downright outlandish. I feel sorry for the boy who would sit for hours considering the day he might uncover his purpose on earth and share some miraculous discovery with the world. I shake my head. I can no longer share anything with anyone, barely any strength left to breathe.

I glance out of the window towards someone walking along the canal, nothing on their mind other than the dimming evening light. I have no idea how long I watch them, my throat closing in quiet defence, hidden behind my mother's heavy curtains because I have nowhere better to be. I allow my unfettered attention to drift, a strange new personality developing from the darkest areas of my sickened mind. Until the accident, I was unaware and unconcerned about the suffering of others, disability of no real relevance to me. I guess I was part of the ignorance, part of the problem. Maybe *this* is my penance.

No one takes the afflicted seriously, do they? No one understands who such people are beyond a limited assumption of what is deemed *normal*. I once believed I knew what normality looked like, pretended I was just like them—a normal kid, a normal *son*. Yet, those days are long gone, a shift already made I can never undo.

I wait until my mother and my sister, Lizzy, leave the house before heading downstairs, her calls in my direction hitting deaf ears, finding myself propped against the open kitchen door because there is nowhere else to be. It's still warm outside and I slip quietly into the garden, the heavy evening air lingering, the sun dipping gently on the horizon. Lizzy's dance classes and summer club are the only things my sister can claim for herself these days, the only time her day does not revolve around me. It's probably just as well she can't see me like this. As much as I enjoyed my brief hour with Newton earlier, *this* is my real life, my real world, surrounded by people who will never understand me, will never appreciate who I am.

I'm a different person now, no longer the Jack Monroe everyone remembers, a not-so-innocent journey confirming this painful shift. Yet, since waking up in a hospital bed with the Grim Reaper as an unwitting companion, I have thought of little else other than to show those who see nothing beyond the mundane of each day, just how fortunate they are to be *alive.* I have dreamt of helping them see each other with kindness instead of sickness, with empathy instead of hate, thinking the impossible, planning the irreversible. Now, because of the two males I encountered yesterday, *everything* will change, the unwitting actions of strangers set to destroy the lives of many before cancer destroys mine.

I check my rucksack is still inside the garden shed I hastily thrust it, a place no one ventures, confused by its contents and struggling to absorb my recent unthinkable deeds. This bag has oddly become my protection from a world I don't understand, the items inside providing solace from my daily battles. My mother finds it funny how it hardly leaves my side, but I can't leave it lying around to be discovered, painful thoughts written in my diary, a second cordless drill now covered in blood, my unfounded actions the reason I have been forced to hide it behind the lawnmower. Damning evidence, if anyone asks. Which they will.

I glance towards the house to ensure it's still there before creeping through the garden gate, glad no one is home to notice my escape, heading silently onto the canal path behind our house. A middle-aged man is perched on a bench some distance away. I pause, assume he is about to recoil in obvious shock. But he simply glances my way and nods, returning his attention to the newspaper in his grasp, far more important things to deal with than me. He doesn't notice my damaged features, does not linger over my skin. Or if he does, he says nothing. I don't know how I feel about this, used to being subjected to open ridicule, obvious hatred, bullied until eventually, inevitably, I was forced to take matters into my own hands. Forced to do the *unspeakable*.

I guess I'm searching, hunting, hoping to catch someone's eye, if I can, my presence too much, their attention offering an unhealthy resolve to this day. It's ridiculous, I know, yet something inside has changed. I can't go back, can't retract my failings. A dog walker passes by, glancing briefly in my direction, the female in question thankfully unable to conclude much in the fading light. I can't offer a natural smile but I nod all the same, holding my head as high as I'm able, the illusion of confidence created by yesterday's madness and my mother's conspicuous lipstick. It has the negative consequence of making me look insane, unable to connect with others on a genuine level. But she merely smiles and moves on too, more interested in her dog than me.

I need to recharge my depleted energy levels, that's all, to be alone with my thoughts for a while. I don't intend to go far. I'm mindful of my surroundings, hoping to reclaim a little clarity, a little dignity. Before the accident, strangers rarely bothered me, their thoughts and opinions none of my business. Now, I'm on constant guard, unaccustomed to being baulked at, whispered voices no more potent than the breeze buffing my body.

'Hey, *ugly!*'

I look up, unsurprised by the outburst, fully aware of the makeup applied in haste. I wrongly assumed the canal path beyond our garden would cocoon me. How deluded must I be?

A scrawny, average-looking male is staring my way, his angry persona hidden behind his own twisted features. I should have anticipated the ridicule, things I can't change becoming a perfect storm of events set to steer me the wrong way. Yet, it seems I can't escape trouble now, a bitter cycle of contempt emerging from people like *this*. I ignore him, even when he throws a stone that hits my head. I honestly don't know how much more I can take.

'What's wrong with your face?' he asks when I stop mid-stride, his own nothing more than a twisted mass of muscles I'm unsure he knows what to do with. He points to my lips, to the right side of my face all twisted and taut, the crooked smile I applied in haste. 'Are you supposed to be a clown or something?' He laughs, sounding more like a child than an adult.

I'm sure it's because of what happened yesterday and not because I'm weak, but I don't initially react when he grabs me, my legs buckling beneath my weight. The sight of my seemingly defenceless body gives way to a torrent of abuse in the form of kicks and punches, forcing me to close my eyes, willing this moment to end. I take a breath only when he does, when silence befalls this unassuming space.

He adds nothing further to the position we have found ourselves in, doesn't utter a word. Only his heavy breath lingers. I can already feel the bruises on my face, iron-rich blood coating my lips, blurring what's left of my vision, a black eye mocking me when I blink. I *always* have a headache. That's nothing new. I can only imagine how I must look to him.

He laughs, less committed now, already bored of my company, bored of inflicting pain he has no idea runs deep. He motions to move on, ready to leave me to my fate. I glance around. The man on the bench is gone, the dog walker included.

What people fail to appreciate is although I *look* weak, I am unwilling to succumb to the reality of my condition just yet, not ready to yield to the inevitable. I rise slowly, tapping his shoulder with the rubber end of the crutch he has wrongly assumed my weakness. He turns around, a lingering smile still on his lips until I slam the metal rod against his jaw, my anger emerging from his. He falls, lands hard, does not get up. I punch him a few times until I tire from the effort, tears burning my eyes, my soul. I don't turn around as I walk away, leaving him to the same fate he planned for me. I scoff, knowing how lucky he is.

I *didn't* bring my drill.

Fifteen

Jack

I've not exactly considered the consequences of my actions or what they mean for my family, merely hoping someone might appreciate my predicament while I still breathe the same air as them. I'm considered ugly, I know that. Painfully accustomed to unapologetic looks and whispers behind well-placed palms, other people's reactions no longer shocking. I shock myself whenever I steal a glance at my reflection so why would I expect others to react differently? What surprises me is their ignorance, the way they see only what they want to see, outer appearances more significant than what exists inside, bitter words retained behind ill-meaning gossip. I think about the boy on the bus and the man in his bath, merely wanting them to understand what it is like to be Jack Monroe. Yet, it has triggered something in my head, changing my values, my views, the intricacies of life forever beyond my limited perception.

I don't recall getting back to the house or tripping over the kitchen rug, but I find myself staring up at the ceiling, my faithful dog by my side, a look on her face saying more than words ever could. Star tilts her head, wonders what has happened, licks my wounds, my tears—just an innocent attempt to make things better. I suck in a lungful of air as pain jolts through my chest, a vile taste of iron in the back of my throat. My face is throbbing and I struggle to pull myself upright, my dulled reflection in the refrigerator door confirming what I already know. My blinded right eye is swollen closed, angry blood pulsating beneath my trembling touch. I wince at the pain, try not to scream, desperate to claw back my unclaimed dignity.

How dare other people judge so harshly the things they don't understand? How *dare* they treat me like this? Is it wrong to confirm I care nothing for the man I've just this minute left by the canal, unconcerned by how badly he might be hurt or if he's *dead?* I doubt he would have behaved differently if he knew the extent of my injuries, the reason I am what I am. Nothing about me would alter his opinion, acceptance only ever skin deep, it seems. I feel sorry for him, to be honest. His life is destined to follow a path of bitter hatred, his bullying ways and emotional baggage carried lifelong.

The house is silent. Too silent. I *hate* what I have done to my family, what the world is doing to me, my loved ones at the sharp end of an impossible situation promising no comforting conclusion. The last memories they will have of me are as I am now, unable to speak, unable to eat without help, incapable of using the toilet without a chaperone or be seen in public without a reaction. It's uncomfortable to acknowledge. Yet, those who know nothing of my traumas brand me a freak, someone who should be kept as far from decent people as possible. I can't continue this way. It's not fair.

I lift my rapidly failing body from the floor, the earlier adrenaline wearing off, my throbbing bones mocking my movements as I struggle to pull myself upright. I linger over several photographs pinned to my mother's notice board showing a happy family, the people in *this* house long passed the point of feigned pretence. I touch the smiling faces, wishing I could go back and relive those perfect days. A holiday in the Caribbean, if I remember correctly. I was six, Lizzy was one, a normal family day at the beach, smiling, laughing, having fun. We were happy back then, happy to live in simple bliss, no concept of the dark future awaiting. My father must have been drinking by then, but no six-year-old sees such truths, do they? He abandoned us in favour of alcohol long ago, his way of hiding from problems he could never undo. I was eight when my parents finally split, their problems oddly far worse *now* than they were back then. I can only imagine what my illness has done to aid their downfall, the arguments they have whenever they think I can't hear. My father doesn't realise I know everything about his depression, understanding him more now than I ever did before.

If I'm crying, I can no longer tell, my eyes too swollen and bloodshot, stroking a dog who has shown me nothing but love, whose affection and devotion never wavers. Out of everyone I know, Newton aside, of course, I think I will miss Star the most. I no longer recognise my cumbersome appearance, unaware how far my mood has shifted until I take a pair of scissors from the kitchen drawer and hold them against my cheek. I have to offer my family more than they see each day, to display a simple smile, even if it will never be a genuine expression. It won't hurt. I'm already in too much pain for my actions to register anything of value. What else can my body subject me to it has not already tried to take? I hover next to the kitchen sink, my thoughts blurred, my mother's lipstick smudged. If I'm going to do this, I must hurry, get it over with.

I want nothing more than to smile again and feel something beyond the agony of hidden turmoil no one will ever understand. I'm not the first victim of society to carry out such a savage act of self-sabotage, won't be the last. "Joker" from Batman pops into my head. He's a fictional character in a comic book, the invention of someone's imagination. Yet, like him, I feel the pain inflicted onto me by society, forever alone in a crowd, my mask nothing but false hope of a life I wish I had. It's a shame the thing in this room is a product of society's imperfect making, nothing left of the person I should have become.

I open my mouth and insert the cold blades between my bloodied cheeks, nothing left of my face to damage anyway. I take a deep breath and begin to slice, unfeeling metal chopping savagely into soft flesh, unfeeling hands trembling. There is a sudden rush of heat, a shocking pain, yet my fingers are unwilling to relinquish control until my right side matches my left, balancing the abhorrent malice I'm thrusting painfully onto myself. Muscle and skin succumb to my demands as I follow the contours of my mother's imperfect lipstick. I have cut deep, I know, pieces of flesh already peeling from my lips, exposing my teeth, my cheekbone, my jaw. Yet, I'm unable to register what I've done until a torrent of blood pours over the kitchen floor.

I drop the scissors and stagger into the hallway, feeling nothing, tasting nothing but bitter liquid as blood pours from my mouth. Someone else's reflection stares back in disgust from a mirror on the wall. He looks hideous, whoever he is. Yet, for the first time in months he's smiling, the right side of his face matching his left, an angry curve pointing violently towards his damaged cheek. The stranger begins to grunt with forced laughter, his so-called *normal* side pulled taut in surprise, his shoulders and chest juddering with the effort. Tears sting his eyes, burning his wounded face, the new Jack Monroe on full, uncensored display. I am glad Star can't see this moment, can't witness what I've become. She is distracted, in the lounge chewing a bone, unaware, uninvolved. Her frantic barking would no doubt alert the entire neighbourhood. That's the last thing I need.

Sixteen

Newton

I spent the rest of that day distracted, leaving Jack several unanswered messages, questioning my judgment, my integrity. Why he refused to help me so bluntly I couldn't say, but I subsequently left a university meeting under the false guise of ill health, in a bad mood, my headache no better for painkillers that did nothing other than provoke a dry throat. I arrived home to a pile of mail pressed against my front door, junk mostly, nothing of value, almost failing to notice an envelope bearing a solicitor's logo. I glanced at it blankly, making a mental note to take a closer look when I was in a better frame of mind. I then made myself a coffee and a cheese and pickle sandwich to deflect thoughts I didn't want in my head, no intention of eating it, merely going through the motions, as always. When my phone rang, I was shocked to see Jack's number lighting up my screen, his inability to speak making this moment all the more disconcerting.

'Jack?' I panicked, jumping to my feet, my impromptu actions causing several books to slide sideways on a shelf. I was speaking as if the poor boy could respond, as if I was waiting for an answer.

A gurgling, something sounding as if he was banging an outstretched limb against a hard surface.

'Jack, is that you?'

More gurgling.

I took a moment to register what was happening, forcing myself to think rationally. 'Bang twice if you can hear me.' I practically yelled into my phone.

Two loud thumps echoed in the background.

Shit.

'Are you at home?'

Two more thumps. Was that a *yes?*

'Stay exactly where you are. I'm on my way.' My phone was balanced precariously under my chin, my car key already in my hand, my shoes sliding around the hallway floor in protest of my searching feet.

I left my untouched sandwich on my dining table and raced into the street, still speaking to Jack, still trying to reassure him everything was going to be okay. I considered calling his mother but she would ask what was wrong, her ensuing panic worse than mine. I didn't want that on my conscience, didn't yet have the answers. I was thankful they didn't live far away, parking carelessly across the driveway, unconcerned by pedestrians or neighbours, my haste seeing me stumbling around like a fool. I didn't bother locking my door, no time to check I'd closed it as I raced across the gravel.

'Jack?' I thumped desperate fists against his front door, needing a response to ease the burning sensation in my throat. Jack couldn't speak so had no reason to call me, especially under the current circumstances. The only rational explanation I could conclude was this was an emergency.

No answer.

'Jack?' My heart was thumping dangerously in my chest, my lips dry, my mouth quivering. I peered through the lounge window to gain a better vantage point, noticing the empty sofa, one of the magazines I'd bought him now discarded in a heap on the floor. I rang the doorbell again, my mobile phone pressed against my strained ear to ensure I could hear his unstable breath on the other end.

'Jack, I'm outside. If you can hear me, make a noise, *please?'*

I was yelling into my mobile, my shoes crunching hastily against loose gravel I kicked absentmindedly into the borders. I needed him to appreciate my panic, my desperation. I could think of nothing but Jack's cancer, trying not to overthink what I had no control over as I made my way around the side of the property. I opened the gate to the muffled sound of a German Sheppard barking frantically behind a set of closed French doors leading into the kitchen. Her attention was set now on me, jumping at the glass, her wagging tail and uneasy mannerisms expressing urgency for an event I was still to discover. She had blood on her legs. I wondered if she was hurt but she wasn't limping, didn't seem to be in any pain.

I scrabbled around inside my pockets, pulling out sweet wrappers, tissue paper, and used train tickets before I found what I was looking for. Jack's spare key. He'd given it to me a few weeks before his accident, oddly, his foresight something neither of us expected to become advantageous. For emergencies, he'd said. I was to tell no one, certain his mother would neither approve nor understand. Ironically, he couldn't have known I'd one day need it. I was glad I still had it, in fairness, my tendency to lose things circumvented by the wallet I never left home without.

I didn't confirm it, would never mention it, but I knew *why* Jack didn't want Rachel to know I had a spare key to their home. I appreciated his emotions more than most, the poor kid locked inside his head long before the accident took his identity, unable to talk about important things or the hidden pain he was already in. This key was Jack's connection to normality, to *me*, knowing I'd be there for him, should he need me. Neither of us assumed it would be under these circumstances.

I nervously unlocked the double doors, taking the dog by her collar so she wouldn't escape and make my day worse. She looked pleased to see me, at least, despite trailing bloodied pawprints around the kitchen. I checked her over. She wasn't injured. I couldn't decide if I was glad or *terrified*, trying not to overthink what I couldn't yet see, knowing this blood was Jack's.

'Jack?' I was tired of talking to myself, asking questions that offered no response.

Star barked again and raced into the hallway, willing to

answer my question when no one else could. I followed. I'm not sure what I expected but the sight of him on the floor wasn't it. There was blood everywhere, his already damaged face barely recognisable. *Jesus.* I raced forward and knelt by his side, unappreciative of what had happened, unsure what to do or how to react. He made a strangled noise when he saw me, the look in his eyes as telling as the expression he clearly didn't know how to convey. He pointed to a pair of bloodied scissors some feet away, the entire right side of his face sliced open, skin hanging loose, his teeth and jaw exposed. The poor kid looked horrendous.

'Christ, Jack, what happened?' It didn't bear thinking about, didn't warrant a direct confirmation. He was shaking, crying, his bruised features a mass of unrecognisable tissue and bone. I tried not to baulk, tried not to express my shock. 'Who did this to you, Jack?' I sat him upright, knowing he couldn't tell me, merely needing to assess the situation, take a closer look. It was obvious the boy had been attacked, yet the idea of such a thing happening in his own home was not something I found comforting. My last visit consisted of drinking his mother's tea, talking about nothing important, trying not to make Jack's illness about *me*.

I called his mum but it went to voicemail. It was probably a good thing. This was not how a mother should see her child, the thought of conveying such a terrifying message over a recording wholly inappropriate. I swore, apologised to Jack, my thoughts dissipating beyond unacceptable ideas swamping my head. I knew this was a crime scene but needed to stem the flow of blood, no time to wait for an ambulance *or* the police, the idea of him bleeding to death where he lay *not* something I wanted on my conscience.

I searched frantically, carefully, knowing I was contaminating the space, yet thinking *only* of Jack. I found a clean towel in the utility room and wrapped it around his face, trying not to hurt him, trying not to overthink the protests of pain escaping his quivering mouth. When I scooped him into my arms, I was shocked by how light he was, no time for anything other than immediate action. I cradled his fragile body against mine as we headed out to my car, everything hazy, blurred. I could barely think straight, barely remembered to lock the kitchen door behind us in my haste. The boy held onto me tightly, unable to speak but clearly glad I was here. He was conscious. For now, it was the only thing that mattered.

Seventeen

Newton

The drive to the hospital took forever, every set of lights slowing my progress, traffic in every direction mocking my decision to drive instead of calling an ambulance. I cursed several times, apologising more than was necessary, wishing Jack had the capacity of mind to laugh. I missed Jack's laugh, missed the sparkle that lit up a room. I parked sideways in an ambulance bay, unconcerned by parking tickets or irritated paramedics. Jack was losing consciousness, his blood loss and my yells for help provoking panic I wasn't sure helped anyone. My shirt was now a shade of dark red in places, several gasps of horror emerging from those around us as I lifted his fragile body from the passenger seat, manhandling him uncomfortably through a set of double doors. A few people stared.

'What happened?' A nurse yelled as several hospital

staff raced towards me, ready to take him out of my hands. I didn't know the answer, could barely respond.

'Help him, *please*.' It was the only thing I could offer. My brain throbbed, my muscles ached, my voice catching my throat like shards of glass. I could barely breathe, could barely acknowledge this moment, forced to watch helplessly as the poor kid was taken away. I should have been thankful his condition would be assessed, at least, his serious wounds attended. Yet, the only thing I could think of was his mother and how she would react to the news of what had happened.

'Are you okay, sir?' The nurse approached me. She could clearly see I wasn't, the smile she gave unappreciated, my own struggling breath worsening by the second. I felt dizzy.

I shook my head. How on earth was I meant to explain *this* to Rachel? What would I say? Where would I begin?

'Are you able to tell us what happened?' The question was simple enough yet I didn't have the answer.

'I found him on the hallway floor.' I doubt I would ever get the image out of my head.

'Yours?'

'His.'

'Was he alone?'

'Yes.'

'Was he conscious?'

'Barely.'

'Do you know how this happened?'

'No.'

I was taken to a relative's room, given a cup of strong

black coffee and a box of tissues, asked if I needed anything else. I shook my head, grappling my phone from my pocket while struggling with my thoughts, knowing the phone call I was about to make was set to make things worse.

Rachel answered on the second ring. She sounded upbeat. It wasn't ideal, almost made me vomit to think I was about to ruin what was left of her day.

'Professor Flanigan. I didn't expect to hear from you again so soon.' She sounded flustered, as if her life and my presence were overwhelming, too much to do and not enough time to do it. I wasn't confident she didn't blame me for that, got the impression she didn't like me very much.

'I'm at the hospital.' It was the only thing I could say. I closed my eyes, taking a breath I wasn't sure I could manage. 'With Jack.'

'*What?*' I sensed whatever she was doing was no longer important, her full attention now on me. 'How are you with *Jack?* What happened? Where is he? Is he okay?'

I didn't have answers to the questions aimed towards me like bullets shot from a loaded gun. For the first time in my life, I was speechless, too shocked to respond with anything of value.

'Where's Mark?' Rachel spluttered, sounding panicked.

'Sorry?'

'He was meant to be popping to the house to keep an eye on Jack while I took Lizzy to her dance class this evening,' Rachel continued, clearly unsure why she was even speaking to me. 'Is everything okay, Professor Flanigan? I need to speak with my husband. *Now.*'

I didn't know anything about Jack's father other than he

and Rachel had separated years earlier, didn't know of any apparent arrangement they'd made on their son's behalf.

'He called me.' My eyes were still closed, this room temporarily removing all logic from my thoughts, a heady smell of blood and disinfectant the only lingering reminder of where I was.

'*Mark* called you?' Rachel sounded shocked, as if she couldn't appreciate why he would want to. I didn't know Jack's dad, had never met him.

'No. Jack called me.' The thought was ridiculous, the memory of the last hour impossible. Rachel clearly wasn't grasping the situation.

There was a short pause and a scoff that honestly didn't help. 'How could he have possibly done that?' She sounded annoyed now, certain I was winding her up, wasting her time, this phone call concocted for fun.

'He didn't speak directly to me, but he was in trouble. I found him on the hallway floor.'

'Who's?'

'Yours.' I paused, tired of explaining myself. 'I'm afraid he's been badly beaten up.'

'My God. Is he okay?' The poor woman was yelling now, crying into the phone, her shock and turmoil apparent.

'I'm not sure. He's with the doctors.' All I wanted was to give the poor kid a hug.

'I don't understand why you took him to the *hospital* without calling me first?' Again, with the accusations. She was lucky I'd found him. She didn't ask how I managed to get inside the house, didn't assume Jack wasn't capable of letting me in.

'I tried calling, but it went to voicemail. There was no time.' It was true. She didn't see the state of him. I couldn't confirm it. Not like this.

'Sorry, I didn't realise you'd called me.' She sounded distracted now, as if she was searching her mobile for the evidence.

'It doesn't matter.'

'I'm on my way.' Another pause. 'Professor Flanigan?'

'Yeah?'

'What the *hell* happened?'

I couldn't tell her, couldn't confirm the state of her son when I found him. I thought about the scissors Jack had highlighted, wishing I'd had the foresight to bring them with me, the offending object potentially covered in DNA and fingerprints of his attacker, Jack's blood still all over them. Instead, I'd left them on the floor, no time to think about things I now realised might be important, vital to any case Jack or his family might want to initiate.

'He's in safe hands,' I found myself confirming sullenly, unable to answer her question. I then headed outside to locate a clean shirt from the back of my forever cluttered car.

***

Rachel was on her mobile when she burst through the A&E entrance, her face flushed, the day over, openly berating her child's father for actions he had no control over.

'Where is he?' It was the first thing she asked when she saw me, hanging up abruptly and dropping her phone on the floor. It skidded under a chair, prompting me to retrieve it. I handed it to her. She didn't thank me.

'He's with the doctors,' I confirmed, unsure what else to say, glad she didn't have to see me covered in her son's blood. I didn't know how to comfort her, nothing to say that would make this better.

'I *need* to see him.' She was crying, her body trembling.

'They're doing everything they can.' I was trying to convince myself he would be okay, yet I couldn't remove the image of his damaged face from my mind. I doubt I ever would.

'I don't understand what happened.'

She wasn't the only one. 'I'm not sure where to begin.'

'Try me.' She glared at me, her eyes unmoving, her arms folded stiffly across her chest. She looked angry, terrified, as if she was about to be sick. 'I don't understand why he called *you* instead of me. I'm his mum.'

I shrugged. I didn't know any more than she did, didn't know what else to add. I offered to get her a coffee while she went to find a doctor, the woman almost triggering an argument with security staff before someone realised who she was and took her to the relative's room. I found her sobbing into her hands, handing her a coffee she refused, gulping my own because I needed the comfort. A doctor was with her, his face almost as ashen as Rachel's.

'Jack has sustained a deep facial laceration,' he confirmed, 'including severe bruising to his face, ribs, and legs.' It was clear he had been beaten, yet by whom we were still to uncover. The doctor paused, glancing my way, his confirmation not yet fully appreciated. 'He will need reconstructive surgery. Several operations.'

'Oh…My…God.' Rachel stumbled to her feet, the mere thought of her boy in such pain too much for her troubled mind to comprehend. She glared at me as if it were my fault, sobbing again, her trembling hands covering her mouth, the wall she was pressed against offering only stony silence. 'Who would do such a thing to my boy?' She glanced my way as if she believed I might tell her. I didn't know. Jack was a likeable kid, fun to be around, a laugh.

I reached forward and rubbed her shoulder, a futile attempt to soothe emotions neither of us understood. It didn't help but she didn't push me away. I thought about the scissors still on the kitchen floor, a sudden urge flooding my brain to get to them before someone else did, before vital evidence was lost.

'I'll be back in a minute,' I stated, stepping out of the room, pulling my mobile from my pocket, my own hands still shaking. I dialled Paul's number, berating my friend for taking so long to answer, unashamedly about to take his attention from pressing police matters. I hoped he would still be at the station. The only important thing right then was Jack, beaten badly enough to trigger an investigation, the potential weapon still where his attacker had left it. I was glad the house would be empty for a while, his sister unaware, his father *Christ* knows where. I still couldn't recall if I'd locked the door, not even sure what had happened to the dog.

'Hey, Newt. How's it going?'

'Do you have a moment?' I grunted into my ageing mobile, no time to acknowledge him or ask about his day.

'For you my friend, always.' Paul's simple affection

would usually calm my nerves, ease the tension. Not today.

'Can you send someone over to Jack Monroe's house? It's urgent.'

'Who?'

'My student, Jack.'

'The kid with the brain tumour?'

'The very same.' As if the poor lad wasn't going through enough. I didn't appreciate Paul's apt analogy yet didn't comment, recalling the day I'd told him about Jack, my university work not something we often spoke about. Paul had made me a coffee, one of those rare occasions he allowed his human side to shine through.

'Is everything okay?'

I explained about Jack's earlier phone call, the state I'd found him, my impossible dash to the hospital. I felt guilty I hadn't collected the scissors when I had the chance, wrapped them in plastic, protected the evidence. It would have saved time, resources, my nerves.

'I'm sorry to ask, but I was too busy dealing with Jack to consider bringing them with me. They might confirm the identity of his attacker.'

'*Jesus.* Yes, of course. Leave it with us. Thank you for your quick thinking and swift actions, Newt.' A pause. 'I hope he's okay.'

So did I.

'Thank you,' I muttered, relaying Jack's address before hanging up and confirming I'd leave the spare key with the hospital reception desk so one of his team could collect it. In my haste, I forgot to tell him about the dog. I'm sure it didn't matter. Star was a friendly enough animal. I hovered outside the hospital for a few moments, hoping the evening air would help calm my racing heart. It didn't. I couldn't tell Rachel about the scissors until I had something concrete to say, couldn't confirm what I didn't yet know. For now, all I could do was hope her son was okay. He didn't need more shit adding to his existence. None of them needed such a high level of stress thrust upon their depleted lives.

Eighteen

Jack

I'm fully expecting the fallout, yet the sight of my mother racing through a set of double doors still shocks me, this hospital bed offering no protection from her pained glare. As much as I have anticipated her reaction, I'm still upset by it, my mother becoming the one person I never thought would look at me how she is now. Her face is flushed, her eyes confirming I'm the cause of her suffering, her mind along for an excruciating ride. Rachel is always so well presented, so beautiful, yet looking at her now, it's impossible to appreciate the superwoman I used to admire. I'm glad it will be over soon. My absence will make her life better, no need to worry once I'm gone. She can finally get back to what matters. Anything other than me.

'My Goodness, Jack, who did this to you?' My mother's eyes dart from me to the doctor, hoping one of us will provide the answer, looking around as if she can't believe I'm once again in such a vulnerable position.

I don't know how long I've been here but my face is bandaged and I can't open my mouth, can't confirm any wrongdoing. I look as if I suffered brutally at someone's savage wrath instead of my own. She takes my hands in hers, pulling me close, hoping to keep me safe from the harm I've already inflicted onto myself. I'm grateful when Newton steps into the room, a cup of coffee in one hand and a smile on his beautiful lips. I want to smile in return, thankful for his company and the support he has shown. Yet, when he winks, I burst into tears, prompting my poor long-suffering mother to do the same.

I have skirted normality for a while, something dark twisting violently inside me long before this day began. Yet, lying in this bed, a dressing over my face and bruising over my body, I despise the looks they give each other when they assume I can't see. My actions have wrongly confirmed injuries they believe are from an attack, just twenty-four hours provoking several incidents I've no capacity of mind to discuss. They don't know I did this to myself, would never understand why.

'Jack, can you *please* tell me what happened?' My mother is still waiting for answers she will never want to hear. She hands me my notebook and pen before wiping her nose with a tissue, her sniffles the only sound in the room making sense. 'And where the *hell* is your father?' She glares at me, then at Newton, hoping he can answer that question, too.

I place the notebook on the bed and shake my head,

turning the pen around in my hand because nothing else will hold my attention. I'm unwilling to acknowledge my absent father right now. I suspect he's drunk somewhere, as usual, the man rarely sober these days. He barely speaks to me when he sees me, stays in the kitchen or the garden, Star's company more interesting than mine. He can hardly look at me, his own son, scarcely has anything to say. I assume it's because of the way I look and not because he hates me, although he wasn't much of a dad before everything turned sour, far too absorbed with himself. I can still feel him struggling to take a shard of mirror from my hand, the blank look he gave me when he did.

I can't explain what happened beyond spinning thoughts I have no control over, subdued by events I will never change. My mother's presence is cementing my decline into an undeserved lull, a deep despair I can't escape. I glance at Newton, no longer confident I did the right thing by calling him. Yet, what else could I have done? It didn't take long to realise my mistake once the initial elation of my tumultuous actions had worn off, seeing the blood I'd spilt, the horror I was causing my family. I didn't want my mother or my sister to find me like *that*. I vaguely remember the moment Newton saw me, the look on his face as he scooped me from the floor. I close my eyes against unwanted memories, fresh bruising mocking my stupidity, my ultimate actions making things worse.

'Why won't you tell me what happened, Jack?' My mother is still sobbing, growing increasingly frustrated by my absence of words and my father's absence entirely. She stops short of grabbing my shoulders, shaking me, demanding a response I'm not yet ready to give.

Even if I could answer I doubt I would.

I did this to myself, Mum. Sorry. What can I say?

She wouldn't understand anyway. Who would? None of them appreciate a forced smile is better than *no* smile, this world unforgiving without laughter, my life worthless without joy. They would lock me away for my own good and theirs, no doctor able to heal my damaged mind. I would die in a lonely room, strapped to a strange bed, those in white uniforms in charge of my end.

A doctor steps forward, unconcerned by our one-sided conversation or my mother's twisted face set in shock.

'We will need to keep him in for a few days to monitor the damage and check for signs of infection,' he says, speaking to my mother as if I'm not in the room, already assuming me not of sound mind. They discuss my stroke, my cancer, my wounds, fully aware what these fresh injuries mean for me. A healthy individual would take weeks to heal, months. Nobody expects me to heal at all. It has taken twenty-seven stitches to reassemble my face, so they say, more surgery and skin grafts required, operations I don't want, time I don't have. I don't want to address my actions, don't need to dwell, too much in my head I now wish to forget. I appreciate the words they aren't using, confirmations they're not making. They are only prepared to make allowances for me because I'm dying, my home a better place to live out my final weeks than an unforgiving hospital bed.

I glance towards my mother, the doctor, then Newton, neither of them offering what I need. I shake my head, motioning to sit up, swiping scratchy sheets from my legs in temper. I'm lashing out, behaving like the very child they all still believe I am. The only thing I want is my bed, my dog, *Newton Flanigan*. My face hurts. More than anticipated, if I'm honest, a row of stitches holding it in place, the drugs they gave me failing to contain a pain I've hidden too long. I glare at Newton, silently pleading with him to understand my predicament, this day's conclusion *not* my intention. When he looks my way there is something in his eyes I don't want to see, his pupils dilating, his mannerisms softening. He sees how scared I am, unable to express the emotion in front of my mother.

'Why don't we give Jack some space?' he queries, resting a hand on her arm, guiding her from the room. There is nothing I can do but watch as they talk out of earshot, flinching every time Newton glances my way.

A cloud of suspicion has settled over me now, it seems—each person searching for evidence that does not exist, discussing unknown facts to decide a relevant course of action, pointing fingers my way. It's probably my imagination, my troubled mind. But I can't help how I feel. Sad, depressed, borderline suicidal. I doubt I will ever explain why.

I wait until everyone has left before I ask for a mirror, a nurse carefully peeling away the dressing from my cheek, revealing the gruesome wound beneath. My right eye is still drooping, still mocking me, still vile, yet my mouth has now joined the chaos. A large patch of unnatural red curves into an unforgiving smile, meeting my eye in surprise, a neat row of nylon thread keeping my gaping injury in place. The nurse tries to reassure me. But something significant has changed, something I can never speak of. I feel it in my gut. I shake my head towards the odd-looking young man staring back, absolutely no idea what happened to him, no idea where I go from here.

Nineteen

Newton

I left the hospital exhausted, reminding myself several times of Jack's young age, the boy barely out of his teens, still very much a child at heart. He had been through so much in such a short space of time, his trauma disguised by dressings now hiding a painful truth. I was glad it was me who had found him, me he'd called. He didn't deserve this. None of them did. I dumped my ruined shirt in a nearby bin and drove to the police station, desperate for information, hoping Paul would still be there, keen to know if he and his team had been to the house. All I wanted was confirmation those incriminating scissors were safe.

Paul was in his office, hunched over his desk, multitasking as always, managing his staff, his email, his priorities. He looked stressed, the sternness on his face nothing new.

'Newt, just the person. I was about to call you.' He glanced up, smiled, picking a mug of tea from his desk already long cold.

I smiled back although it wasn't an expression I felt like sharing. I had Jack on my mind, his blood literally on my hands, unconvinced I'd done a good enough job of appeasing his mother. I was yet to confirm how I'd found the boy, unwilling to express the extent of his injuries. I'm not sure anyone would want the gory details, that boy's savaged features not an image I would ever get out of my head.

'Did you send someone to Jack Monroe's house?' I asked, flustered by the thought of what I'd found there today.

'We did, yes.' I don't know why, but the way my friend looked at me made me assume there was more to his comment, unappreciative of what he was about to add.

I sighed. 'And?' I sat down.

Paul rubbed his forehead, pressing stressed lips together as if considering his next words. 'We took a good look around as you asked, saw the blood inside the kitchen and hallway.' He was looking at me with an expression I couldn't understand.

'Okay. Good. And did you get the scissors?' I couldn't stop thinking about them, the panic arising from Rachel if she'd found them, the shock too much for her to deal with. I imagined the look in Jack's eyes as he faced his attacker, the poor kid at the end of some brutal event I didn't yet wish to acknowledge. I sighed again, unaware my reaction was prematurely unwarranted.

Paul shook his head. 'I'm afraid not.'

'What? Why?' I couldn't understand what he was saying. He'd promised. 'But I left the kitchen door key with recep—'

Paul shook his head, cutting me off mid-sentence. 'We didn't go inside the property, in the end.'

'Why?' I repeated, getting to my feet, placing hot palms on Paul's desk to steady myself. My head was spinning, black dots flickering rapidly behind my uncertain eyelids. 'How did you expect to find the scissors if you weren't even *looking* for them?'

Paul raised his hand towards me, a gesture meant to calm an irritation he could clearly see elevating. 'Because we had no just cause for entry.'

'*Jesus*, Paul. I asked you to do me a favour.' I was probably overstepping the mark, but I didn't care. I didn't ask for much. I tried to think back, attempting to recall what I did wrong, what I did with the dog. What wasn't he telling me? 'Since when do you allow little things like warrants and legalities to deter your investigations?' I assumed this was the reason for his failed entry, the reason for his vacant, non-descript glare. Paul didn't usually buy into such limiting concepts. It often got him into trouble, but like me, my friend had his own way of dealing with the law.

'I assume you know Jack's family have a dog?' Paul was leaning back in his chair, unconcerned by my elevated vocals or rapidly reddening cheeks.

'I do yes. Sorry, I forgot to mention her when I called earlier.' Star was a brutish-looking German Shepard, but she was soft as a pillow, would lick you to death if you let her.

In fact, the only injury she was likely to inflict was a dead leg if she sat on you. Why wasn't he answering my question?

'The dog was barking when we got to the house.'

'So?' That was a *good* thing. At least I hadn't lost her in my unwitting haste, hadn't left her outside to run off and create further drama for the family.

'So, if Jack was attacked inside the property, Newt, don't you think the dog would have alerted someone? Fought off a potential intruder, left behind some kind of damning evidence?'

'How do you know the dog *didn't* fight off Jack's attacker?' I narrowed my eyes, unable to predict Paul's thoughts or where he was going with this. I would have fully expected Star to protect him, exactly how *I* should have. It didn't matter from who or what. I recalled the blood on her paws, her frantic desperation to raise my attention. Why was this important?

Paul ignored my question, getting instead to his feet, staring out of the window as if he had all the time in the world. 'According to several neighbours, the dog has been fairly quiet all day. In fact, the only time they claim to have heard her barking was when they saw *your* car parked outside and again after we arrived this evening. Apparently, anything out of the ordinary will trigger Star's barking. The walls in those newly built homes are like paper. Nothing remains private in that neighbourhood for long, so I've been told.'

'I'm still not getting your point.' It was annoying, to be honest, the idea of neighbours witnessing my arrival, yet failing to notice Jack's intruder, his predicament or my urgent intervention. I stared blankly at my friend, no words of value finding traction, no comforting consideration to think a neighbour might have been watching us, peering through a nearby window, ignoring the carnage.

'Think about it, Newt. If Jack was attacked in his own home, no family dog would allow such a thing to happen without someone hearing the commotion. That dog has a loud bark.' Paul turned to face me, waiting for me to appreciate the words unwilling to settle in my head, muttering under his breath, 'and probably a painful bite, too,' before giving me a sideways glance.

She did indeed have a loud bark, although I wouldn't know about her bite potential. Why was this relevant? 'What are you saying?' I was staring into space, trying to picture the scene, the image of Star's blood-coated paws still vivid in my mind.

'I'm saying whatever happened to Jack did *not* alert his dog. Don't you think that's strange?' Paul was glaring at me, waiting for the penny to drop.

'You think Jack might have known his attacker?' I hadn't considered the thought, hadn't expected the revelation.

Paul shrugged. 'I'm not so sure about that. Even if Jack knew his attacker, his distress would still alert the dog. '

'Then what am I missing?' I know I was stressed, but I honestly couldn't appreciate what Paul was trying to say.

My friend was wearing his detective brain, mine too clouded by what had happened to think straight. I also needed coffee. 'How did you gain entry to the house?' he asked, calmly folding his arms across his chest.

'With the key I gave you.'

Paul nodded, more to himself than to me, confirming in his own head what wasn't yet in mine. 'The property was secured?'

'Yes.'

'Okay. So, tell me something. If the property was locked and you had to unlock the door, how did Jack's attacker leave?' He took a deep breath before continuing. 'The windows and doors were all secured from what we could tell, no sign of any break-in.'

I narrowed my eyes.

'Jack *does* know his attacker.' I had to sit down, Paul's revelations not forthcoming. Securing the property when they left meant they were close to the family. Either that, or they were cold, calculated bastards. I couldn't imagine a friend or family member wanting to hurt Jack, his father's absence a sudden concern. 'Shit.'

'I don't think it's as simple as that.' Paul licked his lips, taking a sip of cold tea that made him gag.

'Why?' What was I missing now?

Paul paused, allowing me to absorb his words. 'Because even if Jack *was* attacked by a known associate, a neighbour would have heard the commotion, Newt. If the kid was fighting for his life, it would have alerted the dog.'

He wasn't about to let that go. 'So, what are you saying?'

'At this stage, we can't be sure it isn't a self-inflicted injury.'

'You think Jack did this to *himself*?' The thought made

me feel sick.

Paul nodded. 'It's probably not what you were expecting or hoping to hear.'

I glared at my friend. He wasn't wrong. I was hoping for support I assumed he could offer, a full investigation. Yet, for the first time in my life I was genuinely troubled by his unfailing professionalism, his detective nose far more astute than mine, it seemed. I desperately tried to think back to my time at the house, Star the only other living creature who'd unwittingly spread Jack's blood around, aside from me, and I'd been careful to skirt around what I genuinely believed was a crime scene.

'Then what on earth happened?'

'You're probably going to need to ask Jack.' Paul turned back to the window, nothing more to say.

I was trying to add two and two together, coming up with ridiculous answers, my brain creating every possible calculation aside from the one that mattered. The truth.

'Surely, he wouldn't hurt *himself*? Surely, he wouldn't do something like *that*?' I knew Jack was suffering, locked inside his head, forced to deal with things no kid should. But I *knew* Jack. He wouldn't put his family through such an ordeal.

Paul shrugged again. I didn't like the look he was giving me, sickening thoughts now racing through mine.

'Do you still have the key?' I reached out my hand, shocked by how much it trembled, glad when Paul placed it into my open palm without comment.

'Don't do anything stupid,' he called after me as I left his office. 'You can't fix everyone else's problems.'

Twenty

Newton

It was getting late by the time I reached Jack's house, in a daze, unsure what I was going to do or what I hoped to find. I was convinced I'd either be chastised for my uninvited interference or add to the family's problems, but I couldn't allow Rachel to come home to the sight of her son's blood *or* those scissors, wherever they were, couldn't force her to relive the drama. The only thought plaguing my head was that Jack *couldn't* have done this, no other choice but to hope Paul was wrong.

I opened the door to a pitch-black, silent house, thankful no one was home to witness the chaos. I flicked a light switch, the kitchen and hallway floors still smudged with red, exactly how I'd left them, the blood now dry in places, a horror scene of carnage I'd never forget. Star was in her bed, her face, nose and feet dotted with pink, her wagging tail oddly comforting. I hosed her down in the downstairs shower room before letting her into the garden to dry off, barking, happy to be free, unconcerned as she chased a cat across the lawn.

I sighed, grabbing kitchen roll and disinfectant from a nearby cupboard, keen to wipe away all traces of this day before the family returned, Jack's trauma lingering like a scab unwilling to heal. The house should have been a crime scene, this incident a sensitive matter, but instead I began the arduous task of removing evidence, placing several bloodied towels in the washing machine so Rachel wouldn't have to. Under normal circumstances the police would be here, logging details, searching for clues. It was unnerving why they weren't, to be honest, Paul's uncertainty weighing heavily on my mind. As far as he was concerned, no crime had been committed, no evidence to support any supposed attack and fully convinced Jack had injured himself. Even as I looked around, I could see no sign of anyone else having been here other than me.

I found the scissors under a cupboard in the kitchen, hidden from view unless you were looking. I still couldn't understand why Paul hadn't collected them anyway, couldn't appreciate his detachment. I grabbed a carrier bag from a kitchen drawer, careful not to touch them as I wrapped them up, wondering what I was meant to do with them now I had them. I didn't want to believe Jack did this to himself, convinced there was more to the story. I placed the scissors in my glove compartment for safekeeping, making sure the house was presentable and Star was safely inside before I left, ensuring the place looked, at first glance, as it always did.

I arrived home to the confirmation that Rachel was spending the night at the hospital with her son, her text message short and to the point. She sounded exhausted. Lizzy was staying overnight with a friend, knowing only her brother had been rushed to the hospital. I'm certain Rachel no longer cared where her ex-husband was. She thanked me for being there for her son, her previous hardness softening slightly. I considered calling her but assumed she wouldn't need further intrusion so I sent her a brief message telling her to contact me if she needed anything, then took a well-needed shower.

I'd almost forgotten about the letter I'd earlier discarded next to my now dried-out sandwich, a much-needed coffee calling from my kitchen. I accidentally took a bite before realising my error, dumping it in the bin while tearing open the envelope, my hands shaky, a comforting sound of coffee beans grinding in the background. The only reason I hadn't binned it already was because it reminded me of a different letter, years ago now, though still as painful. It contained my divorce papers, my failed marriage not something I thought much about these days, my ex-wife exiting my life long ago. But because of a long past trauma, this new letter caught my attention. I doubted it would be anything important, of course, just more junk for the recycle bin. Yet, I scanned the contents anyway, needing to read the words twice, wholly unsure what I was looking at. I stood by my open kitchen door, convinced the darkness was creating hallucinations, eventually calling my sister-in-law because I needed her opinion.

'You've done *what?*' Steph's raised voice didn't help the situation, my foggy eyes still unable to confirm what I was reading.

'I've inherited a cottage.' The idea sounded ludicrous, the paper in my grasp obviously a scam.

'From who?'

'That's the thing. I don't know. Some great aunt I wasn't even aware existed.' I read the letter aloud as Steph pondered my news, nothing of this moment making sense. 'Someone called May Packman. According to this, the property is in Bridgechurch.' I stared at my wheelie bin, several flies buzzing around the top, hoping for a late-night meal. 'Who's Great Aunt May Packman?'

Steph laughed. 'Actually, Newt, now you come to mention it, I vaguely recall Isaac saying something about an aunt on your mum's side of the family, but no one has seen or heard from her in years.' She paused. 'I *think* her name was May, but don't quote me on that.'

'Why don't *I* know who she is?' Although my brother was four years older, it did *not* make him privy to information I wasn't. I recognised the surname. My grandmother's maiden name.

'I don't know, but if the house is in Bridgechurch, it might be worth a bit.'

Steph had a point. Bridgechurch was a stunning picturesque English village situated midway between Eastcliff and Shelby, a location I'd driven through many times, had thought nothing of living there beyond slight envy for those who did. The place could be nothing more than an oversized shed, a ruin, already fallen into the sea.

Completely worthless.

'Why don't you call the solicitors and find out?' Steph sounded slightly annoyed I hadn't already done so. 'If by some miracle, the letter is genuine, the kids and I could do with a holiday.' Steph was never one to drop subtle hints, choosing instead to say it like it is, laughing with excitement I feared would be short-lived.

So, the following morning I did as I was told, confirmation the letter *was* genuine coming my way via a strong male voice. I had inherited a cottage from my grandmother's sister on my mother's side, of all people. I'd never met my grandmother. She died when I was a baby, didn't even know she *had* a sister. Having no other family, May had listed my brother and I as the sole beneficiaries of her will. The details were outdated now, nothing recent to confirm Isaac was dead. He wasn't married when the will was drafted, no clause allowing the inheritance to pass to Steph, so it meant the house was all mine. May had resided in a care home until her recent death at the age of ninety-eight, no children, no husband, her siblings already in their graves, our dwindling family unit tiny in comparison to most. That's the thing with getting old. You run the risk of outliving everyone you know. May didn't know Steph, had never met her great-great nephews. It's a shame. She would have liked them.

May had seven thousand pounds in a bank account, the remainder of her dwindling savings after care home costs took everything else, her funeral arrangements already in place. I immediately gifted the money to my nephews. It would one day help with university costs if they needed it, would help Steph if they didn't. I wasted no time in telling her the news, yet was unsure I *wanted* a cottage. I could barely maintain my flat, too much going on in my life for such a colossal distraction. Still, I didn't want to sound ungrateful, wasn't about to mention my concerns. I was still convinced this was a prank. If all else failed, I could gift the place to Steph. She deserved it far more than me.

Twenty-One

Jack

It is two frustrating days before they tell me I can go home. Forty-eight mind-numbing hours of relentless nothingness while sucking my meals through a straw because I can no longer open my mouth wide enough to do anything else. It adds further humiliation to the way I feel, exhausted by unfeeling strangers who, despite their best efforts, don't care about me. I have been struggling to eat unaided as it is, my recent actions now making things worse. I've lost weight, my clothing baggy, my bones mere twigs beneath my sallow skin. They want to keep me in this place longer but appreciate I don't have much time left, my self-inflicted injury something I must now live with until the end. Luckily, my low mood and obvious dispirit provides the fuel for my pending discharge, released under strict instructions I rest, my bandages kept dry, returning to the hospital immediately if anything changes. I glance at my mother as the doctors confirm this, knowing she won't let me out of her sight, unwilling to leave me alone to create further unwanted chaos.

I have insisted Newton take me home today, *only* Newton, my persistence made clear via outlandish sign language I'm sure does not exist. It doesn't matter. My mother received the message well enough. The last thing I need is her negativity, her frustration aimed towards strangers instead of the one person who might offer the answers she seeks. *Me.* I'm refusing to communicate because I don't need further drama adding to this week, unwilling to write an explanation of what occurred on the notebook she carries now wherever we go. The hospital staff assume I'm in shock, unsurprisingly, my injuries enough to unnerve anyone. Newton assumes I'll open up in my own time, confirming I'll tell the police what I can, when I can, when I'm ready.

My professor is standing by my bed, helping me to my feet, my overnight bag in his hands and a false smile on his face. I despise the way people look at me, sympathies they can't sustain flashing across their faces whenever they realise I'm unable to answer their questions. Because of this, I've found myself avoiding communication on *any* level. It isn't comforting, not pleasant to find myself so alone. I stare out of my professor's dusty car window as Newton drives me home, listening to his overworked fans churn dust and debris around the interior. He speaks of nothing involving *me*, unfortunately, jabbering on about some house he has inherited, my eyes kept closed because I can't bear to look at him. I glance his way just once, wondering how he would react if he knew the truth, how he would look at me then.

When Lizzy races through the front door, she looks happy to see me, yet I automatically shrink down in my seat. I can't have my sister witness what has happened, can't bear the thought of what she might think. Instead, I wait silently until Newton takes the hint, taking her inside, offering a sideways look neither appreciate. Lizzy is asking questions, as always, desperate to say hello. She doesn't understand the drastic change in her big brother, has unfortunately been protected from the truth. I hope one day she will understand. I hope we both will. I want to cry, hold her hand, tell her how I feel, yet no tears emerge, no emotions able to bring forth any response that would mean much now anyway. I'm jolted only from my wayward deliberations when Newton taps the window, popping open the door before I'm ready for the intrusion, the smile on his face only making things worse.

'You okay, kiddo?'

I'm no *kid*. I wish he would see *me* how I see him, treat me like an adult, his equal. Instead, I look down and nod, willing him with everything I have inside to hold my hand, if he can, keep me safe, climb inside my damaged soul and save me from a world I hate. As it is, I'm forced to climb into the heady lunchtime air without his help, thankful for his company, yet unable to express anything of value. I hesitate, my heart in my throat, wondering if I'm about to make a mistake before banishing all caution and throw my arms around him. I'm failing to hold back emotions I'm certain will give me away, but I don't care. His scent is familiar, muted aftershave matching my own, the coffee on his breath, the shampoo he uses.

'You're welcome,' he laughs, believing my embrace is nothing other than gratitude for today's lift home, failing to appreciate the significance of anything else.

I *love* Newton Flanigan with everything I have, yet how can I tell him? How can I express what I've done or explain who I am? Instead, I must allow others to create their own assumptions of me, reaching their own conclusions in their own time. It's not my fault what has happened, not my fault what happens next. After all, I'm not responsible for the thoughts and actions of *others*. No one holds that kind of power. Not even me.

Twenty-Two

Newton

I drove Jack home as requested, unsure what I was going to say or how I was going to say it, my struggling breath made marginally better by a breeze blowing through the open car windows. Despite the unforeseen incident shifting something we hadn't yet addressed, I couldn't imagine he might want to hurt himself.

'...And so I collected the keys yesterday but haven't seen the place yet, don't even know what it looks like.' I laughed, trying hard to engage with Jack and share something of value he might appreciate. He didn't answer, instead sank into his seat the moment his sister raced through the front door to greet us, the poor kid left hovering on the driveway. He didn't look at me, didn't acknowledge my news or his sibling.

I climbed into the warm air and greeted the fifteen-year-old, her response merely to glance my way as if I were an alien. Before today, we'd never met. It was a shame. She seemed a nice enough girl, had a kind enough face, a warm expression I would like to know better. I took the hint, explaining Jack needed a little space, waiting patiently until she was back inside the house before attempting to reach him. He wasn't usually this aloof, his younger sister too important to ignore. When he gave me a hug, I wasn't expecting *that* either.

Rachel was standing by the front door, a look on her face I hadn't seen before. She seemed pleased to see me for once, pleased I was here.

'Everything okay?' she queried, glancing nervously my way, something on her mind she wasn't expressing.

I nodded, unconvinced by the smile I offered, uncertain I knew how to help.

'I just wanted to say thank you, Professor Flanigan,' Rachel breathed, stepping aside to allow me inside the house as Jack headed absentmindedly towards the staircase. He didn't look back, didn't offer any gratitude for the time I'd given up.

'Please, call me Newton. Is everything okay?'

Rachel shook her head, lowering her voice. 'I don't know how to reach him. I'm at the end of my tether.' She was close to tears, close to the edge, desperate for her boy to come back from wherever he'd gone.

I thought about my newly acquired cottage, my good news overshadowed by events unfolding in this house. 'He could probably just use a change of scenery, some fresh air,' I found myself confirming as I glanced towards the ceiling, wondering if he could hear me from his room, if he was listening, if he cared.

'If you have any suggestions, I'm open to a discussion.' Rachel shrugged, assuming I didn't.

So, I told her about my cottage, the fact I knew nothing about it other than it was by the ocean, set on Jackson Crest Point, the quaint village of Bridgechurch a place you'd miss if you blinked. It housed a six-hundred-year-old church overlooking the North Sea, a narrow bridge flanking a dwindling stream, a shop, a post-box and approximately twenty scattered homes, Great Aunt May's included.

'It might help him to do something *normal* for a change.' I smiled, steadily forgetting what normality looked like. Besides, I needed a second opinion on the cottage, Jack potentially the perfect person to offer his untethered, albeit silent, viewpoint.

'It sounds idyllic.' Rachel shrugged, momentarily glad of the distraction.

It did. It ran alongside the perimeter of Chestermill Woods, set along a narrow dirt track. Sounded a bit spooky, if I thought about it. Especially at night.

'I guess you could ask him.' Rachel didn't look convinced, didn't seem to believe I could reach her boy on any level now.

'Would you like me to talk to him?'

She nodded sullenly, closing the front door while absently chewing a piece of tissue in her hand. She glanced towards the stairs, frustrated thumping already emanating from Jack's room.

'Second door on the right,' she confirmed. 'Can I get you

a drink?'

'A black coffee would be good, thank you,' I nodded, offering a weak smile. 'Two sugars.' I needed all the sustenance I could get, already on the bottom step before she could change her mind. Star padded out of the kitchen wagging her tail, her nose nudging my leg. At least she was no longer coated in blood. I thought about Paul's theory, knowing if someone had attacked Jack, this dog would know it, her nose into *everything*.

'The dog seems to like you,' Rachel called my way as she headed into the kitchen now herself. I didn't dare tell her how we already knew each other.

Jack's bedroom door was covered in "keep out" notices and handwritten signs denoting a teenager's domain instead of the adult he was becoming. I tapped gently, breaking the stillness around me.

'Jack?'

No answer.

'Jack. It's Newton.'

I heard a shuffle, a spring, a ruffled duvet.

I sighed, straining to position my ear as close to the door as I could. 'Can we talk?'

Still nothing.

Sensing I was going to be outside this room for a while, I allowed my knees to bend, sliding onto the carpet, grateful for Star's willing attention. I stroked the dog's head, thinking of what I might say to a young man in obvious turmoil, how I would feel in his position.

'Have you had Star long?' I asked. She was nuzzling my neck, licking my ear.

No reply.

'I bet she's a great guard dog. I expect she could fend off *anyone* who tried to get into this house.' It was a deliberate statement, a way of expressing my thoughts without saying what I wanted to say, Jack's closed door of no real concern.

Nothing. Only the sound of Star's heavy panting and my strained breathing engulfed the landing.

'She probably would have made a good police dog,' I continued. She certainly looked healthy enough, alert, intelligent.

Another shuffle. I sensed Jack's heavy breath on the other side of the door, no doubt wanting to answer my questions, if he could, already questioning my thoughts, my motives. As long as I'd known him, Jack had an infectious enthusiasm for everything, especially anything I said, forever taking notes, making me laugh. He knew my morning routine, right down to how I combed my hair, the shampoo I used, how many coffees I drank. *Too many*, he'd often complained with a roll of his amused eyes. I'd long to see that again.

I glanced towards the ceiling, pressing my face close to the door panel so he could hear me better. 'You can *always* tell if a dog has a good soul, Jack, by how much they understand what's going on around them.' I was stroking Star's ear, her head nuzzled in my lap, her large brown eyes watching mine. I imagined her camped outside his room or on Jack's bed when his mum wasn't looking.

'You *can* talk to me, you know,' I called out softly, knowing he could hear me clear enough, knowing he was listening. I could hear his breathing and Star's, the dog already comfortable, ready to fall asleep if I let her.

'If there is something you can't tell your mum, you *know* I'm always here for you.' It was true. Jack knew. 'I was wondering if you fancied taking a drive out of town with me tomorrow? I need to look at the cottage anyway.' I paused. 'I could do with your opinion.'

Another shuffle, followed by a click as a lock slid sideways. The bedroom door creaked open, causing Star to jump up in excited response, wagging her tail, trying to nudge her way into Jack's room. I got to my feet, my knees aching with the exertion, feeling older than I wanted, weaker than I once did. Jack was positioned behind his door, his damaged face peering through the crack. I couldn't tell, but I assumed he'd been crying, his sniffles hidden behind emotions he obviously did not want to share.

'May I come in?' I queried, offering the most sympathetic smile I could muster.

Annoyingly, Jack's mum took that very moment to head upstairs, a mug of coffee in one hand and a worried expression on her face. Jack slammed the door, making her jump.

'Everything okay?' she asked gingerly as she handed me the mug, a trail of hot liquid running down the edge.

'It will be,' I whispered, taking the coffee, taking a sip, wiping a free hand over the wet ceramic so as not to spill any on the carpet. 'Thank you.'

She nodded and took Star by the collar, guiding her downstairs, holding back tears, her eyes swollen from the relentless agony these last few months had provoked.

'It's okay, she's gone,' I whispered once we were alone

again. 'Please, don't make me talk to you through a closed door.'

I was forced to wait in silence for a further few seconds before the door slowly creaked open and I was finally allowed inside. Jack kept his back to me, shuffling towards his bed, his only protection being the duvet he pulled firmly over his head, despite this room being too hot for such an indulgence.

Jack's room was impressive, large enough to house a king-sized bed, an armchair *and* a sofa nestling around what appeared to be a sixty-inch television, the room segregated into distinct zones. He even had his own ensuite. It reminded me of the studio flat I once shared with a friend of mine during my university days, only posher, bigger, cleaner. The curtains were closed, the room plunged into semi-darkness despite the bright sunlight outside. It was typical of a young man, with posters on the walls, computer games scattered across the floor, game controllers in various states of health lying on a nearby rug. I closed the door. I didn't know if I should but I sat on the edge of Jack's bed anyway, the boy looking everywhere but at me. His bandaged cheek hid a wound that would probably never heal, the scar forever reminding him of what had happened. There was a broken mirror on the wall. I didn't want to conclude how it got that way.

'That's better,' I said instead, smoothing my trousers, the duvet, my soothing voice meant to calm us both as I pressed eager lips around my coffee mug. I wished today's conversation could have been held under better circumstances, wished I could do something eventful. 'I wish you would talk to me,' I found myself muttering between sips.

Jack glared my way as if I was mad for making such a statement. It made me smile, briefly.

'Your mum makes good coffee,' I added, ignoring his glare and his narrowed eyes, enjoying this simple pleasure. It was true. I'm sure I heard Jack scoff. I ignored that too. 'I know things are terrible for you right now but when have you and I ever *not* been able to talk? Metaphorically speaking.' Jack usually never stopped talking, his forced silence now somewhat unnerving. He must have been going through hell.

Jack shrugged, picking up a notebook which he scribbled an untidy message onto, before holding it towards me.

How exactly do you expect me to TALK?

I laughed. I couldn't help it, his bright personality screaming from his pained handwriting even when he wasn't trying.

'Well, if you're not talking to me *now*, Jack, I don't know what you'd call it.' I winked, causing him to narrow his eyes even further, a shake of his exasperated head making me grin. 'You know as well as I do communication is more than verbal cues alone.' He knew I was right, couldn't dispute the statement even if he could vocalise his thoughts.

I finished my coffee and placed the empty mug on the carpet, reminding myself to take it with me once Jack and I were finished, careful not to leave a stain. I didn't wish to give Rachel the wrong impression, didn't want her to think badly of me. 'Let's start again, shall we?' I smiled, offering the boy a look of genuine concern.

Jack nodded.

'So, how *are* you?'

Fine

'Seriously?'

Jack shook his head, fresh tears threatening to fall. He knew I could see through his lies.

'Do you want to tell me what *really* happened?' It was a direct question, one requiring a direct answer before I either exploded with unanswered theories or throttled the kid for his uncontrolled actions. Despite not being able to directly confirm it, he'd led everyone to believe he'd been attacked, his black eye and bruised ribs a clear indication of *something*. I just didn't know what.

Jack's eyes widened, a shocked expression appearing on his face. His cheeks had reddened, his lips dry with unspoken confirmations. He hesitated before writing a response, his pen dangling in his hand.

I was beaten up

'*Were* you?' I couldn't help asking, the words leaving my lips before I could stop them. 'Because I have a distinct feeling you're not telling me the whole story.'

Jack pulled the duvet around his body in an attempt to fend off my unappreciated words, his brow screwed into a tight knot.

'Okay. So, who beat you up?'

A shrug.

'Where did this happen?'

Down by the canal

Jack could barely look at me, obviously didn't want to relive his trauma.

'Please tell me what happened?'

I sensed he didn't know what to say or how to explain. He stared at the blank television screen for a moment before writing a response.

Some random dickhead attacked me when I went for a walk. I don't want to talk about it

'Tell me about your mouth, then?'

Jack Swallowed. I could tell his face hurt, his dressings preventing any natural movement.

What about it?

'What did you *do*, Jack?'

There was a pause, more scribbling.

Nothing

'Jack?'

A sigh.

'*You* did this, didn't you?'

Jack took a moment to think, looking my way briefly before eventually nodding slowly, his eyes facing the floor, his mind in turmoil. He couldn't keep the truth from me now. I wouldn't let him.

'Why?' I honestly couldn't understand it.

More scribbling.

I just wanted to smile again

His handwriting had become aggressive, his unspoken words breaking my heart. Jack was always smiling, always laughing. Now he could do neither. I pointed towards his face, terrified of the answer I already knew was coming. I closed my eyes, Paul's suspicions unnervingly correct.

'I want to understand. Why would you do something like that?'

Jack's tears were falling freely now, nothing able to stop them.

Because I hate being ME

And there, written in black ink was the answer I was dreading. I didn't know what to say or how to make it better. The only thing I could do was continue my questions, try to understand the obvious contempt, no chance of ever getting to the crux of Jack's problems. I was glaring at him. I couldn't help it. It wasn't meant as malicious. I was just worried, terrified I would never reach him.

Jack swallowed. He still wasn't looking my way.

'I thought someone tried to *kill* you.'

No answer.

'You frightened me.'

Jack glanced up, my words hitting hard, his damaged face dissolving into a young boy again, the infectious teenager who lit up my lecture rooms.

How did you know it was me?

'I didn't. Not at first. But I was worried about you so I asked a friend of mine to come to the house and collect the scissors because I believed they were evidence in catching whoever did this to you. I couldn't allow that to go unnoticed, could I?'

Jack shook his head. He knew I couldn't.

'He's a police officer.'

Silence.

'He suspected you might have injured yourself because of Star, of all things.' I laughed. It was inappropriate. 'Because she didn't bark,' I confirmed, my voice automatically rising. I couldn't help it. I sounded like the kid's dad, not the friend he had come to rely on. Jack looked terrified. He paused before writing again.

Impressive

It was, although I probably wouldn't tell Paul. I'd never hear the end of it. 'Agreed.' My turn now to look away, embarrassed I hadn't realised this simple fact for myself.

What happened to the scissors?

'I have them. They're safe.' For now.

A nod. He could still barely look my way. The thought of cutting open his own face made mine tighten in shock.

'I thought they were evidence of a *crime*, Jack. You *must* understand. You know I work with the police. I just wanted them to help you, that's all.' I glanced around the room, not assuming for a moment his mum had queried their disappearance, probably not yet even aware they were missing. We wouldn't be having this conversation if she had. Like me, she would have made her assumptions, marching Jack to the police station, making him provide a statement, his actions documented on record. If she thought her son had been attacked by a pair of scissors from her own kitchen, I'm not sure how she'd react. If she knew he'd done this to himself, she would never recover.

Jack sighed.

I'm sorry

He glanced towards the far side of his room, wringing his hands tightly together as if searching for absolution. I pretended not to notice.

'Are you going to tell your mum the truth?'

Jack shook his head, his embarrassment obvious.

'She believes someone attacked you. She's already spoken with the police.' Rachel didn't know it happened in her own kitchen, of course, wouldn't have been able to deal with that. As far as she was concerned, the attack happened outside the family home, my cover-up something I would now have to live with. She wouldn't appreciate my interference, certainly wouldn't understand why there would be no ongoing police involvement.

Someone did attack me

'By the canal?' I sounded flippant, no longer sure I believed him.

YES

'Great. Do you want to press charges?' Sarcasm.

NO

'Okay.' I paused, careful how I worded my next comment. 'I won't say anything if you don't want me to.'
When Jack looked my way, I saw something I couldn't fathom. Shock.

Why are you helping me?

The kid looked puzzled.
'Because I'm your friend.' It was true. I hoped he'd appreciate the depth of my statement. Despite being his university professor and twice his age, I'd do almost anything to protect him. If his mother knew what he'd done, she would send him for a mental assessment, force him to sit in rooms designed to dissect his mental health, talking to

strangers who didn't know him or his needs. The poor kid didn't need any more stress in his day.

'So, how about that day trip?'

Jack shrugged. I took that as a yes.

We sat together for a while, *chatting* about the little things, the video games I'd given him, the magazines he'd now read several times, nothing else to do while lying in a hospital bed, nothing further discussed about his self-inflicted injury. Jack had scars I felt ran far deeper than any damage he could do to his physical appearance. If I could make even the tiniest difference in his life, I would. I owed him that much. I eventually left him to get some rest, heading downstairs, my empty mug in my hand, too many thoughts on my mind.

'Did he talk to you?' Rachel was hovering by her open kitchen door, a tea towel in a trembling hand, a vape in the other, an apple pie cooling on the table. Star was outside, chasing something. I couldn't see what.

'Kind of.' I didn't want to elaborate.

'Did he agree to your day out?'

I nodded. *Kind of.* 'He will be okay, you know.' I wanted to believe my words, yet wasn't sure which of us I was trying to convince. I could only hope my statement rang true, feeling somewhat uncomfortable I was unable to share Jack's secret. It wasn't mine to tell.

Twenty-Three

Newton

Despite the overbearing heat and my ageing car, it was nice to do something other than mark essays and dissect police files. I glanced to my left, watching Jack stare out of the window, a fast-moving breeze blowing his hooded top across his cheek. He didn't engage with me, merely sighed whenever I glanced his way, his eyes kept low so I wouldn't see what lay behind the perpetual sadness. I appreciated why he felt his hoodie protected him, but it couldn't be comfortable, not in this weather. His mum must have washed it recently, a strong scent of washing detergent drifting across my nose.

The roads twisted haphazardly in front of us, narrowing in places, meandering around bends, adding to the hypnotic atmosphere, the beautiful English countryside never failing to impress. The cottage was aptly named, "Fisherman

Jacks", a name I was profoundly amused by, keen to share, believing it might cheer Jack up and give him something to think of other than his declining health. He released a sound of joy when I told him, his elevated grunt telling me he was impressed by the concept, even if he couldn't express it, the idea of some fisherman called *Jack* once living there, briefly lifting his spirits. I didn't mention it was probably more likely because the place was set on Jackson Crest Point, *"Jacks"* therefore becoming an apt nickname for the location. I imagined there would have been plenty of fishing to be had, though, once upon a time.

The cottage overlooked the ocean, or so they told me, set along a private lane leading to a private beach, the two-acre plot flanked on one side by woodland. It was perfect for walks, to lose yourself amid nature in all its glory, to escape. My aunt rented the place as a holiday property, a company in charge of the bookings. I could see how it might attract many guests. Yet, I didn't know what to expect, didn't anticipate the impossible images in my head to match the reality I was about to witness. I assumed the place would be run down, overgrown, my great aunt in no position to keep it maintained. I was glad I had Jack for company. He would at least give me something to think of other than ageing relatives I didn't know I had, ageing properties I didn't know how to maintain. It didn't matter how subdued he was. Fresh air would do him good.

Bridgechurch was tiny but beautiful, a quintessential English village flanked by chocolate-box cottages, wildflowers, wild bees and rolling countryside overlooking a stunning sea view. I didn't see the cottage at first, already passing a row of trees denoting the turning before Jack noticed my error, pointing frantically to a hand-painted sign next to the road because there was nothing else he could do. I stopped, reversed a few feet, grateful there were no other cars behind us, thankful I'd brought him along.

We drove beneath the trees, emerging on the other side to the sight of a whitewashed nineteenth-century cottage, complete with a pretty blue front door, sandstone driveway and wrap-around garden. I wasn't expecting it to be so beautiful, so well-maintained. I think my mouth had fallen open. I'm sure if Jack could have moved his, he would have reacted in a similar way.

Instead, he glanced towards me, nodding wildly as if asking my permission to explore, popping open the car door before I'd brought it to a halt. A wave of fresh, sea air engulfed us, the sudden rush as breathtaking as the view. Jack was already halfway down the path before I could stop him, his crutches of no obvious relevance. Yet as I watched him go, his muddled persona appeared unforgiving, almost as if it had mutated into something dark, the poor kid still trying to maintain a personality he was clearly losing a grip of. There was a moment where he seemed to look my way, but it was fleeting, turning his attention to a set of steps leading to the beach. He waved. I waved back. And then he was gone, leaving me alone in this strange place, a strong sea breeze cutting sharply across my face.

The first thing I wanted to do was call Steph. I'd promised to video call her as soon as I arrived so she could share this unfathomable moment, offer her verdict, her opinion. She was as excited to see this place as I was. But I equally wanted to give my attention to Jack, this day as much about him as anything. He didn't know it yet, but I'd made a genuine effort, loading the car with his favourites — cartons of chocolate milkshakes, sausage rolls, cheesy twists, chocolate bars already melting in their wrappers. I didn't care how old he thought he was. To me, he'd always be that bright-eyed kid who'd wandered into my lecture room with a beaming smile and not a care in the world. It was a shame he'd never now grow into the man he deserved to be, would not live long enough to find his genuine happy place on earth.

I found him on the beach picking seaweed from rock pools, his pockets filled with shells and pebbles, his toes coated in sand, jeans rolled to the knees. I tried not to notice how thin his legs looked. Being here seemed to help him find a glimpse of normality in a cruel world neither of us really understood. Christ knows the poor kid needed the respite. So did I, to be honest. He waved excitedly when he saw me, his eyes shining with life I hadn't seen in a while. From a distance, he looked just like the Jack I remembered, this place enough to lift his mood. It almost broke my heart.

He spent the next hour exploring in silence, oddly at peace with his surroundings. I wasn't anticipating such a stunning location, the images I'd seen briefly on paper *nothing* compared to the reality greeting me. The outskirts of Chestermill Woods were set boldly along one side of the property, a dense line of trees rolling casually towards the sea, halted only by a cliff edge and powerful waves crashing against the rocks. Nature at its best. For a while, I almost ignored the issues this place would come with, a septic tank

I'd need to maintain, a boiler requiring an annual service. I doubt I'd get much internet access. I assumed those who booked a holiday here were looking for an escape.

The cottage itself was well presented, with sash windows set on either side of a brightly painted front door. It was immaculate. I knew instantly my nephews would love it. So would Steph. I visualised many holidays here, summers, birthdays, Christmas, the occasional lazy weekend away from life's stresses. The perfect getaway location.

In contrast, I expected the inside to be crammed with old lady trinkets and hastily gathered items suitable for passing families, not anticipating the vintage interior, the likes of which could rival a glossy magazine. The paintwork was fresh, recent, with books and plants set purposefully along shelves and tabletops, whitewashed floors in every room. The soft furnishings were well cared for, cushions plumped, the place only cleaned yesterday, a log-burning stove ready for long winter evenings, logs piled high in one corner. The plants looked healthy. I touched one. Artificial, thankfully. No television. Good.

Jack headed upstairs, traipsing through every room, his enthusiasm matched only by what this place might promise. The kitchen was spotless, two bottles of wine on the table as a welcome. One white, one red. I wondered if this was the treatment all guests received or if Great Aunt May had arranged this for *me*. I assumed it was the former. I grappled with the keys until I found one that unlocked the back door, opening the kitchen to a flood of bright sunlight across the flagstone floor, the view outside just as breathtaking from this angle. I felt as if I could stay here forever, my Eastcliff flat somewhat boring and rundown in comparison. I would probably continue to rent it out. It seemed the easiest option. I was still waiting for the catch, for someone to wake me up and laugh, two properties in my possession because of generous family. I only owned my flat outright because of the money my brother left me in his will, this cottage now joining the list.

Although I'd brought Jack here to cheer him up, he was finding it easy to avoid me, locating anything to distract his attention. I was in the garden hypnotically watching waves lap against the shore when he finally joined me, his feet bare, his cheeks flushed with vigour I sorely missed.

'You okay?' I handed him a mug of coffee. I'd forgotten to bring a straw. I hope it didn't matter.

He nodded, taking in a lungful of clean air. I almost didn't notice his scars, his pain, or the fact he was about to die. I smiled, knowing his mum would thank me for something I'd done right today.

'Glad you came?'

Another nod. He turned to look at me, the undamaged side of his face pulled into what would have been a beautiful smile under normal circumstances. It made my heart lunge for the life he would never now have. I blinked, turning my attention to the outside table laden with the snacks I'd brought, a buttered French baguette now joining the feast, also courtesy of my late aunt's holiday package, two cups of coffee, mine already empty. I'd put the wine in the fridge. Someone else would appreciate alcohol far more than me, Jack in no position to be drinking.

In my haste, I'd forgotten Jack couldn't open his damaged mouth wide enough to eat solid food, having been on liquids for a while. I was subsequently forced to eat most of the food myself, in uncomfortable, embarrassed silence. Jack pretended to be happy with a milkshake or two, plastic straws luckily supplied by the manufacturer. Although he said nothing, this was the most he had communicated in weeks, psychically relaxing, content to be away from Eastcliff and a life almost over. Sitting here, overlooking a wild rolling ocean and steadily setting sun, I hoped the kid was okay. It didn't matter how short-lived this moment would be or the reality facing his future. We didn't need to explain ourselves or express our thoughts. We would come here again. Before it was too late. This didn't have to be a one-off. Jack's life didn't have to end any other way than how it should, surrounded by those who loved him. I just needed to check the bookings first.

I turned his way, a thought popping into my head. 'Maybe this could become our new *Happy Place*, hey Jack?'

Jack looked at me, a twinkle in his eyes confirming I'd made his day.

Twenty-Four

Jack

I was unsure what today would bring aside from a one-sided conversation and sea air I didn't feel like enduring, ambling around some stupid old house no one had cared about in years. But oddly, once I was there, I felt different. I wasn't expecting the place to be set in such a stunning location, an incredible sea view by all accounts, dense woodland a mere stone's throw from the door. You could lose yourself, forget the world exists. I oddly now *love* Fisherman Jacks almost as much as I love Newton. I hope he doesn't sell the place. I'd ideally like him to think of me whenever he goes there, the name of the cottage perfectly apt for such an occasion. In fact, I've spent the last hour wondering who Jack was. A fisherman, obviously.

I didn't expect to feel so downtrodden when we were forced to leave, the drive home exceptionally long, listening to Newton's chatter in feigned agony, his plans for the cottage, his hopes, his dreams. *None* of them include me. He even misjudged the moment entirely when he spoke about planning a Christmas there, glancing my way enthusiastically before falling silent. We both know I won't be here by then. I hope he doesn't forget me when I'm gone.

I'm forced to watch in stunted silence as Newton leaves my house, his head down, his sleeves rolled up, his luscious hair glued to his forehead in places because of the heat and the stress I have unintentionally triggered. I can't help but feel lost, saddened by his lowered mood, knowing I'm the reason so much has been left unsaid between us. He did a genuinely lovely thing today, taking me briefly from my problems, showing me his cottage, a potential new life in the making. I *could* show a little gratitude. I tap my bedroom window, hoping he will understand my emotions, despite my behaviour and my perpetual absence. I'm irritated with the world as a whole, that's all, frustrated by things he doesn't yet know, everything slowly destroying me.

Newton glances up and I wave. He waves back. He doesn't smile. I wonder what he's thinking. I hope he doesn't hate me. Yet again, no one can hate me as much as I hate myself. I pull away from the window and slump onto my bed, tears I don't wish him to see spilling over my flustered cheeks. I can't have him see my weakness, can never show him my faults. The seagulls outside remind me of today, intensifying a recollection of waves crashing against the rocky coastline—a tiny but picturesque beach enough to placate me for the rest of my life if I were to live long enough. I couldn't help but peel off my trainers and socks, rolling my jeans to my knees, searching rock pools for shells and pebbles to bring home, keeping the memory of this day safe while I can. It was nice to know Newton was close by, should I need him, yet far enough to afford the space I wanted. I could have sat outside all evening, thinking nothing of Eastcliff or the very thing that has become my life. I desperately want to circumnavigate the humans I have been forced to endure, avoiding conflict where I can, Fisherman Jacks a fragment of a much bigger future I will never now know.

I found an outbuilding some distance away but I didn't tell Newton because I'd forgotten to bring my notebook and had nothing to scribble on. I assume he will discover it for himself at some point, has probably already seen it on the property details. It looks like an old boathouse. Judging by the name of the cottage, it probably is. He allowed me to explore, like a child, searching cracks and crevices, cupboards and hiding places, lying on his bed for a moment because of exhaustion. I was shocked by how well-cared for it is. Vintage elegance at its best, no trace of any fishermen now, barely a trace of the old lady who owned it. I can see us living there, my professor and I, no one to judge, to mock, to tell us we can't be together. I sigh. In another life, maybe. He called it our new *Happy Place*. If only things were so simple.

I consider sending him a message, apologising for my low mood and inviting him out for a coffee. It would be my way of saying thanks, nothing else capable of undoing my mistakes. Instead, I listen as his car drives away, wanting to race into the road, chase him down, lie in front of his tyres until he sees my truth. Unfortunately, I don't want to face anyone, not even my mother when she comes to say goodnight. Eventually, everyone goes to bed, allowing the house to fall silent after several attempts to rouse me from my darkened room go unreturned, my only response being the note I thread beneath my closed door when she threatens to kick it in.

I'm okay, I confirm. *I just need to be left alone.* For now.

I lie on my bed listening to my sister talking softly on her phone in the next room, wishing I could do something *normal* like that, wishing things were different. She should be asleep and is eventually told off, the house falling into a deepening silence that disturbs my uncomfortable discord. I wait until the only sound is a gentle snoring from behind a closed door before I pop open my own, creeping downstairs, my breath held, my feet bare. It has just turned midnight, too late for attention, yet too early for sleep. Star greets me in the kitchen, her wagging tail confirming her unwavering affection as I pull on my trainers and my hooded top, unclicking the back door, heading into the night. Under normal circumstances, I would take her with me, but tonight I have other plans.

The sky is brightly lit, stars shining overhead, a large moon guiding me with ease. I don't need to think where I'm heading, already on autopilot, venturing along the canal dressed in black, perfectly hidden in the darkness despite the pure white bandages covering my damaged features. I have followed this path many times in the dark, a habit I've formed of late, my crutches creating noise I can't help. I head past an unused allotment, the space overgrown, full of weeds. It's still warm but I shiver anyway, thinking of Newton, no doubt in his lounge drinking coffee, marking essays that should include mine. I doubt he's asleep. He never sleeps. I enjoy the walk, the peace, the silence, my trainers padding softly over the dewy ground, my struggling breath keeping me company in the din. The darkness used to frighten me as a kid, but there is nothing here now more worrisome than *me*, no demon other than the one inside my head. I have become the very thing people are afraid of, the one thing they turn from whenever I approach.

It takes around twenty minutes to walk to Newton's home, his basement flat along Clarington Avenue a place I secretly know well. The property forms part of what would have once been a grand row of Victorian houses, the highlight of our little town back then, so they say. I pause, wondering what I would do if he moved to his cottage permanently. I would miss him. Yet again, I will be dead soon anyway, no need for me to walk this way again.

A comforting light is shining through his front windows as I approach, the space visible enough behind curtains he has drawn in haste. I creep silently down his steps, narrowly missing a passing cat, watching with bated breath through glass that needs a clean. I gasp at the sight of him stretched across his armchair, his legs on a footstool, a coffee in one hand, a book in the other. He's talking aloud, yet to *whom* I don't know. Knowing Newton, probably himself.

For the last few weeks, I have been watching Newton closely, mostly at night when everyone is in bed, when prying eyes are closed and no one can see my misgivings. No one knows. I don't ever intend to tell. I quietly observe him through the crack in his curtains, absorbing his routine, his quirks, his body. Few people know he listens to classical music, when alone, reading a book, always non-fiction literature about killers and the psychotic mind, the man I *adore* forever drinking coffee. I wonder if I will one day become one of his subjects, someone to dissect from the confinements of a draft-filled lecture room.

I'm deluding no one but myself, I know, but I have seemingly *never* been popular. Maybe if I were, my friends would have noticed. As it is, none of them came to see me after the accident, no one left in my life now to care what happened to the friend they once believed they knew. Months of silence tells me everything I need to know. People are your friends *only* when it serves them. Watching Newton this evening, I realise he is the only one left who cares.

Twenty-Five

Jack

What I like the most about Newton is the comfortable clothing he wears after his shower, the type reserved for privacy and *special* people. Very few people know this, his attire usually far more formal. I watch silently as he enters his bedroom, a towel around his shoulders and jogging bottoms hooked over his hips, no socks, no shirt. It's a shame his bathroom window is frosted and therefore unwilling to allow a glimpse of his naked form, his body shielded from view. He rubs his hair vigorously, leaving it to dry naturally. I rarely see him use a comb, preferring to run his fingers through the ends to smooth them, as if that's enough. He doesn't go to the gym, yet in my opinion, he's not in bad shape. Not for a man of his age.

I almost hold my breath. I can't help it. I like seeing him dressed now the way he is—handsome, someone I admire, harbouring thoughts I can barely admit. There are exactly eighteen years between us, our shared birthday *almost* a shared destiny. The twelfth of July is the best day of the year. I don't care Newton is almost twice my age, or the scandal we would create if we began a relationship. I love to challenge the status quo. So does Newton. Besides, I'm not a *child*, no longer a teenager. It's a shame I haven't told him how I feel, a shame I will never express in words the thoughts I've kept in my head. Only in my perpetual silence have I dared dream of a future with this man, dared imagine the impossible. It would be a short-lived future now, I know, but the possibility still lingers.

'Jack?'

I turn sharply to see Newton standing by his open front door, his dishevelled hair and flushed cheeks more alluring in the light cast behind him than I can tolerate. I didn't notice him, too busy imagining the impossible to realise he was watching.

I offer a wave I know must look pathetic, stepping into the light of his hallway because there is nowhere left to go. I *hate* the way I look, how people look when they look at me. Yet, Newton looks at me now as he always has, the same kind eyes, beautiful teeth, charming smile.

'What on earth are you doing out here by yourself?' he asks. 'It's late. Does your mum know where you are?'

I dislike his tone, the way he is openly chastising me as if I'm a child who needs discipline, a boy who needs his mother. I swear, if he folds his arms defensively across his chest the way *she* does, I might punch him in the face. Luckily, he does no such thing, stepping to one side instead, allowing me entry to his private domain. I have never been inside Newton's flat before, the place warm, inviting, a strong whiff of coffee drifting on the evening air along with a heady scent of shampoo. It makes me want to take a deep breath and never exhale.

'I'm calling your mum. She'll be worried.' Newton closes his door and heads towards his mobile phone still perched on the very chair he was earlier relaxing in.

I wave my arms, shaking my head, angry with myself more than anything for sneaking around, undetected, undeterred, uninvited. I merely want to *talk*, that's all, express my emotions, ask his advice.

'She doesn't know you're here, does she?' Newton stands motionless in the middle of his lounge, his mobile in one hand, a towel around his shoulders, concern written all over his face. He looks so handsome, so incredibly beautiful. I love the way the light catches his damp hair.

I shake my head, willing myself to shake these ridiculous thoughts from my mind. Newton is barefoot, dressed now in a t-shirt pulled tight across his chest, the tiniest threads of hair peeking over the top. I want to kiss him, hold him, stroke that hair, twist it around my fingers until I fall asleep. I want him to hold *me*, stroke my cheek and other places already aroused by his presence. I turn sharply, fearing he might notice. I take a seat, crossing my legs, trying so hard not to cry I almost bite my tongue in half. Like Alex. I don't want to think about that, don't wish to behave like a child. I'm *not* a child.

Newton notices my troubled emotions and sighs, tossing his phone onto a nearby table with a thud. 'Are you okay, Jack?'

His question is warm, thoughtful, kind. I shake my head. No. Far from it.

He walks over and sits by my side, close yet so far away. I want to wrap my arms around him, his steady breath strong in my ear. Instead, I linger in silence, nothing else for me to do.

'Can I get you a drink? A glass of water, a cup of coffee?'

I shake my head again. I don't wish to put him to any trouble. I shouldn't be here. Embarrassingly, I have been trying to learn sign language, although I'm not very good and only very basic communication symbols are being retained in my damaged head. I blame my tumour, my memories steadily dissolving along with my rotting brain cells. I close my fingers into a trembling fist and rub a circle across my chest, a simple sign for "sorry".

'It's okay,' Newton replies. 'You have *nothing* to be sorry for.' He smiles. I can't bear his kindness any more than he can abide my silence.

I have too much to be sorry for. If only he knew. Newton rubs my shoulders, an innocent gesture, yet it spurs something inside I can't subdue. I burst into tears, my damaged face made all the more ugly because of my reaction, my eyes red, my nose sore. He pulls me into a hug and we sit for a moment, just the two of us, no sound in this room aside from Newton's breath and my berating heart. I'm so very fond of Newton, and he of me, I'm sure. Yet, the fact I am *gay* but have never told him haunts me daily. I want to communicate this truth. I owe it to myself to at least try. This has to be a sign, surely, forgive the expression. If nothing comes of this, I can run into the night, run away, die in some dark space away from them all. It's probably all I deserve.

I reach out and touch his leg. I don't know what I'm expecting. Something *wonderful*, despite everything telling me otherwise. In my thoughts, he reaches back, touches mine, has done so many times. We entwine as one, our naked forms expressing with ease what I can never express with words. I blink, pushing away such impossible ideas, surprised when Newton doesn't turn away. I look steadily into his eyes. They are so beautiful, piercing blue with flecks of green. Or is it the other way around? In this light, I can hardly tell. Dare I allow myself the possibility to dream? He smiles. I want to embrace him, my groin groaning with misplaced anticipation I have nowhere now to place.

'Do you want to talk about it?' His breath is so close to mine it's almost painful.

I nod, licking my lips in anticipation of something I'm not brave enough to initiate.

'Coffee. Then whatever this is we can discuss it. *Then*, I'll drive you home. No arguing.' Newton gets to his feet, forcing my hand to slip from his leg. If he noticed the moment I felt between us, he doesn't say, doesn't change his behaviour towards me. Instead, he heads into the kitchen humming, leaving me to deal with the swelling in my pants, still breathless, still hoping. I get unsteadily to my feet, my head hot now, wishing I had words to express my feelings. I'm a lost puppy, nothing more. Lost, uncertain. *Pathetic*.

'Under normal circumstances, Jack, I'd let you sleep in

my spare room, but I'm sure your mum would prefer me to take you home,' he calls my way with a smile, his hands busy taking mugs and spoons from nearby cupboards and drawers.

I hold my breath, his words hitting me in the chest like a hammer, the idea of *sleeping* just a few feet from him more than I can stand. I watch from the doorway as he places a mug under a coffee machine, loud mechanics grinding beans into hot liquid, frothing milk into a thick foam before he pours it on top. He turns around, smiles again, handing me a tall glass mug, a long thin straw standing to attention inside it.

'Latte. Two sugars. You look as if you need it.' He offers a wink I take as a sign to drink up, say nothing, behave. Newton stares at me longer than I find comfortable. I wish I knew what he was thinking. 'Jack?' he asks eventually, waiting until I'm halfway down my coffee before he speaks again, busy scooping a thick layer of frothy milk into my mouth with my finger. I glance his way, the man casually leaning against his sink, his arms folded, his brow furrowed. He looks hot, in more ways than one. 'What are you *doing* here?'

It's a simple question. A question I have so many answers to. I'm here to apologise, to express my gratitude for being there for me when most people are not, to show my beloved fondness, to tell him I *love* him. I hang my head and stare at my mug, watching a layer of creamy milk slide down the side. I press a closed fist against my chest and rub it in a circle.

I'm sorry. So very, *very* sorry.

'Sorry for what? For coming here tonight, refusing to engage with me at the cottage, or for getting angry about young Ben?' Newton has a kindly tone. It is hardly appropriate. He grins. It makes me want to kiss him.

I hold three fingers towards him. All of the above. I'm sorry for everything. Sorry for loving him. *Sorry for breathing.*

Newton sighs a little too deeply. I try not to take it personally. 'You have *nothing* to be sorry for, Jack.' His words are heartfelt, genuine. I hate them. 'What you have been through over the last few months is nothing short of miraculous. Seriously. You've coped far better than most people would. Better than *I* would.'

I glance his way, wondering how much of his statement is true and how much is designed to make me feel better. It doesn't matter. It's still nice to hear. I drink my remaining coffee and place the empty mug on the countertop, nodding my gratitude for the simple pleasure.

'You're welcome,' Newton replies, offering a sign of his own, touching his fingertips gently against his chin before arching his open palm towards me. 'And you're *always* welcome here, any time. I hope you know that. Or we can drive out to the cottage again. I really enjoyed today.'

I feel a tingling in my nose, my sinuses filling with emotion I'm not yet ready to share. I don't want to burst into tears again, but I can't help how I feel. Newton sees my distress and comes over to embrace me, holding me against him as if I'm a fragile doll in need of restoration. He strokes my head, my hood pulled back, unconcerned by patchy hair already falling out in clumps, allowing me to breathe in his scent, his larynx pressed against my cheek. I like that he's taller than me, able to protect me, *save* me.

'Come on. I'll drive you home. You look exhausted.'

Before I have time to prepare myself for the distance or tell him what I came here to say, our embrace is over, our private moment gone. He slides his feet into a pair of worn shoes and grabs his phone and keys, stepping into the night, waiting with a wide smile for me to follow. With nothing more to do, I head outside, a deep chill biting into my bones. It isn't cold. Newton drives me home, chatting about anything and everything, suggesting he and I attend sign language classes together, that he could use a refresher course. I sit in the darkness pretending to look out of the window while stealing glances his way whenever he looks distracted.

I *love* Newton Flanigan. I just wish I knew how to tell him.

Twenty-Six

Newton

I drove Jack home, calling his frantic mother on the way while the poor kid held my phone in the air because I didn't want it sliding around the dashboard. I struggled to calm her down, her continued apologies unrequired under the circumstances. It wasn't her fault, wasn't Jack's. I could understand her anger though, her frustration borne from her son's poor health and inadequate decision-making. Yet, I was subsequently left to ponder far more than I should, contemplating the boy's state of mind more than was healthy for my own. He couldn't communicate, but I was keen to get around such an unfortunate fact with my unwavering enthusiasm. This evening, however, something felt different. I couldn't tell what. We sat in feigned silence once again, the second time today this had happened. It was something we *never* did, always keen to fill the space with chatter, despite Jack's silence, closing the gap I could now feel growing between us.

As it was, he climbed into the darkness with not so much as a glance backwards, walking towards his front door with his head bent low, his chastising mother waiting with arms folded across her chest. He didn't look my way, instead disappeared so delicately inside he could have been a cat. Rachel nodded, smiled, then closed the door with a click.

I got home and made myself a coffee, checking the time, wondering if I should text Jack to ensure he was okay. However, it was gone two o'clock now and I was certain he would be in bed. I should have gone to bed myself but couldn't sleep, too much on my mind for such a luxury. There was something different about Jack tonight, something sad, forlorn, almost isolated. I couldn't tell why. As a psychologist, I was furious I wasn't able to help him, lift his mood, talk about the issues troubling him. I understood his emotions. I wasn't an idiot. But this was more than his cancer, more than his injuries. I hoped today hadn't been too much.

I considered calling Steph but thought better of that, too. She wouldn't appreciate my intrusion at this hour, wouldn't like being woken up to appease my mood. Instead, I read for a while before drifting off, waking some time later to the sound of my buzzing phone, daylight creeping through the open bedroom window. My sister-in-law always started her day with a text message, this morning no different. It was never anything extravagant, usually a single emoji denoting her mood, her day ahead, her thoughts on nothing in particular. This morning's emoji was an upside-down smiling face. It made me laugh, matched my mood. I sat upright, a stiff neck and a damp pillow to contend with, my duvet barely ruffled. I couldn't remember the last time I'd slipped into such a deep sleep. Must have been the sea air.

I picked up my mobile and dialled her number.

'Jeez, you're up early.' Steph sounded busy, as always, sorting the boys, making sure they ate a decent breakfast.

I glanced down, shocked I was still dressed in jogging bottoms and last night's hastily acquired t-shirt. I never left the house in anything other than smart trousers, a shirt, and a tank top to complete the professional professor image I was unintentionally going for. Most people made jokes at my expense, but I didn't care. Tank tops were comfortable, practical. They didn't have to be fashionable. I didn't tell her I'd driven across town to Jack's house dressed like *this*. Aside from Jack, no one could see me in the dark.

'How did you get on at the cottage?' Steph made it sound as if I was considering buying the place rather than somewhere I'd been gifted without warning.

I smiled, recalling yesterday's escape, hoping it wasn't a dream, feeling bad I'd forgotten to send her the video I'd promised. Jack jumped into my thoughts again.

'You'd love it. The boys would love it.'

'So, what's the plan?'

I knew what she meant. Am I selling or keeping?

'I haven't decided yet. There's no rush I guess.' I wasn't sure how I could afford to run two properties. I now had two lots of council tax, two sets of bills, maintenance I wasn't convinced I was up to. Owning two properties was a big responsibility. I was glad it still had a few holiday bookings, enough to cover any upcoming bills. Right now, I had more important things on my mind.

'Do I look gay?' My question came from nowhere, seemingly taking my sister-in-law by surprise, the scoff she aimed my way loud and unexpected as she practically choked on my words. I was staring at my reflection in the hallway mirror, unsure what *exactly* I was looking at. My hair was ruffled. I smoothed it flat.

'What are you *talking* about?' I could tell she was trying not to snigger at my passing comment. It wasn't funny.

'It's a serious question.' I ventured into the lounge and stretched my arms behind my head, peering through the window towards the street above, wondering, not for the first time, what others thought of me.

Steph was openly laughing, unable to speak through her unrequired amusement.

'It's not funny. Why do people always assume I'm gay?'

Another laugh, followed by a cough, done with meaning, no doubt to gather lost composure. 'Who assumes you're gay?' I couldn't see her but I could visualise her features, her grin, tears of amusement no doubt streaming down her cheeks.

I thought about Jack. *He did.* Obviously. I'd tried not to notice how he touched my leg, how he'd leant expectantly towards me, his breathing far heavier than it should have been. I saw the glint in his eyes, the bulge in his trousers, the words he wouldn't have said even if he *could* speak. The only reason I hadn't rejected the poor boy on the spot was because he would have taken it badly, assuming my shocked reaction was due to his looks. It wasn't true. I just wasn't gay.

'I always seem to attract the attention of men.' I did. It wasn't the first time I'd been the subject of unwanted male affection. Probably wouldn't be the last. Maybe it was *me*. Maybe I had that effect on people.

Stephanie was beside herself now, laughing so hard I'm sure she dropped her phone on the floor, a few moments passing before she answered.

'Newt, you're so funny.'

'Stop it. Seriously, Steph, do I *look* gay?' I was standing in the middle of my lounge, pacing up and down, unsure what else to do. I needed a shave, a haircut, a coffee.

Steph didn't immediately respond, too busy trying to catch her breath and cease her incessant giggling before she offended me. 'It's not how you *look*, Newt, it's how you behave.'

I narrowed my eyes. 'How do I behave?'

'You get too close. You allow yourself to be taken in by some very vulnerable people.' She had stopped laughing. Finally.

I was stunned. Stephanie was right, I did, although I hadn't looked at it that way, hadn't considered the possibility. I had to sit down, my legs suddenly like jelly. Not only did I get too close, but I got inside the minds of people I should have kept at arms-length. Not that I wanted to keep Jack at a distance, but he *was* vulnerable. He was still young, had only just turned twenty, missing his birthday because of a coma none of us saw coming, a tumour no one knew about, an unfortunate stroke making everything worse. He was barely out of his teens, still just a kid. No wonder he presumed my attention meant something more.

Until last night, I was unaware of Jack's sexuality, didn't deem it important. It wasn't something I spent much time thinking about. It was none of my business, our time best spent talking about other things, the human mind, the universe, the simple ways in which we might make this world a better place, if we could. However, I could see now how I'd unwittingly taken things too far, led him along a difficult path, led him on. *Shit.*

'Newt? You still there?'

I'd almost forgotten Steph was on the other end of my phone, her throwaway words biting into my brain like a shark. I took a breath. 'Yeah. Still here.' Still behaving like an *idiot.*

'I hope you don't mind my bluntness.' A spring in the background sounded as if she'd sat down now too, probably in her lounge, away from the boys. 'You have a good heart. It's just... not everyone is like you, Newt. Not everyone has your innocence.'

Innocence? Steph made it sound as if I was a child, a sexless being, a eunuch, someone with no desire to be loved in *that* way. I was none of those things. I was just busy. My relationships with women were often complex, the needs of my short-lived girlfriends often factoring lower than my own, my ex-wife included, my thoughts anywhere but with them. It was hardly my fault I was too preoccupied to notice. I thought about Alice Baker, about how much I liked *her*, never daring to tell anyone other than Paul for fear of open rejection.

'So, you definitely don't think I *look* gay?' I just needed the confirmation. I had no problem with homosexuality, of course. We are all different, each and every one of us trying our very best. I just needed the confirmation I hadn't somehow flagged myself as something I wasn't.

'No, I do not. Besides, no respectful gay man would look twice at you.' Steph was still chuckling, her sarcasm unappreciated.

My eyes automatically widened, my brow furrowing into a defensive response I wasn't expecting. She had a point about that, but I could pass as *fanciable*. I think. I could use a haircut, new clothes, cleaner shoes. I wasn't bad looking, though.

'Why? What's *wrong* with me?' I queried. I couldn't help myself. The idea that men might not find me attractive suddenly didn't sit well.

Steph didn't answer my question. She didn't need to. 'Stop worrying about unimportant things. Go and have a good day, and Newton?'

'Yeah?'

'For the love of God, *relax*.'

Twenty-Seven

Jack

The morning seems normal, at first glance, the outside world waking up to its own reality. Lizzy is in the bathroom singing, Star in the garden barking at a bird. Yet, mine is anything but. I'm still reeling from last night, from the last thing Newton said to me, so much I wanted to say to *him* left dangling mid-air. I can still feel the warmth of his body, if I close my eyes, his lingering breath, the way he looked at me. I still want to imagine the impossible.

Everyone knows I'm not in a good place, last night's actions leading only to a drive home in profound silence. I always assumed I would find my place in this world, eventually. It's a shame this will never now happen, the accident silencing me in more ways than expected. I can never truthfully express who I am, no words left to convey how I feel beyond sign language basics and scraps of paper thrust aimlessly towards those I love.

Hi, Mum. I'm gay. Sorry I didn't tell you before I lost my ability to speak. I also killed a man. I'm sorry about that, too.

Maybe she will place such a declaration in a cupboard for safekeeping, recalling the moment her son came out of his own, removing my confession with scissors currently in Newton's unwitting possession.

I climb out of bed and pick up a money box that has sat on my dresser for as long as I can remember, throwing it in temper across the room. It hits the wall and smashes, allowing coins that have not seen the light of day for years to scatter over the carpet. It doesn't make me feel better. I feel chastised, openly rejected by Newton, subjected to hatred by people I don't know. I was going to tell him my thoughts, my feelings, explain about the boy on the bus and the man in his bath. Now, the only thing I feel is shame.

'*Jack?!*' My mother races up the stairs and bangs on my door. 'Are you all right? I heard a noise.'

I don't wish to acknowledge anyone, least of all my mother, irritated my frustration has drawn her unwanted attention. I unlock my door, unconcerned by the look she gives me as she races inside. She has not replaced the mirror I broke. I no longer want to see my face.

'I heard a smash. What happened?' She is glancing around, her desperate gaze attempting to locate some problem she now assumes exists, her eyes falling to pieces of broken ceramic on the floor, stepping on coins that, like me, lost their shine some time ago. She looks at me with sympathies I don't need, unwilling to relinquish the pained look she now lives with. 'Are you all right?' she asks again, knowing I am anything but.

I nod, rubbing my closed fist in a circle across my chest. I spend every waking moment apologising for something, saying sorry for things I can't change. Yet, the only problem in this room is *me*.

'It's okay.' My mother's tone has softened, despite the shocked expression lingering. She assumes it was an accident. 'I'll clear it up.'

I shake my head. No. It doesn't matter. Nothing matters. Nothing will *ever* matter again. I wave my arms, ushering her out of my room, several ineffective protests leaving her worried mouth and mine, my cheeks ashen, teeth clenched. I slam the door and lock it. It matters little I will never be the fun-loving, cheeky young man everyone remembers, what I am *now* unimportant. Even my sister has been told to stay away, speaking only from doorways because she is unsure what else to do, watching her brother from afar before being ushered elsewhere. It's not her fault. She is only following instructions, listening to what everyone else believes is right.

Since the accident, I have rarely been exposed to the people we live amongst, this last week the most I've experienced of their unfettered judgement. It's not a subject we discuss. Instead, we live as if it's just the four of us— myself, my mother, Lizzy, Star, the wildlife thriving in the large garden behind our home. I have been checking my newsfeed for updates regarding the man I left in his bath, unable to get the image out of my mind, unable to talk to Newton, even though he *saw* the body, knows full well what happened. I have already convinced myself it was an accident. After all, I didn't intend to kill him, did not want to hurt either of them.

A tiny knock against my closed door jolts me from my deliberations.

'Jack?'

Lizzy.

I glance up, knowing how long it has been since we held a conversation, held each other, had a laugh. I clamber to my feet, concluding swiftly that nothing would be worse than my sister hating me because of what I have become, the idea of being cast into exile by my family more than my frazzled brain can consider. The irony is not lost on me that humans rarely stop to absorb their surroundings, mostly too self-absorbed to appreciate anything beyond the assiduous activities of their day. If Alex Jefferson had not stared at me he might still be alive. If Ben Harris had walked the other way, he wouldn't have spent a night in the hospital.

I open my door to the sight of my little sister hovering uncertain, her face a telling reminder that none of this is acceptable. She smiles, her eyes glistening with tears she is attempting to prevent. 'You okay?'

It's the first time in months she has spoken directly to me, the first time I have acknowledged her attention. I nod, holding back tears of my own, wishing things were different.

'Mum is trying her best, you know,' Lizzy whispers, ensuring our mother can't hear.

I nod. I know. I don't know what else to convey. We look at each other for a moment, my sister's eyes resting briefly on my damaged features before she looks away, her own pain too vivid. I looked after her when our father left, took her under my wing, our mother left to deal with the fallout of raising two kids alone. I haven't been able to speak to my sister in months. It's not something I want to dwell on. I will be gone soon enough, poor Lizzy left behind to pick up the pieces of not just *her* life but our mother's, too.

She smiles again, her eyes meeting mine briefly before she rushes forward and throws her arms around me. We hold onto each other, our tears falling for a future we will never now share, for a childhood we can never relive.

'I'll never forget you, Jack,' she tells me before pulling away, racing into her bedroom and closing the door with a slam, no time for me to react.

I take a deep breath. I will never forget *her* either. She's my little sister. *I love her.*

I race downstairs and head outside, irritated by the limited time I have left, no consideration for a world I know little about, time no longer on the side of the freedom I deserve. I want to speak with Newton, but what would I say? Nothing he would not openly reject, I know. My mother is hanging laundry, a warm breeze lifting the sheets along with her mood when she notices my approach. She smiles, grateful when I nod in return, holding my arms out for a hug. She smells of seaweed and cucumber shampoo.

'How are you doing?'

I nod. There is nothing else to say. As it is, the morning has lowered my mood. I need an escape, to be somewhere that does not involve continued mollycoddling, private tears and overbearing attention, to find my *happy place* again. My mother wouldn't understand. She assumes my place is here, with her. But I'm not a child, not sure how many more weeks I have left to give. I need space, somewhere to think. Newton's cottage is too far, but there is one other place I can go. My Aunt Ruth is currently in London, her job as a government official often taking her away for weeks. It's probably just as well. My mother won't like the idea, but an empty house is exactly what I need right now, somewhere to be other than here.

***

'No.' She is already shaking her head before I have even finished scribbling my sentence on the notebook she insists I carry in my back pocket.

Why?

'Because your aunt is not there to keep an eye on you and I would never forgive myself if anything happened.'

I'm not a kid

'But you *are* my responsibility, Jack. I can't agree to this.'

Just for a couple of nights. I need space

'No.'

One night then?

'Why?'

Because…

I take a deep breath, careful about my next sentence, trying to ignore the expression on my mother's face. I should be grateful she cares.

…I'll be okay

There is nothing more to add, no other words to plead my case. My mother looks at me, a damp pillowcase in one hand, a peg in the other, tears forever in her eyes.

'All right. *One night*. I'll call Ruth and let her know the plan. But I'm dropping you off and picking you up first thing in the morning. Clear?'

I nod, grateful, relieved that, if nothing else, I can at least clean up any mess I might have overlooked when I attacked Ben, unable to correct the carnage I caused in Alex's home. I can still see the look on his wife's face as she raced into the street, can still see Newton's smile as he greeted me in the darkness last night.

***

I don't allow my mother to step through my aunt's front door when she drops me off, leaving her instead to hover in the street, an overnight bag in her outstretched hands and a frown on her worried face. I give her a hug, look deep into her eyes, and then I'm gone, bolting the door against her protests. The bag contains food she assumes I'll need, bottles of water, homemade soup, fruit smoothies. Anything I will not have to chew. I love my mother but I don't need her overbearing affection, not today, her son no longer the boy she once knew. Newton and I used to laugh about our happy place, an empty lecture room once everyone had left, *his* happy place being the coffee he drinks to excess, his family in London, his job. My happy place is here, inside *this* house, deep below a building where even my aunt does not venture. I close my eyes, thinking of his cottage.

It takes longer than anticipated to clean my aunt's hallway floor, blood dried to a dirty brown hue still lingering in places if you look hard enough. I scrub splatter marks from the walls, repositioning a rug to cover a stubborn stain. It will have to do, I guess, nothing to be done about the damage caused other than conclude my day in peace. I head into the kitchen and pull open a creaking door leading to my aunt's basement. As far as basements go, this one is not so bad, not your typical creepy domain. Aside from the odd spider looming in shadowy corners, there are no damp spaces, nothing sinister clinging to the walls in the dark. Well, nothing I haven't put here, anyway. No. Aunt Ruth has ensured this space is perfectly adequate for her nephew to use as I wish, free to come and go as I please. The walls are painted a muted white to allow in as much light as possible, a tiny window in the far wall enough to protect this space from the perpetual dark. Decorated how I like it, a lush carpet covers the stone floor, bookshelves along one wall, a sofa bed housing mismatched cushions because my aunt throws nothing away.

It looks like a bedroom, only larger, taking up the entire ground footprint of the property. In one corner sits my 'studio', a place for me to craft, to create, to learn, a large table flanking the centre, storage for every eventuality. I come here whenever I need an escape from the world, when my mother's house feels oppressive and small, when nothing and no one can appease my mood. My aunt *never* comes down here. She trusts me, appreciates the privacy she knows I need. I wouldn't like her snooping around anyway. There are secrets here, things I can't share with anyone, Newton included. This domain has become my private space, my escape, the only place in the world right now that feels right.

My *happy place*.

Twenty-Eight

Jack

My mother has messaged me several times since I've been at my aunt's, ensuring the last few hours already feel like an eternity. It's her way of checking on me, unconcerned by how irritating her relentless questions are.

Have you been able to warm your soup?
Have you taken you medication?
Do you need anything else?

No, to each of those questions, although I don't confirm my infuriation, do not wish to invite the stress. The only thing I need is silence, time to think, freedom to imagine something beyond the realms of a life I wish wasn't mine. Only when my aunt sends a message confirming she has left ice cream in the freezer do I feel a little better.

Newton lives just three streets from Tolbert Street, his home easily accessible from a canal path I've now become painfully familiar. It's not the *only* reason I have insisted on being here tonight, but it scratches an annoying itch, this place far closer to my professor than I would otherwise be. As far as my mother is concerned, I'm planning a quiet evening alone, to be in bed by ten, this night meant for space I can't find in my own home. She assumes I need time away from routine and familiarity, unaware I have other plans, the darkness becoming my unwitting protector.

I lose track of how long I sit amid the weeds and moss beneath Newton's lounge window, spots of warm rain tickling my frozen cheeks—my professor unaware of my presence, my thoughts, my desires. I don't wish to draw attention. I do, however, want to bang frustrated fists against his front door, throw my arms around him, express my desires in actions undeserving of words. Instead, I absorb his life and his quiet routine from a distance, only heading to my aunt's home and her cold bed once Newton is soundly in his. I envy the time others share with him and the private conversations we no longer have. His evenings are mostly spent alone. These are the times I allow myself to dream, to think the impossible, to imagine a life beyond my own.

Sleep does not come easily and I wake fretfully in the early hours, forgetting where I am, only locating composure when a cockerel's call jolts me into painful reality. My mother has left more messages, hell-bent on treating me like a child, one of her possessions. It matters little how often I have sent Newton messages during the night myself, waiting with bated breath for his replies. I ignore the irony. Sometimes he forced me to wait a few seconds, sometimes several minutes. When he made me wait an entire hour, I almost threw up. My mood was only softened with each response, his perpetually bright tone making my adoration grow just that little bit stronger. I climb out of bed, barely managing to swallow a few sips of lukewarm water from a glass next to my aunt's bed, my pills catching the back of my throat in protest. My recently stitched face is still sore, the bruising turning a sludgy green, my feet aching from last night's endeavour, my clothing still damp where I sat outside in the rain.

After the accident, I was advised to keep a diary. Those pages have become far more important now than expected. I plan to leave it for Newton as a gift on his doorstep. Nothing major, just a little something from me to him, something to express my fondness and how much I miss his bright conversation and intoxicating company. My unforgiving story is written with love, spiral bound and personalised by yours truly. It contains just fifty-seven pages, nothing epic, but expresses in words what I can never say aloud. Newton will read it and will understand. He will come to me then, I'm sure. He will want *me* as I want him. I have been careful not to disclose everything, needing to keep some secrets to myself, for now. It reads like a love story. Newton will know it's about us, *our* story. I'm certain he will appreciate what I'm trying to say that words no longer afford me. After all, Newton Flanigan is a renowned psychologist. He understands more than most.

I watch his front door from behind a neighbouring bush,

waiting until he leaves for work, hovering in forced silence as he picks my diary from his step. I'm glad it's no longer raining. I wouldn't want my hard work to be ruined. I have wrapped it in a plastic bag along with a simple note reading, "For all the wrongs I want to right". I've not signed it. There is no need. Newton will know it's from me.

He glances around, no doubt trying to locate me in the morning haze. It makes me smile, inwardly. He knows me better than I know myself. I anticipate him reading it after his shower, when he's alone, when no other thoughts will distract him from me. I'm almost disappointed when he heads inside, emerging a few seconds later without my gift, climbing into his car without a single glance back. How long will I be forced to wait until I learn of his thoughts? How will I gauge his reaction if I can't see his face?

I wait for what feels like forever before I take a chance and cross the street, heading down his front steps, my bated breath held firmly, my probing hands outstretched. For some reason, I can't recall him locking his flat door. I need to investigate. I owe him that much. I'm his *friend*. I expect it to be locked, surprised when the handle turns easily, the door opening without incident onto his silent hallway. Newton can be terribly forgetful at times. We have this unfortunate fact in common. Luckily, he lives in a relatively good neighbourhood, but he should be more careful, opportunists everywhere. It matters little I have now taken the very same opportunity, no one appreciating my good intentions, if they caught me, my presence merely to rectify the error made in haste.

I hover with uncertainty before stepping inside, closing

the door behind me, hoping I've not been seen, hoping he will not return and find me like *this*. My diary is on a shelf next to his unopened mail, several pairs of shoes piled in a corner, his favourite jacket hanging from a nearby hook. I consider having a tidy round, but I'm sure he'll notice. Instead, I head to his bedroom. It's the one place I'm drawn to, the only room I *want* to be. It smells of shampoo, hand cream, and Old Spice aftershave, this space surprisingly neat compared to the rest of the flat. I suspect he comes here only to sleep, many of his belongings discarded in other areas of his home.

I sit on his bed and run my hands over his sheets, imagining him here, by my side. I can't help it when I lie down, burying my head in his pillow, absorbing his smell, his presence. I don't intend to stay long. Yet, when he sends me a message an hour later, I'm still inside his home, nowhere else to be, my vibrating mobile phone threatening to expose my position, my emotions, my needs. I yank it from my pocket, grunting with annoyance at my own pathetic failings. I don't recall falling asleep.

Thinking about you, Jack. Hope you're well.

Newton's message brings a lump to my throat. I step into his sun-filled hallway, unconcerned someone outside might see me, half expecting him to be standing there, waiting. It feels as if he can see into my heart, as if he already knows where I am.

I message back immediately.

Likewise. You okay?

I need to appear casual, unconcerned either way. I don't want to frighten him or tip him off to my position, yet I find myself waiting for his reply with bated breath, my mouth trembling with anticipation.

Busy, to be honest. Have a lot going on at the moment. We'll catch up soon, promise.

I take a breath, my heart sinking.

No worries.

It's a lie, of course. I *do* worry. Immensely.

There are no further messages and I wait for over thirty minutes before I realise he has moved on to something else. I imagine his laughter, the conversations he will be sharing with other people, the coffee he will be drinking to excess. It makes me feel sick. How can he behave so casually when I'm all alone and frightened?

I want to call him, to interrupt his day and draw his attention to me. My teeth are clenched, my closed fists ready to punch something, *anything*, hovering between impossible insanity and an escape I will never find. I glance around. What am I doing here? I only wanted to see what he thought of my gift, but he hasn't mentioned it, has not even *looked* at it by the way the bag is mostly untouched.

Frustration is building. I don't want to do anything foolish so I search for a spare key before leaving his flat, ensuring the door is firmly locked before heading along the street, sidestepping two strangers who glare at my exposed features, their shocked looks something I'm growing obscenely tired of. I want to scream, yell, punch something. But I do no such thing. Instead, I glare back, those women unaware how much I want to throttle them where they stand, Newton's flat key now firmly in my possession.

***

I wait in the silence of my aunt's basement for three and a half painful hours, willing my phone to ring, for Newton to notice my absence, the window blind pulled closed for fear of being seen. I ignore my mother's incessant messages, only jolted from my private musings when she comes to the house to collect me, forgetting the spare key *she* keeps to hand. I carefully bolt the basement door from the inside because I don't want her to find me like *this*, allowing her shouts to go unanswered, her footsteps more frantic with each empty room she finds. She is crying, I can tell, calling my father from the kitchen because she wrongly assumes I'm missing.

Eventually, she leaves and the building falls silent, my muted phone already too heavy, too imposing. I send her a message to alleviate her stress, making up a ridiculous story about spending time on the beach before heading home, and I'm finding the fresh air invigorating. I tell her I'm sorry if I've worried her. I don't care if she believes me. I then message Newton, pressing "send" before instantly regretting my decision, immediately wanting to retract my words.

I hope I haven't done anything to upset you.

I stare at my phone, wishing I hadn't sent such a ridiculous message, the scent of his sheets still on my skin. I sound desperate, pathetic, weak. A few aggravating minutes later, Newton responds.

What on earth makes you feel that way? ☺

His message is accompanied by a smiling emoji, his comment casual, upbeat. I'm almost overwhelmed by the attention he doesn't even know he's provided. I can't directly ask what he thought of my gift, can't yet expose my intentions.

Not sure.

I sound like a sulky child.

Is everything okay, Jack?

I stare at my mobile, unsure how to answer, wondering why I began this conversation in the first place.

Jack?

I'm fine.

I'm far from fine. I am, however, *desperate*, weak, keen to tell him everything about *everything*, when I can, oddly convinced he'll understand. My diary initially had an inclusion at the back, confessing to the attack on "bus boy" Ben Harris, and Alex Jefferson, who I've nick-named "bathtub man". However, I tore it out, unwilling to provide anything to potentially see me locked away before I'm ready. My writing is metaphorical, a musing, nothing to conclude my reality. I didn't set out to kill, merely to hinder, to change their views, their reality. I'm keen to speak with Newton about these incidents but don't know where to begin. For now, I guess it will have to wait.

You can message me anytime, Jack. I hope you know that.

Newton's words are heartfelt. I like the way they make me feel, replying before I can chastise my eager fingers.

Can we meet up?

I need to see him.

Sounds great. When were you thinking?

Tomorrow?

I hold my breath. There is a pause, as if he is considering my question, checking his calendar, contemplating his reply.

Tomorrow is out, unfortunately, but I'm free on Friday.

I stare at my phone, my damaged mouth agape, convinced Newton has just agreed to a *date*. I can barely keep my fingers steady as I type back, my heart racing, my lips twitching.

Okay, sure. Your place?

I'm trying to sound casual, although I can already imagine what we will do with our private time, his place a location I'm oddly now familiar. We might even drive out to the cottage, weather permitting, discover one of the bedrooms he has not yet slept in. We can christen the place together, imagine a life other than this.

Meet me at Billy's Bar at twelve-thirty.

My heart sinks and I message back.

No. I don't want to be seen in public.

I can't believe he has wilfully asked me to expose myself, metaphorically speaking. Panic is rising in my belly. I thought he understood. I assumed we would be *alone*.

Jack, you must stop putting yourself down. Your scar is healing and your facial muscles are nowhere near as bad as you think. You're still Jack Monroe. Still beautiful. ☺

Another smiling emoji.

I stare at my mobile, unconvinced what I'm reading, my brain struggling to comply. The only thing I catch from this statement is Newton thinks I'm *beautiful*. For a moment I no longer worry about damaged facial muscles, unhealed scars or being in public, nothing else important when I'm with my man.

Okay. Sounds good.

I close my eyes against my surroundings. *Shit.* This really *is* a date.

Twenty-Nine

Newton

My back was pressed against a wall, metaphorically, morally, and in reality, yet not even the oppressive panelled walls of this silent lecture room were willing to keep me upright. Coffee and laughter were calling from a nearby staffroom, my sanity lingering over a failed hope of justice. To add insult to injury, there was little I could do to help Jack's muddled mindset, Paul's latest murder case on my mind, nothing concrete pointing us to where we needed to be.

I felt as if I was letting Jack down on some level, my abrupt disappearance from his tainted life something I should have dealt better with. It had only been a couple of days since he'd stood in my kitchen, but he was messaging me constantly now, every half hour. I didn't know what to say, my replies kept purposefully light and upbeat. I didn't want him to believe anything was wrong, yet our last encounter had pivoted a shift in our relationship, the changing dynamic not something I was confident we could retain.

I'm sure he'd tried to kiss me, although I can't be certain it wasn't my imagination, my wayward senses, a joke. I assumed we were friends, Jack and I. Mutual allies in a world neither understood. Now I wasn't sure what to think. I didn't want to hurt his feelings, didn't want to offend him. But how could I tell him I wasn't interested in a relationship like *that?* It was pathetic. I was a grown man, a professional, capable of holding conversations with psychopaths and serial killers. Surely, I could tell the boy I wasn't gay.

I didn't know what to make of the gift on my doorstep, my already heightened suspicion aroused that Jack might have been loitering outside again, watching, waiting for me to do something of interest. I couldn't recall how I'd spent last night, probably wouldn't have noticed the footprints below my windows if it hadn't rained so heavily. As it was, a distinct pattern of circles denoted the presence of crutches, several indentations left in the mud. It reminded me of the photograph currently pinned to a whiteboard at the police station, blood-tinged circular stains on Alex Jefferson's hallway rug something I now couldn't get out of my head. Were they crutch marks? I took a photograph, making a mental note to confirm this possibility with Paul, Ben Harris already openly stating *his* attacker walked with crutches.

I glanced around at the empty chairs, my students not due to return here for another two weeks, knowing Jack would never return, a void already created no one would fill. It was ironic. Jack was my most promising student, the one amongst everyone I taught who would have gone on to do great things. Inevitably, I spent my day writing up several assignments on temporal lobe function and how damage to this delicate area affects personality, wanting to share my thoughts on the side effects of this condition. There is often a distinct disturbance with what those afflicted see and hear, selective attention provoking difficulty in identifying and categorising objects. There can be a struggle in learning and retaining new information, as well as impaired factual and long-term memory. I outlined an assignment on perseverative behaviour, too, leaving Jack an unread message that oddly added to my frustration.

He was vulnerable. I needed to deal with this delicately. I thought about calling his mum again but I didn't want to get the boy into more trouble so decided against it, for now. Meeting him in public might be the better option, a way for us to talk openly while in the unassuming privacy of a quiet corner. We could have a drink, attempt to get our relationship back on track. I deliberately suggested we meet at Billy's. It was the perfect place, no chance of finding ourselves alone, yet private enough to talk unhindered. *I* would be the one doing the talking, anyway, and I was deluding no one by giving the kid false hope.

***

It was late afternoon by the time I left the eerily silent university, the police station my next planned stop, the day threatening to slip by without me. I was ready to pass out,

221

still musing over a gift I was only fifty per cent confident was from Jack. I'd briefly flicked through the journal he'd left me, wishing I hadn't, unsure what to make of his words or his *obvious* desire for us to start some kind of relationship. It had played on my mind ever since. Because of this, I was struggling to turn my attention to the Alex Jefferson murder, the case so far returning no viable results, our brief attempts to question Ben Harris remaining unrewarded. He was still claiming he couldn't remember much, unwilling to tell us more about his attacker. It was frustrating.

'Maybe you should arrest him?' I scoffed openly. I wasn't serious, my comment nothing other than a passing thought, a throwaway gesture. But Paul gave me one of his looks anyway. 'Joke,' I muttered flatly, resisting the urge to pull a face, roll my eyes, laugh.

'Newton has a point, Paul.' DI Tony Avery was looking blankly out of the incident room window, his arms folded across his chest, staring at nothing in particular. 'The kid must know *something*.'

I glanced his way, impressed by the unexpected gesture of support, the timing oddly appreciated. Tony and I conversed only in passing, nothing more, nothing to ever cement a potential friendship or convey a mutual understanding. I got the distinct impression he didn't like me very much, equating the reason to my profession, my appearance, my ill-considered dress sense. Tony did not understand psychologists. He'd confirmed it several times. He didn't see their value, especially when it came to policing. He was a hard-working copper, preferring to see the bad guys for what they were instead of *who* they were, ensuring they were locked away as quickly as possible so he could move on to the next case. He did not ask questions as to their state of mind or what prompted their crimes. Tony didn't care about such things. He was like Paul in that respect.

Paul shook his head, turning his attention instead to Alice. She was busy making me a coffee.

'Baker, did you manage to trace Ben's movements for the day of the attack?' he asked.

'Nothing concrete, Guv. CCTV footage from the bus showed him with some of his friends just before three o'clock but they were thrown off due to unruly behaviour and subsequently went their separate ways. Ben doesn't show up again until a camera in Tolbert Street picks him up around thirty minutes later, racing into the road and clutching the side of his head.' She crossed the room and handed me a cup, our fingers momentarily brushing.

'Do we know what happened on the bus?' Paul was standing by the whiteboard, a pen in his hand, too many thoughts in his head. CCTV was still fairly limited in some residential streets, even in a growing town like Eastcliff, no view at all from the other side of the road. You could blame a lack of funding for that. Government cutbacks.

'A minor disturbance, by all accounts. The driver confirmed the kids were taunting some disabled guy and an elderly lady stepped in to have a go at them. Eventually, he was forced to kick them off.'

'Disabled guy?'

'Yeah, although the CCTV footage doesn't show much more than the back of his head, unfortunately. He was wearing a hooded top and was careful to keep his face covered. Seemed to know where the cameras were.' Alice looked embarrassed she didn't have all the details, didn't have an identity.

'That reminds me,' I pitched in. 'The circular marks on the Jefferson's rug could be crutch marks.' I glanced around, hoping to provide the team with something useful, ready to pull my mobile phone from my pocket and hoping I'd remember where photos were stored. I wasn't good with technology, was the reason I still drove an old-fashioned car.

'Do you want me to look into it?' Alice asked, already on her feet.

'Well, yes if it's not too much trouble.' Paul shook his head in frustration, throwing his pen onto a nearby desk before heading into his office, leaving Alice biting her lip, glancing around the room.

I followed, closing the door behind me.

'You don't have to act so aggressively. We're all just trying our best.' I was whispering, hoping Alice wouldn't overhear. It was hot, the unusually long summer taking a toll on everyone.

'I have a dead man in the morgue and a kid who, for whatever reasons, *won't* speak to us. I need results.'

'He says he can't remember much.' It wasn't Ben's fault, wasn't Alice's. I recalled his Spiderman pyjamas, the way he'd admitted to the bullying, the kid far more vulnerable than I wanted to confirm.

'Yeah, and I don't buy it.' Paul took a deep breath and ran his hands through his hair, most of it staying in an untidy position on the top of his balding head. He looked stressed.

'Well, someone had just drilled his *skull*, in case you'd forgotten.' My turn now for the theatrics.

'Exactly.' Paul glared at me. I knew what he meant. He liked to tie up cases quickly, tick boxes, move on. But sometimes the details didn't add up and cases were left to fester, families left to suffer.

'I'm not sure if this is of any help, but I remembered a serial killer from around ten years ago who drilled the skulls of his victims before leaving them to bleed to death because he liked how the blood left the body.' I was referring to "The Gimlet", the guy popping uncomfortably into my head a few days earlier. I had a lot of experience with those types of people, studied a lot of killers.

'Who?' Paul was staring at me. I wanted to smooth his hair, get him a glass of water, a cup of tea.

'His name is Darius Jacobs.' I didn't know if Paul had heard of him and I didn't ask. I hadn't thought of him in a long time, didn't really want to think of him now.

'Why am I only just hearing about him *now?*' I couldn't discern my friend's features but his eyes had widened, as if he assumed I'd been withholding vital information.

'Sorry. I forgot.' It was true, other things on my mind. I was only human.

'But you think he might be our guy?' Paul's face had lit up, his cheeks brightening with the thought of the potential victory I'd unwittingly provided.

'Hardly. The guy has been in Manor Hill for the last decade.' I didn't mean to sound so blasé, didn't mean to scoff. Paul couldn't be expected to know the details of every criminal investigation in the country. Darius lived in the North until his conviction, murdering three local men including a dog. Although technically a serial killer, he wasn't considered national news, his killing spree limited to a personal network of three unfortunate sods he worked with.

'Then why are you bothering me with your theories?' Paul sighed, chewing a piece of skin from his fingertip before slumping painfully into his chair.

'Because I've met him before.' It was a few years ago now, though, and a lot of time had passed since then. 'I've booked a visit with him tomorrow. Wondered if he could shed some light on why someone might effectively be copying his methods. He might remember me, might be willing to help.' If I asked.

'You've actually *met* this guy?' Paul sat upright, his eyes widening.

'Yeah.' I felt my cheeks redden. 'I was required to assess whether he was mentally fit to stand trial.' It was the first time I'd been asked to do something so important, my first case. I remember being nervous as hell. I didn't mention this to Paul.

'And *was* he?'

'No. That's why he's been in a high-security psychiatric facility for the last decade instead of prison.' I almost rolled my eyes, stopping just in time, glad Paul didn't notice.

'But you think the killer might be a copycat?' Paul got to his feet, thrilled by the idea I had now placed in his head. He pointed a knowing finger my way, an excited look on his face.

I shrugged. 'Worth looking into, isn't it?'

Paul nodded, the pained grin he gave me not worth discussing. To be honest, there wasn't much to say about that.

Thirty

Newton

Manor Hill wasn't the type of psychiatric hospital you'd visit if you had a choice. Used not only for the mentally ill, it also doubled as a secure unit for those deemed *permanently damaged* and unfit for society—criminals considered too vulnerable for the prison system brought here because there were few other places in the UK to house them. The building was very much like a prison in some respects, only filled with doctors and shrinks instead of wardens and cells, the same locked doors and rules keeping offenders at bay. I'd been there once before, to enquire about a patient whose name still haunted my dreams. Serial killer David Mallory was set to remain here for the rest of his tainted life, our time together brief yet poignant. I wish I'd never met the man but, unfortunately, fate had other plans. He claimed responsibility for thirty deaths, his murderous streak spanning no less than two hundred years because he was convinced he had lived the lives of three reincarnated serial killers. He was insane, of course, but he still lives rent-free in my head, the knife wound to my stomach showing me how close I was to becoming number thirty-one.

I was almost glad the time I'd spent with Darius Jacobs had been limited to a police station in Leeds after his initial arrest. I wondered if the two men spent any time together or if they'd ever mentioned what they had in common. That they both knew *me*.

From the outside, the building appeared like any other modern industrial space, flat roof, large windows, unassuming façade. Yet the inside disguised a warren of corridors leading to hidden areas, little furniture, zero personality. It matched the people who lived there, deadened by their unfeeling lives and bland existence, their days isolated, most of them left to rot. I doubt many received visitors.

'Doctor Flanigan,' the receptionist stated brightly, greeting me with a wide grin and an outstretched hand as she opened the security doors, a cool rush of air hitting me in the face from the air conditioning behind her. 'How lovely to see you again.'

'Likewise, Janet,' I replied, surprised she remembered me, shocked I remembered her, our last encounter made under somewhat uncomfortable circumstances.

I returned her gesture, my smile as fake as the spindly plant standing in a corner, signing the visitor's book while she attached a sticker to my top, my name written in capital letters across its face. Lanyards were not suitable for certain patients, hard plastics more than capable of causing unwanted injury. I glanced at Janet who said nothing, yet I fully understood why. No one wanted to be strangled by a dangling cord or stabbed in the eye with a piece of broken identity badge. I was told to leave my belongings behind the reception desk before she led me along a narrow corridor and down a set of steel steps that seemed to go on forever, my footsteps echoing loudly in an attempt to keep up.

The entire place felt like a tomb, no windows to lift the heaviness clinging to the air, no personality aside from the occasional poster hanging lifelessly from bare walls. Even the floor was unpolished concrete, limited funding allocated to the damned, it seemed. I tried to ignore several muffled screams in the distance, shouts becoming lost amongst our footsteps, the unassuming reception space above a far cry from the cold interior of the room I was led into.

I had a vision of long-term patients living underground, away from society, their minds left to fend for themselves, natural light left wanting. I wondered if Darius Jacobs would remember me, our previous encounter short-lived. My job was to assess his mental state, that's all, to confirm if he was of sound mind, fit to stand trial. Back then he had offered nothing other than unwavering silence, leaving me to conclude he wasn't. How would he understand what was required of him when he was unable to tell me his name? It was ultimately my fault he'd subsequently spent ten years locked away, his isolation made permanent because of his silence. No one assumed he would be well enough for release. I assumed no one cared.

I'd brought my old notes with me as a reference, just in

case my memory needed jogging, the documents on "The Gimlet" carefully checked for staples, paperclips, anything he could use as a weapon. I was told to keep to my side of the table, to keep my hands to myself. I recalled his crimes well enough, had memorised the police interviews, assumed I knew what to expect. But I wasn't prepared for the man who awaited me on the wrong side of a thin-legged table, his features as grey as this building. He'd changed, and not in a good way.

'Doctor Flanigan, how nice to see you.' He rose to his feet when I entered, his wrists shackled by chain to the table, his ankles hooked into steel rims around a chair bolted to the floor. I was surprised he was *speaking*, my shocked reaction not going unnoticed. He reminded me, in a vague way, of Hannibal Lecter, yet older than I remembered, thinner, frailer. I presumed he would have held his hand towards me if he could, expecting me to shake it. I was glad for the handcuffs, my inability to immediately acknowledge him *not* something I anticipated. If I had any notion of relaxing once I'd re-familiarised myself with Darius, I was deluded, his face telling a very different story, his memories clearly as vivid as mine. I wasn't sure I liked that he remembered me, didn't want his private musings in my head. I'm sure he remembered everything, only here now because he wanted it this way.

'Thank you for agreeing to see me,' I stated boldly for the purpose of self-preservation, my words echoing violently around the room. I did not wish to give away my nerves, my position. We sat down, the bolted chair beneath me cold, unfeeling, almost as unmoving as Darius's stare.

He looked at me as if he couldn't believe I was here after all this time, in the flesh, his eyes drilling a metaphoric hole into mine; excuse the expression. Yet, I saw nothing inside his but a decade of unanswered questions, his absence from society highlighted only by his ageing appearance. I remembered Darius because of the way his left eye drooped, the damage due to an unconfirmed accident. It had never quite healed, his face now predominantly misshapen by a lopsided smile. I tried not to stare, tried not to think about poor Jack. Someone flicked a light switch, allowing a tube of glass to buzz and flicker overhead.

'So, what can I do for you?' The question was simple, his continued stare unappreciated. 'I was surprised by your request to visit. I do not see many people these days, as you can imagine.' Darius looked crestfallen, the shape of his face appearing hollow in the shadows of the overhead bulb, forlorn somehow, as if he was no longer in the room. He shuffled uncomfortably, his worn shoes scraping the worn flooring, setting my teeth on edge.

Upon first appearance, Darius Jacobs no longer looked menacing, his balding head and creased features a telling reminder of the passing years, an old man now, nothing more. Yet, I vividly recalled the way he looked back then from the photographs in my file, the day of his arrest as clear as it was all those years ago. He once owned a thick head of jet-black hair, his eyes like raw steel. Yet, his penetrating stillness had faded to a dull glare, his grey hair matching his grey skin. He hadn't aged well.

'Are you privy to outside news, Darius?' I asked, the sound of his name provoking uncomfortable memories. I glanced around, fully aware of the cameras surrounding us.

Darius shook his head. 'I have heard nothing from the *real* world for almost a decade, Doctor Flanigan.' He glanced around now too, searching for a window that didn't exist, for answers he couldn't explain. 'They tell me I am not yet ready to return up there.' He looked up at the ceiling. It made me nervous. He didn't exactly have a kindness about him. You wouldn't want to be on his radar.

'A few days ago, a man was found dead in his bathtub. The side of his skull had been drilled. It killed him instantly.' I didn't wish to divulge too many details, didn't want to provoke something in Darius to throw off the balance of this conversation. I didn't mention Ben, didn't tell him how lucky the boy had been.

'Really?' Darius's eyes lit up. 'How delectable.' He smiled. I could see he was missing some teeth. David Mallory jumped into my head again, the man who had claimed to have murdered thirty people still lurking within these very walls, somewhere.

'I was hoping you could help me with a few questions.' It never failed to amaze me how these people think, death something they find almost alluring. Yet again, if death didn't excite them, they wouldn't kill.

'Oh? And how can I help you?' He sat up straight, his attention caught, the idea of feeling important for once, not something he could disguise.

I nodded. 'I recall there were three victims.' It wasn't a question. We'd been here before.

Darius nodded a reluctant confirmation, closing his eyes briefly, his own memories lingering. 'Four. Don't forget the dog.' The dog was his first victim, found after his arrest and subsequent search of his house. It had been dead a while.

'According to several handwritten notes found at your property, you drilled holes in their heads because you thought it would be *fun*.' I'd brought my notes with me, paperwork on Darius Jacobs I was hoping to forget. I reached into a carrier bag and pulled out a thin file, embarrassed I didn't own a briefcase or anything to make me look professional. Darius did not look impressed.

Another nod.

'I'm hoping you can share your reasons behind such unusual activity. Aside from the basics, we never really got to the bottom of why you did what you did.' We didn't, in fact, speak at *all*.

'Why do you want to know of my past now, Newton?' He looked momentarily flustered, calling me by my first name because he wanted a reaction.

'It's Doctor Flanigan,' I corrected, sitting up straight now too, oddly offended. I wasn't sure it was relevant, knowing he was merely trying to wind me up by using my first name. I didn't look at him. 'And I'm asking because it might help us catch our current killer.'

Darius smiled. 'I'm intrigued. You obviously believe someone is copying my work, *Doctor Flanigan*. Surely you have your notes to look through?' He glanced towards my slim file, his eyes unmoving, cold. I didn't like the way he emphasised "Flanigan" as if I was a child who needed placating, his tone borderline patronising. Until recently, I'd almost forgotten he existed, his callous crimes unworthy of my attention.

'I wrote a book about you a few years ago, but at the time you'd given me *nothing* to fully understand your motives.' The book was a scholarly piece really, something the university allowed me to hand to my students to help with their studies, nothing major. It *was* published but had only sold a handful of copies, my students becoming the few people in the world who ever feigned their excitement, my sister-in-law proudly keeping a copy on her bookshelf.

'I'm in a *book?* How wonderful.' Darius's eyes lit up again.

I nodded. 'You claimed you found the crimes fun, and you liked the sight of flowing blood, yet I *know* there must be more to your story.' Things he didn't deem important to express in the ramblings found in his home.

'And you were able to write about me based on my notes?' Darius scoffed. Laughed. 'Impressive.'

'I did.'

'And what is this book called?'

It wasn't relevant, but I told him anyway. '*Lesser-known serial killers and their motives.*' I probably could have come up with a better title, but it didn't matter. It was a means to an end, that's all. Written years ago. I'd forgotten most of what I'd said. He wasn't the only killer I'd included in the book, but oddly he *was* the one I found the most disturbing. Aside from David Mallory. If I'd known *him* when I wrote the book, he'd have been in there, too.

Darius smiled. 'Lesser known?' He licked his lips.

Another nod. I was not about to give him undeserved notoriety.

'Of course,' he muttered, his smile slipping. 'And you're

right, Doctor Flanigan. We never did get to the *crux* of the problem, did we?' He narrowed his eyes, deep in thought, glaring my way with a twisted grin I wasn't confident I appreciated. 'Yet, you never *asked* me to provide information for such a book.' He tilted his head, his eyes maintaining a cold focus.

I swallowed. *Correct.*

'Why not?'

I took a moment to think before answering, before launching into the questions I'd concocted for this visit. I needed to understand him, to appreciate what made him who he was, why he drilled holes into heads. It had been a long time since we'd last shared an interview room, a long time since permission to question him for my book was declined. I couldn't tell him this was the *real* reason I'd been forced to improvise. Darius had many nights to think about what he did whereas I'd spent many nights trying to forget.

'To be honest, I don't remember.' I smiled, not wanting him to see my lie.

'Then I am more than happy to tell you whatever you want to know now.' Darius sat upright and cupped his frail hands together, his nails bitten to the quick, his thinning skin marked with age spots and deep lines running across his rough knuckles.

'Why a drill?' It wasn't something he could deny, his victims' bodies containing the evidence. It seemed too focused, too calculated. Downright wrong.

'Do you know what temporal lobe damage does to a person, Doctor Flanigan?' Darius was grinning, toying with me.

I nodded, thinking about poor Jack again, subjected to a private hell I couldn't begin to contemplate.

'I do, yes.' I glanced at the drooping mouth Darius tried to disguise, his thin body trembling beneath its unfortunate weight.

'Good.' He glanced across the table towards where a security officer stood facing the room, his bulk impressive, his pristine white uniform denoting nothing of his personality. 'Because, it has taken almost forty years from my life, Doctor Flanigan. And I'm sure, in time, it will take the rest.'

I wanted to tell him he didn't look sick, not like poor Jack, but thought better of it. Despite not having a terminal brain tumour, he looked *sicker* than anyone I'd met, mentally speaking. I glanced towards his frail body, realising too late Darius was watching me, the man no doubt now crippled by his condition. I refrained from searching the room for a wheelchair, assuming his injuries would have, by now, taken his mobility, too. Instead, I kept quiet and allowed him to talk in his own time, oddly annoyed he *could* still share a conversation while poor Jack could not.

'I can't walk very far these days. My brain won't allow for such an indulgence. Yet, it took a while to relearn to speak, my memory loss, paranoia, and aggression forming my existence for so long I honestly don't know how else to live,' he continued, staring into space as if my presence was of no relevance. 'Brain injuries can be permanent, life-altering, *terrifying*.'

Again, my thoughts drifted to Jack, his traumas, his

young age. 'What does any of this have to do with drilling holes into skulls?' I couldn't help asking. I didn't need his life history, his past traumas. It was hot in here, despite the rattle of an air conditioning unit overhead.

'I'm getting to that.' Darius smiled, more to himself than to me, recalling a life long past. He was too calm. I didn't like it. 'Imagine feeling as if you're constantly having a stroke, a stroke you know won't heal. My injury came about after I was kicked down a flight of stairs by a group of homophobic men. I was seventeen.' Darius paused. 'I didn't expect such a drastic change to my personality, but it felt as if overnight, I became someone else.'

'A killer?'

'No, Doctor Flanigan, not a *killer*. A muser, an overthinker. A man who just wanted to be understood.' He whispered 'still does', assuming I wouldn't hear, automatically attempting to get to his feet in response to his rising temper. His chains clattered violently, metal on metal, prompting the security officer to place a heavy hand on his shoulder, ensuring he took a breath, took his seat, calmed down. He wasn't going anywhere.

'Understood, *how?*' I asked, glancing briefly towards the officer whose name I didn't know, thankful he was in the room. He didn't look at me.

Darius sighed, in a seated position again now although no calmer for the shift, it seemed. 'Are we not all *made weak by time and fate, but strong in will to strive, to seek, to find, and not to yield?*'

'Tennyson.' He didn't need to quote literature to me.

A smile, a twinkle in his otherwise blank eyes. He tipped his head my way, seemingly impressed I knew to whom he was referring.

'And were you?'

Darius narrowed his eyes. 'Was I what?'

'Understood?'

He smiled. 'Are any of us?'

He had a point, and it was a very good question. Time does indeed make some men weak, yet wilful to strive for better, to search for more than there currently is.

'What were you looking for, Darius?'

He looked at me as if seeing me for the first time.

'Answers, Doctor Flanigan. *Answers.*'

Thirty-One

Jack

The location of "Healing Heads" does not look much from the outside and my mother makes me check the address three times before she is satisfied we are in the right place. She says a group counselling session might help process things, yet sceptically, I'm not sure. It matters little what *I* want anyway, such places designed to help me digest my condition and come to terms with my fate. I don't want to go, but my mother has insisted on driving me because she no longer trusts my judgment. If only she knew the half of it.

A shabby-looking, badly painted sign is the only proof this place exists, no windows, no personality, just a thin column of red bricks set back from the street. If it were not for my mother's continued interference, I would probably walk away and leave her to it. Until now, I have refused all counselling, my tumour no less active because I choose to keep my thoughts to myself. I assume this is my penance, what I deserve.

'I'll come in with you,' my mother states as I climb from her car, the heavy evening air once again too much for my brain to contend with, a thunderstorm brewing overhead. 'I can sit at the back. You won't even know I'm there.'

I shake my head. The last thing I need is to be watched. She means well but I feel more like a child now than ever. For once, I would like her to treat me like an adult. I reluctantly head towards the door, leaving my mother in the street, unwilling to look back, unable to say goodbye. This place unnerves me. I don't know why. Probably because it cements an irrational reasoning I don't belong here, forced against my will to endure the torture. Oh, the irony.

'Well, hello there,' a tall male calls out absently as the door springs shut on my mother's incensed features. He turns around, smiles, doesn't seem concerned by my appearance. 'You're a little early, but the others should be arriving socn. I'm Larry. I run the group here, in case you were wondering.'

I wasn't.

He flicks several light switches, flooding an ample-sized room with a panel of light showcasing dusty bare flocrs and forgotten brick walls. There is very little furniture apart from a stack of tired metal-legged chairs discarded against the wall, a table in the corner housing a tea urn, cups, milk, sugar. Larry busies himself setting out the chairs, leaving me hovering, wondering what to do, unprepared for the footsteps filling the desolate space behind me. Several people burst into the room, pausing only when they notice me. I hold my breath, expecting the worst.

'Is this the new recruit?' a woman asks, excitedly heading my way. Like me, she is walking with crutches, her head covered by a scarf, her skin blue with veins spread unevenly across her face. She smiles. Takes a seat. Doesn't seem concerned by my twisted features staring back.

'Yes, this is Jack, everyone,' Larry offers, setting out the last of the chairs in a questionable circle configuration, my company expected. I'm annoyed he knows my name, has obviously encountered my mother.

I glance towards the door again, desperate to run, if I can, careful not to look at anyone in particular. It's cold in here, despite the overbearing heat outside and I wonder if the coolness is my imagination, my very own "death grip" waiting to claim me when I'm least expecting it. I'm offered several nondescript introductions, listening to nothing in particular as I edge closer to the door, merely waiting for my opportunity to leave.

A woman called Carrie begins the session, this hour meant to share experiences and express emotion. Everyone is looking at her with such compassion, it feels almost alien. No one has looked at *me* that way since my accident, my mother aside, of course. And Newton. I'm deliberately zoning out, unwilling to listen to strangers speak of their doomed lives when mine is about to end, frustrated I've been forced here against my will. I don't need the intrusion, don't care about the smile she offers or the tears she spills. I'm *not* listening to a word she says.

Despite my discontent, Larry has a courteous manner,

putting the group at ease, seemingly thankful for how everyone is coping with their brain tumour experiences. None of them stare at me, luckily, my face of no obvious consequence to their day. I assume they have their *own* demons to deal with. None of them even notice when I slip from the room, my new "group status" seemingly of less interest to them than it is to me. I sigh as the door snaps shut, my relief obvious, heading into the street, those strangers left to enjoy each other's company far more than they will ever enjoy mine.

I assume my mother will be waiting in the car, but I don't see her so I take the opportunity to escape while I can. Before I'm seen. Before this day declines into all-out anarchy. I'm tired of living in the darkness of my peevish mind, my aunt's basement offering only temporary refuge. I slip away unnoticed, the evening swamped heavily now by claps of thunder and pouring rain, hurried strangers keen to be elsewhere. Yet, the only thing I need is fresh air, time to think, a moment to clear the thoughts I don't want in my head. I've been musing over Newton's words, the *date* he has vaguely confirmed, sending him several messages to confirm we are still okay for our twelve-thirty arrangement on Friday. I was careful not to use the term 'date' and his prolonged silence is making me nervous.

When I catch a glimpse of my face in a nearby shop window, my reality is brought into blinding focus, hovering uncomfortably as rain soaks my skin. From this position I look almost unrecognisable, my features distorted by water obscuring the glass, what's left of my hair damp, my eyes hollow. I despise what I see, what I've become, my past a place merely belonging to someone else now. I'm growing increasingly frustrated, no longer concerned for those I have hurt, unwilling to acknowledge the two people already punished for their poor judgment. I'm sick of living in the shadows of everyone else's assumptions. I'm not sure if it's the thunderstorm or merely my twisted mind, but whoever should look at me the wrong way this evening is destined to appreciate just how vengeful I can be.

Of course, those looking at me *now* are doing so only because of my lowered mood, my newly acquired "smile" nothing but an ugly scar stretching across my face. The stitches remain, my wounds nowhere near healed, more time and attention required to achieve this ultimate end. I stare at myself in a nearby bus shelter, my aim simple, my thoughts oddly calm.

I don't like the way my mood is tipping but I embrace it anyway, wanting notoriety before I'm dead, to be remembered by a society I believe loved me once. Anyone brave enough to look at *Jack Monroe* the wrong way runs the risk of becoming a target. I plan to watch them, stalk them, changing their lives in a way they can't imagine. My body tingles as I think of the lessons I will teach, prompting others to see the world how I see it, righting wrongs I believe have been made against me. My mission is to show them *all* a different side of normality. *My* normality. I don't want to kill, merely to share the trauma I go through, the emotional pain I can't escape. Surely that's not difficult to understand.

The sky is thick with heavy clouds and flashes of electricity, freshly formed puddles dampening my trainers, tipping my already failing sanity. I stop, look skyward, wonder how many evenings I have left, how many sunsets I will witness before my life is over. This storm is provoking something deep, something I can't change. There is, after all, a killer inside me, cancer feeding endlessly off my body, my mind, my soul. Bathtub Man's death was a problematic side effect of the skills I'm still developing, what happened to him *not* entirely my fault. Bus Boy is still alive. *I think.* I just wanted them to see the world beyond their limited existence. It's too late for me. This is now just part of the game.

I'm waiting for the inevitable, ready to take an obvious next step along a path with no end, no future to hold my failing attention. When a middle-aged couple pass by, their shock is undeniable. They look at me, then each other, wondering why their eyes can't accept this uncomfortable vision before them. I'm not about to ignore it. I tilt my head, wishing I had the capacity of mind to laugh, staring at them as they stare at me, armed with far more than my instincts, my head always full of pain. If I could question their reasons, I would. If I could speak, I would ask what makes *them* so perfect. Instead, I follow them through the dampened streets, onto the silent canal path, keeping my distance at first, then at a pace to match theirs. Eventually, the male turns around, uncertain of my dangerous motives, unaware of his fragile fate.

'What's your problem?' he asks in the dark, rainwater dripping off his head.

I can't speak, can't reply. Instead, I stare at them blankly.

'Are you listening to me?' he yells, unconcerned by his elevated tone or the weather. 'I said, what's your *fucking* problem?' The male is speaking as if he needs the interjection, his words an automatic escalation. Yet, I can see he is far more afraid of me than I am of him.

I stop, pondering my next move, my next thought. The female looks nervous, anxious. She should be. I walk towards them, undeterred by their presence or my own deep-rooted fears, pushing the male hard enough to dislodge his balance. He's not expecting what happens next, tumbling down the embankment like a soft toy, all squeaks and squeals, the canal's watery edge no escape, his bones taking the impact of his incoming weight. It's not helpful to admit, but I feel oddly powerful, righteous, more so than I have the right to express. I lunge towards him, ignoring his pathetic attempts to fight back or the woman's screams, the man cursing again now, hoping to draw attention to our predicament. I slam a nearby brick across his head, not hard enough to kill, merely to silence, to express how I feel. The woman is still screaming, grappling inside her bag for something, probably her mobile phone to call for help, to end this thing while she still believes she can. Her makeup is streaming down her face. I can't tell if this is because of the rain or her tears.

'Please, don't hurt us,' she whimpers, staggering along the canal path as I follow, her wet shoes slipping and sliding in the mud. I stop. Take a breath. She doesn't appreciate how her taunts have already hurt me. It's ironic. She probably doesn't care. She certainly doesn't seem bothered about her male companion lying on the ground behind us, her thoughts only on self-preservation. I use my crutch, satisfied only when the metal length connects with her head. She stumbles forward, adrenaline taking over as I slam her body to the ground. I don't want to hurt her, but I must silence her, too. She is yelling, hell-bent on raising attention, kicking out, catching my cheek with her shoe, sending unforgiving pain into my head.

I don't intend my overreaction, but I grab her head and slam it into the wet grass, my full weight on top of her now. I only stop when she stops struggling, only willing to release her when she finally lies still. I'm exhausted, rolling onto the sodden ground, my breath heavy, the blackness of the sky enveloping me like a coffin. I wait for my heartbeat to settle before getting to my feet again, ensuring the female won't come after me before retreating towards the male. She is no longer moving.

I carry a drill with me now wherever I go, at the bottom of a bag everyone assumes carries nothing but my medication. I wish I could say I don't know why such objects have become an unrelenting part of who I am, but I do. My anger has been building for a while. There is nothing I can do about that, nothing I can say to change the outcome. I contemplate boring into his flesh, then his skull, mindful to stop when I feel pressure. I've researched in detail the thickness of a human skull, how far I need to drill, have practiced in the silence of my aunt's basement many times. I'm not very good, haven't always been able to meet my requirements. Too deep and they die, not enough pressure and the only thing proceeding is a headache and a scar as a reminder. I glare at this man, wanting him to *feel* what I feel whenever I open my eyes, waking up tomorrow to find his world has changed forever. Like mine.

I wait in the darkness, uncertain, nothing but the sound of my breath and the falling rain for misplaced company. I almost change my mind but my anger runs too deep. My victim is exactly where I want him, his body dampened by rainwater pooling beneath his fractured limbs. I kneel on unstable knees, ready to drill his skull with unsteady hands. I plan to leave him limping. Like me. They will think he has suffered a stroke, initially, prompting a journey of recovery never to arrive. Only when he is well enough for visitors, will I then go and see him. If I live long enough, that is. He won't have the capacity to tell anyone who I am, and together we will share our understanding of the private world we will have in common. Maybe *then* will he realise the error of his ways, seeing the world how I see it, feeling how I feel when someone like *him* treats me as if I'm nothing.

I'm on autopilot, only stopping once my deed is complete, only taking a breath when I'm covered in blood. I sit by his side for what feels like forever, waiting, the falling rain mocking us both. He does not move. Neither does the female I earlier knocked unconscious. I begin to panic, wondering if I have killed them both, two more deaths to add. It is almost dawn before they are found, a leadless dog following a trail of blood I have honestly not intended to create.

Thirty-Two

Newton

It was still early when I received a call from Paul asking me to attend another crime scene, in my kitchen contemplating my day and a wave of thoughts racing relentlessly through my head. It did not fill me with comfort to know I'd been in bed while two people were being attacked, the nearby canal path just a couple of streets from my flat. I arrived to heightened police activity, their presence preventing unwanted onlookers, blue and white tape wrapped around bushes in haste. Hazy fog drifted over the murky water, disguising the incident, an ambulance crew already in attendance.

'What happened?' I headed down a set of slippery steps onto the towpath, carefully where I trod, Paul's disgruntled features too much for my exhausted mindset. I was too tired to smile, the hour too early for pleasantries.

'A dog walker came across a middle-aged couple around an hour ago.'

I glanced behind my friend, unable to see much beyond the activity preventing my view. 'Are they okay?' I wondered if dog walkers ever considered how exposed they were to untold crime scenes, usually the first to locate unfathomed incidents the rest of us are happy to avoid. Buying a dog should come with a warning.

You might see things you're not prepared for, your dog sniffing out dead things in unspeakable places. Still wish to proceed?

'Our witness initially thought the male had suffered a stroke,' Paul confirmed, unaware of my thinking.

'How so?'

'Because he was mumbling, the right side of his face drooping, the poor sod unable to move his mouth.'

'So, why do you need me?' It was still early and I hadn't yet had a coffee, my mind not able to absorb Paul's words. People have strokes every day. It's an unfortunate fact of life we mostly ignore until it happens to us.

'Because stroke victims don't have holes drilled into the sides of their heads, Newt.'

'Another one? *Shit.*'

Paul nodded. 'The dog walker assumed the blood on his head was caused by a fall. He couldn't have known differently. He was just glad the guy was breathing.' Paul took a breath. 'But, unless fate has somehow intervened, it seems we now have another victim of Black 'n' Decker on our hands.'

'I beg your pardon?'

Paul smiled, glancing my way in response to my question. 'Black 'n' Decker.'

'You called him Black 'n' Decker?'

A nod.

'*Why?*' I gave him a blank look, my eyebrow slightly raised.

'Because he uses a hand drill the same as tradesmen.' Paul was looking at me now as if the nickname was obvious, my confusion unrequired.

'Seriously?' I scoffed, shook my head.

Paul shrugged. 'We couldn't think of a better name.'

'Really?' I couldn't help the face I was pulling.

'Can *you* think of anything better?'

I couldn't, but he was putting me on the spot. It wasn't ideal. Maybe if I had more time. 'Well, I can't call him *that* in my Flanigan Files. It will sound as if I'm writing a DIY manual.' I thought about The Gimlet, wondering how long it had taken them to come up with Darius Jacobs's nickname 'You said there were two of them?'

Paul glanced along the path, the lingering mist unhelpful. At least it was cooler now, last night's storm finally clearing the air. 'Yes. A female was found a few feet from the gentleman, although, to be fair, she wasn't spotted until the dog sniffed her out. She was hidden amongst the long grass, floating face down in the canal.'

'When you say floating face down—'

'Dead.' Paul confirmed, his tone flat, cold.

I shuddered.

I wondered about the type of person who would do such a thing, musing over my recent discussion with Darius

Jacobs, still uncertain about the type of killer who would drill holes into people for fun.

'By the way, how did you get on with Jacobs?' Paul asked as if reading my mind, his face a telling expression of stress, exhaustion, too much on his plate and too few resources to support his underfunded team. I hadn't spoken to him since my visit to Manor Hill, didn't know how to report my non-descript findings.

'The only thing I discovered is he has lived with temporal lobe damage for the last forty years.'

Paul gave me a blank look. 'I thought you'd met him before?'

'It seems there was a lot I didn't get to know about Darius Jacobs the first time around.' He didn't speak during our first meeting, merely stared blankly into space. I didn't know at the time he *couldn't*. The only thing I could do was confirm he was not of sound mind, stamping a box placing him in a psychiatric hospital, locking him away from rational society until someone deemed him worthy of anything better. I didn't mention this to Paul. I was young, naïve, newly qualified. Darius Jacobs was my first real case. I kept this to myself, too.

'What caused the damage?'

'Some accident he was oddly vague about.' I thought about his words, his blank expression, his underlying persona, wishing I'd questioned him on a deeper level. It was, after all, my job. 'He said it left him overthinking everything, a dramatic change to his personality leaving him wanting to be understood by those who didn't appreciate how serious his brain injury was.' I thought about the

Tennyson quote he'd provided, the look of feigned intent he'd given me. Then I thought about Jack. I didn't mention *that* to Paul, either. He wouldn't appreciate the connection. There might not *be* one. 'He said he was looking for answers?'

'To what?'

I shook my head. 'Life, probably.'

We watched in silence as the woman's body was placed in the back of a private ambulance. Paramedics were still with the male, keen to get him to the hospital. At least it had stopped raining.

'Go with him,' Paul instructed. 'Let me know *if* and *when* he's up to talking.' My friend was already heading towards his car.

'Where are you going?'

'I have two murders to solve.' He offered a brief wave. Didn't look back.

***

Hospital coffee was cheap, but it was hot, and right then, exactly what I needed. I hovered along a corridor, trying to keep out of the way, trying not to look as if I was a victim of some unsuspected event. The injured man was Desmond Malkin, a taxi driver who'd lived in Eastcliff his whole life. The dead female was his wife, Sarah.

'Detective Newton?'

I turned around to see the same doctor who'd assessed young Ben Harris heading towards me. 'Flanigan,' I corrected. *Doctor,* if we were being one hundred per cent

253

correct, although I didn't mention it, didn't confirm I was *not* the police officer he already assumed me to be.

He nodded a vague apology, more pressing matters to address than my name and non-existent police status. 'Mr Malkin is awake if you want to see him.' He stepped towards the lifts, pressing the button several times in quick succession, in an obvious hurry. I could relate to that. 'We've just moved him onto a ward if you'd like to follow me.'

'Is he okay?'

'You mean, is he able to *talk* to you?'

I did. I didn't confirm that either, merely nodded weakly.

'He's conscious. For now, that's a good thing. The rest is down to nature, I guess. And time. He seems okay on the surface, though.' He glanced my way. 'Any closer to catching this drill person?'

I shook my head, unwilling to mention Paul's flippant comment regarding *Black 'n' Decker*. It was *not* a name I wanted to stick. I was shown onto the ward, a nurse already waiting to take me to Desmond's bed, the man on his back, a bandage around his head, monitors everywhere. I didn't know if I would be able to speak to him, didn't know the full extent of his injuries.

'He's very tired,' the nurse confirmed, keeping her voice to a whisper as we entered the room. 'But he *is* awake and insisting he speak with the police.'

I shot her a look. 'He's talking?' I didn't anticipate he would be well enough yet to communicate.

'He didn't have a stroke, Mr Flanigan. The man was

attacked. And he is very lucky to be alive.' She had a point.

'You with the...p...police?' Desmond's disgruntled voice reached me the moment I stepped into the room, his newly acquired stutter a painful side effect of what he'd been through. He tried to sit up, his injuries consisting of a bandaged head and bruised ego, his slurred speech imperative, a tremble in his arm I hoped was there before the attack.

'Yes. I'm a clinical psychologist.'

Desmond nodded. 'Where's Sarah? Where's my... w...wife? Nobody's telling me a...th...thing.'

I pressed my lips together, Sarah Malkin's fate not yet confirmed, knowing I'd now have to do the unfortunate honours. I moved a chair from a nearby wall and placed it next to his bed, taking too long to answer, too long to sit down. He reminded me so much of young Ben—the same swelling, the same bruising, the same drilled hole in his head.

'Do you have someone we can call for you, Mr Malkin?' I asked eventually, the coffee in my system dissipating with words I hadn't even spoken.

'The doctors have already...a...asked me that. No. It's just me and...S...Sarah now. And our dog...C...Chaffy. Where is she? Where's Sarah? Has someone checked on the...d...dog?' He looked worried, had every right to be. I was about to destroy his world.

I shook my head. 'I'm sorry, but it isn't good news, I'm afraid.' I couldn't offer anything else, could barely look at him. There was a moment of silence, a fleeting second where I couldn't bring myself to speak, inwardly cursing Paul for leaving me to break this news alone.

'*No!*' Desmond breathed out painfully, the shock of words I hadn't yet uttered slamming him in the chest like a missile. 'Please, God, tell me she's....o...o...o....' The man began to sob, snot, and saliva streaming down his bruised face.

I shook my head sullenly, wanting to help him finish his sentence, if I could, absorb his burden. 'I'm so sorry,' I repeated softly. 'I'm afraid she was already dead when they found her.' I hated breaking this type of news. I sounded cold, unfeeling. Like Paul.

Desmond burst into a fresh wave of tears, his trembling arm shaking violently, his bottom lip quivering with almost as much force. 'You've *got* to get the...b...bastard who did this,' he spat, aiming poisonous words into the air. He reached forward and grabbed my arm, desperate for me to hear his plea.

'Did you see the person who attacked you, Mr Malkin?' I needed to know. It was the reason I was here, the reason Paul had left me with this unpleasant task in the first place. I stared at his closed fist around my arm, his grip diminished, his weakened state *not* his fault.

'Oh, I saw him all right,' Desmond snapped, removing his hand from my sleeve, struggling to sit upright, monitors bleeping wildly as his heart rate and blood pressure shot up. A nurse rushed into the room, expecting the worst before noticing Desmond's troubled features. She looked at me with sympathies I didn't need, turning around and leaving us to talk in private. The machines were still bleeping. Desmond didn't care.

'I can pass any information onto the police so you can get some rest,' I confirmed. He looked as if he needed it. The last thing Desmond wanted was Paul by his bedside quizzing him for information, *drilling* him for details, excuse the expression. I glanced around, knowing Paul had orchestrated this moment so I'd be alone with the man, the rest of his team conveniently elsewhere.

Desmond nodded. 'Sarah and I were heading home from the…p…p…pub. I didn't take the taxi. Didn't want to lose my…l…license.' He closed his eyes, tears falling. 'We took a shortcut along the…c…canal. It was raining so we didn't want to hang around for long. He was just staring at us in the…d…dark.'

'Who?'

'The w…weird guy.'

'Weird guy?'

'Yeah. Looked like something out of…h…horror film, all pale-faced and dark-eyed.' Desmond raised a shaky hand to his face, his own eyes wide, his skin flushed. 'Had a…s…scar on his…cheek. A d…drooping eye.' He looked at me as if he couldn't understand the confirmation. 'When S…Sarah looked at him he got angry. I yelled…b…but he didn't even have the decency to…respond.'

'He didn't say *anything*?'

'Nothing.' Desmond was thinking back, concentrating, his memories too painful, his damaged brain uncooperative. He was luckier than Alex, yet not quite as lucky as Ben.

I was taken aback, young Jack springing into my thoughts once more. He had a scar, too. A large one. It ensured that, even when he wasn't smiling, his lip curved unnaturally upwards, his senseless self-mutilation done so the poor kid could achieve the expression. Oddly, it had worked, to an extent. And, just like Mr and Mrs Malkin's attacker, Jack had a drooping right eye and couldn't speak. I sat upright sharply, an uncomfortable thought jumping into my mind, heavy air catching my lungs. I shook my head. It couldn't have been Jack. That boy was a delight to know, wonderful to be in the company of. Or, at least, he *used* to be. I made my excuses and left Desmond with the nurses, confirming a full statement would be taken in due course. I then stood in the corridor and called Alice, my own trembling hands barely keeping my phone steady.

'Newt, hi. How are you?' The sound of Alice's voice was my one unfortunate weakness, this moment no exception.

I closed my eyes, needing no distractions, no limitations. I couldn't think of my needs, right now. 'Listen, did you get the details for the elderly lady who was on the bus the day Ben Harris was attacked?'

Rustling paper. A clicking keyboard.

'Erm, yes we did. Anne Clarence. Lives along Old Grove Lane.'

'Have the police spoken to her yet?'

'I assume they will have done.'

'*Yes, or no?*' I didn't mean to snap or express my frustration. I liked Alice. More than she knew.

More clicking. 'She made a statement just after Ben's attack.' Alice paused. 'You okay, Newt?'

I was far from okay but I had no reason to feel the emotions steadily swamping my mind, nothing concrete to link Jack to the victims other than a vague description from a grieving man.

'What did she say? In her statement?' I'd closed my eyes. All I could see now was Jack's face.

Alice fell silent. I assumed she was reading something on her computer, clarifying any information before committing herself to my unfounded questions. 'She said she witnessed several boys, Ben included, bullying a young man on the bus.'

'How young?'

'She didn't say. Apparently, she didn't get a clear look at him because of his clothing but claims he didn't try to fight back, didn't even speak.'

'Not a word?'

'No.'

'Did she say what he looked like?' My eyes were still closed, Jack's face still looming large in the ensuing darkness.

'Only that he was wearing an expensive tracksuit top of some description, the type with a hood, dark trainers. Nothing out of the ordinary aside from he was a disabled man.'

Shit. 'And his *face*?' Jack's was the only one I could *see*, confirmation of his innocence the only thing I needed.

'Nothing. Mrs Clarence said the male faced away from her during the entire journey. The CCTV footage from the bus and a nearby street has confirmed this. She didn't get a clear look at him, Newt. Just that he walked on crutches and kept his hood pulled over his face. Assumed that's why those kids were picking on him. You know what teenagers are like.'

'And she gave no description other than that?'

'Nothing we can go on. Sorry. Was there a reason you're interested?'

I couldn't tell her my thoughts, wasn't about to put poor Jack In the frame for something he might not have done. I couldn't accuse him of assault or potential *murder*. I wanted to be wrong, couldn't express my concerns. Not yet.

'Nothing concrete. Sorry to bother you,' I said instead.

'No problem.' A pause. 'Hey, Newt?'

'Yeah?'

'I'm always here, okay?'

Alice's declaration should have been the tonic I needed, her kindness never wavering, no matter what was thrown our way. It was why I liked her. As it was, I had too much on my mind to think of my *own* future, a young kid about to lose what was left of his to a potential legal battle I wasn't yet convinced was Jack's fault.

'Thanks, Alice,' I muttered instead. 'Have a good day.'

***

I headed home in a bad mood, telling Paul that Desmond Malkin was awake and ready for questioning. I confirmed what he'd told me, knowing it wouldn't take long for Paul and his team to put two and two together, only a matter of time before they questioned Jack as to his whereabouts last night. Although I couldn't confirm it, I knew he would have been at home, with his family, where he belonged. I considered sending him a message, warning him about what was coming, but what would I say? Where would I start?

Hi Jack. Hope you're well. Found a dead woman and an injured man down by the canal this morning. Says they were attacked by a male with a scar on his face and a drooping eye, a bit like yours, and the guy walked with crutches. Wasn't YOU was it?

Yeah, as if.

Instead, I got home to another gift on my doorstep. A bag of toffees. My favourite. They were from Jack, his beautiful cursive handwriting and flowing language unmistakable. I felt like crying. *This* was the type of kid Jack Monroe was. Kind, thoughtful, considerate. The type of person you could depend on in a crisis.

Thirty-Three

Jack

I've inadvertently spent the early hours of this morning crushed into a painful position beneath a bush, hiding amid the rot and the rats, waiting for my recent *victims* to be discovered. I have no idea why I didn't leave them to their fate and go home, yet just like with Alex, I was unable to leave until I witnessed the results of my actions, unwilling to relinquish responsibility until someone else took control. I didn't mean to fall asleep out here, the cooler evening air and overwhelming exhaustion enough to comfort me for a while. I know my mother will call the police if I don't show my face soon, wearing out her expensive carpet, the coffee in her system keeping her on edge.

I've lost track of time, that's all, physically sick to the pit of my stomach by the thought of an act I'm still unconvinced is mine, my murderous streak not yet revealed in all its infected glory. As it is, I barely recall getting home, my feet and brain numbed by an event I'm certain I imagined, forced to wait in silence until the scene was cleared. They took the female away in a body bag. I assume that means she's dead. I can't comprehend what will happen to the male now, the human skull far weaker than anticipated, my drill too heavy for my depleted limbs, my *favourite* one lost somewhere inside a dead man's bathroom.

'Oh my God, Jack, you look terrible.' My mother races into the hallway when she sees me, pulling me into a shaky embrace, smelling of alcohol, sweat, and goodness knows what else. Her exhausted tone matches mine but I'm in no position to tell her what she wants to know, my emotions far beyond what she sees.

'Where have you been?' She's looking at me as if she can't quite believe I've worried her so much, unable to appreciate my absence.

I shake my head. I don't want her drama right now, no explanation fathomable anyway, even if I could offer one.

'I called your aunt but she hasn't seen you. Newton hasn't seen you. None of your friends have seen you in months.' My mother's address book sits on the kitchen table. I have no doubt she called every contact in it.

I glare at her, angry Newton now knows I've been out all night, not the first time he's been forced to deal with my disappearance. I can't look at her but confirm from the mess in the kitchen she has been up all night, two empty bottles of vodka on the table. If she notices my dirty clothing or the blood on my hands, she says nothing.

'We're going to be late.' She glances at the clock, no time to discuss the matter now, no chance for me to take a breath. 'Why don't you go and wash up and I'll meet you in the car.' Today is my fourth chemotherapy session, my treatment ongoing because my mother will *not* accept I'm dying.

Another head shake, firmer this time, my reaction borderline violent.

'Jack, I'm coming to the hospital with you. I *always* come with you.' She is staring at my hands, a tremble in one I can no longer sedate.

Not today. I'm defiant in my mannerisms, firm in my stance. I have been through too much over the last few days and I *can't* sit in a room and pretend everything is okay.

'But Jack…' My mother trails off, leaving me in no doubt as to her disappointment.

I shake my head again. I need to do this alone. It's not negotiable.

***

The *only* good thing about cancer is when you have it, you can pretty much do what you like without consequence, your every action excused, your failing emotions taken readily into account because no one knows what else to do. People no longer see *you* but your illness, everything you do and say accepted with a strained smile, fake composure, ill-placed acceptance. Nobody can fix it, so instead they brush over it.

I arrive at the hospital with a growing sense of fear I try

to bury at the back of my mind, the taxi driver unnervingly quiet as he avoids looking in his rear-view mirror. I climb into the morning air, regretting my decision to come alone, nothing I can do about this now. I feel violently sick, the poison they are about to inject me with set to make everything worse, no support network to lean on, feeling oddly sorry for myself. I can't go through something like *cancer* alone but I equally cannot abide my mother's overbearing tone. Not today. The very thought leaves me trembling with misplaced regret I'm not prepared to acknowledge.

I sit anxiously in a waiting room surrounded by soulless faces, each one as nervous as me judging by their expressions, their chewed lips, bitten nails and tapping feet displaying a shared anxiety none of us want. They don't speak, barely look my way, thankfully unconcerned by my appearance. They all have at least one other person with them, yet I have spent the last few weeks pushing people away, absorbed only in my unforgiving world, wishing things were different. Now I *need* someone, I have unwittingly found myself alone. I've always been stubborn, I know, but this is a step too far, even for me.

I'm taken to a quiet room while nurses busy themselves preparing my treatment, perched uncomfortably on a worn chair that digs into my protruding bones. I'm destined to die a painful, agonising death, alone if I'm not careful, in a jail cell if I'm not mistaken. I wonder briefly if this is some kind of fitting karma, but I try not to dwell on the details, on things I can't change. Cancer *kills* people. That's all I need to know. A nurse comes into the room with a needle too big for my shrivelling veins and I try not to notice that either, the woman thankfully gentle as she attempts to find one momentarily eluding her efforts. She has a quiet look about her. It tells me she has been here many times, many sick people infecting her day.

'You're quiet,' she states casually as she hooks my medicine bag to a pole. I stare at the poison, knowing it will make me sicker than I already am, secretly wishing for this to be over so I won't have to suffer anymore. I wish I could smile, offer false reassurance. It might make *one* of us feel better. 'Try not to worry,' she continues, unconcerned by my silence or distorted features. 'You're in good hands.' She softly pats my shoulder.

I don't *feel* in good hands. I feel terrified, despite having already accepted the idea of dying. What else is there to say? Yet, my mouth feels dry even before a single drop enters my veins and I think I might throw up.

'Would you like something to drink?' she asks as if reading my tainted mind.

I nod, pointing to an elderly man by a window drinking what smells like coffee, curling my forefinger and thumb into the shape of a C while holding two shaky fingers from my other hand towards her in the hope she will understand what I need.

Coffee. Black. Two sugars. Exactly how Newton takes his.

The nurse pats me again and leaves the room, leaving me to survey my surroundings. The gent by the window is unconcerned by my presence, far too absorbed in his own, a hairless child quietly reading with its mother in the corner. I can't tell if the child is a boy or a girl, hair loss having taken the poor thing's identity, its skin as pale as the walls around us. It makes me uncomfortable. Fragile looking, the kid looks a terrible sight, life and laughter long gone from its fractured features. I must have been staring because the mother glances my way, offering an understanding smile that brings a lump to my throat. I nod, attempting a smile of my own in a failed attempt to diffuse my embarrassed presumptions, looking away too quickly as tears fill my eyes. For a moment I almost forget my own afflicted appearance. I'm glad she does not stare at *me*.

Instead, I flick through a discarded leaflet, uninterestedly scanning information about cancer crammed onto cheaply printed paper, too many terrified fingers flicking through these pages before me. There are many side effects to deal with depending on what medicine you are given, the type of cancer being treated, other factors to take into consideration. Looking at this poor child I can see why many fear it. I stare at my drip, watching drop after drop of poison disappear into my body, hooked to a primitive and dangerous treatment oddly not changed much in decades. When the nurse returns with my drink, I have already lost my taste for it.

An hour passes, then two. Although I can't see what I look like, I no longer recognise the man I've become, my mind a tangled mass of troubled ideas. My cheeks have the feel of a sunken ship, my clothes hanging from my shallow frame as if my body is made of coat hangers, my clothing clinging on in vain. I surmise if Newton could see me like this, he would be mortified. If my mother saw me, she

267

would be heartbroken. I want to scream, punch walls, run away.

Why me? *Why me?*

I'm still in my own tainted world when Newton strolls into the room, his sudden appearance visibly shocking. His beaming face is alive with enthusiasm, untroubled by the sight of me sitting here waiting to die, unconcerned he is about to see me at my worst.

'Hey, kiddo,' he chides, settling himself onto a chair next to mine, placing a carrier bag at his feet. Something inside chinks, like glass. A coffee jar, no doubt, maybe two. He leans my way and touches my arm. 'Hope you don't mind a visitor?' His question is heartfelt, yet I'm both stunned and aggravated, knowing my mother has told him where I am. I take a breath, warmed by his presence, absorbing his aftershave, his grin. I'm mortified I don't look my best.

Newton smiles. I know he only wants to check on me, initiating light conversation teetering on the implausible. But it's the last thing I need. There is a reason I wanted to be alone today. Yet, I find myself wanting to reach over and touch him, hug him, hold him close. I want to feel his breath against my fingertips, tell him how he makes me feel. It takes everything I have to stop myself from leaning towards him, stealing a kiss I need, blinking away tears I do not.

Newton stays with me throughout my treatment, convincing me not to be angry with my mother after a lengthy explanation falling mostly on deaf ears. She's worried about me, didn't want me enduring chemotherapy alone. She *loves* me. I understand all of that. Yet, it changes nothing. I close my eyes while he talks about the weather, my treatment, of getting strong enough to beat the odds. But at no stage does he touch on the subject that matters, does not acknowledge *us*. He chats nonstop until my bag of gloop is empty and my session has ended, buying me a coffee in the hospital café because he needs one more than me. He talks about life, the world, his cottage, everything he wants to achieve from life. It feels natural, normal, almost beautiful. I don't want this moment to end.

'I know you probably don't want to talk about it, but where *were* you last night?' Newton looks at me as if he honestly cares, genuinely has my best interests at heart.

I shake my head. He does *not* want to know, wouldn't understand even if I could explain.

'Your mum said you weren't at the counselling group when she came to pick you up, and despite several frantic calls, you never came home.' Newton tilts his head, making me hang mine in shame. His smile has slipped, his tone now painfully serious. 'Come on, Jack. What's going on? When have you and I never talked about things *this* important?' He is looking at me like a professor, not the friend I sorely miss.

I glance his way, knowing he's right, yet there is nothing I can say to change the facts. I press my lips together and close my eyes, recalling last night, just another in a growing list of stupidity. Where would I even begin?

'I got your journal.' Newton changes the subject, surprising me when he reaches into his bag and takes it out, placing it on the table in front of him as if he is planning on reading me a bedtime story.

My mouth falls open. In my haste, I'd completely forgotten about my gift, about words I can never say aloud. I feel my cheeks redden, my throat dry despite the coffee coating it. My eyes widen, imploring him in silence to tell me what he thought of it, how it made him *feel*. I hope he won't judge. I poured my heart into my diary, expressing everything I feel for him, attempting to explain who I am. I assume he can't be upset with the contents. After all, he's here, keeping me company, a look on his face I want to remember forever. It's a shame I can't yet tell him about my drill obsession, about the things I do in private. I find myself thinking of our date instead, about Friday and the hope it might bring. I nod, hoping Newton understands I *do* want to talk to him. When the time is right.

'I guess we can discuss this later,' he says, running a free hand over the card exterior. 'For now, I need to get you home. Your mum will be having kittens if I don't get you back safely.' He laughs and gets to his feet, pausing for a moment before looking my way. 'Jack?'

I glance up.

'Don't *ever* do anything like that again, okay? You scared your mum. You scared me.'

I rise unsteadily to my feet, my legs like jelly, the coffee we shared only moments earlier threatening now to make an abrupt reappearance. I amble slowly around the table and lean towards him, glad when he responds with a hug.

By the time we get home, I'm exhausted, yet Newton is still chatting, still laughing. For the first time in weeks, I oddly don't feel sick.

'By the way, Jack,' he calls my way as I climb out of his

car. 'Thanks for the toffees.' He winks before driving away, leaving me breathless for the genuine gratitude he has shown and the twinkle I see in his eyes. I've forgotten all about those toffees, forgotten I *can* do nice things. Sometimes.

Thirty-Four

Jack

As soon as I get to my room, I send Newton a message, thanking him for his time, his kindness, his patience — expressing in a text the words I can't say aloud. I withhold thoughts I don't have the guts to confront, ignoring my mother when she calls me to dinner, staring at my phone, a lump in my throat that has nothing to do with my treatment. I'm waiting for something good to happen, that's all, my delusions keeping me company when no one else can, annoyed when twenty minutes pass before he replies. When a love heart emoji pops up on my screen, I croak into the afternoon air, attempting a laugh I will never achieve, unconcerned by the massive dose of chemotherapy set to have me throwing up in the toilet before this day is done.

To quote Leonardo DiCaprio, I am on top of the world. I

don't imagine anything reducing my heightened emotions today, my demanding mother included. I refuse the soup she has prepared for me, blaming the chemotherapy instead of Newton's infectious presence, telling her via aggravated sign language I'm going out for a walk. I'm no longer concerned about passing strangers. What can they do to *me* that I haven't already done to them? I'll be fine by myself, but I wear my hooded top, all the same, pulling it over my head to prevent unwanted attention, nothing on my mind other than Newton. My mother peers readily through an open upstairs window. She waves. I don't wave back. She means well, only wants what's best. I'll apologise later, give her a hug.

I find myself strolling through a nearby park. It's peaceful, calming, isolated from the rest of a crazy world I've developed a profound dislike for. It's funny, really. Before the accident, I don't recall ever complaining about life or a potential lack of it. Yet, somewhere along the way, I became just like those grumbling people I claim a vivid dislike for, begrudged by how life has done me an injustice.

A dog barks, darting towards the outstretched arms of its owner, an apparent prospect of some tasty treat bringing temporary joy to this creature's life. It turns excitedly, burying its nose in a patch of long grass, wagging an ever-curious tail, waiting to be congratulated on some amazing discovery it has made.

'What is it, girl?' I hear someone laugh, enjoying the infectious enthusiasm the dog has for what will no doubt turn out to be a discarded crisp packet or cigarette end.

It sits down, panting, stomping a heavy tail into the

ground as its owner, an elderly woman, kneels next to it. She says something I can't hear, oblivious to everyone else's problems, mine included. I recognise her immediately as the old lady from the bus, automatically motioning my weakened body towards this stranger who, for the briefest of moments, had my back. I must thank her somehow, offer my gratitude. If I can. She glances my way, a smile on her face, her otherwise boisterous dog under perfect control. There's not a hint of shock in her eyes. I wonder if she remembers me. How could she *not?* It's early September now, a couple of weeks before I should be returning to university, pleasant enough despite last night's storm. Beautiful colours cover the shapely paths, making it impossible to see where wildflowers end and the walkways begin. I release an audible sigh, allowing it to disperse into the afternoon air.

'I love animals,' the old lady calls out brightly. 'Don't you?'

I nod, momentarily grateful for the distraction, thinking of my own dog, wishing I was well enough to have brought her with me.

'And then we get old and struggle to keep up with them,' she confirms with a chuckle, moving her arthritic body steadily towards mine while playfully stroking the dog's fur. The animal tilts its head to one side in excitement, a lopsided tongue displaying expectant joy.

She reminds me of my mother in some ways, only older, wiser. The old lady. Not the dog. The way she pulls a strand of grey hair from the corner of her mouth, allowing it to moisten as it slides between her lips. The way she stands, her arms calmly by her side, confident, relaxed. For a moment, I almost lose track of where I am, failing to notice the tears in my eyes, the dog busy sniffing my crutches in some frantic attempt to chew off the ends. I would *love* to grow old. I wish I had such luxury. If only this lady appreciated the irony of her words.

'You look lost, young man,' she states instead, a look of intent on her face as I find myself staring back, a blank, unapologetic expression on my own. She isn't wrong, is not looking at me how everyone else does. I am indeed lost. Yet, aren't we all?

I wipe my eyes with my sleeve, giving her my answer without saying a word.

'We used to come here all the time,' she continues, oblivious to the memory she has triggered, long pauses left between her words, unconcerned by my silence or tears she can't mistake. 'My husband loved it here.'

She smiles but I notice something behind her ageing eyes confirming a different story. Is it loneliness? I can't tell from this position, but I expect she must miss him. I try not to overthink how rude it is of me to assume this poor woman's husband is dead.

'But I'm always with him. And he's always with me,' she mutters, her words fading now to a profound whisper I might have missed was she not standing so close. I want to ask her to explain but I can't, so I don't try. I don't know this lady. She doesn't know me. Eventually, she glances my way as if her thoughts have cleared, her illuminated persona resuming. 'So, what's your story, young man?' She asks, her question emerging as if genuinely believing I have one.

I hang my head, no words to express my situation even if I *could* speak.

'You have the look of a man who has lost something important.' She's not wrong. Is it *that* obvious?

I shrug, attempting to hold back tears I know have already fallen, exposing my weakness, my fragility. Why would this woman want to hear *my* problems?

She calmly strokes the dog at her feet, leaving me wishing Star was this good on walks. 'Time has a strange way of working itself out, my boy,' the woman states firmly, picking up two heavy looking shopping bags. 'That's if we are lucky enough to grow old at *all*.' She looks at me. I know what she must be thinking, almost as if she can read my thoughts, my emotions. *She sees me.* Probably clearer than I see myself.

Instinctively, I step forward and take the bags from her grasp, hooking each one around the handles of my crutches, shaking my head when she protests. She has given me her time today. The least I can do is return the favour, offer the compassion very few show me. I'm not even sure she remembers what she did for me that day, in no position to comment on the past, present or future.

'Well, thank you very much, young man,' she expresses instead, ambling steadily onto the high street with me now in tow, a smile on her face and the dog on its lead. If I could smile, I would, knowing her kindness aided me, despite what happened before and after. We walk together as if we are old friends, the dog stopping periodically to sniff the ground, have a wee, pick up a stick. She talks about the weather, the state of the country, the economy, querying nothing about my condition or the reason I've not spoken a word since we met. Maybe she already knows I can't.

Eventually, we stop outside a tiny cottage, its picturesque location offering a stunning sea view, reminding me of Newton's. Although my family home is close to the seafront, too, I don't have a good view from my window, the front of our house facing the wrong way. All I see from my bedroom is the driveway. The old lady opens her door and the dog races inside, barking with excitement, glad to be home. I hesitate when she invites me in, but the least I can do is ensure her shopping is safely delivered. I don't intend to stay long. I unhook the bags from my crutch handles, placing them on a tiny kitchen table, surprised when she lifts out a packet of chocolate biscuits and hands it to me.

'Thank you for your kind help, young man,' she says, waiting keenly for me to take them. 'Go on. It's okay. You've earned them.' She laughs, noticing how my eyes have lit up.

It has been a while since someone did anything this nice, Newton and my mother aside, of course, a while since I ate anything *this* delicious. I have been unable to swallow solid foods since I woke up from my coma, apple puree the only sweet indulgence my mother allows. Besides, sugar loves cancer, apparently. It matters little how much *I* love sugar. It is yet another thing Newton and I have in common, grateful for the soft centred toffees I consume in private. I take the biscuits, knowing I will give them to him on Friday. He deserves them far more than me.

Thirty-Five

Newton

I was strolling along a busy high street when my phone rang, overthinking the passing afternoon, not expecting Alice's vocals to seize my attention.

'You busy?'

'For you? Never.' The words slipped out before I could stop them, Jack and coffee the only things on my mind until now. I stopped, closed my eyes, hoping she hadn't heard the tenderness in my tone or the eager expectation in my thoughts. 'Everything okay?' It was too late for me to sound professional. I merely hoped I hadn't made her uncomfortable, hoping she would appreciate I was tired, overworked, hot.

'Remember the elderly lady who stepped in to help the male on a bus who was being bullied by Ben Harris and his friends?'

'I do.'

'Well, she called the station an hour ago. Says he helped carry her shopping home.'

'When?'

'This afternoon. Want to come with me to speak to her?'

I was shocked by Alice's request, Paul busy elsewhere with Tony, the rest of the team already assigned other missions. I wished I could see her face and gauge her expression.

'Sure. Want me to meet you there?' I was trying to sound casual, failing, oddly convinced Paul had put her up to this and momentarily wondering where I'd parked my car. Although I couldn't see her, I could tell she was smiling, either grateful for my help or grinning at *him*, an index finger pressed over his lips to shush any potential laughter.

'You got a pen? I'll give you the address,' she confirmed instead, leaving me questioning everything.

***

Alice was waiting for me when I arrived at number one, Old Grove Lane, propped against her car looking stunning, as always, the afternoon sun fading now to a grey sky once again threatening rain. She smiled when she saw me, her casual mannerisms ensuring I accidentally left my door unlocked, realising my error only after I'd walked away. She shook her head, rolled her eyes, smothered a grin.

We were greeted by a spritely female in her late sixties, dressed as if she was about to go for a run, her healthy flushed cheeks and broad smile making me feel inadequate and out of shape.

'Thank you for coming to see me,' she confirmed, stepping to one side so we could enter her home. 'But I'd have gladly come down to the station.' Anne Clarence stepped back, her cosy space smelling of sea air and home-cooked meals. A dog was curled up in the corner. It lifted its head, didn't get up.

'That's honestly not a problem, Mrs Clarence,' Alice confirmed. 'We're glad you called us.'

'It's Anne, please,' she laughed. 'Mrs Clarence was my husband's mother's name and I don't wish to be reminded of *her*.'

She winked.

We were standing in her front room, the downstairs consisting of two small rooms, nothing more, the kitchen barely visible behind a narrow doorway. Two mismatched sofas were nestled around a log-burning stove, wooden flooring throughout, several rugs underfoot. The space was inviting, with trinkets on the windowsill, cushions on the chairs, a little coffee table beneath the window. On it was a small vase of violets, oddly reminding me of my mother.

'You said over the telephone you think the man from the bus carried your shopping home for you?' Alice was holding a notebook, ever the professional.

'I did, yes. Poor thing.' Anne smiled, glancing between us. 'May I get you a tea, coffee?'

'Two coffees would be wonderful, thank you,' Alice confirmed, automatically answering on my behalf. I gave her a grateful smile. She knew me well.

Anne headed into the kitchen to put the kettle on,

clanging pots and pans noisily, speaking to us over the encroaching volume. 'I recognised him as soon as I saw him, although I'd say he is more a *boy* than a man,' she called our way, hovering inside the doorframe briefly, a teacup in her hand. 'I didn't get a very good look at him when we were on the bus, but when that young man helped me with my shopping earlier, I *knew* it was him.'

'How?'

Anne smiled. 'Two things stood out. Firstly, he was walking with the same crutches. I remembered because one of them was covered in stickers.'

'And the second?' Alice was writing, unconcerned.

'He wore a distinct hooded top with a large, embroidered motif on the back. He was wearing the same one today.' She paused. 'I'm not sure if I mentioned this in my initial statement.' She looked embarrassed.

My spine stiffened. 'What was the motif?'

'Some kind of dragon, I think.' Anne drew a shape in the air with her free hand as if trying to recreate the image. 'Very beautiful.'

I sucked in a lungful of air. Jack owned something similar, his right crutch covered in stickers because he said it would take the attention off his face. I was almost frustrated I hadn't viewed the bus camera footage for myself. I might have cleared a few things, ruled Jack out of the equation, saved the stress.

'Can you describe it?' I almost didn't want to know, happy for Jack to reside in a perfect world of invisibility, my own seemingly deluded. I could hear Desmond Malkin's words in my head.

Anne shrugged. 'It was fairly large with detailed embroidery. It didn't look cheap, either. Not something printed you'd get from a high street shop.' She glanced my way. 'I probably *should* have said this in my earlier statement.'

Alice nodded, prompting Anne to go on. She looked uncomfortable but tried to hide it. This had obviously not yet been investigated.

'He kept his hood up during the bus journey and was facing away from me, so I got a far better look at his clothing than his face. But having seen him up close today, I can understand why those kids were taunting him.' She glanced our way, her discomfort not going unnoticed.

I stood perfectly still, unable to move. I think my feet had welded themselves to a rug. Anne was still looking at me.

'And why's that?' Alice was writing, oblivious to the thoughts now spinning around my head.

'His poor face. It is terribly scarred.' Anne pointed to her right cheek. 'I could never forget a face like that. He has a wound stretching outwards from his mouth that doesn't look healed, poor kid, and one eye hangs down as if he has suffered some kind of trauma.' She turned around and ventured back into the kitchen to make our coffee, returning moments later with a tray of mugs, biscuits, milk, sugar, spoons, and a steaming coffee pot.

She had just described *Jack*.

'You didn't say anything to him did you, about his injuries, I mean?' My voice emerged as a thin whisper, this small room and the lingering summer heat to blame, should anyone ask. Jack was sensitive about his injuries.

'No. Of course not. What kind of person do you take me for?' Anne shook her head as if I was insane to ask such an impertinent question. 'He seemed a really nice young man, as it goes. Although he didn't speak a word during the entire time we were together.' She stood in front of the fireplace, motioning us to sit down and drink her delicious-smelling coffee.

'Not one?' I felt as if I was being strangled, glad I wasn't wearing a tie today. Not that I ever did. Unless I was called into court to give a character reference.

Anne shook her head. 'I thought he was shy, but I get the impression he's probably mute.'

'So, you didn't get his name?' Alice was innocently asking questions, unaware I already *knew*. She looked frustrated, searching for answers she had no idea I could provide if asked.

'No, sorry, I didn't think to ask. But how many young men do you know living in Eastcliff with scars like *that*? I'm sure it won't take you long to track him down.'

I sat down, then got to my feet, suddenly panicked by what I knew was coming. Jack was in no fit state to undergo a police interview, cautioned under oath, locked in a cell. He wasn't up to it, wasn't something he'd take lightly, not something his mum would appreciate. Jack wouldn't be involved with Alex, Ben, *or* the Malkin's. I couldn't comprehend any of it.

'Are you okay, Newt?' Alice asked, noticing my unease, getting to her feet now too, mine suddenly unsteady. We hadn't even touched our coffee.

'I'm so sorry Mrs Clarence… Anne, but I've just remembered something important. I have to go.' I turned towards Alice briefly before motioning towards the front door, a mere five paces between myself and a handle that felt hot in my grasp.

As I stepped outside, I could hear Alice conveying her thanks, her apologies, the thick air feeling as if someone had placed a bag over my head.

'Newt, what's wrong?' Alice was behind me now, her hand already on my arm.

'Nothing. I'm fine,' I lied, unable to catch my breath.

'You don't look fine.'

Anne Clarence was standing in her doorway, her previously disinterested dog by her side as if my sudden exit was important, as if it could read my thoughts. I stumbled into the street, leaning against my car for air I wasn't convinced was coming my way any time soon.

'Is everything okay?' Anne called out.

I didn't reply.

Alice nodded blankly on my behalf, offering the old woman a well-meaning smile before putting a well-placed hand on my arm. 'Newt, you're worrying me. *Talk* to me. I've never seen you behave that way before.' She looked genuinely worried, confused.

'Not here.' I yanked my car key from my pocket, needing a moment to think, Anne still hovering behind us, still wondering what twas wrong. I didn't need prying ears listening in, didn't want to confirm my growing suspicions.

'You're going *nowhere* in this state.' Alice snatched the key from my grasp, leaving me reeling. 'Let's go and grab a coffee somewhere. You can tell me what the *hell* is going on.'

I didn't want to but I followed Alice to her car, not about to argue, climbing into the passenger seat while she continually glared my way, my key now firmly in her possession. 'I'm fine,' I lied again.

'Clearly, you're not.'

We drove to a tiny coffee shop overlooking the bay, the place closed during the winter and overcrowded in the summer. Luckily, it was empty this afternoon aside from a woman sitting outside with three kids drinking milkshakes.

'Okay, spill. And leave *nothing* out.' Alice was already seated by a window, her hair and skin catching the afternoon haze in all the right places. She was beautiful, even with a stern look on her face.

I sighed. Where should I start?

'I'm sorry.' I was. I couldn't convey my words any clearer.

'About what?' Alice wasn't backing down, wasn't willing to let this go.

'Promise me you'll keep this to yourself?' I closed my eyes, opening them to Alice's narrowed glare that made me uneasy.

'I can promise nothing of the sort.'

'Then I can't tell you.'

'Newton!'

I always knew I was in trouble when friends called me Newton. I sighed, picking a menu from the table, desperate for a distraction. 'The young man. The one Anne Clarence spoke of.'

'What about him?'

'I think I *know* him.' I almost held my breath, the very thought Jack could be involved lodged uncomfortably in my head.

'*What?*' Alice leant across the table, her mouth dropping open. When she pulled her mobile from her pocket, I knew what she was about to do.

'Please, don't.' I automatically reached for her hand but she was too swift, pulling away, offering me a sideways glare I knew not to mess with. I still had Desmond's words racing around my head, Anne's now joining the confusion, the reason for Ben's bullying all too clear. If it took me less than five minutes to conclude Jack was up to his neck in this thing, the poor kid would probably find himself in custody before the day was out.

'What the *hell* is going on?' Alice was whispering now, the look on her face confirming nothing good, the look on mine saying it all.

'It has to be a mistake. Just give me a few hours to clear this up. Please. I promise I'll explain everything as soon as I can.'

'You can explain right now.' Alice was still holding her phone, an index finger hovering over the "call" button. 'Or you can explain it to *him*.' She turned her phone towards me, Paul's name displayed on the screen.

I shook my head. She didn't need to do that. 'He's one of my students. His name is Jack Monroe.' I couldn't believe I was saying his name aloud, whispering only because I didn't want to believe it. Jack was a *good* kid, a great student. A friend.

'Okay.' Alice was too calm. I didn't like it. 'And you

think he might know what happened to Ben Harris?'

I shrugged. 'Jack's a good kid.' I needed to confirm it.

'I never said he wasn't.' She glared at me, a crinkle forming in the centre of her forehead. I wanted to smooth it out. 'Whatever this is, you don't need to protect him. For Christ's sake, Newt, if he knows something about Ben, he might help us find whoever attacked the others. I don't have to remind you we have two dead people on our hands.' She glanced around to ensure no one was listening, the waitress conveniently now on her way over to take our order.

Alice was right, but something told me Jack was far more involved than I wanted to admit, the idea of expressing it aloud too much for my inferior brain to deal with.

'What aren't you telling me?' Alice narrowed her eyes again, realising there were more revelations to come.

I swallowed something uncomfortable. Whatever it was didn't taste very nice. I needed to change the subject before I said something I'd regret, opening my mouth before realising I was just about to.

'Why don't you come over to my place tomorrow evening?' I found myself blurting towards her. 'I'll cook us dinner, get a nice bottle of wine. I promise I will explain everything about Jack then. Just don't mention this to Paul. Not yet. *Please.*'

'Newton Flanigan, are you asking me on a date?' Alice looked momentarily surprised, a sliver of a smile curling the corners of her beautiful mouth. Her cheeks were flushed. I concluded it was the heat. My imagination.

I nodded.

'If you like?' I shrugged, attempting to appear casual, my facial muscles almost as tight now as Jack's. To be honest, I fully expected her to blow me out, say no, laugh.

'What can I get you?' the waitress asked, cutting across our private conversation, a disinterested look on her face confirming she hadn't been listening, didn't care about my obvious embarrassment.

Alice kept her eyes firmly on me while she ordered two cappuccinos and a chocolate brownie, an extra scoop of ice cream, two spoons. She waited until the waitress had walked away before answering, her lips parting as her mouth turned knowingly into a grin. Her surprise did not go unnoticed, despite no longer being able to look at her. She was deliberately making me squirm.

'Okay, you're on. But on *one* condition.'

'*What?*' I glanced her way briefly, noticing the glint in her eyes before pretending to read the menu to distract myself, peeling the edges with my fingertips because I could think of nothing else to do. I might have been holding my breath.

'Cook something not reheated from a tin and if you *don't* explain everything you know about this student of yours and why you don't want Paul to know about his involvement just yet, I'll go straight to him so you can explain it directly.'

I glanced her way, grinned. Yet, it was from sheer embarrassment, nothing more, wholly failing to disguise my shock. I was a reasonably good cook when the moment called for it, although aside from my sister-in-law, my ex-wife, and a couple of fleeting girlfriends, very few people knew. It wasn't my fault the moment rarely called for anything these days other than a microwave and the coffee I drank to excess. I was a simple man. Easy to please. I didn't mention that, either. Instead, I made my excuses and took a slow walk across town to retrieve my car, turning down Alice's offer to drive me because I wanted some air. Christ knows I needed it.

Thirty-Six

Newton

The first thing I did when I got home was discharge the contents of my stomach into the kitchen sink because there was no way I was making it to the bathroom. I was unsure if it was because of Jack, asking Alice on a *date,* or what I now knew was coming for him causing my stomach to launch, but it wasn't holding back. By the time I was able to draw breath again, the day was already at an end. I barely made it into my bedroom, sitting on the bed with my hands over my face in a vague attempt to stop the room from spinning.

I was glad Alice had at least agreed to my dinner request, my impulsive outburst more "spur of the moment" than "planned invitation". I needed to change the subject, that's all, deter the moment, more time required to work out what I was going to do. Besides, I *never* would have been brave enough to ask her of my own volition, no matter how often I'd thought about getting to know her on a personal level. It wasn't as if I was terrible with women. I just hadn't had many good experiences with them, had never quite surpassed my own impossible failings. Tomorrow's date could kill two birds, so to speak, my impromptu outburst something I would have never managed under normal circumstances. I wanted to explain what I knew about Jack, *needed* to share my thoughts. I knew she would understand. Eventually.

I ventured into the dimming evening light, grateful the earlier rainclouds had passed. I needed to get out of this place for a while, needed some air, a chance to speak with Jack, if I could, ask him what on earth was going on. I'd only have to take one look at his face to confirm my ill-considered fears, my ill-timed accusation. I hoped he would forgive me. I didn't take my car, choosing instead to walk along the canal, this time of day perfect for reflection. Walking always cleared my head, helped me process ideas, muse over impossible considerations. I pulled my mobile from my pocket but changed my mind. What would I even say to him?

Were you on that bus, Jack? Did you attack Ben Harris? Did you kill Alex Jefferson? Oh, yeah, and where WERE you last night? Were you down by the canal? Did you attack the Malkin's, too?

By the time I arrived at the house, I was ready to change my mind, avoid the confrontation entirely and allow the police to deal with this in their own way. I'd been with him earlier, for Christ's sake, at the hospital, the poor kid undergoing *chemotherapy*. He looked vulnerable, terrified. The last thing he needed was my interference or my unfounded accusations. I hovered on the driveway, unsure what to do, unconvinced I had this right. Yet, I was here now and if all else failed I could merely say hi and leave. I didn't have to stay long, didn't have to trigger unwanted drama for the family.

There is an old saying going something along the lines of "you never really know what you've got until it's gone" and with Jack the meaning was unmistakable. He was never part of the crowd, always standing out in his own unique way, his interpretation of the world something I found inspiring. However, since losing his ability to speak, he seemed lost, as if something inside him had already died. Yes, I noticed the sideways glances others gave him when they assumed no one could see, the whispers they shared when they believed no one could hear. But I should have realised something was amiss, should have seen this coming. Life can be cruel, the people in it fickle.

I held my breath as I knocked a clenched fist against his front door, the sound of Star's barking elevating my nerves. I felt sick again, unsure what I was about to begin, unconvinced I should even *be* here.

When the door opened, it was Lizzy's smiling face greeting me, Jack's sister the one person in all this who had been seriously forgotten. Her long hair was hanging loosely around her tiny shoulders, headphones draped around her neck, distant music fizzing from within. She looked innocent, sweet.

'Mum's not in at the moment,' she stated flatly, automatically stepping in front of Star who was now desperately trying to get to me.

I hesitated, wondering how it would look if I asked to see her twenty-year-old brother, if I could come in for a coffee. I was old enough to be his dad, old enough to know better.

'Is she with Jack?' I asked instead, keeping my tone casual, the smile I offered fake, oddly wrong.

She nodded. 'Yeah. He wasn't feeling too well after his chemo session, so she's taken him to see the doc. Do you want to come in and wait for her?'

I wanted to ask if he was okay, if there was anything I could do to help, but instead I found myself shaking my head. 'No, thank you. Tell her I called round. I hope your brother is all right. Tell her I asked after him.' I nodded, turning to leave, leaving Lizzy none the wiser as to my intentions.

***

I found myself ambling along a well-used path that would have led to the beach if I'd walked far enough, an overwhelming urge to scream into the air emerging from nowhere. I was thinking about my brother now, how he died before his time, life little more than a collection of days destined to end us *all* at some point. I pondered as I walked, mulling over life, death, lingering too long over the fact I would never get to know the *real* Jack Monroe. Was a cruel twist of fate destined to send him to his grave a sad and bitter young man, twisted into something he wasn't?

I glanced around. This location aptly fitted the way Jack's life was destined to go, brambles and bracken twisting around delicate wildflowers, strangling their growth, suffocating their survival. I closed my eyes, trying to recall a time in *my* life when I felt at peace, poor Jack too young to think about death. It was ironic. How many of us think about mortality until faced directly by it?

I stood by a tree and sent him a message. If nothing else, I wanted him to know I was thinking of him.

Hope you're okay.

I pressed send, staring at three pathetic words on my screen that, in the scheme of things, meant nothing. Yet, it was the only thing I could think to say, everything else paling into insignificance. How could I question a dying boy about crimes he couldn't have committed? I thought about Anne Clarence, her confirmation about what could *only* have been Jack's appearance, his sticker-covered crutches, his dragon motif hooded top, the description Desmond gave of *his* attacker. I kicked a stone, trying to convince myself Jack must have lent someone his top while equally knowing he couldn't lend them his *face.*

By the time I got home, I was exhausted. Did I want food? No. Did I need food? Yes. Could I be bothered to make food? *Absolutely not.* I slumped onto my sofa, snippets of painful memories lodged in my brain, attempting and failing to push Jack to the back of my mind. I thought endlessly about people, the universe, the point of life, my first *official* date with Alice. I still couldn't believe I'd *asked* her to come here. I should be elated, should be jumping for joy.

As it was, the next few hours passed in a blur of self-created drama. I binned everything making my flat look untidy, which as it turned out, was quite a lot, searching online for the perfect recipe to aid my culinary mission before eventually settling on a chilli. Chilli was easy, I didn't have to overthink it, and everyone loves chilli, don't they? Coupled with a salad, I wouldn't have to overthink our evening either. I then called Paul, my curiosity too much, hoping Alice had kept her end of the bargain. I was glad when he responded with genuine surprise, the tone in his voice prompting all-out excitement.

'You did *what?*'

'I asked her on a date?'

'No way. Shit, I honestly didn't think you had it in you.' Paul was openly shocked at my impulsive forwardness, his voice continually moving in and out because he was too busy laughing.

'Ha ha, yes, very funny.'

'How on earth did *that* happen?'

I appreciated why Paul was asking, but I couldn't tell him it was my way of deferring something I didn't wish to speak to the police about until I had it straight in my head, until I'd spoken to Jack. I felt bad, knowing how much I liked Alice, only asking her on a date to throw her off the scent of something I couldn't yet ascertain. I was grateful she hadn't mentioned anything of value to Paul. Alice was discreet. I knew she would keep her word. She was good like that.

'I thought you'd be pleased. You can stop chiding me now.' I rolled my eyes.

Paul had been goading me for over a year about Alice, including my obvious lack of confidence when it came to women. Alice was a good listener, a good friend. But so was Paul. I felt bad they were both currently in the dark about something *so* important, usually the first to express my theories, my ideas. I was usually right. This dinner was my way of sharing my thoughts on a sensitive matter I wasn't certain existed, the idea of getting Alice alone for longer than a passing moment, still too much to consider. Jack was *innocent.* I was sure of it. I just needed time to prove it.

'I'm glad for you. I hope it works out. You deserve it, Newt.'

Paul was usually the first to crack a joke at my expense, especially when it came to my non-existent love life. However, he sounded subdued, unusually quiet. There was something was on his mind, something he wasn't sharing.

'Are *you* okay?' I couldn't help asking. He sounded sad, deflated. I couldn't tell why.

'Oh, don't you go worrying about me,' he scoffed, throwing off my genuine query with a statement I didn't believe for one second.

Now I *knew* something was off.

'Paul?'

Paul fell silent, his cast-off words falling on deaf ears. 'Adele has gone to stay with her parents for a few days.'

Shit. I wasn't expecting that.

'Why?'

'She said I'm never home, that she never gets to see me anymore and when she does, I'm apparently not even there.'

She had a point. 'You *do* work a lot.'

'I'm a detective. It's my job.' I could tell Paul was frustrated, chewing the skin from his fingernails, clicking his tongue over his teeth, his stress levels higher than he was willing to acknowledge.

'Have you spoken to her?' It seemed logical he would want to speak to his wife.

'I will.'

'When? *Christmas?* One of the girl's birthdays?' My turn now to turn on the sarcasm.

'Thanks for that,' Paul muttered. I don't think I'd ever heard him sound so downtrodden.

'I just mean, if you don't fix this, you won't have a marriage left to stress over.' It was true. I'd seen it many times, plenty of broken relationships resulting in catastrophe, those I'd previously dealt with often ending up in hospitals, prison cells, or graves. I paused. 'Are the girls okay?'

'Yeah. Ashley says her mum is being overdramatic and Chloe is currently on holiday with her boyfriend so isn't aware of what's happening. She doesn't come back until next week and I'm hoping Adele will be home by then.' Chloe was eighteen going on thirty. Ashley was sixteen, both girls old enough for Paul to assume they were fine.

'Okay, so why don't you go and see her?'

'I just told you, she's at her parents?'

'So?'

'*So* they won't want me to speak to her.'

'How old is she? *Five?*'

Paul sighed loudly.

'Where do Adele's parents live?' The way Paul was behaving, it may have been on the other side of the world.

'Bridgechurch.'

I smiled. I couldn't help it. Sometimes things are just meant to be.

'Perfect.'

'How?' I could tell Paul had sat upright by the crack of his knees, the groan I would have otherwise mistaken for frustration.

'My cottage. It's perfect. Cook her something nice, tell her how you feel. Spend some time with your wife, Paul.' Christ knows he deserved it.

'The cottage you inherited?' Paul didn't sound impressed. I'd barely mentioned the place, had only been there once. Despite our alleged friendship, we rarely spoke of our personal lives.

'You haven't seen it. It's stunning.' It really was. 'Seriously, go and rekindle your relationship. The place is isolated so you won't be disturbed. I'll drop off the keys later.' For once, I felt I was doing something good, something positive. After the day I'd had, I needed this. I momentarily wondered if any holidaymakers were booked in, but didn't overthink it. I'd check later.

By the time we'd finished our conversation, Paul sounded mildly more positive for my efforts, thanking me in his own way for my support with a grunt I took as gratitude. I took a shower, shaved, momentarily considered a trip to the barbershop for a much-needed haircut before changing my mind. I pulled my best shirt from my wardrobe and hung it on the back of the door, an unconscious choice, done to ensure I understood my date with Alice was real. It didn't matter about my ulterior motives. I thought about being sick again but changed my mind. Now wasn't the time for such an indulgence.

Thirty-Seven

Jack

I harboured big dreams when I was younger, things I wanted to do, achievements I assumed I'd make. Yet, like everyone else, I always believed there was time. My reality now is very different, forced to live within the confines of what other people believe I should be doing, enduring unhelpful demands for however long they presume I can. I've never felt so alone in my entire life, my physical pain *nothing* compared to the emotional trauma I've encountered. Nobody truly understands what is happening to me, *their* silence forever weighing on my mind. I can't share my experiences, forced instead to remain hidden in the darkness. It matters little now, I guess. I just need to get through this thing. After today, I'm sure things will be all right. I am not a killer. I am Jack Monroe. Besides, if I were to show myself in all my unfounded glory, I would surely give myself away.

I don't know what Newton sees when he looks at me, but I'm glad he doesn't hate me, the one good thing left of the world I remember. I can't explain it, can't express why my mind has shifted in such a volatile way, but I no longer recognise who I am. Newton is my chance for something special, almost inconceivable to believe we might find what most already have. I've been given the opportunity to reclaim a little normality today, that's all, a chance to glimpse what life might have been, were things different. We have never discussed matters of the heart, he and I, and he doesn't yet know I'm gay. But, neither does he appreciate his potential to save my soul, no time left in my life for anything else. He holds my wellbeing in his hands, nothing so solid as what is set in stone.

I have ensured I'm dressed well today, spending a little too long in my bathroom, reminding myself briefly of the old Jack. The Jack who would spray himself liberally with deodorant and aftershave, who would sing in the shower, ensuring his hair was on point, his clothing on-trend. I began shaving a while ago but between the accident, chemotherapy, and my savage mistreatment, looking in a mirror is the last thing on my mind. Any potential stubble has been hindered by scars and toxic chemicals, the hair on my head wispy, ugly. *Like me.* I've shaved my head this morning, my hooded top no longer offering the image I was never really going for in the first place.

My mother is wondering why I'm making all this effort, shocked when I emerge smartly dressed and smelling of Newton, our taste in aftershave oddly the same, my features on full uncensored display. I dare not tell her about my date. She wouldn't approve. Yet, the only thing I care about right now is providing Newton with a good impression, to show him the person I *want* to be, the person I still am on the inside. It's already too late for a first impression. My mother queries what I'm up to, a smile on her lips she can't control. I can't say, even if I could explain. Instead, I leave the house with my heart in my throat, a crumpled packet of biscuits in my pocket, my wounds exposed for the first time in months. I can't allow external judgment to cloud my thoughts, can't allow anger to control me. This day is far too important.

Billy's Bar is not far from my house, luckily, a simple walk seeing me arrive early, an empty table in the corner easily able to hide me until my guest arrives. We said twelve-thirty. It is only a quarter past. I order a hot chocolate using a piece of paper I've pre-scribbled my requirements on, planning ahead as always, requesting they bring Newton's coffee when he arrives. He won't appreciate cold coffee. The waitress is all smiles until she sees my face, barely able to contain her shock. I nod my acknowledgement, in a good mood despite everything, things about to change for the better. I sip warm chocolatey liquid through a straw, keeping one eye on the door and the other on my surroundings, the last few pages of my diary tucked safely in my pocket. I hope Newton will appreciate the effort I've made, the precious contents I carry.

Ten minutes pass, then twenty. Newton is now precisely five minutes late. I need to calm down, take a breath, panic hardly a good look on me. Besides, nothing good ever comes from heightened emotions. It has taken everything I have to venture into the world like this, exposed, no hooded top to provide the shield I've sadly become heavily reliant upon, no crimson lipstick to shame others into submission. *Nothing* is hidden, this day seeing me coming out openly as a proud gay man. I swallow, panic rising in my chest for what I'm about to do, glancing towards the door every time it opens. I consider sending him a message but it would look desperate, so I hang on for a further ten minutes, the feeling I've been stood up rising rapidly in my chest.

If he has changed his mind, I honestly don't know what I'll do, nothing able to calm the mood such a gross misdemeanour would provoke. The waitress comes to my table and asks if everything is okay. She can barely look at my face, instead pretends to be distracted by the pad in her hand, her pen, her hair, other people. I nod, glancing towards the floor, then the door, wishing Newton would hurry up and save me from this misery. At one o'clock, I know something is wrong so I send him a message, a disgruntled one, hovering nervously outside the doorway and wondering what has happened. Newton is a good man. He would *not* stand me up. At least, not deliberately. Maybe his car has broken down. He certainly complains about it enough. Maybe the police have taken his attention, taken him to a crime scene they believe more important than me. Even so, he *would* have messaged me, called to explain his absence. At least I would know why he's late. I glance nervously along the street, glad he can't see my tainted thoughts. I have a connection to the man, that's all, not a stalker mentality.

I reluctantly return to my table, ignoring the strangers

who stare my way and the continued rustle in my pocket from chocolate biscuits melting steadily, the urge to scream into the air painfully strong. My aim is to wait as patiently as I can, avoid the conflict, their hatred, my wrath. But I have barely sat down before my nerves get the better of me, this place suddenly too hot and unfriendly. I clamber into the lunchtime air, my half-consumed drink left on the table and the staff a little confused. Staring at my mobile is not helping and neither is the breeze continually buffing my body, leaving me exposed, vulnerable, weak. Until now, I've been in a good mood, a *great* mood, the best I've felt in a while—a real effort made on my appearance to ensure I don't embarrass anyone. Now, I feel every eye upon me, everything I am on painful, ugly display; a rat in a glass box, a freak.

I stumble along the street in an attempt to look as if I know what I'm doing, not exactly heading anywhere in particular, not wanting to venture too far. I still believe he will race around the corner at any moment, full of apologies, his hair blowing wildly, his cheeks flushed pink. Yet the further I walk, the more I realise how alone I am, no one coming to my aid. I message him again, my words as irritated as I feel.

Where the HELL are you?

Nothing, just a blank screen mocking me.

With no other option, I begin the arduous journey to his flat. If I must sit on his steps all afternoon, I *will*. I still have his spare key in my possession. Maybe I will let myself inside, giving him no choice then but to explain himself. I'm subjected to many sneers, the outside world as frightening today as it ever was, car horns showcasing disdained disgust, horrified mothers pulling children out of my reach. In all fairness, it might be my frustration they can see, my body language hardly rational as I stomp my crutches along the pavement, my facial muscles tight, my expression unforgiving. As much as I want there to be a rational explanation, a simple reason, something tells me I've been rejected, stood up, let down, the one person in this world who I thought cared about me, seemingly equally capable of *vile* abandon.

This is not how I saw today going, not how things were meant to be. The only thing I need is my professor's unwavering company and the strong smell of coffee forever following him around. By the time I get to his flat, I'm out of breath, my uncertain legs throbbing, my nerves worse than anything I imagined my confession of love and murder might be. From the tightness in my face to the way I'm wringing my hands together in a knot of painful extremities, I know how horrific I must look.

I take a breath and nod slowly, more to myself than anyone else, no one here now to witness my wrath, thank Goodness, *nothing* coming close to the way I feel. I feel sick, chewing my lip, knowing I can provide Newton far more than the frustrated grunts he has grown accustomed. If he let me. He doesn't yet know I've been practising my speech, a therapist providing several semi-successful sessions over the last couple of weeks. It was my secret, hoping to share important words in public I've been forced to relearn in private, hoping to say things aloud today I can barely contain in my head. If nothing else, I need to confront him, devastated my *best friend* has hurt me like this. He is no better than the rest, it seems. How dare he behave so cruelly?

I stumble down his weed-ridden steps, his front door key in hand, wanting to chastise him for his failings, my heartbeat pulsating in my throat. I am forced to hold onto the wall so I don't fall and create more problems, glancing casually through his lounge window, reeling immediately at the vision staring back. I can't see clearly but I *can* see a bottle of wine, two glasses, the smell of strong perfume and music drifting from his open window.

You have GOT to be kidding me.

Surely Newton is *not* entertaining someone else? I narrow my eyes, noticing a fleeting movement inside as I catch a glimpse of a female figure through the glass. Dressed like a tart, her curled hair falls across her bare shoulders as if she believes she might somehow attract *my* man's attention, her gloss-coated lips making her look cheap. I don't see Newton. The woman is laughing, probably at some joke he's telling her. From where I don't know, but she's on her mobile phone, I think, something about dying of thirst while she waits. How dare he put the need of some female ahead of me? I'm beyond distraught, so close to tears it is fast becoming a physical pain, nothing left now but to show my true identity and express the agony he has savagely thrust upon me.

I take those biscuits from my pocket and slam them on the ground, stamping on them twice, my frustration aimed the wrong way. If all else fails, Newton Flanigan *will* see the real Jack Monroe today.

Thirty-Eight

Newton

When Alice called to confirm she wasn't able to make our dinner arrangement as planned, I was tidying my flat. My heart lunged, the idea of her changing her mind oddly not something I'd considered. I felt rejected, not something I wanted to admit. Luckily, I didn't have to worry, her reason merely a forgotten prior arrangement she'd made with her mum. She asked if we could change our dinner to lunch instead. *Yes.* Yes, we could. I think I might have punched the air, sighing with relief into my phone.

Lunch would be less formal anyway and therefore induce fewer expectations. It should have helped my nerves, eased my anticipation, but I still managed to spend an hour racing around like a fool, double-checking ingredients for a simple meal I was now unconvinced I could cook. She arrived on time, exactly one o'clock, yet I wouldn't expect anything else, forever in awe of Alice's perfection. She stood in my doorway looking and smelling amazing, her hair like something from a magazine. *Jesus.* I think I may have stared at her for a while. What was I *thinking?*

'Are you going to let me in or do I need to stand out here all afternoon?' Alice was smiling, rolling her eyes, licking her gloss-coated lips.

'Of course. Come in.' I stepped back, almost tripping over my clumsy size nines in the process, glancing around to ensure everything was as it should be. Like Alice, my flat now smelled pretty good, my chilli happily entertaining itself on the hob, a pre-prepared salad in the fridge. I had dug out my best plates, knives, forks, glasses. My dining table looked quite impressive. I'd even purchased a bottle of Bollinger, the attendant at the off-license assuring me it was a good brand for a date. I had no idea if Alice liked red or white wine, if she drank wine at *all.* To be honest, I was too nervous to ask.

I couldn't help watching her bottom as she floated through my front door, glancing my way before her smile forced me to look away. 'I didn't realise how nice your place was,' she confirmed, sounding surprised. I was too anxious to conclude if she was joking, too flustered to initiate banter. I *could* make an effort occasionally, if I tried.

I smiled back, hoping she hadn't noticed my anxiety, my thoughts hell-bent on laughing at my inferiority. 'I try.' It was the only thing I could think to say, knowing the effort taken to make my place look this good at such short notice. I assumed I had the whole afternoon to organise things, any other plans I might have arranged for the day now firmly cast aside. She was either being overly kind or genuinely liked it.

We headed into my lounge. At any other time of the year she would have been wearing a coat and I would have offered to take it, but as it was, she was wearing nothing but a summer dress hugging her figure in all the right places, her bare shoulders tanned, well-proportioned. I tried not to notice, tried not to stare at the sunlight glistening through the thin material, her bare legs going all the way up to her—

'Are you okay?' Alice's question jolted me from my ridiculous deliberations, back to this impossible moment. She was staring at me, staring at her, thinking things I shouldn't.

'Sorry, yes, of course.' I sounded like an idiot. Who was I kidding? I *was* an idiot, an idiot to believe someone like Alice would ever look twice at me. Yet, here she was, in my flat, waiting for attention I wasn't sure I could give. I could hear Stephanie's advice. *Keep calm, keep cool and, for God's sake, keep your mouth shut.*

I reached for the wine I'd earlier placed on the dining table, the bottle already warm despite being in the fridge all morning.

'Bollinger Champagne. I'm impressed.' Alice nodded towards the bottle in my hand, a cheeky smile on her lips.

Champagne? Jesus, that explained the price tag. No wonder the off-license attendant was keen to sell me a bottle. When I peeled off the foil to expose a cork, reality came back to bite me. *Shit.* I glanced towards Alice who had already settled herself on my sofa, my expression blank, my thoughts disappearing into a whirlwind of nothing. Despite the effort I'd gone to, I'd forgotten to buy the one thing I needed, the one thing I didn't own. A corkscrew. Posh wine was not something I *ever* kept in my flat. I was not a big drinker, only ever drank coffee.

Alice noticed the horrified look on my face and burst into unapologetic laughter. 'Seriously?' She knew me well, knew my life was usually far simpler. I was happy with a takeout meal, a jar of coffee, my existence boring, predictable, easy.

'Sorry. I forgot.'

'I can go and get one if you like?' Alice rose to her feet, ready to head out of the door. She was still smiling, at least, her eyes glimmering with potential fondness for the bumbling twat standing in front of her.

'No, it's okay, I'll go.' The last thing I wanted was for Alice to leave. She might not come back.

It was embarrassing, but I asked her to keep an eye on our lunch so it wouldn't burn, heading into the lunchtime air to source the one thing I hadn't even considered. She called me before I'd made it twenty feet along the street, my ringing mobile mocking my every movement.

'Am I supposed to be stirring this sauce?' She was laughing. I imagined her in my kitchen, barefoot, flush-cheeked, her mobile phone balanced under her chin. If I owned an apron, I imagined her wearing that too, naked beneath, my *dessert* awaiting attention.

'Turn it onto simmer, and yes, thank you. I'm so sorry.' I was mortified, the only time I'd asked Alice to sample my culinary delights and I'd left her to manage it. I'd left the pre-prepared salad in the fridge, the chilli blipping away on the stove. I thought I'd done well. What a fool.

'Well, at least I get to nose around your flat while you're gone,' she chided. I couldn't see her but knew she was still smiling, her tone light, amused.

I stopped mid-walk, wondering if she was serious, thinking about everything I'd hastily stuffed inside cupboards and under my bed. I wasn't sure if I liked the idea of Alice snooping around my bedroom, glad I'd scrubbed the bathroom top to toe. I couldn't even remember if I'd put my pants in the laundry basket.

'Help yourself,' I replied instead, hoping she was joking, trying not to sound concerned either way. I felt bad she was alone, chastising my wayward memory as I walked towards the nearby corner shop.

'Hurry up, or I might die of thirst.' She was jesting, I know, making fun because that's what we did. We had both spent enough time with Paul to appreciate the banter, had known *me* long enough to understand that's what I expected. But, despite my underhand reasons, I honestly wanted today to be special. Was this too much to ask?

'I've got this, Newt. Don't be long.' She rang off, leaving me jogging along the street, out of breath by the time I reached the shop, stressed, hot, annoyed. It wasn't the look I was going for, not the image I wanted Alice to remember. A lengthy queue forced me to wait for what felt like an eternity, only locating a corkscrew when a staff member directed me to the right shelf. I began overthinking everything, my appearance, my hair, wondering if my clothes were good enough for the likes of Alice Baker. She was a great dresser, a good-looking girl, never a hair out of place. Even when questioning potential suspects or calming terrified victims, Alice was always perfect. At least, as far as I was concerned.

I messaged her twice to apologise, receiving a "not a problem" response and wondering if she meant it. When I noticed two missed text messages from Jack, I could have kicked myself in the face.

Today was Friday, the day I was meant to be meeting him at Billy's for a coffee and a chat I got the distinct impression he needed more than I did. The poor kid would think I'd stood him up, unconcerned by his needs until now. I had, I guess, too busy thinking of my non-existent love life to give him a moment's thought. I took a breath and dialled his number, knowing my words would not yield any response but needing to explain myself anyway, express why I'd stood him up. I didn't mean to forget. I had no idea what kind of excuse I would provide.

His phone went to voicemail so I left him a message, blurting out I was an idiot and that work had once again taken over my morning. I hoped he was okay. It was only a white lie and a white lie was better than the truth. I must have apologised several times before I hung up, cursing when I did and forcing a young woman to glare sideways my way. I apologised to her too and silently cursed the queue.

Thirty-Nine

Jack

My anger ensures I fail to notice the missed call from Newton, his *pathetic*, apologetically weak voice slamming against my ears like a sledgehammer. He is *very* sorry he missed our coffee date, apparently. Something important came up at work he could not get out of. I scoff, knowing he's lying, his rushed words making things worse, a pulsating drum at the base of my skull confirming my growing frustration. I know *exactly* what he can't get out of, knowing full well what he wants to get into. I genuinely believed we had a connection, he and I, a trust no one understood. Now, I don't know what to believe. I fight tears threatening to drown me where I stand, blinding me to a truth I don't wish to confront—the actions I must take now, not something Newton will appreciate.

I peer angrily through his lounge window, keeping low,

out of sight. The female has fallen silent which probably means she is no longer speaking to him, his attention no longer on her. I still don't know where he is but I try not to overthink my choices as I creep along the side of his property, down a narrow alleyway, my crutches cushioned silently underfoot. I unclick the latch of his dilapidated rear gate, the thing never locked, thankfully, finding myself in Newton's courtyard, an area potentially passing for a garden, if he tried. I can tell he rarely comes out here other than to discard his rubbish, ironically my turn now to do the same.

I keep low, hiding behind a fly-invested wheelie bin, trying not to gag at the stench of rotting food, glaring with frustration through his kitchen window. The female is inside, stirring a saucepan, bringing a spoon to her mouth every few seconds to taste the mixture, adding something from a container that, from this position is hard to see. She has her back to me, does not notice me watching.

My heart is in my throat as I creep through the open back door, knowing it won't take much to alert her to my presence, glad I haven't needed to use Newton's spare key. Soft piano music is playing in the background, keeping her entertained, her annoying humming something I find most irritating. There is a strong smell of chilli in the air, blending with unfamiliar perfume making me feel sick. Hers, no doubt. I creep up behind her, silent, swift, determined.

To be honest, the way I feel now, I don't care if she turns around and sees me, nothing good coming her way. I'm about to change the status quo, about to change her day. Without hesitation, I grab her around the throat, the unexpected motion taking us both by surprise. The spoon drops to the floor with a clatter, my response almost humorous when she yelps in shock. I place a hand over her mouth, dragging her backwards, pulling her unceremoniously off her feet. She can't scream, can't call for help.

We are on the floor now, struggling against each other as I muffle her screams beneath my outstretched palm, my intention to knock her out, if I can, nothing on my mind aside from revenge I'll shortly serve cold. Newton needs to pay for what he's done, needs to appreciate how his decisions have consequences. I was prepared to bare all today, bare my soul, explain my feelings with honesty. Now, because of his deception, I no longer have such an option. I already know in my heart if *I* can't have him, no one will.

I'm knowledgeable in the art of karate, yet aside from my family, very few people know. I don't attend the classes anymore, of course. For obvious, untenable reasons. But I haven't forgotten the training. A single sharp chop to her carotid artery sees this creature fall under my unwitting control, my next move not yet fully considered. The temporary sedation is more stun than knockout. I don't want to kill her. Not yet. Not unless I have to. And, should that time arrive, there will be no hesitation. Believe me.

I ensure Newton is not in some other room, unaware of my actions and this unfolding event before searching drawers and cupboards, unconcerned by the mess I'm making, swiping his carefully placed plates and glasses over the floor. By the time I return to the kitchen, I have rope and a pair of socks I fashion into a gag, tying this wretch up, shutting her pouting mouth, her continuous groans confirming nothing good.

Although a slim-built woman, she is still heavy and I'm forced to drag her through the open kitchen door, unconcerned by her torn dress, the bruising to her hands, her legs, her ruffled hair. I need my crutches to walk with, unable to get far without them. Yet, adrenaline has oddly taken over, seemingly enough to ensure my increased strength, allowing me temporary access to the man I *should* have already become.

Newton's car key is on a hook in the kitchen and I grab it, no other way to get this whore away from here than in the boot of his car. I hastily check the street to ensure no one can see us before manoeuvring her body towards it. She is beginning to protest beneath her gag, already awake, shocked by what is happening, a graze on her head where she fell. She is struggling so I punch her hard in the face, my fist connecting violently with her jaw. She falls silent, her heavy breath enough to ease mine. However, Newton's car boot is too high for me to lift her body into, my own too weak despite my best efforts, so I'm forced to manhandle her onto the back seat instead, unconcerned she might break an arm, a leg, her *neck*.

I love the solace of my aunt's basement but there is only one place I can think to go, one place in this world where I can gather my thoughts and consider my next impossible move. Although I have been there only once, it seems a fitting location somehow, somewhere I might express my emotions, explain things to Newton, if he will listen. I'll send him a message later. Once we are settled. Once I have calmed down.

I feel sick, far from stable, far from any reality I assumed today would bring. It's lucky I know how to drive although I never passed my test, did not get the chance, always assuming there was time for that, too. I drive hastily away from Newton's home, unconcerned by the mess I've now left him, my chosen destination the only place that matters. I need to think, to work out what I'm going to say when I see him, what I plan to do to this bitch while I wait.

I keep one eye open for the police and another on the stranger in the backseat, knowing I'm making a mistake, yet unable to do a thing about that. She is motionless, at least, her pretty head lolling to one side, her arms tied behind her back, her mouth gagged—wholly at my mercy. If I could punch her again, I would, but I'm too busy driving so instead I glare loathingly from the rear-view mirror, wishing Newton had not brought me to this. I'm thankful the cottage is located in a quiet village, this unassuming Friday afternoon seeing most of its residents elsewhere, hopefully too old or too ignorant to notice me.

I park as far from prying eyes as I can, past the house, along the narrow track running adjacent to the sea, ensuring Newton's old car is positioned behind the dilapidated boathouse I located previously. A fresh sea breeze catches my lungs, bringing tears to my eyes for what will *never* now be, recent memories still lingering, recalling another day here, a better day, one so very different to this. I waver. My previous so-called *victims* were kept within the safety of the town I grew up in, behind a wall I've unwittingly built.

Being here feels different. I don't know why.

I'm temporarily unconcerned by the contents on the back seat, only remembering my "package" when it wakes up and threatens to ruin my quiet contemplation. I yank open the rear passenger door, dragging the female to the ground by her hair, no consideration for her wellbeing or mine, my reality already in tatters. She attempts to fight back but can barely move. Despite everything, I'm still stronger than she is, stronger than most people realise, emotionally, if nothing else, my feelings driving my actions, my frustration driving me insane. I've lost count how many private hours I've spent fighting my injuries, my illness, my mind.

When the woman attempts to speak through her gag, I don't want to hear what she has to say, punching her again to ease my own frustration, nothing else to do. I can't bear her tone, her appearance, screaming into her bloodied face for the agony thrust upon mine, my troubled voice fractured, broken. Although I can barely form words in any coherent order, I can still form sound, the one I make now wholly unappreciated by the confused look she gives me. I'm crying unapologetically, tears streaming down my cheeks, snot dripping from my reddened nose, glimpses of teeth exposed through a wound that will never have time to heal.

She doesn't appreciate what she has done, her fault I'm forced to drag her roughly along a rocky path towards the boathouse, unconcerned when she falls, her bound hands unable to prevent the sound her head makes as it hits the stony ground beneath. Then there is silence, nothing other than a bracing wind to catch my attention, a seagull in the distance, the rustle of nearby trees.

Forty

Newton

I headed into some much-needed fresh air after an unprecedented wait in line saw me tapping my foot, chewing my lip, cursing my feigned stupidity. Our lunch was threatening to burn in my absence, Alice certain to leave if I took much longer. I jogged along the street, hot, flustered, keen to get home, needing to apologise and terrified my first impression had been left somewhat wanting. I still hadn't mentioned Jack, hadn't explained what I didn't yet want to address. There was an unopened packet of chocolate biscuits lying next to my steps, the pack half flattened as if someone had stamped on it.

'I'm back,' I called into my empty hallway, half laughing, half kicking my shoes into a corner. It took a moment for me to register the strong smell of burning, racing into the kitchen to find an unattended saucepan, the contents ruined, smoke already reaching the ceiling. I turned off the heat, cursing myself and my forgetfulness, momentarily wondering where Alice was. Surely she wouldn't leave the pan to burn dry? Surely she wasn't that insensitive?

'Alice?' I called out, expecting her to be in the toilet or the lounge, noticing a discarded spoon on the floor, chilli sauce splashed against my cupboard doors. A gnawing sensation tugged at my gut, along with a growing concern I couldn't place. Something felt wrong. I didn't know what. It took a moment to register the mess, the crockery I'd earlier laid on my dining table smashed over the floor, nothing of my carefully prepared lunch remaining. The bathroom door was open, no sign of Alice anywhere.

'*Alice?*' I yelled, sounding panicked. I did not for one second assume she had anything to do with the mess, yet I oddly didn't expect her to answer. The kitchen door was open so I headed outside, my forgotten rear courtyard used only by rats and the milkman. I wasn't expecting my gate to be open either, a discarded item unexpectedly catching my attention. Alice's shoe.

Confused, I picked it up and headed out into the street, my heart in my throat, wondering what had happened, where she was, and if my growing panic was justified. I called her name again, my wavering tone echoing violently as I scanned the pavement. Yet, Clarington Avenue was empty now aside from a dog walker some distance away. He was picking up poo, his hand deep inside a plastic bag, his attention elsewhere. Then I noticed something else. My car was missing.

The first thing I did was call Alice's mobile, mine trembling in my grasp, the soft tone unbearable. I was in the street, in my socks, confused, wondering why she'd take my car when she had her own, unsure why she would leave her *shoe*. A moment of hysteria arose as I registered the sound of a ringing mobile close by. I glanced around, wondering if, by some cruel twist of fate, someone else had the same one, yet there was no one here but me, the dog walker already gone. The sound continued as I headed back inside, Alice's ringtone becoming louder with each uncertain step I took. I found her phone in her bag where she'd left it, along with her purse, her keys, her lipstick.

I couldn't think, nothing of the last thirty minutes registering with my overanalysed considerations, my rational thoughts replaced by fear. I took a step back, leaning against my hallway wall for support I knew it wouldn't offer, wondering what to do next. Alice had left in a hurry, by the looks of it, leaving our lunch to burn, to potentially start a fire. She wouldn't do such a thing knowingly. Yet, neither would she leave her shoe by my gate. None of this made sense. Even if, by some weird coincidence she'd been forced to leave abruptly, she would have taken her own car, not mine. She wouldn't leave her phone or handbag. I'm fairly sure she would have told me she was leaving.

I glared at her discarded shoe, the truth hitting me harder than anticipated, my legs suddenly numb. She hadn't left of her own accord. I was about to dial Paul's number when I remembered my apparent well-planned mission to save his marriage. If my good deed had worked, he would be with his wife at my cottage, his phone turned off, my suggestion to take a few well-needed hours for himself something I now regretted. I cursed, no other choice but to call Tony, hoping he would come to my aid instead.

'Has Alice stood you up already?' He was laughing, trying not to snort down the phone, his joke only meant in jest.

'Something's happened.' I wasn't sure what, wasn't confident I knew what to do. I could barely think, could scarcely hold my legs in place.

'Christ, what did you do *now*?'

My throat was tight, my heart pounding like a drum in my head. I didn't do anything. 'Shut up and listen,' I snapped, unappreciative of his snippy tone and constant bad attitude towards me. Now was not the time for games.

'Okay, you're worrying me. What's up?' Tony was no longer laughing, no longer mocking my spontaneous date with DS Alice Baker.

'Alice is gone.'

'Gone?'

'As in, not here.' I was trying not to panic, trying to keep my hands steady in a fumbled attempt to hold my phone against my ear.

'I take it the date didn't go well?' I'm sure I heard Tony sigh, his relief unfounded, his unrequired laughter muffled.

'No. I mean, yes, it was going fine. I think.' Right now, I didn't honestly know what to think.

'Newt, you're not making sense.'

I know, and this conversation wasn't helping. I tried to calm down, attempting again to explain what had happened.

'I went out for a corkscrew and when I came back, Alice was gone.' I automatically looked around in case, by some ridiculous miracle, she was behind me, laughing, ready to confirm the joke I wasn't yet a part of.

Another laugh. 'So, she got bored of waiting. I can't say I'm surprised. Have you tried calling her?' I could tell he wasn't grasping this conversation, the seriousness of the situation floating in the air like poison, mocking me, judging. What did he mean, he wasn't surprised?

'No. Tony, you're not getting my meaning. She's *gone*. I think someone might have taken her.'

'*What?* What the hell are you talking about? What do you mean, *taken?*'

I shook my head, glad at least I now had his full attention.

'Her mobile and handbag are still here, as is her car, but my kitchen and lounge look as if they've been ransacked and I found one of her shoes by my back gate. *My* car is gone. Why would any of this happen unless her leaving wasn't by choice?' I automatically glanced towards a key holder on the wall, my car key no longer where it should be, the spare flat key missing, too.

'Jesus Christ.' I could hear Tony grabbing things, his radio, his keys, calling out to several nearby colleagues. 'Stay there. I'm on my way.'

His tone was finally serious. I didn't know whether to be relieved or throw up. I wracked my brain to figure out what I'd missed, what I could have done differently, what events I was currently incapable of concluding.

Jack.

This was all about Jack. Always had been. I hadn't noticed, hadn't given him a second thought. I'd sent him a weak, desperately pathetic message, forced to *lie* in order to save my own skin, to save a date I'd made in some ridiculous attempt to help him. I'd given our coffee meeting little consideration, had made Alice my priority.

I closed my eyes, registering the irony, trying to think back to the last time we'd spoken, to the last time I'd seen him. I'd stood him up, two disgruntled messages on my phone proof of his frustration. I'd made him feel unwanted. I tried to tell myself it was a simple mistake, but Jack wouldn't have seen it that way, the poor kid vulnerable. I thought about everything I currently knew, everything I'd not yet confirmed with the police. An unsavoury thought popped into my head of Jack coming to my flat and finding Alice here instead of *me*. His mind was fragile, his thoughts confused, enough going on in his life at the moment for him to take my absence as rejection.

There was evidence all around to confirm *someone* had been here; broken crockery, a broken plant pot, scuff marks by the door, remnants of chilli sauce no doubt leaving stains I'll never wash off. I attempted to retrace Alice's steps, following her potential movements, recalling our earlier conversation. She'd laughed, mocked my inability to remember a simple item I now had no idea what I'd done with.

When I found something else out of place, I almost didn't want it to be real, my eyes fixated on a discarded object in the corner of my lounge. I stepped forward, picking Jack's notebook from the floor. It looked as if it had been thrown across the room in temper. I turned it over and opened the cover, the truth right there for the taking. Tucked inside was an envelope addressed to me. I didn't dare contemplate what it said, no other explanation now needed as to what had happened here today. Jack never left home without this pad, had become heavily reliant upon it.

I'd withheld vital information from the police, had placed Alice in danger. I glanced around, my eyes focusing on nothing that made sense. I should have just told her what I knew, should *never* have triggered this moment. I fully suspected what Jack might have done, yet chose to keep quiet because I didn't want to believe it was possible.

Where did that leave me, and where the *hell* did it now leave Alice?

Forty-One

Jack

I love Newton Flanigan with everything I have, and he loves me. Of that, I'm certain. He has been my protector, my caregiver in a world often alien and wrong, the only one who understands my formidable existence. However, his once innocent and gentle affection has wavered, bringing about today's unfathomed torture. I desperately yearn for his touch, yet it is something I'm seemingly unfit to know, *his* fault things have come to this. Whoever this woman is, she is attractive, and I appreciate what Newton might see in her. It's a shame her hair and makeup are now ruined, bruises formed across her cheek where I hit her, clothing torn where she struggled. I have no idea who she is. All I know is she took Newton from me when I needed him the most, turned his head, his attention.

The boathouse would have made a perfect hiding place,

but because of this wretch's unconscious condition and my failing enthusiasm, I find myself unable to drag her body the twenty short feet to the run-down and weather-damaged building. It seems my earlier strength has failed me, my earlier wrath dispersing. I imagined us sitting beneath the missing roof watching the sky and trees peek through the wind-beaten beams, waiting for Newton, wishing for absolution. Instead, I sit on these rocks and wait impatiently for my guest to wake up, only a matter of time before he realises what I've done. I lean uncomfortably against cold stone, angry waves lapping against my body and hers, the tide already on its way in. She didn't complain when I pulled her from the car, did not cry out when she hit the ground. I'm unsure what I think about that, not even convinced I care.

I didn't expect to be placed in this position, did not assume today would go like *this*. Still, we are where we are, what is done is done. I lean towards her, methodical, careful, my companion too quiet, no protests to stave off my encroaching attention. I scoff. Even if she *does* wake up, she can't go anywhere. I anticipate the moment she attempts to free her binds, trying to speak through the gag pulled tight across her mouth.

The only thing I wanted today was to meet Newton, enjoy a coffee, go for a walk, weather permitting, tell him my truth. I visualised us walking along the canal together, or the beach, arm in arm, listening to the birds, a breeze against our skin, sharing the laughter I miss. In my head, we spoke about what mattered, using whatever means necessary to communicate, discussing the wildlife around us, the beauty and wonder of nature, life in general. *Us.*

He would have asked openly about my sexuality, I'm sure, about my inability to look people in the eyes for fear of what I might see. I would have explained what I fear the most, what I fear when Newton looks at me. His questions would have been kind, not pointed, not like everyone else's, his mind merely curious about the connection we share. And I would have been as honest as I could without frightening him away. He is, after all, amazing like that. He might have even shared a kiss.

This woman, whoever *she* is, has singlehandedly taken our moment from us, from me, ruining our date, ensuring I probably won't get a second chance now. There will be no walk along the canal to distract my hunger, no honest discussion about the things that matter. I always believed I could trust Newton, knowing he would protect me, no matter what. Now, I honestly don't know *what* to think, can't appease the deep burning inside.

I want to send him a message, explain my unprecedented actions and today's ruined plans, but I doubt his thoughts will be with *me* right now. I regard the woman in my company as I stare at her blood-soaked head, wondering who she is to him, stopping only when my hands reach her throat. Yet, she *still* does not move or attempt to recover her dignity, her unspoken words nothing but an assault on my overburdened ears. I reach into my pocket for my notebook, knowing Newton's envelope is inside, the last pages of my diary meant for his eyes only. For a moment, I don't understand why my hands feel nothing but the insides of my clothing, shocked to discover it's gone. I clamber to my feet, scanning the immediate area, only recalling what I did with it when my infected memories remind me.

'Aarrgh!!' I yell towards the unconscious woman, needing everything I have inside to scream against the bracing sea air, wanting her to acknowledge me, disgruntled when she does not move. I couldn't have predicted today's actions, didn't intend to do anything bad. I merely needed time to think, to bring things back under control. I'm not going to lie, the idea of killing her was strong in my thoughts for a while, a wild concept forming that once she's gone I get Newton to myself. Yet, my throat aches and my head hurts, the sound of my own strangled vocals making such considerations impossible. If I killed her, Newton would never understand. He wouldn't want to know me after that, I'm sure. I doubt he would want to be my friend. Would he see who I am or only what I've done?

If my recollection serves me correctly, I've now drilled the skulls of three people. I think. However, I've not exactly been keeping tabs, unable to witness the outcome of my work. I'm beginning to wonder if I've been in too much of a hurry, too stressed to take my time and therefore unable to do the job properly. I was interested in carpentry a few years ago, my aunt's basement subsequently filling with tools, off-cuts of wood, drills. Any other day, I would have taken this woman there, a drill to her head the perfect end to it all. But Aunt Ruth is due home today. And besides, I now feel more at home here.

The woman's hair is blowing in the breeze, her motionless body mocking me, her relationship to Newton something I will never understand, unfortunately. Yet, I can't see the rise of her chest, no heartbeat to comfort me when I need it. It's my imagination, I know, an impossible conclusion sent to ensure my unwitting downfall. It would be ironic if she was already dead, someone else's demise once again on my conscience. But this is *not* my intention, I promise. I stare at her for a while, unable to touch her for fear of what I might find, unable to conclude anything good.

'Argh!' I call out again, softer this time, my weakened voice snatched painfully on the breeze, fresh tears lingering.

But she still does not move. With trembling fingers, I move a piece of sand-covered hair from her face, unprepared for her blank expression, her wide eyes staring at nothing, her perfect lashes damp. I reel backwards. There is no life there now, only shock, horror, an unprecedented pain neither of us have expected to endure. I know she is dead even before my brain registers this truth, my own death advancing rapidly.

I stagger to my feet, my crutches no longer helpful, my legs crumpling against uneven rocks that graze my shin. Even the breeze has fallen silent. When childish tears begin to fall, they are ready to claim my reality, my life. I glance around, nowhere left to go, nothing left to do. I know full well what this means for me. I can't allow Newton to see the monster I've become, the person I could have been existing only in my darkest fantasy. If all else fails, at least I'll die knowing I made it out of my teens.

Newton once told me we only ever see things from our own perspective, our private world all we really have. I guess he was right. I glance at the female's pale features, wondering if she wasted her life as I did, wishing I knew when I awoke this morning what I sadly know *now*. I don't even know her name. I should have known better than to embark on a journey set to seal my fate and the fortunes of everyone I know. Yet, no matter how hard we try, none of us truly know what we are doing, burdened relentlessly by the confinements of our limited perceptions. There's no going back for me now. What is done is done. I guess I'm already dead.

Forty-Two

Newton

'What the *hell* is going on?' Tony yelled as he rushed through my open front door, flustered, out of breath, several officers behind him offering the same pained look. I wasn't ready for the intrusion, my thoughts and damaged possessions all over the place.

'I'm sorry.' There was nothing else for me to say. If I hadn't tried to protect Jack, none of this would have happened. Alice wouldn't now be in danger.

'I need you to tell me everything. Talk me through *exactly* what happened. When was the last time you saw her?' Tony was red-faced, clearly terrified something had happened to a highly regarded colleague. I didn't know if he'd told Paul, wasn't looking forward to the fallout when he did.

I shook my head, couldn't believe the day had shifted so

violently. 'I went out to get a corkscrew.' I was in a daze, my trip to the shop a seemingly simple task.

'And what else? *Think, Newton!*' Tony was already in my kitchen, several other officers searching my flat, gathering evidence, turning this day on its head. My home was now a crime scene instead of the romantic setting I'd intended. I handed someone Alice's shoe via an outstretched evidence bag. My fingerprints were on it. I didn't know if it mattered.

'I was meant to be having coffee with a friend, but Alice agreed to a lunch date and I lost track of time.' I was thinking about Jack, knowing I could no longer protect him from what was coming.

'What friend?'

I swallowed. 'He's a student, really.' Hardly a *friend*. I couldn't think, in my own world, in shock, the last image I had of Alice still vivid in my thoughts. I could still smell her perfume.

'What about him? What does your student friend have to do with Alice?' Tony grabbed my shoulders, bringing me back to the present moment, forcing me to look his way.

'His name is Jack Monroe.' I still couldn't believe he would be involved, despite the notebook in my possession and eyewitnesses to confirm otherwise. He didn't even know Alice.

'And what is so special about this Monroe kid?'

'He's been struggling. I've been trying to help him, *support* him.'

'And?'

'Okay, before I say anything else, *promise* you won't be angry?' I closed my eyes.

'Shit, what have you done?' I hated it when Tony looked at me the way he was now. Although he and I had never been friends, I respected him as a person, a police officer, an ally.

I had little choice but to explain our brief visit with Anne Clarence, what Desmond Malkin had confirmed, how I'd suspected Jack might have been involved, asking Alice to keep quiet on suspicions I had no right keeping to myself. I didn't mention Jack's vulnerabilities or my own stupidity.

'Okay, and why am I only hearing about this *now?*' Tony was still glaring at me. I swear if his eyes narrowed any further, he'd go blind. He glanced towards a nearby colleague who offered a non-committed shrug, his expression equally as blank. Detective Constable Noah Bates usually spent his days at the station, his job to follow up on important leads and investigate potential suspects. I assumed he was only here now because Alice wasn't, an extra pair of hands needed in Paul's absence.

'Because I *begged* Alice to keep it quiet until I could figure out a few things.'

'Jesus Christ. What the *hell* am I missing? Figure *what* out?'

I paused, unsure of my next words. 'I think Jack Monroe might be our drill attacker.' I still had Paul's ill-placed analogy in my head, *Black 'n' Decker* not a name I would be using anytime soon.

'Are you fucking *serious?*' A vein was pumping violently in the side of Tony's head. I tried not to stare. He was glaring at me as if I'd lost the plot. So was everyone else.

'He recently cut open the side of his face with a pair of scissors. Has a huge scar running from his mouth to his cheekbone. It still isn't healed. Probably won't.'

'Don't tell me this was the same incident you *begged* Paul to go to the other day?'

I nodded. 'Sorry.' I didn't mention how terrified I now was, Alice in serious trouble because of my actions. Jack's profile wasn't on any police file, his fingerprints and DNA not in the system. He wouldn't have been flagged on the police database. The poor kid had barely left the house since he came out of hospital, a death sentence over his head none of us wanted to acknowledge.

'You damned well will be if anything happens to that girl.' Tony shook his head, snatching his radio from his pocket, calling this in. 'Will Jack Monroe be at his house now?' Tony was serious. I felt sick. 'Newton?'

'I don't know.'

Tony glared at me before he stormed into the street, giving me no choice but to follow. I climbed into his car like a chastised child, beyond numb, my lunch date ruined, Alice *God* knows where, her parked car mocking me where it sat.

We drove to Jack's house in aggravated silence, Number Seven, Moreland Crescent suddenly an oppressive location. Tony's car was equipped with flashing lights and a screaming siren, his temper doing nothing for my fragile mood or bitten fingernails. I didn't assume Jack would be at home. He wasn't *that* stupid. But if anyone could shed light on where he might be, it would be his mum. I didn't know what Paul was going to say when he found out what had happened, his pre-arranged afternoon not the romantic occasion I'd anticipated.

'Professor Newton, hi. Is everything okay?' Rachel was far too calm, a casual hand on the doorframe, a dry smile on her lips. She looked as if she'd been drinking, an open bottle of wine on the kitchen table in the background, a strong smell of alcohol in the air. She wasn't initially concerned by my arrival until she noticed the police cars behind me, her driveway peppered now with unwanted activity and uninvited guests.

'Rachel, hi, do you know where Jack is? It's vital we find him.' I was out of breath, failing to remain calm, Tony's face beyond frustration.

'Why? What's wrong?' Rachel's smile slipped, her attention now fully caught.

'I can't say.'

'Newton, you're worrying me.' She motioned forward, wavered, changing her mind as she clung to the doorframe, hovering on unsteady feet in her hallway.

'Mrs Monroe, it's imperative we find your son,' Tony pitched in, his impatience uncontrollable, his face beet red.

A pause. She glanced at me, something passing across her bloodshot eyes I took as fear. 'Is he in trouble?'

I shook my head but it was a lie. Jack was in big trouble. 'Do you know where he is?'

'Well, if it was down to me, he would be in his room, safe. Yet, just lately he's been so distant. More so than usual.' I appreciated the melancholy tone of her voice, the pain in her eyes, the reason she was drinking in the afternoon. 'If he's not hanging around outside your place then he might be at his aunt's.'

'And where is that?' Tony again.

'Tolbert Street. Number Fifty.'

Tony looked at me. I knew what he was thinking. 'Does he go there often?' he asked, the contorted look on his face confirming his thoughts, knowing Tolbert Street was the location of the Ben Harris attack. He didn't say anything about that.

Rachel nodded. 'My sister Ruth spends a lot of time in London so she lets Jack use the house whenever he needs space.' She hung her head, her words slurred now, sounding genuinely worried she'd somehow contributed to her son's decline. 'Which is far too often these days, I'm afraid.'

It made sense. If Jack had taken Alice, he wouldn't want to be disturbed, wouldn't want to be out in the open. I felt sick thinking about it.

'Is your sister at home?' I was grateful for Tony and his logical questions, my brain seemingly unwilling to cooperate.

Another nod. 'She should be. Do you want me to call her?'

'No, thank you.' Tony stormed across the driveway, nothing else to add, leaving me staring blankly into space. He hadn't even said goodbye. Yet, I had nothing of interest to add either, so I conveyed my thanks to Rachel before climbing into Tony's car.

'Tolbert Street? Seriously?' Tony was shaking his head, glaring at me now as if he believed I'd been keeping secrets, was somehow involved.

'It might be a coincidence.' I didn't even know Jack *had* an aunt. Certainly didn't know she lived in Tolbert Street. It wasn't something I'd have kept quiet about.

'A coincidence? Really?'

I shook my head. No. It seems I didn't know Jack very well at all.

Tony made an unimpressive three-point turn on Rachel's driveway, his raging car almost as angry as him. If anyone was going to get hurt today, none of us wanted it to be Alice. I could barely comprehend the thought of her in danger, knowing I'd brought this on myself, brought this on her.

My head was throbbing, my heavy eyes littered with painful images that made little sense. I still hadn't told Tony I'd found Jack's notebook, oddly unwilling to divulge things I wasn't ready to accept. It was in my pocket, the thing staying there until I had more answers.

Ultimately, I saw it as my job to ensure Jack didn't become yet another statistic of this failing world, to protect him, if I could, from everything. I honestly don't know why. Maybe because I felt sorry for him. Responsible. Guilty. I knew the police would never see the kind, thoughtful boy he once was, only the brutal killer I wasn't even certain he'd become. I had no idea how to explain my thoughts aside from a profound knowledge I could never determine, Jack's emotions too raw, his true identity not yet disclosed.

Forty-Three

Newton

Ruth Miller's property was an unassuming average terraced house on an average Victorian street, several wheelie bins stacked against ageing brick walls, cars crammed like sardines against crumbling kerbs. I didn't believe it held any secrets, despite what I now feared about Jack. The kid had duped me, lied to me, leaving a trail of destruction and failing to appreciate our miscommunication until it mattered. Tony glanced briefly my way as he climbed out of his car, a worried expression on his face. He headed for the front door, joined by DC Noah Bates and two uniformed officers I'd never met. He liked Alice. We all did.

'No. Please. Not like this.' I clambered after him, pulling him to one side, hoping he'd understand. I was begging, practically on my knees.

'Newt, what aren't you telling me?' He was glaring at

me as if I was an idiot, beyond furious, beyond trying to work me out.

I sighed, knowing I needed to share what I knew, yet unsure how. There was no going back for Jack now.

'I'll explain everything later, just let me do this alone. I promise, if Alice *is* there, I'll get her out, I swear. Trust me on this.' I needed Tony to appreciate the delicacy of the situation, Alice's limited timeframe, Jack's unconfirmed emotions. The poor kid's mental health depended on it. So did mine. 'Isn't this what I do for a living? Isn't it what the police pay me for?' I didn't mean to sound condescending, the police merely doing their job, too.

We were hovering in the street, Tony wavering now, uncertain, unsure what to do for the best. I could deal with sensitive situations like these far better than him, better than any of the officers in attendance. I knew it. Tony knew it. We were wasting time.

'Okay. But any trouble and we're coming in.'

I nodded. I knew *that*, too. I knocked the front door, hoping no one would answer, wishing I had this wrong, several disgruntled police officers now standing in the street behind me.

'May I help you?' A tall woman in a dark grey suit answered the door, her blonde hair tied back, slim glasses perched on a slender nose. She looked nothing like Rachel, did not look pleased to see me.

'Ruth Miller?' I queried, wholly wishing she would tell me otherwise.

The woman nodded. 'Is everything okay?'

'I'm sorry to ask, but is your nephew here?'

'Jack?'

I took a breath, the sound of his name making my skin prickle. 'Correct.'

'No. Sorry. I haven't seen him.' She glanced behind me, casting nervous eyes over the police. Tony was on his mobile, kicking debris into the road. I didn't know who he was talking to, didn't know if Ruth was lying. 'What is this about?' she queried.

'My name is Doctor Newton Flanigan,' I found myself confirming, my voice almost a whisper. 'I'm a clinical psychologist with the police. We need to find Jack, but are worried about his state of mind. May I come in for a moment?' I pulled my ID badge from my pocket. 'I just need to ask you a few questions.' I didn't confirm I was also Jack's university professor, someone he once considered a friend.

Appreciating my outwardly calm tone, Ruth opened the door, allowing me to step into her quiet hallway. I was unsure what I might find here, knowing the chaos Jack had already caused. Yet, there were no sounds from within to verify my suspicions and I wavered, wondering if I had this wrong. I gave Ruth a brief smile, holding my breath, unconvinced I knew what I was doing. I half-expected Jack to walk into the room, his cheeks flushed, his arms outstretched for a hug.

'I have to admit, Jack has been acting very strange lately,' she stated, a worried look on her face.

'How?'

'Well, he hasn't allowed me access to my basement for weeks.' She glanced towards her kitchen, her features uncertain, an uncomfortable smile on her lips. 'I assumed it was a privacy issue, this year not exactly helping his state of mind. He's a young man. Deserves his own space.'

'But?'

'But I wasn't expecting him to *padlock* it.' Ruth turned and headed into her kitchen, pointing shakily towards a closed door in the corner.

'Your basement?'

Ruth nodded, her embarrassment obvious.

'Do you have a key?' I knew the answer but asked anyway.

She shook her head. 'I'm sure I've heard noises coming from down there, but I haven't dared ask Jack about them. I'm not here that often as I work in London. I trust my nephew, Mr Newton.'

I'm sure she did. So did I. Or, at least, I used to. The padlock was a Yale, nothing special. 'May I?' I asked, knowing the police would break it if I didn't.

Ruth nodded again, stepping out of my way. I didn't want to admit it, but I was fairly good at lockpicking, my ability formed from years of dealing with those less stable than most, my brother at the wrong end of a wayward childhood for a while. This wasn't the first time I'd been forced to improvise, probably wouldn't be the last. I took a paperclip from my pocket and fashioned it into a length of wire, twisting it haphazardly until the lock clicked open. I made it look easy. It wasn't.

I didn't look at her but could tell Ruth was nervous by the way she was biting her lip. I didn't tell her I *hated* basements, or that I'd spent a cold night in one a couple of years ago, courtesy of David Mallory. I glanced towards Ruth as if this was just an average day, creaking open the door because I didn't know what else to do. I felt I was betraying Jack's trust as I descended the steps, the padlock still in my hand, hating the sound of my shoes as they clacked loudly against creaking wood. Every breath I took was heightened. I half expected him to be waiting in a corner, Alice tied to a chair, a drill in his grasp, my arrival too late.

The first thing I noticed was the smell. It wasn't a typical basement smell but something else, something I couldn't place. I grappled around until I found a light switch, shocked by what met my adjusting eyes, unsure what I'd walked in on. The walls were covered in writing of all shapes, sizes and colours, some of it neat, carefully worded, other phrases scrawled in untidy scribbles highlighting bitterness I knew could have only come from Jack. Some words were written in pen, others in paint, some barely legible they'd been there so long. There was no continuity, merely reckless rambles of a deluded madman, voicing in ink what he couldn't say aloud. I suspected some of these impressions were written long before his accident. Probably before he met *me*.

I'd never heard Jack swear, yet words I was uncomfortable repeating were sprawled across the room, hate-fuelled obscenities cascading down every wall. The space was otherwise well-decorated, naturally lit in places from a far side window throwing a soft haze across a piled carpet. I couldn't help placing my hand over my nose, unable to confirm what was violating my senses until I noticed a row of steel cages along one wall.

'Is everything okay?' Ruth called my way from above, jolting my thoughts, elevating my shock. She was standing at the top of the stairs, either unwilling or unable to descend. I couldn't tell which. I wondered if the stench was as strong up there as it was down here.

'All good,' I called back, hoping she would remain where she was, for now, some of Jack's words unfit for a lady.

I forced myself to read a few, regretting my decision, my heart breaking for Jack's obvious suffering. By the time I'd made it across the room, I already knew what was in those cages, Jack's open ramblings casting a painful truth onto a life I'd sadly misunderstood. It seemed the journal he left on my doorstep wasn't the only place he expressed his thoughts. I pressed my hand over the envelope in my pocket, wondering what revelations were still to come.

The smell grew stronger with each step I took, nausea increasing as I cast shocked eyes over several dead animals lying in urine-soaked filth, blood drying over their matted fur, most of these creatures unrecognisable. I barely made out the shape of a rabbit, I think, a mouse, something with a long bushy tail. A squirrel, probably, if I had to hazard a guess. I didn't want to, but I opened a groaning cage door and prodded a soft mound of fur. It moved, still warm, still *alive*, my brain unwilling to confront what was happening.

I reeled backwards, blinking away the impossible, unconvinced I hadn't imagined what my eyes were not yet prepared to acknowledge. The fur moved again, a shrill sound leaving its quivering lips. It was clearly unwell, whatever it was, drooling, banging its head against the cage, blood seeping from a hole drilled into the side of its head.

'What's happening down there?' Ruth called out again, her anxious tone unhelpful, already on the top step.

I glanced up. How was I meant to answer? 'Nothing,' I yelled instead, reaching forward to slam the cage door shut. I didn't want whatever was in there to escape, did not anticipate the chain reaction it triggered as more fur moved, highlighting yet more animals in agony. Most of the creatures were dead, thankfully, but three were clearly very much alive, left to die unnaturally, painfully.

I caught my leg against a nearby table, shocked when a copy of the very book I'd written all those years ago fell to the floor. I picked it up, recalling my recent visit to Manor Hill, remembering Darius Jacobs's enthusiasm when I told him about it. I flicked through the pages, several notes in the margins expressing Jack's thoughts, ideas he wanted to try, techniques he was hoping to master. A profound understanding of Darius's apparent motives were highlighted in red along with an over-enthusiastic appreciation of mine. Jack wasn't here, but his secrets were, several blood-crusted drills stacked neatly in a corner. Trophies. My theory about a copycat killer was right.

I removed the notebook and envelope from my pocket and stared blankly at vital evidence I'd deliberately withheld, knowing the police would soon search this place and mine, Jack's time almost over.

'Mr Newton?' I turned to see Ruth behind me, staring in bewilderment at her ruined basement, her eyes unable to acknowledge what she was seeing. She took one look at those animals and screamed. I didn't know what to say to make this better, did not know her nephew at all.

The envelope was in my hand, my name emblazoned in capital letters across the front. I crumpled it in my grasp, unable to relinquish my grip, unwilling to give it to the police until I'd read it at least once. I *had* to know, had to at least try and understand who Jack Monroe was. I didn't dare contemplate how this all looked for me. I would deal with the fallout later.

Forty-Four

Jack

Newton, if you are reading this, it probably means I am either dead, locked away, or about to lose you forever. As dramatic as this may sound, I hardly assume it matters. I hope you will one day understand why things had to end how they did, why I could never explain in person the things I've done in private. This entire thing began innocently enough, I hope you appreciate, mere taunting, nothing more, just banter from strangers who knew no better, a journey I took to escape my mother. I'm glad he didn't die, that kid. I think you said his name was Ben. I didn't mean to start this, I promise. Never meant for things to go the way they did. I hope you believe me. I hope you don't hate me. I'm so sorry about the others. Alex Jefferson, and the couple by the canal.

Alex's day was sealed the moment he saw me, although I try not to think about what happened, the two of us thrown together by circumstance and fate. I wished only to remain anonymous, yet if I had the capacity of mind to focus on my surroundings instead of my doom, things might have been different. As it was, that day was set to conclude otherwise, triggering a torrent of hatred leading to the downfall of several people. Destiny was already in control by then, you see. I just wasn't aware of the details. I should have walked away, but he provoked my anger and so I attacked him. I only hit him once. Well, maybe twice. But I promise you the idea of drilling his skull came only from thoughts I had in private. I didn't expect it to become a reality until it was too late.

For as long as I've known you, I have loved you, but it's probably too late to tell you now. Once you know my truth, I'm sure you'll no longer care. But I can't die without you knowing who I am, what I am, why things turned so sour for me. I am not a killer, Newton. I hope you know that. Things went wrong, that's all.

If I had more time, I would right so many wrongs, leaving the world a better place than it might have otherwise been without me. As it is, time is running out for me, for us, for everyone who claimed to love me. I had dreams, ideas I never shared beyond the realms of impossible thinking, destined now to leave this earth with nothing other than what they'll bury me with. I can barely see, can no longer think, karma finally coming for me. I can still smell your aftershave, though, if I breathe deeply enough, can feel your arms around me in the dark. In my dreams, of course. I don't understand why I always feel so cold. I guess that's because I'm dying. I would like to remember us, if I can, and the time we spent together.

In my aunt's basement, you will find a copy of the book you wrote a few years ago, notes in the margins, should you choose to read them, my thinking inspired by yours. Read your book and the notes I made. Understand it. Understand me. Only then will you find the closure sadly no longer afforded to me. There are other things down there too. Things I'm truly ashamed of. Tell my aunt I'm sorry.

You always used to tell me you would walk through broken glass to protect those you love, yet ironically, I have been looking through nothing else for months. It has savaged my life, my soul, leaving behind wounds that will never heal. There is honestly nothing more I can say about that, other than I'm genuinely sorry. Sorry for everything.

Jack

Forty-Five

Newton

'Well?' Tony glanced my way as I stepped through Ruth Miller's front door, fully anticipating Alice to be with me, shocked when she wasn't, the blinding light unable to retract images I'd probably never forget. I didn't know which was worse, the afternoon air out here or the alien atmosphere I'd just encountered, Jack's painful confession lodged in my head.

I swallowed, unsure how to convey Jack's actions, unconvinced Tony would understand. 'They're not here,' I stated instead, glancing behind me, a shaken Ruth already speaking to an officer, untold horrors awaiting their attention. 'But you might want to send the RSPCA down to the basement.'

'Jesus Christ, *why?*' Tony sounded as if he half-expected me to confirm some gruesome discovery, his eyes widening, his voice rising.

I had no idea how to explain. 'Animals. Mostly dead. What seems to be holes drilled into their heads.' I could barely speak.

'What do you mean, *mostly* dead?' I'm sure Tony's vocals had tightened. Mine certainly had.

I couldn't reply, couldn't articulate the chaos I'd uncovered, Jack's letter quivering in my grasp. I still didn't believe his involvement as I handed Tony the recently opened envelope along with Jack's notebook and battered copy of *my* book, nothing else for me to do with them.

'What's this?'

'Evidence.' Everything they needed to convict their killer wrapped up in a neat little bow. No doubt exactly how Jack had planned it. He loved being in control. I used to find such things endearing. I felt sick again, the overwhelming rot of Ruth Miller's basement already too much.

Tony scanned the items in his possession, flicking briefly through Jack's musings, a pained expression on his face. 'Okay, so where the hell is Alice?'

I shook my head.

Tony swore, muttering words he didn't wish to share with the rest of us. 'Where would he go? Newt?' He was glaring at me as if I knew but was choosing not to say. *'Think.'*

I couldn't think straight let alone answer his question. He hadn't taken her to his house. His mum would know. He hadn't brought her here. He *had* taken my car despite not having passed his test, unconcerned for the law or public safety. I glared at Tony, a wayward thought jumping into my head.

'What?' He glared back, uncertain, his expression nowhere near as confused as mine.

'My cottage.'

'What cottage?' I hadn't told him about it, hadn't yet shared my good news. I wasn't even certain he knew that Paul was currently meant to be there with his wife, attempting to rekindle a relationship I was no longer convinced needed my interference. Tony was looking at me as if I'd lost the plot. Maybe I had.

'It's a long story,' I muttered. 'I'll explain on the way.'

***

We notified Paul ahead of time as to our pending arrival. I didn't tell him what had happened, didn't want screeching police sirens alerting Jack to our presence, tipping his mood, his balance—a very strong possibility he would do something stupid. As Tony's car snaked along the narrow track, I momentarily wondered if I should rename the place. *Fisherman Jacks* was hardly an appropriate memory to be left with under the current circumstances. Yet, the building was over two hundred years old, hardly the properties fault.

'Jesus, you kept this place quiet,' Tony stated as we climbed into the sea air, this location as breathtaking now as I remembered, the second home I'd barely acknowledged. Paul's car was parked on the driveway. It didn't make me feel any better.

I couldn't see *my* car, didn't know if Jack was here, merely taking a wild guess, that's all, a stab in the dark.

Alice was our main priority, our only concern. I glanced around, hoping to catch a glimpse of movement, *anything* to tell me I had this wrong. The air was clean, yet unmistakably thick, as if something was lingering, waiting for attention. I couldn't tell what. My last visit here was designed to entertain Jack, yet I was feigned to admit I still didn't know much about it. It had a boathouse, I think, but where, I had no idea.

'What the hell is going on? Why did you sound so vague over the phone?'

A familiar shout confirmed Paul's presence, my friend already heading out of the front door, his cheeks flushed, his feet bare, shirt undone. I hoped this meant he and Adele had made up, my isolated cottage more than enough to create a romantic atmosphere.

Tony was the first to intervene, as if my existence was unnecessary, the way he looked at me suggesting he believed I was somehow involved, had instigated it all.

'I'm sorry to interrupt you, boss.'

'What's all the fuss?' Paul looked concerned, confused, his brow furrowing tightly against his reddened skin. His wife Adele appeared behind him and waved, all smiles and ruffled hair, the urgency of this moment not yet confirmed. She winked at me and I offered a strained smile, knowing I'd done at least one good thing today. I wondered if they'd found the wine in the fridge.

'My student,' I pitched in, weaving back, closing my eyes briefly against events I didn't want to be true. 'The one I told you about.'

'The one with cancer?' Paul asked, vaguely recalling the

kid with the brain tumour.

I nodded.

'What about him?' Paul was buttoning his shirt, his ruffled hair telling of a private moment interrupted. He looked embarrassed. Now was not the time to ask how he and Adele were getting on. Very well, by the looks of it. I was thankful they seemed okay, grateful my plan had worked.

'Have you seen him around here?'

'No.' Paul looked briefly over his shoulder, his tone mildly sheepish. 'I've been kind of busy.' He narrowed his eyes. 'Why? What's wrong?'

'Alice is missing.' Tony couldn't help his aggravated tone, spitting the confirmation towards Paul like venom. 'I didn't want to tell you over the phone but we think this *Jack* kid might have taken her.'

'*I beg your pardon?*' Paul glared at me, his shock apparent, his marital activities forgotten. 'I thought she was going to yours for lunch?'

I nodded, annoyed with Tony for blurting it out so abruptly. 'I'll fill you in on the details later, but right now it's vital we find Jack. Have you seen anything suspicious since your arrival?' I didn't have time to explain, more important matters to address. I glanced around, unable to see much beyond my own increased panic. I didn't anticipate Paul had seen *anything* aside from the inside of a bedroom.

'Well, I did hear a car earlier but wasn't taking much notice, didn't assume it was important.'

'What car?' Tony asked.

Paul shrugged. 'If I knew I was meant to be looking out for one I might have checked.' He sounded agitated now too.

'Shit,' Tony muttered, his fists clenched.

'He *has* to be here somewhere,' I pitched in. I *knew* Jack, knew he'd want to go somewhere he could think, feel safe, his attention forever set on *me*. I didn't for one minute believe he would hurt Alice, yet my mind shot back to those animals in his aunt's basement, the painful words written on her walls. Who was I kidding? I didn't know him at all, only realising now what he was capable of.

Several marked cars were beginning to arrive, my cottage lit with flashing lights and police uniforms, the entire location more like a television drama than a quiet getaway.

'Over there!' Paul jolted me from my private thoughts, pointing towards the beach, his face a knot of strangled lines. I followed his pointing finger towards a figure some distance away, a dark shape staring towards the house, watching us, watching him.

Jack.

Thank God.

'*There* you are!' I found myself calling loudly, knowing he couldn't hear, knowing I sounded stupid. I was almost sick with relief, merely wanting, for now, to pretend everything was okay. I sounded far calmer than I was, needing him to believe I was happy to see him, thankful I'd found him, glad he was safe. I headed in his direction, waving frantic arms above my head, my mind attempting to convince me it didn't matter what he'd done, hoping we could fix this. Somehow. I was hoping he could shed light on some very dark matters, tell me where Alice was, confirm she was safe. In reality, I was absolutely terrified.

'I've been leaving you messages,' I found myself yelling against a sea breeze oddly now turning cold. 'I called you earlier. Didn't you get my message?' I smiled, thinking only of Alice, hoping she was okay, glancing around in case I caught a glimpse of her beautiful face, her summer dress, those bare shoulders earlier catching my attention.

Jack turned and disappeared from view, away from my line of sight, my vision temporarily impeded. He didn't acknowledge me, didn't seem glad to see me, his newly shaved head highlighting the cancer I'd tried for a while to ignore. I glanced at Paul, Tony, then Noah, watching helplessly as they jogged towards the beach, oddly concerned now for *their* safety, too.

For a kid who walked with crutches, I was surprised by how swiftly he seemed to evade us, already some distance along the beach by the time we reached it. It was flanked on both sides by high cliffs and bracing waves, no potential for Jack to disappear around the bay, unless he swam, which I didn't imagine he was well enough to do. Paul knew this. So did I. The kid was going nowhere. Uniformed police officers were already blocking the lane behind us, a police helicopter scanning nearby woodland, watching, waiting, preventing his unwanted escape.

'Where could she be?' Tony called my way, his legs stumbling over uneven shingle.

'The boathouse.' It was the only place I could think of, despite never having seen it, never having been there. I didn't know if Jack knew about it, his explorations achieved mainly without me.

'You have a boathouse?' Tony asked, his day becoming ever more bizarre.

I shrugged. I guess.

I wasn't sure what Tony was thinking, couldn't read his thoughts.

'There!' Noah yelled, our attention pulled towards something in the distance. I began to run, prompting Paul, Tony, and several officers to follow suit.

The boathouse was tiny, tucked into a cove, soon to become unreachable by the rising tide if we didn't hurry, the structure on the verge of crumbling into the sea. It would have been the perfect place to keep a fishing vessel, once upon a time. My car was parked against a crumbling wall, out of the way, impossible to see until you were upon it. I slipped and skidded across several algae-covered rocks, reaching the bottom step of what probably used to be the entrance, most of it long gone now. I was unsure what I was going to find, my heart threatening to leap from my chest at the sight of a familiar shape lying motionless some distance away.

Alice.

Tony reached her first, pressing his weight against her body so she wouldn't slide unexpectedly into the rising tide, his hand already clamped around her head.

'Somebody, *help me!*' he screamed, his voice wobbling, his tone tight.

Everything seemed to slip into slow motion after that. I broke into an unsteady run, unconvinced I wasn't about to make things worse by falling into the sea and drowning, frantically counting each unstable step I took. I *should* have confirmed what I knew about Jack long before now, should have placed Alice in the picture instead of danger.

'Are you okay?' I was yelling into the air, talking mostly to myself because I didn't know if Alice could hear me. It took a painful moment to register she wasn't moving, still hoping she would respond.

'Newt!' Tony glared my way.

I glared back, my shock obvious.

'Call an ambulance. *Now.*' Tony's face had lost its colour, his ashen cheeks as pale as Alice's.

I stared at Alice, unsure what was happening. I was desperate for her to speak to me, anticipating lifting her to safety, already creating the joke we'd make about this later. Yet, Alice remained silent, her bright eyes open, unblinking, Tony's trembling hands cupping her body. He could barely look my way as he removed a gag from her grey lips and stroked her hair. Her mouth fell open. So did mine.

'What's wrong?' I knew. I just didn't want to hear it.

Tony didn't reply. Instead, he and Noah carefully hoisted her body over the rocks away from the water's edge, none of us willing to acknowledge what was happening.

'Hey, Alice,' I chided loudly, 'Maybe we should rearrange our date, hey?' I was trying to make light of a very serious situation, trying to make a joke. It wasn't working, my words mere white noise dissipating quickly.

'Will you just call that *fucking* ambulance,' Tony screamed, attempting to jolt me from my ridiculous daydream. He was already performing CPR.

It took a moment for reality to kick in, for my brain to shift into painful focus, my surroundings sharply picking up pace without me. Alice wasn't breathing, her open eyes unseeing, her body unresponsive. Yanking my mobile from my pocket, I struggled to dial 999, my fingers unwilling to cooperate. I could barely think straight, could not acknowledge Paul as he shifted his attention to Jack, already on his radio to nearby colleagues.

Someone was asking questions but I could scarcely understand them, forced instead to convey muddled words towards an unsuspecting emergency operator.

No, I did *not* know what had happened.

No, I did *not* think the patient was breathing.

Tony was brilliant. He grabbed my phone, performing desperate chest compressions while relaying Alice's unresponsive condition to the woman on the other end, an ambulance crew already heading our way. Paul was barking orders, his officers shifting into swift action, turning their focus towards Jack. I didn't know where he was, could no longer see him. I merely stood on the shoreline, Alice's lifeless body matching my useless brain, the sleeve of Tony's torn shirt wrapped around her blood-soaked head. She had bruising over her cheek, swelling on her lip. I couldn't confirm Jack hadn't drilled her skull, could not imagine the outcome. I, on the other hand, was a spare part, in shock, beyond useless. Of all the things I'd anticipated from today, this wasn't it, Jack's actions something I was not yet ready to accept. This wasn't how I wanted to introduce Fisherman Jacks to my friends, not how I'd anticipated our first date.

An ambulance arrived within minutes, yet the whole

thing felt wrong. I tried to intervene but was pulled away sharply as desperate medics failed to restart Alice's heart. I couldn't imagine she would die. Not like this. If I was crying, I couldn't tell, my body numbed by impossible events of the day, taking a toll I hadn't expected.

I lost track of reality after that, several minutes passing in a haze of vomit-induced panic. I vaguely recalled Paul patting my arm as he passed by, his face blank, the uncertain way Tony rose to his feet in defeat. Noah glared at me. So did everyone else. They didn't need to say anything. This was *my* fault. I know.

I watched as paramedics carried a stretcher along the beach to the awaiting ambulance, still working on Alice's body, my mind still unwilling to confirm what was unfolding. When Adele ran towards her husband, tears in her eyes and trembling arms outstretched, I couldn't discern what was being said. When she fell to her knees and sobbed, my entire world fell apart.

Forty-Six

Newton

I tried to breathe but oxygen evaded me, every painful step feeling as if I was underwater, my body weighed down, my limbs heavy. I couldn't think, could barely hear the commotion unfolding around me.

'Newt?'

I couldn't appreciate why everyone was moving so slowly.

'Newt?'

I wavered, wondering if I had somehow already left this mortal coil, in limbo, this day merely a dream.

'Newt?!?'

A firm tap on my shoulder jolted me back into reality, my mind catching up too fast. I turned to see Paul standing next to me, his hand gripping my arm, his features unreadable.

'What?' I barely remembered where I was, my mouth unwilling to form logical words.

'I said, are you okay?'

I swallowed, nodded. I didn't know *what* I was. I certainly wasn't okay. All I could see was Alice's lifeless body, Jack's demonic form, my unyielding stupidity. I leaned over and vomited, some of it hitting Paul's shoes. He didn't say anything.

'Is she…?'

Paul took a deep breath, clearly holding back tears. He didn't answer. I'd never seen him cry before, wasn't expecting to see him do so now. He pressed a trembling hand over his mouth, his eyes glistening, unwilling and unable to confirm the words I already knew in my head. I glared at him, his face zoning in and out of focus.

'I need you to come with me. *Now.*' Paul wasn't asking. He barely managed to compose himself before pulling me roughly over the shingle, my shoes catching pebbles and shells, my legs stumbling to keep up.

'I'm so sorry,' I found myself whispering, the taste of vomit strong on my tongue, acid burning my throat. I glanced around, knowing none of them appreciated the depth of my involvement, my silence, my hindrance. I wasn't willing to accept Alice was dead because of *me*.

'What do you know about this Jack?' Paul was calling over the breeze, glaring at me, his teeth clenched so tightly I thought he might break one. He was trying to retain professionalism, but I could see his fury, his eyes black with pain.

I shook my head. *Hardly anything.* We were heading

towards the cliffs, several police officers ahead of us, shouting words I couldn't absorb, conveying information I couldn't explain.

'Is he okay?' After everything he'd done, I honestly couldn't believe I was asking.

Paul pointed to where the beach ended and a layer of rocky coastline began, a slim figure standing some feet overhead. I barely recognised Jack, his arms pulled over his head, gently rocking back and forth against an incoming breeze. He was close to the edge, in more ways than one, his frail body buffeted by unspoken words and unconfirmed deeds. How he'd managed to get up there, I couldn't say, but his tenacity was baffling. What on earth had happened to bring the poor kid to this?

'We can't get him to speak to us,' Paul continued. 'Every time one of my officers gets close, he just steps towards the edge.' He looked at me. I looked at him. We'd been here before. Jack was not the first unstable person I'd tried to save, probably wouldn't be the last. 'I can't have *his* death on my conscience today as well, Newt. I need you to talk him down.' Paul wasn't requesting my help this time. He was giving an order.

I wavered, still unwilling to accept Alice was dead, unable to contemplate never seeing her again. I glanced at Paul, his exhausted face displaying his age, his shock, his fear.

'He's mute,' I found myself confirming flatly. I didn't want to go into details.

I was forced to scramble through gorse and knapweed, a rocky coastal path not on my list of strenuous activities today. I emerged out of breath on top of a thirty-foot cliff edge, this part of my property throwing more surprises my way, my thoughts all over the place. I could barely breathe let alone hold a conversation, the outcome of this day promising nothing good. Getting Jack into custody was imperative, for his sake as much as anyone's, the information I already knew only making this moment worse. If nothing else, I needed to ask what had happened, what had gone so seriously wrong.

Tony was waiting for my arrival, his hair blowing in the breeze, his features as knotted as mine. He didn't say anything. I swallowed, nodded, didn't speak to him either. The air seemed even thinner up here, if this was possible, my cottage a mere dot compared to the waves crashing violently against rocks. I thought about my nephews and how much they would love it here.

Instead, I turned my attention to Jack, my trembling hands held in front of me as if I were planning to push him over the edge. I wasn't sure what I was going to say but I needed to do *something* to clarify all this, anything to settle my shattered nerves.

'Just tell me *why*, Jack?' I found myself calling out, wanting an acknowledgement, a reason—answers. 'What did Alice ever do to you?' I didn't want the kid to see my emotions, struggling to hold back feelings I'd never now develop, my uncertain future shifting in a single day, like Jack's. I could feel Tony's discomfort, the way he shuffled next to me, the way he held his breath in response to my question.

Jack didn't look at me, instead remained motionless, his

back to us, seemingly ready to end it all.

'I'm sorry about today,' I called his way, trying to gain his attention. It was true. 'And I know it might sound lame, but you know me. You *know* what my memory is like.'

I tried to laugh before realising I couldn't, considered yelling instead, demanding answers. But when he finally turned around and I saw the look on his face, I changed my mind. He was unrecognisable, his once beautiful eyes swollen with tears, his expression filled with more pain than anyone should know. He coughed, stuttering violently as he attempted to speak, his hands shaking, his head lolling to one side, his damaged mouth quivering with shock. He didn't seem to care about the police standing behind me, wasn't concerned by the commotion.

'S…sorry…Newton.'

For a moment, I wavered, assuming I'd imagined his voice. It had been so long since I'd heard him speak. It took my breath, the sea breeze engulfing what would have otherwise been a powerful moment. His vocals were broken, his throat obviously sore, but he *was* communicating, vaguely.

'When did you start speaking?'

Jack shook his head. It no longer mattered.

'Acc…cident,' he spluttered instead, needing my urgent understanding, my full attention. 'Didn't…mean…it. She…fell.'

I didn't know if this made me feel better or worse, knowing Alice's death was potentially an accident. her involvement merely a case of, wrong time, wrong place. The poor kid sounded desperate, if not a little unwell. I could vaguely see Paul and Noah pacing the beach below, knowing I was trying to do my job, failing on both fronts. No one yet appreciated how badly I'd messed up, didn't know I could have prevented this. They could chastise me later. I deserved nothing less.

'Why did you take Alice, Jack?'

Jack glanced up, the name of the innocent female he'd kidnapped alien to him. He didn't know Alice, didn't know who she was to me aside from someone who had taken his attention. He shrugged, hung his head.

'Did you know she was a police officer?'

Jack's eyes widened, his breathing shallow and thin, the very thought of murdering a copper clearly *not* something he'd intended. He shook his head violently, knowing things were about to get a whole lot worse, staggering from foot to foot, his crutches barely holding his weight.

'I take it you were angry with *me?*' I couldn't quite visualise the moment Alice realised she was in danger, didn't want to place myself on such an unfounded pedestal. Yet, everything Jack did was seemingly about me.

Jack nodded, closed his eyes, could not even look at me.

I felt terrible. I could see the pain I'd caused him, his suffering on full uncensored display. To me, our lunchtime meeting was a simple coffee, a chat, a way to talk about things unsaid. It could be easily rearranged. To Jack it was *everything*.

'I'd never deliberately let you down. You know that, don't you, Jack?' Right then I didn't know *anything*, no honest idea what to think.

'Sor...sorry.'

I didn't know what to say, didn't know if I could stand in front of him and not express the anger burning inside me. Instead, I took a direct route, my intention merely to get him down from this cliff as quickly as possible, the day taking a turn I wasn't prepared for. I wasn't sure how much longer I could look at him, fearing I might snap, push him over the edge, end this thing once and for all.

'I'm your *friend*, Jack. I hope you know that.' I swallowed, no longer believing this was true. Jack didn't need to know.

The boy shook his head, pointing a telling finger my way before he turned around, stepping forward as if to jump, his crutches no longer helpful, my lie stinging him like a slap to the cheek.

'No! Jack, please,' I begged, racing forward, stopping short of grabbing him, making things worse, my hand inches from his. Tony and two uniformed officers followed suit, all-out pandemonium set to follow, the four of us hovering between certain death and justice we weren't even sure we'd get. Waves crashed below, a heavy breeze buffing our bodies. I wasn't sure what to do for the best. If he jumped, I couldn't follow. I couldn't swim. I didn't deem it important to tell anyone until now, my limitations hardly important. I felt ridiculous standing here, knowing Jack's next move might be his last. 'I just need to understand what happened,' I found myself muttering. 'We can get you the support you need. But you hurt people, Jack. You *killed* people.'

Jack burst into tears then, his sobs engulfing the air, his reaction engulfing me. 'You…don't…un…derstand.'

'*What?* What don't I understand?' Nothing came to mind I could begin to appreciate, Alice's death on both our consciences.

'People...stare.' Jack shook his head, failing to shake off his unwanted thoughts. He pointed towards his face, prodding his cheek with an angry finger. 'Ugly...in...visible.'

I realised then exactly how Jack saw himself, seeing *me* as his savour, the one person in this world who didn't look at him with confusion, who always saw the brilliant young man he was, the talented, amazing Jack Monroe who would one day change the world. I sighed, reality *not* my friend today.

'And I let you down today, didn't I, Jack?' I called into the air, knowing I was speaking to myself, Jack no longer listening.

Jack nodded. It was the first honest thing he'd done. He didn't want me to be gay. Not really. He merely wanted me to be there for him, to *see* who he really was. Being gay wasn't the issue. Being *accepted* was.

'I'm so sorry kiddo.' I was. Emotions I couldn't acknowledge swamped my body, every cell tingling with shame, ignorance, regret. I was no different to anyone else who'd hurt him, putting myself and my needs first, forgetting about Jack and his. I tried to think back to the first victim, Alex Jefferson, wondering if I could have done or said something to prevent the events that followed.

'Sorry....about...your...friend.' Jack sounded sincere. I shook my head. It was too late.

He must have noticed the look on my face, the

unspoken pain behind my eyes, because he shuddered, shaking off emotions he no longer wanted. He began tearing at his face, his grunts of frustration dissipating into the afternoon air, stopping only when he'd drawn blood. He glanced my way, closed his eyes, and allowed his fragile body to fall towards the incoming waves and rocks, his damaged soul pulled into the awaiting ocean.

I screamed. So did Tony. Panicking, we lunged forward, barely stopping short of joining him. I stood and watched as several officers below tried to reach him, clawing their way through heavy spray and seaweed, getting nowhere fast, the tide too high, the rocks too dangerous, any potential swim too fraught.

I was forced to watch his broken body rock steadily back and forth, blood and saliva dribbling from his mutilated mouth as waves crashed over his skin. Although still alive, he was already gone, his once sparkling eyes grey now, blank, dead. It was as if the ocean was holding back any hope of help, his frail body disappearing with the truth. The last thing I saw of Jack Monroe was his closed fist clenched tightly against his chest, rubbing his trembling hand in a continued circle configuration, over and over, his eyes set firmly on mine.

I'm genuinely sorry, he'd said in his letter. Sorry for everything.

Forty-Seven

Jack

I didn't mean for things to end the way they did, but I knew I was done for when Newton told me the dead woman was a police officer. I didn't know who she was, I swear. Only that she had taken Newton's attention when I needed him the most. Still, I couldn't take it back or change what had happened, and there was nothing left for me in this world other than to disappear—to sink beyond the grasp of everything I once believed I loved.

I stared at Newton for longer than planned, wondering *why* he was nothing to me in that painful moment other than a concerned stranger; distant, vague, the look in his eyes a telling reminder we would *never* overcome this. I was already dead, anyway, a lingering look towards the ocean below me to confirm what needed to happen next.

I guess, when all is said and done, there was nothing

more remote than the darkness that dragged me to the depths, other than the furthest reaches of space, of course, and yet I will never see the stars again. There was no undoing of what I'd done. Lives were ruined because of me, and all I wanted was to feel *nothing*. It was all I deserved. There would be no quick end, no escape from my torment.

Instead, I stepped forward and descended into a cavernous void, feeling the rocks rise gradually like the creeping tide, the weightlessness of my body surrounded by calm. Newton was above me, yet all I could think to say was "sorry". There was nothing else left. I allowed the darkness to extend its hollow hand and I embraced it as if it were an old friend, my breath escaping my body one final time.

I smiled.

The Case of Jack Monroe

Temporal Lobe Damage versus the Psychotic Mind

Detective Sergeant Alice Baker died on a breezy September afternoon on a beach she would have, given half a chance, adored. She was just thirty-one years old. She lived with her ageing mother and a cat called Taffy, her favourite tipple a cup of tea, milk, no sugar, her favourite food, pepperoni pizza. I never knew what her favourite colour was, what made her laugh, what made her cry, or the songs she sang in the bath, would never get the chance to see where our relationship might have, one day, taken us if fate hadn't cruelly intervened.

When they searched Ruth Miller's basement, they found dozens of letters Jack had written to Darius Jacobs, asking him questions unfit for most ears, pouring his emotions into words unsuitable for any other form of communication. He never posted them. I like to believe this is because Jack didn't really want the answers, that somewhere deep down, he didn't *want* to hurt anyone. He was lost, that's all, like most of us, merely trying to figure out his place in this world, his tortured mind beyond redemption. It was a shame, in the end, it turned him into a hate-fuelled killer. The dried blood found on the drill inside Alex Jefferson's bathroom was matched to a rabbit, its rotted remains still in the very cage it died in, further proof of Jack's unhinged mind.

I have since studied his journal and the extensive notes he'd written frantically inside the book I now wish I hadn't written, and on the walls of his aunt's basement. It was a vain attempt to understand his behaviour and what led to his ultimate end. He was just a kid, had dealt with so much, yet his illness twisted his reality so intensely, it made for difficult reading. He hated the world and what he felt it represented, inspired by a killer I'd unwittingly brought to his attention. If it wasn't for me and my obsession with the human mind, Jack wouldn't have known about Darius Jacobs, would not have copied the insane work of "The Gimlet".

As it was, his mind became filled with an unhealthy obsession to change the world for what he believed would be a better place before death claimed him, to leave his mark, somehow. In his head, the idea of afflicting his suffering onto those who didn't understand his trauma became the only way he assumed he could enlighten humanity. Where books had failed to satisfy his unquenchable thirst for the human mind, mine had the opposite effect, hanging off my every misjudged thought, his own twisting into something rather ugly. Jack's depiction of this world was something he wished naively to share with others, his need for freedom sadly unable to transform him into anything other than the troubled young man he was. He therefore became a product of our tainted society, a killer in the making.

Living with temporal lobe damage is not easy, a blow to the head enough to change everything you know. Jack was young, his life barely begun, forced to endure what most could not. Couple this with an aggressively growing brain tumour and it was always set to become a recipe for disaster. I deluded myself I was there for Jack because, unfortunately, I now know I wasn't, not really, my *only* contribution being the twisted thoughts he absorbed in the dark, thoughts I'd put there, ideas he assumed were real. I achieved nothing aside from aiding his untimely death and the death of someone I was fond of.

Most of us fail to understand the power of the mind when it matters, how easily other people's viewpoints affect us. Rarely do we notice what lies beyond our small worlds, seeing only what we want to see, feeling nothing but our pained emotions. Rarely do we understand each other. Jack assumed there was no other option but to take matters into his own hands, attempting to right the wrongs he believed had been made against him. He was dying, the poor kid just desperate to accept his fate and find his place in a world he wasn't long for. His reasoning wasn't wrong, merely his erroneous methods.

Do I believe his illness turned him into a killer? No. Of course not. He was a frightened young man, an overthinker, a boy whose life was coming to an end. Do I feel his cancer somehow distorted his logic? Absolutely. The human brain is fragile, easily tipped, the slightest shift triggering falsifications we don't always appreciate until faced with the unthinkable. Our realities can change in an instant, our thinking pivoting towards the impossible.

I was certain Jack would become a star on earth for the people who would touch his life—a shining light in an otherwise black and overwhelming world denoting our modern existence. It is a shame fate had other plans. Yet, even if Jack had answered to his crimes, he would not have lived long enough to take the weight of his punishment, his injuries and his cancer punishment enough.

I told him I forgave him last week, although I will probably *never* forgive myself, my words meant as a comfort, nothing more, a way to accept things I should have seen coming. Although I could never offer the romantic love he fantasised about, I wish my young friend could have understood how much he meant to me. I wanted the last thing I said to him to be something profound, something he could hold onto. As it is, I can't recall much now beyond my own infected pain, memories I can no longer abide, emotions I no longer want. I would have liked to tell Alice how I felt about her. I guess she will never know. They never found Jack's body, searching for three frantic weeks before giving him up for dead, his family left to deal with his untimely departure and the deaths of those loved ones we are all still struggling to accept. He killed four people in the end, himself included.

An inquest now hangs over me as to how Alice died and

how my involvement with Jack brought about such tragic consequences. There are questions I need to answer, lies the police still need to uncover about my unfounded connections to a killer I still don't want to believe existed. I don't wish to think any less of Jack, despite everything he did, wanting instead to believe they are both in a better place, wherever *that* is. The only good thing to come from this is I have decided to take swimming lessons in the hope that, one day, eventually, I might find myself in a better place, too.

For now, I will settle for laying flowers on Alice's grave and on the beach where she died, the wild clover growing in the dunes, oddly one of Jack's favourites. I can still feel the gentle pull of the waves against my legs when I close my eyes, my cottage a beautiful place, homely, welcoming, so very peaceful. I imagine the fishing boats moored there long ago, the clang of metal against wood. I will probably never sell the place, despite what logic tells me. I'm not sure I can let it go, too many unresolved memories to cherish.

N Flanigan

Acknowledgements

I didn't anticipate that my background in psychology would one day become useful in writing dark thrillers about the damaged mind. Yet, *The Flanigan Files* has become the one place I can express the pain of those people I've encountered along the way. This is book three in a series I hope to turn into twenty-five novels, each tackling a different damaged mind from a different perspective.

As always, heartfelt thanks go to my publisher Stuart at SRL, whose insight and input has created the perfect ending to this novel. My beloved husband always gives me his 100% support, and the readers who are fully appreciative of what this series can be.

SRL Publishing don't just publish books, we also do our best in keeping this world sustainable. In the UK alone, over 77 million books are destroyed each year, unsold and unread, due to overproduction and bigger profit margins.

Our business model is inherently sustainable by only printing what we sell. While this means our cost price is much higher, it means we have minimum waste and zero returns. We made a public promise in 2020 to never overprint our books just for the sake of profit.

We give back to our planet by calculating the number of trees used for our products so we can then replace them. We also calculate our carbon emissions and support projects which reduce CO_2. These same projects also support the United Nations Sustainable Development Goals.

The way we operate means we knowingly waive our profit margins for the sake of the environment. Every book sold via the SRL website plants at least one tree.

To find out more, please visit
www.srlpublishing.co.uk/responsibility